LION RESURGENT

Stuart Slade

Dedication

This book is respectfully dedicated to the members of the Comisión Nacional sobre la Desaparición de Personas, (CONADEP) whose work on Argentina's Dirty War started the "justice cascade" trend leading to the implementation of new practices that provide more accountability for human rights violations

Acknowledgements

Lion Resurgent could not have been written without the very generous help of a large number of people who contributed their time, input and efforts into confirming the technical details of the story. Some of these generous souls I know personally, others I know only via the internet as the collective membership of "The Board" yet their communal wisdom and vast store of knowledge, freely contributed, has been truly irreplaceable.

I must also express a particular debt of gratitude to my wife Josefa for without her kind forbearance, patient support and unstintingly generous assistance, this novel would have remained nothing more than a vague idea floating in the back of my mind.

Caveat

Lion Resurgent is a work of fiction, set in an alternate universe. All the characters appearing in this book are fictional and any resemblance to any person, living or dead is purely coincidental. Although some names of historical characters appear, they do not necessarily represent the same people we know in our reality.

Copyright Notice

Contents

PART ONE

SOBERANÍA

CHAPTER ONE
TOOLS OF THE TRADE

Karoo Desert, South Africa, October 1981

"And now, ladies and gentlemen, McMullen Industries is proud to present the corporation's latest contribution to the defense of our country, the Boomslang tank destroyer!"

A low, sinister-looking vehicle accelerated out of its hide in front of the gathered crowd and turned to face the six target vehicles parked on the range in front of it. Its tracks threw a cloud of dust as they churned the thin, dry soil of the Karou, almost hiding the vehicle in its own private smokescreen. The Boomslang stopped. Something happened on the superstructure aft of the driver's compartment. Two half-cylinders mounted on the upper decking rotated, exposing the anti-tank missiles mounted on the rails integral to the cylinder. A tongue of red flame shot out as one of the anti-tank missiles streaked across the range, burning up the 4,000 meters to the first target. It hit squarely on the front of the old tank, sending a great pyre of smoke shot with rolling orange flames skywards.

Before the missile had reached the halfway point to its target, the Boomslang fired again. The second missile streaked off towards the target at the other end of the range. This time, the audience gasped in dismay, the missile was obviously flying too high and would overshoot its target. It did. The instant it started to pass over the old tank it had been aimed at, the warhead detonated. Fragments lashed through the thin top armor of the vehicle. The second tank joined the first; reduced to wreckage crowned by the column of black, flame-laced smoke. The crowd erupted into cheers as the implications of a top-attack missile sank in.

The third and fourth missiles followed the same pattern, rapid fire pairs that turned their targets into blazing wrecks. For a second, the Boomslang was silent. Only two targets were left, the outer members of the original line almost two kilometers apart.

Suddenly, the Boomslang fired two missiles simultaneously. The weapons raced across the desert to see which would reach its target first. As it happened, it was a dead heat. Both remaining targets exploded simultaneously. The crowd went wild at the demonstration.

"And, ladies and gentlemen, let's see an SU-130 do that!"

Out on the range, the Boomslang turned around and drove towards the watching spectators. A few meters short of them, it stopped. Inside the driving compartment, the driver reached for the suspension controls. He lowered the nose of the vehicle and raised the rear so that it appeared to be taking a bow in response to the applause. The crowd thundered their approval. Hatches opened and the crew emerged; the driver from his position beside the forward-mounted diesel, the commander behind him and the two missile controllers from their positions just in front of the missile launch rails.

"Ladies and gentlemen, a round of applause for the McMullen Industries Boomslang and its crew!"

Auditorium, McMullen Industries Head Office, Capetown, South Africa.

A thunderous round of applause swept the room as the film finished. The last few inches of the 35mm reel rattled as it went through the projector gate. The hammering as delighted stockholders pounded on the desks built into their seats sounded almost like gunfire; it went on for minutes. In front of the audience, three men sat watching the display with broad grins on their faces. This wasn't the first such applause they'd received at one of these meetings but that didn't make it any the less welcome. Eventually, the ovation subsided and quieted completely as the man at the center of the head table raised one hand.

"Thank you, but I'm pleased to say that we have more good news for you." John McMullen looked at the audience who were virtually holding their breaths. He'd come a long way since he and the two men sitting beside him had started this company up in the desperate days of 1949. He'd arrived in South Africa with a wife, a few sovereigns as capital and very little else. He still had the wife. Now he had children and grand-children to go with her and more sovereigns than he could count. "The South African Defense Forces have, this morning, placed an order for 800 Boomslang tank destroyers to re-equip the anti-tank battalions in all twelve of our infantry divisions."

He paused again as the audience once more erupted into cheers. Eight hundred vehicles was a big order, one that would keep McMullen Industries (President John McMullen, Vice-President Jorgie Vermaak, CEO Deke Van Huis) working full-time for years. A company that was working full time with a packed order book was a sound investment. That meant good dividends for the stockholders. As the audience allowed their delight to subside, one of the stockholders tapped the microphone in front of him.

"I think I express the feelings of us all when I say, congratulations, gentlemen! A great day for the company I am sure. Can we assume that the Boomslangs on order will be armed with the anti-tank missile we have just seen?"

McMullen spoke to the figure on his right. It went without saying that VerTech Inc (President Jorgie Vermaak, Vice President Deke Van Huis, CEO John McMullen) would be supplying the missiles for the new tank destroyer but it did no harm to confirm the fact. Vermaak leaned forward slightly. "I am not sure, John, will you be ordering our Mamba missiles for the Boomslang?"

"Provided the price is right Jorgie, I think you can count on it." This time the laugh in the theater was full-bodied and almost outdid the applause of a few minutes before. Everybody in the room took it for granted that an order for the Boomslang meant an order for the Mamba. Just as certainly it also meant an order for the TV8 diesel engine produced by Van Huis Engineering (President Deke Van Huis, Vice President John McMullen, CEO Jorgie Vermaak). Cartoonists in the South African press never tired of depicting the conglomerate as a three-headed beast wielding a sword against South Africa's enemies. Whether the beast in question was a hound, a snake or a buffalo depended on the newspaper. The three companies were joined at the hip and that was simply how things were. Now the original founders were getting on in years and starting to think of making a graceful exit from the companies they had founded. The next generation were moving up to take their place. Their links were even tighter than those of their parents for the three families had thoroughly intermarried over the years.

"Is the Boomslang available for export?" Another shareholder spoke up as the laughter ebbed away.

"It is indeed, and I am pleased to say we have already had a letter of intent for our first export order. I cannot say who it is from, other than the country in question is European, until the order is signed. We expect that to happen next week and we will announce the customer then. Now, ladies and gentlemen, if there are no further questions?" McMullen looked around, the room was quiet. "We have a lunch buffet in the next room. Please help yourselves."

There would be a good spread out there; everybody knew it. Some companies prided themselves on bringing in rare delicacies and exotic dishes for their company luncheons. Not McMullen Industries. There would be roasts out there, the best meat that money could buy, but simple roasts none the less. The side dishes would be equally simple; vegetables and puddings, roasted, baked or steamed. There was just one peculiarity about hospitality at McMullen Industries. Surplus food was never thrown away. If it wasn't eaten by the guests, take-home packages would be available for them. Any still left would be donated to a hospital, local shelter for the homeless or anything else that seemed appropriate, but never thrown away.

McMullen watched the shareholders leaving the auditorium and sighed happily. He'd never quite lost the feeling of insecurity that had come from a youth spent working in a British shipyard where a man could lose his livelihood at literally a minute's notice. It left him with an urgent desire to ensure that his companies had full order books and for that fact to be well-known to even his lowliest employees. "You think the Brits will go for Mamba, Jorgie?"

Vermaak nodded. "They will. We've got the range edge over the Yank and Ivan missiles and the top attack capability is a big thing running for us. With the armor the new tanks are carrying. . . . . ."

The three men nodded sagely. For their own, wildly differing, reasons, the Americans and Russians both needed to reduce their manpower losses in war. The Americans had an aversion to casualties that was irrational almost to the point of being

9

pathological. The Russians, bled white during the Second World War, simply didn't have the men to lose. One effect of their joint concern had been the development of a generation of battle tanks with massive frontal armor protection. Both the new M-81 Abrams and the T-80 Koniev had frontal armor that was virtually impregnable. The Indian Saradara tank was much the same and it was rumored that the Australian Monash III was also being designed along the similar lines. Vertech had come up with an answer. The Mamba missile would, as the film of the trials had shown, overfly the target and direct a downward-facing shaped charge jet into the vulnerable top surfaces. How it was done was a South African military secret although nobody had any illusions about how long that would last once somebody else got hold of one.

"What does your boy reckon, Deke?" McMullen had more than a professional interest, Bastiaan van Huis wasn't just a conscript serving out his three years in the South African Army, he was the husband of McMullen's youngest daughter, Linda. Their daughter, Kimberley, would be having her fourth birthday soon. They were a good Boer couple: modest, devout and honest, a credit to their upbringing and community. In public, anyway. The Van Huis and Vermaak families had followed in the Afrikaans tradition of large families; after a delayed start, the McMullens had followed suite. Between them, the three had twenty first-generation offspring and the whole lot had run as a pack ever since they were old enough to walk. Eventually, as they'd grown up, they had split into pairs, married and settled down. They still kept together as a tightly-knit group. They kept up appearances and maintained the outward façade of being a set of exemplary young couples. Beyond that, their parents were careful not to ask.

Van Huis stretched his legs out under the table. "Bassie doesn't say too much about what's happening on the border when Linda's around." The other two men nodded wisely. The details of soldiering weren't for the ears of the womenfolk. Logically that was ridiculous; all the Afrikaans and English women were part of the local Kommando and knew how to defend their homes when their men were away. Old habits died hard, especially in the Afrikaans community. "But, over brandy, he doesn't sweat too much about the Caff tanks. Mostly old and they don't use them too well. It isn't even the Caffs that are much of a problem any more. They're never seen on the border any more since they went back into their shell after the Yanks bombed them ten years back. The French have smacked them stupid in Algeria and that put a stop to most of their games. It's mostly tribal groups up there, none of them sane or civilized, and very pleased Bassie is to be in a tank I can tell you. Even an old Centurion."

McMullen looked around, they had the room to themselves while their shareholders were gorging themselves next door. "Might be he won't have to be in an old Centurion much longer. I hear the Army's looking at the Saradara. Big issue now is whether the Army buys them directly from the Indians or whether it gets a license to build them here. We might need to expand our plant if they go for license production. Assuming a good contra-deal can be worked out of course."

"And the contra-deal would be Boomslangs?" Vermaak was grinning broadly at the thought of the huge Indian Army buying his Mamba missiles. An order that size would mean his plant would need expanding as well.

"Could be, could be." McMullen contemplated the same idea with satisfaction. "Now, let's join our shareholders before those vultures eat all the food."

Blackburn Buccaneer S4H XT-279, North Sea.

There was an old joke about the Buccaneer. Blackburn didn't build them, they took a block of solid steel and carved them out as one piece. Known affectionately as 'The Banana' to its crews, the Buccaneer might not be the fastest naval strike bomber around. It wasn't the longest ranged and it didn't carry the largest bomb load but it was undoubtedly the toughest. It was probably also the most stable. Making its attack runs skimming a few feet above the waves meant it had to be. Those were characteristics that were indispensable to use the weapon it carried,. Highball had to be dropped at a very specific speed and altitude. The speed was high and the altitude low. Put together they represented a demanding set of requirements. Too demanding in many ways. Highball had been a brilliant idea when it had first been conceived back in the 1950s but times had changed. Devastating it might be, but using it meant that the Bananas had to approach dangerously close to their targets. A new missile was being developed to replace Highball but that wouldn't be available for years.

Three green lines emerged on the head-up display; two vertical green bars at the side, one a horizontal bar at the base. The art was to keep the bottom line aligned with the horizon while the two green bars moved inwards. When they touched the bow and stern of the target ship, in this case an old A class destroyer, it was time to press the release and drop the two Highballs stowed in the rotary bomb bay under the Banana.

Lieutenant-Commander Ernest Mullback felt more than heard the whine as the bomb bay opened. However, the vibration as the Highball installation spun its two bombs up to speed was very clearly distinguishable from the thumps caused by fast, low-altitude flight and the shaking from the Spey engines. Ahead of him, the target hulk was approaching fast. The green lines on the head-up display edged in towards the old ship's hull. He kept his hands on his controls, using very precise, delicate movements to shift the target to the center of the display panel. This low, this fast, any violent motions on the controls were a recipe for disaster. Another way of killing oneself was to concentrate on the target display to the exclusion of all else. That happened now and then. Usually, it resulted in a Buccaneer flying straight into the sea.

The green lines touched the bow and stern of the target ship. Mullback thumbed the release. Beneath his aircraft, two spherical Highballs dropped clear. This was the remarkable thing. As the bombs hit the surface of the sea, they skipped, a long flat arc that ended with another impact. Another skip then took them closer still to the old destroyer. By that time, they were far behind the racing Banana. Mullback flashed over the target ship long before the two Highballs slammed into its side. That was when another remarkable thing happened, remarkable to those who'd never seen Highball at work anyway. The bombs had a backspin. When they hit the side of the ship, they rolled down it, to explode under the keel. If the bombs were fully charged, the impact was devastating. The Highballs would snap the ship's back and send a jet of water clean through her. A ship so hit would go down in minutes.

But, these bombs weren't fully charged. They just had a small burster and a large amount of red dye. In his mirror, Mullback saw the two bright crimson columns reaching up from the target ship. Both hits were square amidships, right under the single funnel. If they'd been real bombs, that destroyer would be finished. Even now, with reduced charges, her survival was in doubt. She was thirty years old and at the end of her life, her welds had deteriorated, her internal structure decayed. The Navy had done their best for her;

11

everything possible was welded up and the ship was full of empty 55 gallon oil drums. They'd try to keep her afloat as long as they could. Behind him, Mullback saw his wingman make his run. Two more great crimson columns; two more solid hits. Highball may be an ageing weapon but it was still a deadly threat to any surface ship.

"Time for home, Jerry?" The voice over the radio had a broad Scottish accent. Alasdair Baillie was a clansman through and through and wore his tartan proudly. He even had a SAC-like band of the green and dark blue-gray painted under his cockpit.

"Hold one, Jock. We'll see how second section does. They're a pair of Sasenachs you know."

There was a snort over the radio, Baillie and Mullback frequently exchanged good-natured jabs over their respective ancestry and today was no exception. The two Buccaneers curved around and climbed, partly to get clear of the bombing range and partly so Mullback could watch the other two pilots in his flight make their bomb runs. Paul Carter would be fine, Mullback didn't doubt that for a moment. Freddie Kingsman was a newbie and on his first bomb run.

It was hard to see the aircraft, the dark gray of the Buccaneers tended to be lost against the waves and ever-present gray haze that dominated the North Sea. That was, of course, why they were painted that color. In the end, it wasn't the aircraft that he saw first but the white line the concussion waves they generated left on the sea behind them. The two aircraft made their drops, Both Carter's bombs hit dead midships as expected. Kingsman didn't do as well. He picked the wrong angle, left his correction too late and had to pull a tight turn to get lined up properly. By then, he was at the wrong distance from his target and the skips wouldn't align properly. One of his Highballs missed the destroyer, passing in front of her bows. The other actually arced over her and made three or four more skips before finally sinking at the end of its run.

"Sorry, Sir." Kingsman's voice came over the radio, subdued and depressed.

"Not as easy as it looks, is it?' Mullback spoke comfortingly. Everybody had to start somewhere and there were many worse things Kingsman could have done.

"No, Sir. Sorry, Sir."

"Cheer up lad; we all did that at first. Highball's a tricky beast. Get some more simulator time in and you'll get the hang of it." Mullback changed to his internal circuit. "Alex, course for home please."

"Set up, Jerry. We're about 10 minutes out. Carrier Controlled Approach is waiting for us to initiate our run in." Alex Peters was Mullback's 'GIB' – guy in the back – responsible for navigation and handling the electronic warfare systems. Also for looking backwards and making sure no fighters with evil intent were lurking in the six o'clock spot.

As usual, the air control team on HMS *Furious* were on the ball. They brought the four Buccaneers in perfectly. She was an old ship, almost as old as the destroyer her aircraft had just used as a target but the Royal Navy had looked after her and she'd just finished a major refit. One that had taken four of her eight four inch guns and been given new MOG missiles imported from Australia instead. If plans went the way they were

12

supposed to, that would hold her until the new carriers were built to replace *Furious* and her two sisters. If they were built, that was. The government was prevaricating over finding the funding again.

XT-279 trapped perfectly, catching the second wire and halting properly positioned for taxiing off the angled deck. Mullback raised his hook, releasing the wire, and started folding his aircraft's wings. The parking spot behind the island was cramped. The Courageous class carriers were really that bit too small for the aircraft they carried and that meant parking took care. It was always a relief when the Buck was properly in place without hitting anybody or anything.

"How did the new kid do, Jerry?" The bomber squadron commander, Commander Dickie Ravenswood, greeted Mullback as he climbed down the steps from the cockpit.

"Blew it of course. Didn't we all first time out?" Mullback shook his head with memories of fouled-up Highball attacks. "We running to schedule?"

"Don't sweat it, Jerry. We'll have you back in Pompey in time to marry Sam. Assuming she isn't modeling of course. Does The Sun publish on Saturdays?" Ravenswood tried to look as innocent as possible. The fact that one of the Flight Commanders was about to marry The Sun's leading Page Three model was a matter of awed disbelief to the entire carrier air group.

"It does, but they shoot the pages well ahead of time. Make the news up in advance as well you know." Mullback delivered the line deadpan. "Make sure you're at the ceremony and Sam'll give you the racing results for the next meet at Epsom. A week in advance, of course."

Conference Room, White House, Washington D.C.

"I'm afraid, Mister President, that it's only a question of time before the Argentine armed forces move."

"You sound very sure of that Seer." President Reagan drank in the details of the presentation and looked through the satellite imagery with keen interest. "I never realized the detail on these things was so good."

"Those were taken from one of the new Polar Orbit Manned Orbiting Laboratories. MOLPOL for short. Previously, our coverage was always a bit rough that far south, not least because there was nothing down there to interest us. Using a polar orbit allows us much better coverage. We've got three MOLPOLs up now; meaning we do a run over each area at roughly eight hour intervals. When the program is complete, we'll be reducing that to every four hours."

"MOLPOL is a NASA program?" The President had been in office for about nine months and was still getting the fine details sorted out. At least one reason for that was his insistence in learning as much as possible about each subject he was expected to make decisions on. It was that hunger for information that The Seer thoroughly enjoyed. After four years under President Carter, who had treated the Friday Follies as a barely tolerable nuisance, having an audience who actually enjoyed learning for its own sake was

13

a serious pleasure. The Friday Follies had dropped to barely ten minutes and the detailed briefing book that went with it was rarely, if ever, opened. In contrast, under Reagan, the briefing and question session went on for two or more hours and the briefing book was returned dog-eared from heavy use and with annotations in the margins where something hadn't been quite clear enough or where Reagan disagreed with the analysis. They were getting fewer now though. The Seer reflected he'd been getting into bad habits under Carter.

"No, Sir. It belongs to Strategic Aerospace Command. It's part of our target acquisition and identification system. The B-70s can download information directly from the MOLS and use it to finalize their bomb runs. So can the RB-58s. In theory, at least. Anyway, we haven't tried out the system yet, not live. Only on exercises."

"MOLPOL." President Reagan rolled the world around in his mouth. "I don't suppose I can go up to one?"

In the background, one of the Secret Service bodyguards spoke quietly to his thumb, listened and then shook his head. The risk was considered too great. Reagan looked immeasurably sad for a moment, he'd dreamed of going up into space for years but now his position made it impossible. His ride in a Valkyrie, something that was almost a standard part of the orientation process for a new President, had been as far as the Secret Service was prepared to go.

"So if the Argentines move on Chile?"

"Given the way the troop concentrations are being handled, it looks like a coup de main to seize the disputed islands in the Tierra del Fuego area, coupled with major air strikes intended to destroy the Chilean Air Force and an overland invasion aimed at Santiago and Valparaiso in the center of Chile, at Colhaique further south and Punta Arenas in the far south."

"That doesn't sound like a minor dispute over a few islands to me." Reagan re-read the balance of forces being deployed. "This looks like a full-scale invasion leading to a conquest. I thought we'd made it clear we don't allow that sort of thing?"

"We did, Sir, once. But that message got blurred over the last few years and it's only been a question of time before somebody pushed hard enough to test whether the line still held. In many ways, this situation developing is our fault. For many years, we simply ignored South America. Like Northern Europe, it didn't really count in the world scale of things. We had relatively little to do with them, they had about the same to do with us. Back in the Second World War, Brazil sided with us from around 1945 onwards; even sent a few troops to Russia. A brigade or so if my memory serves me well. Mostly they helped out with ASW work in the Atlantic. Chile's got a pretty strong democratic tradition but they kept out of the Second World War although they offered us refueling rights if we had to go around the Horn for any reason. Argentina was strongly pro-Axis right through to 1947. They were an Axis-tilting neutral right up to the time we did the laydowns all over Germany. Post-war they've been the refuge of choice for Germans who still had sympathies for the Reich. It's not surprising they're the ones doing the pushing now."

14

"Then we'd better make damned sure that they know it still does." Reagan paused once again as he re-read the information on the Argentine armed forces. "Can they pull this off?"

The Seer thought carefully and ran the various permutations through his mind. "In fairness, Sir, I don't think they intend a wholesale annexation. At least, they would be really asking for trouble if they did so. I believe their intention is to seize the disputed islands down south and then use the invasion of the center and mid-south as a sledgehammer to force Chilean acquiescence." He paused for a second and ran some more details through the equations. "They may have annexation in mind but that's a hellish big mouthful for a country with serious economic problems. They might pull it off, but it's more likely they'll get a bloody nose in the attempt. The Chilean Army is pretty good and the Andes are a natural defensive wall. I'd guess the Chileans are mining the passes like crazy and possibly blowing some of them up. They'll funnel the Argentines into kill zones and take them down. In the far south, invading those islands will be quite a trick to pull off. The weather down there is foul. So the Argentines may well end up being stalled.

"And there, Sir, lies the real danger. Argentina is a military dictatorship and it faces a lot of internal dissent. My guess is that they're setting this whole thing up to bring about a surge of patriotism from a successful little war. If that scheme falls flat, they'll up the stakes. We know Argentina has nuclear weapons. They're a self-declared nuclear power just like Brazil. They're all too likely to try a nuclear strike to break things loose. Obviously, we can't allow that."

"My predecessor would have done." Reagan's voice was bitter. He was spending most of his time trying to clear up the mess left by Jimmy Carter's disastrous four year term as President. Carter had been obsessed with trying to 'rebuild America's image in the world' and 'atoning for past mistakes.' His efforts to achieve that had done an incredible amount of damage. He hadn't succeeded in doing anything to reduce the fear and resentment that marked other country's attitudes to the United States but he had managed to degrade the respect that came from unmatched power and the willingness to use it. He'd even contrived to damage the Russian alliance that was the foundation of U.S. foreign policy. Fortunately, to the great relief of both governments, Reagan had already managed to repair those wounds.

"Probably not, Sir." The Seer's voice was dry. He'd spent four years trying to make sure that the so-called 'peace initiatives' coming out of the White House hadn't undermined National Security too badly. It had been a hard struggle and he had found it more wearing than most of the wars he'd fought over the years.

"Certainly not. We can thank God that this whole business is cropping up now, not a year or so ago. What would you recommend as our course of action if Argentina does move on Chile?"

"I'd suggest, Sir, that we don't let it get that far. What I would recommend is that we send George Schultz down to Buenos Aires with a stern warning. Basically, tell the Generals down there, 'we can see you, we know what you're up to. Don't.' And do some over-flights of Argentina with B-70s at the same time. A few islands here or there are of no great consequence, and it does nations good to let off a little steam now and then, but this Argentine plan is way beyond that."

Reagan nodded, thinking the implications over. "And if they don't listen?"

"We take out their airfields, naval bases and troop concentrations. Then we ask them, very politely, if their hearing has improved. If it hasn't, we take out everything else. We have to make an example of somebody to show the world that the prohibition on wars of aggression still remains in place. Argentina is as good a candidate as any."

Reagan gulped slightly at that. "I guess we better hope they listen then. Where next?"

"Africa, Mister President. Still a constant low-level war going on there. There's the Caliphate in the North, South Africa down south and a great strip of chaos in between them. Some parts of the region, Kenya for example, are stable and reasonably well-run. Others, like the Congo and the Central African Empire are gruesome nightmares. The South Africans absorbed Rhodesia and the old German and Portuguese colonies but they've stopped there. Smart people, they're holding what they can without over-extending themselves. They just do raiding operations further north to disrupt any efforts to mount a threat against them."

"Ah, not risking Imperial Overstretch." President Reagan was a lot better-read than his political enemies realized and his tastes in books spread widely. He looked around and saw everybody present, including the Seer grinning broadly.

"Definitely not. Something that we, also, are trying to avoid, by the way. We prefer to nuke our mortal enemies into oblivion without a second thought."

"I should hope so!" Reagan put mock irritation into his voice. "Another Russian Front is a nightmare scenario. Any sign of Caliphate involvement in Africa?"

The Seer thought carefully. "There's some, but not much. Ever since the 1973 bombing, the Caliphate has gone quiet. Oh, they're still expansionist and they move into any power vacuums that develop, but they aren't the hyper-aggressive power they were a decade ago. They've eased back on internal repression as well; a little anyway. And their 'Governing Council' these days seems to be neither seen nor heard. The bad news is that they're picking up a little on industrial development. They're building things that a few years ago they wouldn't even have attempted."

"And their military equipment still comes from Chipan?"

"It does, Sir. Arms in exchange for oil; the devil's bargain the Chipanese have been running for three decades now."

"So, if we kick the props out from under the Chipanese, we cut off both the supply of arms to the Caliphate and also their supply of money."

"We surely do Sir. Although, the problem won't be bringing Chipan down, they're folding anyway. It'll be bringing them in to a soft landing. We don't want a spasm of use-it-or-lose it."

"Get your people working on that, Seer. I want to know how we can do it. Another thing; I greatly enjoy reading your briefing books. Is it possible to read them for the last four years? Are they kept on file?"

"Of course, Sir." Naamah spoke up for the first time. "I've got everything on file. Would you like them all at once or one at a time?"

Reagan laughed at the thought of four years worth of weekly situation reports piled on his desk. "A month at a time if you please Naamah. Starting with the earliest ones from four – no, make it five – years ago. If you could give me each set as I finish the previous one, that would be ideal."

"It'll be done, Sir."

"He never read them did he?" Reagan's voice was soft but still the condemnation seeped through. The President had a very personal dislike for his predecessor in office. It was a mixture of big and little things. The big ones were associated with a completely different world view. The little ones were personal. Carter had allowed a degree of casualness that Reagan thought inappropriate for buildings and institutions owned by the American people and just borrowed by their occupants.

"I can't say, Sir. Confidentiality." Naamah's voice was equally soft. She knew that one look at them would tell Reagan that the briefing books had never been opened.

"Very proper. Naamah, I may often forget to say so, and probably will all too many times, but I find your help invaluable. Never think that the efforts you make go unnoticed."

"Thank you, Sir." Naamah knew that even the lowliest member of the White House team was treated with the same respect. It was one of the many differences between the Reagan and Carter White Houses.

"And thank you for the briefing, Seer. Excellent as always. One thing though, a little more care with the grammar and punctuation in the briefing books would be a good thing." The Seer winced at that. Often the only comment he'd had back from Carter on the briefing books was a supercilious typo correction. He grinned ruefully at the President who winked back. Reagan was beaming broadly as he made his way out. He loved the Friday Follies.

Married Quarters, McDill Air Force Base, Florida

"Drink your milk Tommy."

"Aww, mom. . ."

Master Sergeant Selma Hitchins-Yates tilted her head to one side, half closed her eyes and lifted one eyebrow. Thomas Yates, at the ripe age of ten, knew the signs of impending trouble and gulped down his glass of milk.

"There, that wasn't so bad was it?"

"Mom, other kids get chocolate or strawberry flavor for their milk."

"Tommy, that stuff is loaded with sugar. It will make your teeth rot. You don't *like* having your teeth drilled do you?"

"No, but. . ."

"There you are then. Now, school bus is due in five minutes. Have you got everything? Susie? You got everything you need?"

"Yes, Mom." Her two children chorused the answer together, knowing what was coming next.

"Let's see, shall we?" Selma picked up a clip-board hanging from a hook on the wall. "Morning check-list. Lunch?"

"Check." Another two-voice chorus.

"Homework?"

"Check."

She ran down the list, reading off each item in turn. General LeMay had been a great promoter of the check list system and Selma had found it worked just as well at home as it did on SAC's bombers. Of course, it didn't help much with marriages themselves. SAC was a brutal environment for married couples. Up to 70 percent of SAC marriages ended in divorce. The Hitchins-Yates family had been one of the lucky exceptions. Ten years, two children and still together. It probably helped that they were both serving SAC personnel so they both knew the problems first-hand. Selma was prepared to bet that the marriages that failed were between somebody inside and a partner outside.

"Schoolbus?"

"Check!" Both her children chorused the reply in triumph because the yellow bus had just appeared at the end of the street. It would stop there, pick up one batch of children and then come down to her end for the other. That left her just enough time to get her two out there, ready to get on board when the bus stopped.

As always, the schedule worked perfectly. It was a fine day. Humid, of course, but Florida always was. Timing things to perfection really showed its benefit when it was raining but even today it was worthwhile just to have things running efficiently. The children scrambled on to the bus, the driver touched his cap to their mothers and the bus pulled away in a cloud of blue smoke.

Selma waved good-bye and then returned to the house, ready to stack the dishes in the dishwasher and get ready to leave for her duty shift. Her husband was at the table, pouring himself a cup of coffee while something whirred in the microwave oven.

"Why don't you let me make you a proper breakfast? Those oats aren't a fit way to start the day."

Mike Yates chuckled and ruffled his wife's hair. "I was brought up on oatmeal for breakfast, Angel."

She twisted away and looked severely at him. "That is hardly an advertisement. I mean, just look at you. Thin and pale. . ."

The microwave dinged and he took the steaming bowl out and stirred it. "Ambrosia. Nectar of the gods. You got anything interesting on today?"

"*War Queen* and *Spear Woman* are coming in for a full systems check and rebuild. They'll be in for a week or more. How about you?"

"Nothing today. Some simulator time and a lot of paperwork. We've got new target folders coming down for study. Not flying again 'til the end of the week; then we'll be taking *Shield Maiden* down south for some over-flights. Legal ones this time."

Selma laughed. President Carter had tried to stop SAC's habit of over-flying other countries but he might as well have tried to hold back the tide. Deliberate over-flights had been replaced by "navigational errors" if anybody had complained. Few countries had. Even the Caliphate had remained quiet about the continued presence of SAC bombers in their skies. Carter's so-called 'policy' had been reversed within minutes of Reagan taking office. Nobody said so, but there had been a distinct sense of relief at that. Countries might not like SAC knowing what was going on in their territory but they appreciated the fact that a threatening build up on their borders would also be spotted and a potential aggressor warned off. Often the public complaints about overflights had been matched by private messages of appreciation for the information they had generated.

"How are the birds?" Yates was obviously interested and his wife was a prime source of information on the real state of maintenance.

"Overall, pretty good. We've got spares and so on flowing in again. *War Queen* and *Spear Woman* were hangar queens. They always were a problem, so when spares were short, we stripped them. Now we have to replace all the bits we took out. Do a few upgrades at the same time. Anything planned this evening?"

"Not this evening, no. Heads up, though. George and Jenna Pryor are retiring from the PX business and their retirement bash is tomorrow night. We should be there. Nice couple, George was a thirty-year veteran before he retired from SAC and took over running the base PX here as a way of keeping busy. Why do you ask?"

"I know Jenna; heard her reading out a supplier once for sending sub-standard stuff. Anyway, the kids are spending the night with mom and our pops. So we've got the place to ourselves."

Yates nodded. His mother had been bitterly opposed to his marriage to Selma and had gone out of her way to be as unpleasant as possible to her daughter-in-law. Eventually, she had died and Yates's father had retired to Florida, buying a house close to MacDill so he could make up for the time he'd lost with his grandchildren. Selma's parents had met him and the three had become firm friends, taking shared delight in looking after their grandchildren from time to time. Then the implications of Selma's remark sank in.

"Aha."

"That's right, Lover. I plan to be a very bad girl tonight. So hit the ATM on the way home."

Royal Australian Navy Submarine Rotorua, *South of Akamaru, South Pacific*

"Ready to come to periscope depth?"

Captain Steven Beecham tossed the question out to his ops room crew more as a formality than anything else. They had been doing a fast transit under the inversion layer and their batteries had reached a worryingly low charge level. The *Rotorua* needed to come to periscope depth and recharge them using her snorkel. Beecham reflected that the battery charge gauge was the bane of the diesel-electric submarine commander's existence and the ever-present center of his attention. Something the nuclear submarine drivers never had to worry about. There was always talk that the 'next' class of Australian submarines would also be nuclear-powered, but that seemed a long way off, if ever. The S-class boats would be air-independent using Kreislauf diesels. Until they entered service, the *Rotorua* was the best submarine the Australian Navy had. In fact the Improved R class were probably the best class of diesel-electric submarines in the world.

They were also an unusual design. Most submarines used the body of revolution hull design. They looked like an airship, with a single screw at the back. This reduced under water drag to a minimum and made them both fast and agile. The problem was that the design only allowed a single screw. That had significant consequences from a design and equipment point of view. In contrast, the *Rotorua* had a broader hull, a flattened ellipse in cross section, with two screws, moved far out to the sides of the hull. The design had become known as a beaver-tail and it offered a lot of advantages including lack of vulnerability to disablement by damage to a single screw and reduced noise. With both screws out of the stream of disturbed water from the sail, the *Rotorua* had no blade beat to speak of.

"Aye, Sir." Lieutenant-Commander Cardew ran an eye over the boards, checking that all was indeed in order.

"Very good, Number One. Take her up through the level; hold her at one hundred and fifty feet. Sonar, prepare for a complete area scan, check for any surface sound signatures."

The check was a vital precaution, all too many submarines had been run down because they'd surfaced too close to a merchant ship. These days, when tankers, bulk carriers and container ships drew fifty or more feet of water, the chance of a collision was too high for comfort. It wasn't just the big ships that were dangerous; the small fishing trawlers could be even worse. If they were drifting with the waves, there was simply nothing to hear and the first a submarine would know of them was the shattering sound of the collision. A diesel-electric submarine like *Rotorua* would sink the trawler without suffering too much damage but the repercussions, both professional and political, were nausea in the extreme.

Beecham felt the boat move under his feet, heard the creaking in her frames as the water pressure outside changed with the ascent. At some point, they passed through the inversion layer and entered a new world of sound signatures; these included surface ships as well as underwater creatures and machines. That caused a sudden alarmed report from the sonar room.

"Sir, multiple sources of hydrophone effects, all surface ships. They're all around us, Sir. Sound signatures suggest multiple-shaft ships, holding 25 knots."

Beecham knew there was only one group of multiple-shaft surface ships that held that kind of sustained speed: a U.S. Navy carrier task group. His response was instant. "Helm, blow all tanks, get us to the surface now. Before the Septics pick us up and go berserk."

There was no doubt now about *Rotorua's* rise. She was heading straight up. High pressure air blasted her ballast tanks clear; her engines drove her to the surface. The angle of ascent was sharp enough to send people staggering backwards, their ears popping with the changing pressure. Beecham caught hold of a handrail and swung around it, heading up for the hatch that marked access to the sail. In his mind's eye, he could see *Rotorua* breaking surface, her bow lunging into the air before settling back on the surface amid a cloud of spray.

"We're on the surface, Sir."

Beecham didn't acknowledge. He spun the hatch dogs open, went up through the trunk in the sail and then opened another hatch to reach the air beyond. The opening upper hatch deposited a shower of water on his head from where it hadn't had a chance to drain yet. That was just a minor inconvenience. He grabbed a flare gun on the way up. Now he fired it, sending a blue flare arching into the sky. That done, he took a quick look around him.

His guess had been right. He was between two American aircraft carriers; huge ships that dwarfed any other warship afloat. Glancing around, he counted four cruisers and six destroyers; two of which were already turning towards him. Overhead, two Kaman Defender rotodynes were also closing on him. Beecham looked through binoculars at the nearest cruiser. Sure enough, the box launcher amidships that held her Sea Falcon missiles was trained on him as well. *It is*, he reflected, *a chilling experience to have nuclear weapons aimed at me.*

"Signals?"

"Here, Sir." There was a brief pause. "Signal Sir, from the cruiser over there. Message reads 'This is U.S. Navy ship one six nine. Identify yourself."

Beecham shook his head. *Damned Septics, they couldn't make even a pleasant greeting without sounding menacing.* "Make in return. 'This is Australian submarine *Rotorua* in transit. Sorry if we woke you up.' Let's see how they respond to that. What is one-six-nine anyway?"

"She's the *Sacramento* Sir. Improved Long Beach class. The carriers are the *Ohio* and the *North Dakota*."

"*North Dakota?* She's brand new, still running trials. That's a hell of a lot of firepower for somewhere out here. I wonder what they're up to."

"Who knows? I guess it makes sense to the Septics. Doesn't have to be understood by us lesser mortals."

Overhead, the pair of Defender rotodynes were keeping a careful watch on the submarine that had mysteriously appeared in their midst. Cardew gestured at the two carriers that were already pulling away from the virtually stationary *Rotorua*. "You know, if we'd wanted to, we could have got shots in at both of them. We were up, out of the layer, before they could respond."

"And we'd have died ten seconds later. Followed by every city in Australia as soon as the Valkyries could cross the Pacific. Those rotodynes and destroyers aren't screening the carriers; it's the knowledge of what will happen if anybody tries to take a shot at them that does that. Which reminds me. . ." Beecham picked up the bridge internal communications system handset. "Signals, did we collect anything interesting?"

"We got all the radar and sonar signatures, Sir. We're checking them against the threat library now. So far, they're all known. One thing, we got an intercept on a datalink transmission from one of the cruisers to a carrier. We've never had that before. Oh, and I think we got a quick flash of the link from one of the rotodynes to a destroyer but we're still isolating that. With a little luck, we can start trying to crack their encryption."

"Well done Signals. Number One, since we're up here on the roof, we might as well take advantage of it. We'll charge batteries on the surface; men off-watch can come topside. Signals, call Adamstown, let them know we've bumped into our Septic friends out here and they're heading." Beecham hesitated and took a bearing on the departing carrier battle group. "West, on their way to do God-knows-what to God-knows-who. Where do you think they're going, Number One?"

Cardew took only a second to think about it. "South America Sir. Oh, they're heading the wrong way now but that could just be them operating aircraft. There's not that much doubt really. Everybody knows that the Argies are spoiling for a fight with somebody. Chile will be their first choice and I'd guess the Septics are on their way to make a little demonstration of strength off the Chile coast. I'd say of all the countries in South America, Chile's probably the one they're most comfortable with. As are we, of course."

"Signals here Sir. Top-Flash message from Fozzem."

Beecham sighed. A message from Flag Officer, Submarines, more commonly called FOSM was usually trouble. "Let's have it then."

"We're to set course for Santiago in Chile Sir. Run at our discretion but we should plan on getting there ASAP."

CHAPTER TWO
PROFESSION OF ARMS

Salisbury Plain, Great Britain.

It was a reasonably conventional defensive layout; a forward line of observers intended to bring the attackers under artillery fire and channel them into kill zones, a main line of resistance intended to pin them down and destroy them and a mobile reserve of mechanized troops for a counter-attack that would push the opposition Blueforce back into the sea. Blueforce's objective was an area within the defensive perimeter that was supposed to represent a major concentration of command control and headquarters assets. It was actually an old grain silo and disused farm, but nobody was being too picky about that.

Brigadier Strachan looked at his clipboard and noted some comments on the platoon defense layout in front of him. It was a pretty good effort for a newly-commissioned officer. *This young man might have a bright future in front of him. With the right seasoning of course, and a good sergeant to bring him along. A little too much by the book perhaps, some more imagination wouldn't be amiss.* That was the trouble with 'the book;' it was a good servant but it could also be a terrible master. It was always useful to remember that the opposition could read 'the book' as well. That could turn a favorable defensive position into a deadly trap.

"How's he doing Sir?" Sergeant Harper spoke quietly, his voice not carrying beyond the ears of his officer.

"No secured escape route, the position is commanded by high ground on two sides, it's an obvious ambush position and his machine gunners are likely to hit each other. Not too bad for an officer just two weeks out of training. He just needs practice that's all. Needs to get an eye for terrain."

Harper nodded thoughtfully. "We've come a long way, putting the Army back together after That Man ruined us. There were times when I thought we'd never get back to where we were."

"We're not there yet Sergeant, not by a long chalk. Oh, we've rebuilt an Army all right and it's a damn fine one on paper. But, that's where it all is, on paper. Up here," Strachan tapped his forehead, "we're still a beaten army, one that got nearly wiped out here and left the home country to be rescued by the Yanks and the Canucks. That leaves a shadow over everything we do. It's not right and it's not fair, but it's the way things are. It'll remain that way until we win a real one. In everybody's eyes and, worse still, in our own."

Strachan was interrupted by his radio starting to beep. The Umpire's circuit was coming live, suggesting that something was about to happen. Blueforce would be launching their attack soon. Strachan wondered if a Greenforce ELINT group had been listening out for the activation of the Umpire's net to get a first hint of what was happening. He hoped so. It was the sort of initiative that the Army needed. Properly tempered of course. Aye that was the rub.

After the Occupation had ended and reconstruction had begun, the Resistance had dominated the government and armed services in general. They had brought with them their own ideas and experiences based on years of partisan warfare against the Germans and the British Collaborators. Those ideas had included a strong level of contempt for what they considered 'useless administrivia from hidebound reactionaries.' It had taken a long time to convince them that there was a world of difference between partisans and regular armies. Eventually, the two outlooks had been blended and the new British Army created from them. The exercises here today were testing out one part of that doctrine.

"We're under artillery fire Sergeant." Strachan watched Harper, a broad grin decorating his face, get thunderflashes out of the back of the Umpire's Landrover and toss them around the platoon position. He noted with approval how the infantry platoon he was watching took cover but still maintained surveillance of the area to its front and flanks. Despite the unexpected explosions, the officer had his men under control and that spoke well of him.

Strachan took his attention off him for a moment and quickly scanned the horizon with his binoculars. There was movement out there, and he concentrated on it. *At least five Cavalier tanks backed up by a quartet of Bulldog armored personnel carriers.* Strachan reflected that they showed how much the Army was changing as well. Until the mid-1960s they'd used old German armored equipment salvaged after the Occupation had ended. Strachan's old regiment had been driving Panther IIs until the late 1950s. The Cavalier and the Bulldog were the first generation of British built armored vehicles. They were no match for the Russian and American tanks, but creditable first steps. The Cavalier had actually been based on work carried out secretly during the occupation and was a descendent of Britain's last pre-occupation production tank, the Covenanter. Constant refinement had left little of the original vehicle left; the Cavalier had a 20-pounder gun and a powerful diesel in place of a two-pounder and a petrol engine. Not that heavily armored but it was fast and agile. Strachan watched the five vehicles stop and disappear behind clouds of gray as they fired blank cartridges from their main guns.

His radio beeped again and he listened to the message. Harper was watching him. Strachan held up five fingers and waved to the platoon position. Five thunderflashes later, Harper spoke quietly. "You were right, Sir. That position was a bit too obvious."

"Every beginner makes that mistake. An excellent position is a death-trap simply because it is excellent and the oppo can see its value as well. Still, our newbie is keeping his head down so he might get away with it." Strachan took another look through his binoculars. The tanks out on the horizon were still firing but had shifted their aim to other likely positions. They were probing, hoping to get a response from the infantry they were shelling so they could bring in artillery fire on the unmasked positions. Meanwhile, the infantry were working forward in their armored carriers. It was a bit half-hearted; probing and demonstrating rather than making a solid attack. Nevertheless, it was enough to cause the Greenforce commander to shift some of his armored reserve into this sector to try and drive the Blueforce armor off.

That was a fairly indecisive engagement as well. Neither side was really interested in advancing and forcing the issue so the tanks exchanged "shots" at long range. That, at least, pleased the Greenforce infantry who didn't have to put up with the thunderflashes tossed around their position any more. Strachan's radio beeped again. He listened to the message with a smile.

"That's going to liven things up Sergeant. First Airmobile Brigade have just put a battalion assault team behind the objective. Used Junglies to drop in two companies of motorized infantry and a company of assault vehicles."

That was the whole point of this exercise of course, Strachan reflected. The Fairey Junglie rotodynes, so-called after their mottled green-and-black camouflage schemes, had speed and load-lifting capabilities that couldn't be matched by helicopters and they could deliver equipment to areas inaccessible to fixed-wing aircraft. Strachan could picture what was happening now. The Junglies had touched down, dropped their back ramps and were unloading the armored vehicles they carried. Armored was a bit of an exaggeration. The Boarhound armored personnel carriers were splinter-proofed at best, but they allowed the infantry to move fast under a modicum of protection while the Chevalier 'tanks' were the same vehicles fitted with a pair of 120mm recoilless rifles. No match for a regular unit of course but loose in an enemy rear area, they could create chaos.

And that's exactly what they were doing by the sound of it. Strachan switched his Landrover's radio over so he could eavesdrop on the Greenforce communications network. The situation had certainly broken loose back there and he guessed his umpiring colleagues were hard at work sorting out the confusion. He could almost see the little tracked vehicles dashing into the headquarters area while the 120mm armed Chevalier 'tanks' provided fire support. Radio messages on the Greenforce net were already descending into chaos as the signals sections tried to maintain contact under fire and close assault.

"Order, counter-order, disorder." Harper repeated the old proverb with relish.

"And they were *expecting* this to happen." Strachan was fascinated by the way Greenforce was coming unglued as its command control facilities were eliminated. The defense was collapsing quickly as the Blueforce armor up front got the word and started to close on the disorganized and unco-ordinated infantry. Strachan returned his attention to the young officer he had been watching. Despite the confusion and blizzard of disconnected and contradictory radio messages, he was managing a reasonably neat and effective disengagement under fire. Probably the most difficult of all evolutions to pull off. *Yes, this young man had definite promise.* Strachan got the radio message he had been waiting for, fired a red flare into the air and sounded the siren mounted on the back of his Landrover.

"How did they spot us Sir?" It was the young Lieutenant, about 30 minutes after the exercise had been concluded. He'd told his Sergeant to get the men ready to move out, then left him to get on with it. Strachan approved.

"They didn't. But they looked at the terrain and tried to decide where they would put troops if they were defending and fired a few shells at those spots on spec as it were. The place you set up in was an excellent defensive position, so much so it stuck out as a potential target. You'd have been better off setting up in front of it and falling back to it when you came under attack." Strachan glanced at his notebook. "Still, Lieutenant Cross, you did well for your first time out."

"But, with respect, Sir, we lost, Sir." Conrad Cross sounded dispirited by the way events had turned out.

"But you lost well, Cross. Any army can look good when it's winning. It's what happens when everything goes to hell that marks a really good army from those that don't make the grade. You kept control of your troops even when the front was collapsing all around you. That's something to be proud of. You come from a military family?"

"No Sir. My father runs a small house painting business, in Birmingham. He served in the War of course."

"What regiment?"

Cross looked a little embarrassed. "Twenty Ninth Panzergrenadiers, Sir."

"Ah." Strachan acknowledged the German unit designation almost absently, When the significance of the name and designation dropped into place, he looked sharply at the young man. "Your father is Matthew Cross?"

"Yes, Sir. You know him?"

"Heard of him." Strachan decided to prevaricate a little. Some of the details of that case were best forgotten. "He was recommended to one of my officers who bought a house up that way."

Casa Rosada Presidential Palace, Buenos Aires, Argentina

The glass in the windows was both bullet-proof and explosion-resistant. They gave the world a slight sickly green tint when viewed through their impressive thickness. The planning group for Operation Soberanía weren't that interested in looking at the view. They had more important things to consider. The thickness of the glass also served to deaden sound from outside the palace. That meant the noise of the riot currently in progress didn't reach the planning group either. They wouldn't have been concerned with the situation even if they had heard the noise, civil disturbances were for the riot police to handle. They would disperse the rioters and identify the ringleaders. Sooner or later, those leaders would join the long list of desaparecidos, those who had "disappeared" into the maw of Argentina's seemingly unstoppable political security system.

President Jorge Videla looked at the summary file in front of him. "Are we ready to move?" It was his only question.

26

"Yes Sir." Defense Minister Leopoldo Galtieri was confident. Operation Soberanía had been a goal of his for many years and his planning for it had gone back long before the official start two years ago. Even now, with the assault on Chile having full government approval, there were parts of this plan that went far beyond anything officially sanctioned. "We are concentrating the fleet now and refitting the ships for prolonged service. After they have come out of the refit yards, we will start preparing to load the amphibious forces. Fifth Battalion, Naval Infantry, will go ashore at 20:00 on 22 March next year to seize the islands of Horn, Freycinet, Hershell, Deceit and Wollaston. Two hours later, Third and Fourth battalions will land on Picton, Nueva und Lennox Islands and secure the eastern mouth of the Beagle Channel. With our naval infantry in place, we will start the invasion of mainland Chile the next day. Fifth Corps will occupy Punta Arenas and Puerto Natales in Chilean Patagonia while Third Corps will seize Santiago and Valparaiso. We have deployed First Corps northwards to guard against an attack from Brazil. After we have seized Chile, we will hold a plebiscite which will, of course, demand the annexation of Chile into our country."

There was a brief ripple of amusement at the idea of a plebiscite producing any result other than that expected by the people in this room. Videla nodded as he contemplated the assault that had just been described. "Estimated casualties?"

"Between 30,000 and 50,000."

Once more Videla acknowledged the brief answer. It would be a short, bloody war that would end in a major conquest. The surge of nationalism that would go with it would help squash the brooding resentment that had caused the riots outside today and the ones that had gone before. The casualty list would make it easier to describe those who had led the riots as traitors, betraying those who had died to win extra glory for Argentina. The government didn't actually need justification for disappearing those who defied it, but it helped.

The real problem was that Argentina had a financial crisis on its hands of daunting proportions. Inflation was running out of control. The country's trade deficit had become unsupportable and the foreign exchange reserves were running out. Argentina was self-sufficient on its basic requirements. It produced enough food for its citizens to eat well and its oil production was enough to keep the country running but a modern state required much more than that. If something wasn't done soon, a creeping paralysis would start to bring the economy to a grinding halt. Then the rumble of discontent would become a deafening roar.

"Are there any other comments on Operation Soberanía?"

"We cannot move any earlier than the end of March?" The Finance Minister was concerned at the delay might be too long for Argentina's precarious financial position to endure. One of the primary reasons for the operation was to seize Chile's raw material resources so Argentina could exploit them.

"We cannot. The weather will be too bad. March is the earliest and even then it will be risky. The window of suitable weather conditions really is very narrow."

"There is one thing." The Foreign Minister spoke carefully. "We have received some suggestions that the Americans may have some indications of what we have planned."

"So?" Galtieri's voice was loaded with contempt.

"Operation Soberanía is precisely the kind of military action that they have said they will not tolerate."

"I say again, so?"

"Do we really wish to chance nuclear destruction?"

"The Americans are bluffing. Once they may have meant what they say, but those days are long past. That fool Carter made it clear that they will no longer try to interfere in the actions of other countries and who has he been replaced by? A Hollywood actor! We have no need to fear the Americans."

"I hope you are right, General. For all our sakes, I hope so."

Prison Hospital, Puerto Belgrano Naval Base, Argentina

"Pant hard it's nearly there. Just one more effort." The midwife spoke comfortingly to the young blonde woman on the delivery bed while she dabbed sweat from her patient's forehead. The soon-to-be mother sobbed, but tried to gather herself for the last effort.

Across the room, a naval officer glanced impatiently at his watch. "How much longer? We've got more important things to do than this."

"Soon, very soon." The midwife dabbed her patient's forehead again. "Poor lamb. As if being held here isn't bad enough, she had the bad luck to be carrying a baby as well."

Captain Alberto Astrid looked at his watch again. "Bad luck had nothing to do with it. Just get that baby delivered, and hurry up about it."

He started pacing backwards and forwards, still glancing impatiently at his watch. Eventually the sounds of the birth were interrupted by those of a baby crying. Astrid stepped over to the midwife who was now attending to the infant. "Is it healthy?"

"Yes. . . " The midwife started to speak but Astrid held up his hand. "That is all we need to know right now."

"Please, may I see my baby?" The voice from the woman on the bed was weak. That exaggerated her Swedish accent to the point where her Spanish was almost unintelligible.

"No." Astrid spoke with contempt.

"At least, is it a boy or a girl?" She was crying now; a mixture of exhaustion, fear and despair.

"That is no concern of yours." Astrid drew his pistol, held it so the women could see it and know what was about to happen, then shot her in the head. "Orderlies, take that down to the incinerators and burn it."

The midwife was trying to comfort the baby that had started crying again with the sound of the shot that had killed its mother. "Why, why did you do that?"

Astrid didn't even bother to answer. He wasn't accountable to anybody, least of all to a midwife who would not be much longer for this earth if she kept asking questions. He simply gestured to her to follow him as he left the delivery room and walked down a long corridor towards the public area of the hospital. There was a young couple waiting in a side room, an Army officer and his wife. Their faces lit up when they saw Astrid and the midwife.

"Major Mazza, Madame Mazza? Allow me to present you with your new. . ."

"Son." The midwife completed the phrase.

"Son, yes. Take good care of him."

"Oh we will, Captain. This is the dream we have both lived for." Madam Mazza's face was rapturous as she looked down at the infant now in her arms. "We never thought we could have this joy. Thank you Captain, thank you from the depths of our hearts."

"The mother?" The Major looked down at his new son with pride.

"A young woman who loved, not wisely, but all too well. She is delighted her baby has a good home. Major, we must complete the adoption papers. Perhaps you and I can see to that while Madame Mazza tends to her new responsibility?"

Major Mazza nodded and started to follow Astrid out of the room. Before they left, Madame Mazza took one hand from the baby she was holding and grabbed Astrid's sleeve. "Captain Astrid, thank you once more for fulfilling our heart's wishes and making our family complete. You truly are a saint."

Tank Platoon, Transvaal Rifles, South African Border, Just West of Tshinsenda.

"It might be thought that the veroordeel missionaries would have given up by now?" Lieutenant Bastiaan van Huis didn't much like the mission his platoon of Oliphant tanks had just been handed but orders were orders. Besides, his platoon was probably the most experienced around and the poor bloody infantry going with them would need the best support they could get. Van Huis was quietly confident his platoon was the best in the brigade, if not the whole division.

"Perhaps they think the stams need the protein?" Sergeant Anders Lehmkuhl was looking at the map while he spoke. On paper, the job wasn't that difficult. Advance about five miles in, shoot the hell out of the stamkamp, rescue the missionaries and then get back

29

to friendly territory. They'd done a lot worse than that, including one epic that had taken them nearly eighty miles into stam country and then out again.

"They don't really eat them do they?" Private Meade Dippenaar was a newbie. He'd just joined the platoon and had been assigned to tank number five as the loader, making him the lowest of the low. He'd stay there until van Huis had a read on the man and could see where his talents lay. If he didn't have any, then he'd stay the loader of tank number five.

"No, jongmens. Not so often. Usually they do much worse than that." Lehmkuhl knew the bitter truth of what he was saying. There was a very strict time limit on rescues like this. They'd been too late all too often.

"Then why do they keep going?" Dippenaar couldn't see why he should have to risk his life for some people who didn't have the sense to stay out of obvious danger. He accepted that the platoon would have to go; he just wanted a reason why they should. One that he could explain back home.

"Because they believe the Lord will protect them? Or they believe the stories are exaggerated or our propaganda? Because they believe that this time it will be different? The terrible thing is, the worst of the militias across the borders are Christian, or at least they claim they are. They do the atrocities anyway; missionaries and aid workers regardless. So who knows what the sendelings think when they set out? They go because they are who they are and we must try and save them because we are who we are. That's the meaning of being a soldier Doc. We fight for those who cannot, or will not, fight for themselves."

Dippenaar's nickname in the platoon was Doc from his initials. He nodded quietly to himself. He didn't quite understand the answer van Huis had given him but it sounded right and he memorized it for the future.

"What I don't like is the short run." Staff Sergeant Zander Randlehoff was the commander of number two tank and van Huis's second in command. "Why are the stams holding them so close to the border? Don't they realize we'll be coming to get them?"

It was a good question. van Huis had been waiting for one of his men to ask that and he had had a private bet with himself that Randlehoff would be the one. "Why do you think, Staff?"

"Because it's a bloedig trap that's why!" Randlehoff spoke emphatically, the Afrikaans curse spat out like a bullet. "They want us to come straight down here and charge in. They know we're running against the clock and it's the fastest way."

His finger tapped a strip of clear ground between the two great patches of oerwoud that flanked their target. It looked as if a flood at some time had washed the trees and ground cover away, leaving what looked like a roadway through the heavy terrain. "Does anybody want to bet that's soft silt and full of mines?"

The assembled troops nodded. It was common knowledge that Randlehoff was up for promotion to officer and generally agreed that the platoon would be the worse off

30

without him. They could see for themselves that the tanks would bog down in the soft silt and get blown apart by mines and RPG fire.

"And that's why we're not going that way broers. We'll swing north, cross the border five miles north of here where there's hard, clear ground. We'll get the guns to pound on Kawimba. That's another five miles north and with luck the stams will think we're heading there. We've got two platoons of moddervoete with us. One of them will make a feint north to keep the stams thinking we're heading that way. The other will come with us when we swing south and hit the stamkamp from the north. There's a road we can use so we can move fast. Their Ratels can go first; we'll follow as fast we can.

"Once we're in, the stamkamp is pretty simple." He pushed some pictures out over the maps. "Two semi-circular kamps, each with eighteen huts. Cupped between them, three kraals and eleven other huts. That's the civilian area. We try and keep clear of them. Shooting comes from there, we shoot back, but otherwise we leave them alone. Poor bastards suffer more from the militias than any of ours do. Now, see this big one here?" His finger tapped a single large hut a little separated from the rest. "That's where any surviving missionaries will be. If there are any surviving. Now, important thing. East of the main kamp. See this arrowhead? There's seven huts along the main shaft, and there's five on each diagonal. This is where whatever militia is over there live. Way they're laid out, looks like any serious firepower will be in there. So we take them out fast; no need to leave them breathing. Then swing in to grab the rest. Any questions?"

"How many missionaries, Bassie?"

"There were seven; five men, two women. How many left now, we'll find out when we get there. Mount up, broers; we have some hard driving to do."

The meeting broke up, the men going back to their tanks. Sitting in the turret of number one tank, van Huis pulled out the last letter he had received from his wife. It had been a chatty letter, full of news about their family and the rest of their clan. She'd told him how much she'd missed him, how much she wanted him back. Through it all, she'd stressed that she and the family were safe and well, that everything was ready for him when he returned and he shouldn't worry about them She was fine, the children were fine, so he should just look after himself so he could come back to them. It was a perfect letter from a soldier's wife; both loving and reassuring, a letter that raised morale. Bastiaan van Huis knew he was a very lucky man. He kissed the paper, folded it carefully away, then got on the radio to arrange artillery support.

Lankneus Artillery Battery, Transvaal Rifles, West of Tshinsenda

Nobody could ever say that Australian Defense Industries sales division didn't have a sense of humor. The Kunchi 7.5 inch self-propelled gun was a case in point. The weapon had been developed, marketed, introduced into service and sold to several export customers long before anybody had looked up the meaning of its name. It had just been dismissed as another of those strange aboriginal names the Australians liked to use for their weapons. Even when the joke had finally been discovered and the embarrassed laughter had died down, the gunners had to admit it was an apt choice. A 7.5 inch artillery piece with a 60-caliber barrel made for a lot of gun.

It had started life as a version of the 7.5-inch 50-caliber gun used by the Indian coastal artillery. The Indian and Australian armies had been looking for a heavy gun to replace their American M2 155mm Long Tom guns and M115 203mm howitzers. Both armies had wanted the world of course. The specification wa for a gun that could throw a heavy shell a long way with pinpoint accuracy on a self-propelled chassis. The Americans had nothing like it. The Russian guns were mostly 122mm and 130mm and fired too small a shell for the artillerists. Then, the Australian Navy had started looking for a new heavy gun as well and eyes had fixed on the 7.5-inch. There was a problem of course, there were only four of the old 7.5-inch guns left and that was few enough for experimentation. While the gunners had played with the old guns, the designers had got to work with modern design concepts and materials and produced a new version of the weapon. They'd stretched the barrel to 60 calibers and designed a new tracked chassis to carry the weapon.

The 7.5-inch shell itself was impressive. It weighed 200 pounds; twice the weight of the 155mm and – remarkably – the same weight as the shell from the M115. The designers began to realize something. The 7.5 inch was a sweet-spot in gun calibers; one of the places where all the lines converged to give an optimum result. They had been about to start producing new batches of the old shell when a young Canadian engineer had literally hammered on their door. His message had been quite simple. "You're all nuts," had been his first words. It had been an interesting debate as to whether the designers should listen to him or take him into the car park and give him a thorough beasting. At that point, somebody asked his name. It turned out he was Doctor Gerald Bull. That meant two things made them listen. One was he was the youngest man ever to hold a PhD in ballistics and the other was he'd just resigned from the Canadian Armament and Research Development Establishment after they'd cut his development budget.

His point had been quite simple. Artillery shells were atrociously badly designed. The basic layout dated from the First World War and hadn't changed much in the meantime. They were an aerodynamic nightmare. Bull had described them as 'a flying airbrake'. He produced drawings of a new shell, one that was longer than the conventional design and beautifully profiled with extended strakes down the side to stabilize the shell in the gun's barrel. It even had a gas generator; a small burning charge at the base, to fill in the void left by the shell as it passed through the air. The Australian Army had hit a winning combination with its 3.7-inch Nulla long-range self-propelled gun. That had given them a taste for far-reaching artillery, but this new shell looked like something out of science fiction. In a wind tunnel, a conventional shell was almost invisible behind the mass of turbulence it generated. Bull's new extended range full bore shell slipped through the air with barely a ripple.

The ordnance laboratories had made a test batch of 155mm shells to the new design and the results had been stunning. The M2 155mm could throw a 100 pound shell 22,000 yards. The same gun fired the new shell 32,000 yards, equal to the much-vaunted Nulla, and that was with a gun not optimized for the new shell and the ammunition itself that had been hand-made. By the time the new 7.5-inch gun was ready, the design of the shells had been refined and an initial production batch was available for trials. That led to a problem. The instrumented range wasn't big enough for the new gun threw the new 200 pound Extended Range Full Bore Base Bleed shell an astounding 55,000 yards. It wasn't that easy of course. There were development problems with gun, shell and carriage but they'd been straightened out in time. When the new gun was finally unveiled, the Kunchi was the best artillery piece in the world by a large margin. It had been selling as fast as ADI could move them off the production lines ever since.

Staff Sergeant Arend Quarshie looked up at the 40-foot long barrel towering over his head and reflected on how apt the Australian name had been. In the South African Army, the gun was called the Lankneus, the long-nosed one. That meant more or less the same thing. Army humor was pretty much the same around the world. There were eight guns in this battery position. It was one of the three heavy batteries deployed by the Transvaal Rifles. With their unprecedented range, the guns could cover a huge length of the border – or alternatively throw their shells far into stam country the other side.

"You have the fire plan, Staff?" Major Kieran Neumetzger had appeared out of the darkness to make a final check on his battery's readiness. Technically, each of these guns was commanded by a Lieutenant, with a Captain in charge of each two-gun section. There was a reason for the high proportion of officers. These guns could also fire nuclear rounds if needed. However, Lieutenant Kleyn was sick and Quarshie was in command of his gun for the night's work.

"Entered into fire control, Sir. Ready to go when we get the order."

"Very good, Staff. Make sure the men have their hearing protection in place." Neumetzger vanished into the darkness again.

Quarshie picked up the order. "You heard our Major. Get your headsets on. The bosses back in The World don't like deaf employees." He picked up his own headset. It had the radio earphones built into it so the orders and fire direction commands could be transmitted to him and from him to his gunners.

He didn't have to wait long. The word came through on the battery net, "Gun One. Ranging shot." A string of numbers followed. Quarshie repeated them to the gun crew. Behind him, men rolled the long, slender shell from the magazine on the eight-by-eight parked near the gun and slid it forward. He checked the markings on the shell. Black body, white band around the nose. High explosive, common. Quarshie had a repeated nightmare in which he somehow failed to notice the white shell body with fluorescent orange and red bands and the sinister black trefoil, but he never failed to notice the boiling red and black mushroom cloud that marked the full horror of the error. So he checked the shell and checked it again as it was rammed into the breech with the propellant behind it. Six bags, just like the orders said. Then the clang as the breech closed and the whine as the gun elevated and traversed into position and he raised his hand high over his head.

The word came over the radio. Quarshie repeated it, dropping his hand sharply. The gunner pressed the fire button. No lanyards to be jerked here, the shells were fired electrically. The great gun crashed. The sound of its firing shook the ground as the tracked carriage leapt backwards to dig its spade deep into the ground. The barrel recoiled back, the violence of the shot hurled it against the hydraulic recoil buffers that returned it to the firing position. He heard the sound of the shell going out. It was not a shrill, piercing whine like the old guns with their awkward shells, but a soft moan that reminded Quarshie of the times he had spent with a lady of negotiable affection. He even convinced himself he could see the faint red dot from the base-bleed system as the shell went downrange.

This shell wasn't intended to go all the way to its target. It was being tracked by a radar set mounted on the fire control vehicle and its trajectory being compared with the one the fire control men had calculated. From that, they worked out how far from its target that shell would have been and what corrections were necessary to allow for the changes. Then, one of the men in the vehicle blew the shell up in mid-air.

Quarshie's radio beeped again. A new set of numbers came over the link to him. Each gun was getting its own set; only a fool kept his artillery pieces too close together. The barrel moved slightly; a minute fraction to one side, a touch less elevation. Then another shell rolled out of the magazine. The four loaders moved it forward to the loading tray and into the breech. Black body, white ring around the nose.

"Fire for effect!"

Once again, Quarshie dropped his hand. Once again the gun hurled its shell downrange, towards its target deep in stam country. He didn't know where the shell was going, he didn't know why it was going there and, the truth was, he really didn't care too much. It was his job to send the shells downrange with the pinpoint accuracy that everybody expected from a Lankneus battery and that was what he intended to do. The drill was laid down; six shots in the first three minutes, then one shot every two minutes after that. A slow rate of fire compared with the smaller field guns, but they had their job and Lankneus had its.

Free of the barrel of the guns, the shells arced through the air towards their target just south of Kawimba. Photographs had shown a militia kamp just outside the town. The shells were targeted on that. Those who made the decisions hadn't wanted to waste the 7.5-inch shells so they'd decided to devastate the militia huts. Perhaps give the poor stams who lived in the town a few days of peace before another gang turned up to victimize them. For all that, this was a diversion, not the main point of tonight's shoot.

Descending on their target, the 200-pound shells plowed into the kamp. They blew the huts apart, sending steel shards tearing through the mud and concrete blocks that made their walls. The roar of the explosions could be heard miles away, especially at the kamp at Tshinsenda. There, the militia thugs looked at the brilliant flashes, saw the rolling explosions and heard the moan of the shells overhead and made their plans. They knew the Army from over the border would be following up the bombardment. The rival group now under those shells would not survive the night. That meant they could go to the town they had once terrorized to loot, rape and kill. Tomorrow, they could spread fear as they asserted their domination over Kawimba and all who lived there. Tonight, they would watch the destruction of their rivals.

Ratel Infantry Platoon, Transvaal Rifles, South African Border

Second Platoon swung north as they hit the road, heading up towards Kawimba. Their commander had strict orders. This was a feint, a demonstration; it wasn't worth the life of a single South African soldier. He was to take no chances, not do anything other than to make a lot of noise and fire off a lot of ammunition. As it had been explained to him, Lieutenant 'Geldsakke' in the Oliphant platoon was running short on his allowance this month. They had to blast off lots of ammunition so his vader could make some more. Van Huis in the tank platoon was the butt of a lot of jokes about his family's part in the great family of businesses that supplied so much of South Africa's armaments, but there was quiet respect for the fact that he hadn't ducked serving his time or sought out a soft option.

34

Captain Shumba Geldenhuys watched his second platoon head off, then concentrated on his own job. His Ratel platoon was turning on to the road, track was much more like it, and picked up speed. The Ratel eight-wheeled armored personnel carriers could be in Tshinsenda, a little bit over five miles down the road, in just under ten minutes. The lumbering Olifants would be following him as fast as they could but they were slow. They were Indian-built Centurions, descended from British infantry tanks. Geldenhuys knew what that meant. Excellent armor, mediocre gun, poor speed. McMullen Industries had rebuilt them with van Huis TV-12 diesels instead of their petrol engines and 100mm guns in place of the 90mm the Indians had used, but they were still slow. In this action, time would be everything. The Ratels would speed on ahead while the tanks followed behind and reached the battle as quickly as they could. Geldenhuys just hoped they would be in time to help out if things got really ugly.

Outskirts of Tshinsenda.

The monsters came out of the darkness. Their eyes glared white fire, their voices screamed a terrifying battle-howl of fury. The Ratels had their headlights full on and their sirens were blaring at maximum volume to create the maximum level of shock. It didn't make much military sense to do things that way, but not everything that worked had to make sense. This was a technique that had proved useful before and against much more determined opposition than a mob of disorganized bandits who called themselves a militia.

The problem was that things were already coming apart in the chaos of a night action. Geldenhuys had followed Second Platoon along the orange-yellow laterite road all right and found the unmarked side turning easily enough. He'd taken them across the disused and derelict railway line. That's where the trouble had started. The track, it was little better than a path, went through a particularly dense patch of Oerwoud. The reconnaissance photographs failed to show that it was obstructed by fallen trees and partially washed away. The wretched state of the track slowed the wheeled Ratels down so much that Geldenhuys had begun to fear that the Olifants would catch up with him. That was an embarrassing thing for an infantryman who believed in wheels.

The wheels versus tracks argument was one that had bedeviled the South African Army for years. Further south, on the veldt, there was no real dispute. The extra mobility and reliability of wheeled vehicles had led the South Africans to rely on them. But, as the country had expanded northwards, the terrain closed in. Wheeled vehicles were at a disadvantage compared with tracks, as Geldenhuys had just found out. As much as anything else, that was why the expansion had stopped where it did. It would not be many miles further north where the oerwoud changed into real jungle. Up there, even tanks would have trouble maneuvering.

The Ratels struggled through. Eventually they had burst out into a patch of open ground that should have led them to the right position for their attack. They were already more than 15 minutes behind schedule due to the terrible condition of the track they had used so Geldenhuys had hurried his maneuver and swung south too early. Now he faced the job of working his way up the length of the arrowhead instead of taking it all out at once. One part of his mind was screaming abuse at himself. *My hurry, my need to get in ahead of the tanks had screwed everything up and probably cost the kidnapped missionaries their lives.* Geldenhuys looked across at the darkened civilian area, *just where were the tanks anyway?* By the amount he'd been delayed, he'd expected to see them already at work.

35

Two of the three Ratels had stopped. The seven infantrymen in each were already debussing, spreading out in a line beside their vehicles. The 23mm auto-cannon in the Ratel's turret poured fire into the buildings ahead of them. The incendiary tracers set the wooden structures ablaze and lit the whole scene in an eerie flickering orange red light. The militia people in the huts were pouring out. Most were mown down by the nine machine guns mounted on the two troop-carrier and Geldenhuys's command vehicle. More still being picked off by the riflemen on the ground. There was return fire, a lot of it. Most was automatic fire that arched high overhead. Some was rocket fire. The light from the fires and the tracers stained the exhaust trails bright red as they too arched overhead. That was one thing one could rely on when fighting the militias. They always fired high, never allowing for the recoil of their weapons on full automatic.

Across the open ground between the Ratels and their infantry and the huts, Geldenhuys saw the militia who had survived the first savage blasts of fire trying to defend themselves against the assault. He could see them in the shadows cast by the burning huts. Mostly they were standing erect, holding their rifles sideways and over their heads as they hosed out wild, random bursts. He could guess that what was left of the livestock in the kraals behind him were taking the brunt of the gunfire, *that and the poor baastard villagers trying to hide in their own huts*. The white muzzle-flash from the militia's weapons gave them away more than any other single factor. Geldenhuys could hear his own men firing, the slow, vicious crack of the 7.65x54mm cartridges fired on semi-automatic contrasting with the hammering noise of the automatic weapons on the other side.

The South African Army had never believed in the intermediate caliber idea. Their G1 FAS rifles were chambered for a full-powered rifle round. It was based on the old 7.65x53mm sold by Mauser but redesigned, modernized and boosted to much higher chamber pressures. They'd made the case a millimeter longer to stop the new cartridge being fed into old 7.65mm Mauser rifles, but it had turned out that the tolerances were enough to allow the rifles to chamber both. Fortunately, the immensely strong Mauser action meant no serious accidents had taken place. Geldenhuys could see the effects the rounds were having. As each militia rifleman gave his position away, the heavy, high-velocity bullets cut them down.

One man seemed to be surviving. He was standing in the shadows, waving his weapon from side to side as if he was spraying bullets yet there was no muzzle flash from his weapon. Geldenhuys grabbed the machine gun mounted in the small turret on his command vehicle and fired a short burst at the man. He stumbled with the impacts and then collapsed in a heap. Before Geldenhuys could compliment himself, another man ran forward, his chest a bright orange. For a moment Geldenhuys thought the man was on fire, but the color was wrong. The man was firing his rifle, wildly, hopelessly inaccurately, but still firing it. Before Geldenhuys could draw a bead on the man and cut him down, two or more of his riflemen did it for him.

Under his feet, the Ratel lurched and started to edge forward. The riflemen around them moving forward with the armored vehicle. Gunfire from the first group of buildings faded away. The militia had either been killed or run away. That left the shaft of the arrow still to crush before the job was even half done. The infantry had to keep up the pressure on the militia kamp, to divert attention away from the third Ratel and its crew. They were the critical part of the whole mission.

36

A hundred yards or so southwest of where Geldenhuys and most of his platoon were pinning down the militia in their kamp, the third Ratel, its crew of four and the seven infantrymen it carried, were approaching the large rectangular building that had been designated the holding point for the missionaries. Compared with the wild explosion of light, sound and fire from the main gun battle, theirs was a stealthy approach without fanfare or flourish. The Ratel pulled up a few yards short of the building, its gunners ready to pour fire into it if there was any hostile movement. There wasn't. The building was quiet; weirdly, worryingly silent.

Staff Sergeant Lennan de Wilzem braced himself for the sight that he was sure lay in wait for him behind the door. Every instinct that he had was telling him there was nothing alive inside the structure. By every law of logic that meant any people inside were dead. It would be too much to hope for that they would simply have been shot. Instead he knew what he was about to see. Bodies butchered and mutilated beyond any form of human recognition; at least they would be dead. All too often, some were still alive. Trying to keep the contents of his stomach under control, he fired a shot from his rifle, blowing open any semblance of a lock on the double doors, then pushed his way inside. As he did so, de Wilzem rolled to one side and shone a flashlight across the darkened building. It was empty.

Almost sighing with relief, de Wilzem joined his men in quickly searching what was obviously a barn. They pushed through collections of straw, sorted through dark corners, threw open three internal doors. Once they flattened themselves to one side as a mole viper slithered out from a hole in the wall and vanished into the darkness. Human and snake were all too pleased to leave each other strictly alone.

"Building is empty Lenny."

"Up here too Staff."

De Wilzem acknowledged. His reply was drowned out by a roar. The building shook, bringing dust, dirt and insects down from the roof. He was slightly thankful. Shaking a roof like that could bring much deadlier inhabitants down on one's head. Not all snakes were as accommodating as the mole viper.

"It's the tanks." One of the younger men started to move towards the door.

"Bystand waar u is!" de Wilzem yelled at the top of his voice. The soldier froze in his tracks. "If the tankies see you come from a building they will think you are a stam and shoot you down."

That was all too true, not that de Wilzem blamed the tankies. The heavy armor made the Olifants almost immune to shots from the front but the sides and rear were another matter. Not to mention the fact that everybody was edgy in situations like this. The building shook again as the tanks started firing on the buildings ahead of them

They took long enough. The thought ran through Geldenhuys's head as he saw the five Olifants push through the kraals and open fire on the buildings that made up the other arrow-side. The 100mm rounds shredded the wooden structures, sending clouds of fragments billowing into the air. The sudden appearance of the tanks and the vicious crossfore of machine guns from the Ratels and tanks had the desired effect. The firing from the militia kraal started to fade away. De Wilzem knew what was happening, the militia was fading away into the jungle. They'd run and would not come back for hours, perhaps days. That suited him fine. With the militia gone, the skirmish was over.

Tshinsenda, South African Border

"So what happened, Lieutenant?" Geldenhuys was inquisitive rather than condemnatory. He had his own navigational error to temper any rebuke he might have had in mind.

"We missed the turning, as simple as that, Captain. We missed it, Lord alone knows how, and we only realized when we saw the glow of the burning huts behind us. So we turned around and came back."

"You drove to the sound of the guns. Nobody will criticize that." Geldenhuys and van Huis walked through the blasted ruin of the militia kraal while the infantry checked the ruins of the buildings. No sign of the missionaries, but some of the buildings were so badly burned out that nobody would ever know who had been inside. They came across a body, one surrounded by white whispy flakes of some sort of padding covered in orange fabric.

"That's a life jacket; a seaman's life jacket." Van Huis was amazed. "Why on earth was he wearing that?"

"Perhaps it was a fashion statement?" Geldenhuys shook his head. Then an idea came to him. He walked over to where the man he had shot lay. A quick inspection showed why he had never fired his weapon. The bottom plate of his magazine had dropped out and the magazine spring was trailing out on the ground, surrounded by the glittering brass from the magazine. He shook his head. Nothing really surprised him anymore.

"Look here Captain. A double barreled blaster." Two of the infantrymen were laughing. They'd found a body carrying a weird construction, a stockless Arisaka rifle taped to the side of what looked like an RPG rocket launcher.

"Do you think this one had enough magazines taped together?" The figure stretched out on the ground had six of the Arisaka magazines taped together in what the moddervoete called the 69 position.

Geldenhuys looked at the body carefully. "Perhaps he should have used some of the tape to close his flies, hey boys?" The observation got him a roar of laughter.

"Sir, over here." This voice wasn't laughing. Geldenhuys looked across the center of the kamp. The villagers were beginning to come out of their huts. Some women carrying babies were at the front; everybody was moving slowly and carefully, keeping their hands well in view. Sensible of them. Staff Sergeant de Wilzem was moving over to speak with them, or try to at any rate. There was a patois, a mixture of Portuguese, Afrikaans and English, that served for most purposes. Geldenhuys hoped it would here.

De Wilzem spoke for a moment then gestured to some of his men. They ran over to a kraal, one whose stink spoke of the pigs that lived there. The village headman was pointing at the enclosed sty that formed the back wall as Geldenhuys and van Huis joined

38

them. Two of de Wilzem's men and some of the villagers started clearing the dung- and urine-soaked straw away, moving carefully in case of anything venomous hiding in the mess. It wasn't just snakes that could give a man a bite that would put his life in danger. This time, there wasn't anything threatening other than the stink and filth. Before long, the digging had exposed a small wooden patch in the back wall of the kraal. It was cunningly concealed. The tiny hiding hole and pit were lost within the structure of the kraal and the smell meant that nobody would look too closely. The moddervoete ripped the boards away and shone flashlights into the pit. Crouched in the bottom, so closely jammed in that they couldn't move, were the missing missionaries. Cheers rose from the South Africans as all seven were dragged out from the foul pit. They were suffering from spider bites and scorpion stings, but they were alive.

"They hid us. The villagers hid us." The head of the missionary group, a man called Houghan, was speaking to Geldenhuys, shakily, still unable to believe that he was alive and safe.

"You think you are a brave man because you are a soldier, jongmens?" Lehmkuhl spoke quietly to Dippenaar who was watching the scene with horrified fascination. "With your uniform and your tank around you? With your comrades to cover your onderkant? Well, jongmens, look at what real bravery is. Those poor bastaards there have nothing to fight with. Perhaps some farm tools, if they are lucky and if the militias haven't stolen them. If the militias found they had hidden those people, the entire village would have been wiped out and their deaths would not have been pretty. Yet hide them they did because they thought it was the right thing to do. And then they lived with it, for who knows how long, afraid every day that something would give them away or one of the other villagers would try to buy his life by revealing the secret. Those people have more guts than you or I ever will. And don't forget they saved those people, not us. We screwed up. The officers won't admit it but we did. Our clever plan all went wrong and it was those villagers who pulled our nuts out of the fire as well. So remember this next time some siviele tells you that the stams up here aren't worth anything."

The missionaries were being pushed, none too gently, into the back of one Ratel. It was a tight fit, but it was just possible and it was a whole world better than the hiding place they had just left. Around them, the villagers just stared at the armored vehicles. The faces of the men were stoic. Some of the women, especially those with the babies, cried quietly.

"Captain, the militia we drove out, they must be watching. You know what will happen here when we leave."

"Of course, van Huis. But what can we do?"

"Take them with us?"

"That is forbidden. You know that. There will be hell to pay if we bring an entire village over."

"It will be worse than hell if we leave them here."

"Respectfully Sirs." Staff Sergeant Randlehoff spoke quietly, "the men believe it is the right thing to do. The only thing to do. They saved our people, we should save them."

"On nine armored vehicles? How many are there?" No officer worth his salt ever ignored a warning from his sergeant that the men had strong feelings on something. Geldenhuys spoke quickly to the chieftain through de Wilzem. "He says there are about a hundred including the babies. There were more, but that was before the militia came."

"Tell him that all those who want to leave can come with us. We can put some inside your Ratels. More can ride on top and on my tanks. The rest can walk with us. We'll put three of my tanks in front. The other two can bring up the rear. Your Ratels in the middle. That way the lead tanks will explode any mines buried out there. We can get out to the south of this place, there is good ground there to the border. And the border is open. We should know that it is for us to hold it closed."

Geldenhuys nodded slowly. "Very well. De Wilzem, tell the chief we will take the women who have babies inside the Ratels. Order the boys to squeeze up. If there is not enough room, they can walk. Our new jongmens could use the exercise. The old and the very young can ride on the tanks and Ratels. The rest walk between the vehicles. Tell them to step only in the tracks made by the tanks and Ratels."

De Wilzem spoke to the chief who relayed the words to his villagers. As the word that they were going to escape from this militia-plagued hell spread, there was first disbelief and then incredulity. The Afrikaaners were going to take them to something that approximated safety. The Ratels filled up and then overflowed with the crowd of people mounting up. The younger men and women started bringing out what was left of the village's livestock, some pigs, a few scrawny, half-starved cows. The women held chickens under their arms. Geldenhuys looked at the display with something approaching awe. This was an exercise he'd never learned at staff college.

"Sir, the headman asks, can we set the huts on fire? The way we did with the militia kraal. They don't want to leave the thugs anything."

Geldenhuys could understand that feeling. He gave the order. The 23mm cannon on the Ratels snapped out bursts of incendiaries. The burning huts provided a weird, flickering orange backlight as the strange convoy of tanks, armored personnel carriers, civilians and livestock moved out. He shook his head sadly to himself. "If there is an ark waiting in the river when we get there, I will know this all just a bad dream."

"Not a bad dream Sir." De Wilzem also spoke quietly. "We have done good work here tonight."

Six hours later, the sun was rising. The villagers had already started to build themselves a kraal close to the infantry company's base. Geldenhuys had received an ominous message saying the brigade commander wanted 'reasons in writing' by 0900. And van Huis had re-read his wife's letter, then settled down to send her a reply.

"Things are pretty quiet here on the border," he started.

CHAPTER THREE
PLANS AND INTENTIONS

Briefing Theater, MacDill Air Force Base, Florida

"Settle down. A team from Hughes Electro-optics is here to introduce you to some new equipment we will be testing in the near future." That caused the room to quiet quickly. "Doctor Kailie, if you would like to start?"

"Thank you General. Gentlemen, I'm here today to discuss the topic that has been of concern to us all ever since the B-70 first entered service. I refer, of course, to bombing accuracy." A ripple of hostility ran around the room. The B-70 crews were well aware that their average bombing error from the Valkyries was substantially greater than that from the old B-52s. In fact, the surviving BUFF groups still won the bombing accuracy contests at Red Sun, year after year. Doctor Kailie seemed oblivious to the reaction. "Of course, this is quite understandable. The Valkyrie flies at three times the speed of the B-52 and twice the altitude so a degradation of accuracy when using gravity bombs is only to be expected. We note that in the bombing of the Caliphate biological warfare facilities a decade ago, some of the bombs dropped missed their targets by between three and five miles."

Doctor Kailie looked at his audience, blissfully unaware that he was being measured for a lynching. "That's worse than an ICBM, you know."

This time the hostile growl was unmistakable and couldn't be easily ignored. Kailie suddenly realized he was trampling all over very tender corns. "Since then we have managed to correct the situation to a great extent. The new generation of gravity bombs have an inertial stabilization system that detects deviations from the planned ballistic arc and corrects for them. This eliminates errors from varying cross-winds and other atmospheric disturbances. However, this does not change the degree of error built in by the use of higher speeds and altitudes."

"Then give us bigger bombs!" A voice called out from the increasingly restive audience. In a dimension humans know nothing of, deceased General Thomas Power smiled affectionately.

41

"That is only a temporary solution, and in any case there are many cases where the use of larger nuclear devices would be inappropriate. In fact, it would be of great benefit if, in some cases, we could replace nuclear devices with extremely accurate conventional weapons."

"We're not going to ask the ladies to haul trash!" A different voice, but equally hostile. The audience was beginning to surge forward in reaction to Kailie's remarks.

"The ladies?" Kailie was confused.

"The B-70s. Most of them are female." General Carson looked at his assembled crews severely. "Settle down, right now! We have a problem here and, while it might have been addressed more tactfully," now Kailie got the severe look, "it is, nevertheless a serious problem that we have to face. So hear Doctor Kailie out."

Kailie wiped his forehead with a handkerchief. "As I was saying, the problem is a combination of speed, altitude and the reaction time of the bombing system. These are fixed constraints and, as you gentlemen have shown, even the finest training and most highly developed skills in the world cannot compensate for them." He took a chance and looked at his audience. They seemed a little more mollified that they had a few minutes earlier. He heaved a quiet sigh of relief.

"Since the source of error at the drop end is beyond the control of either the crews or the – ahem – ladies, then the answer is obvious, we have to find a way of changing the course of the bomb on its way down so that any errors at the drop point can be corrected as the weapon descends. It is to achieve this end that we at Hughes have been working for the last few years.

"Attaining this end is of ever-increasing importance. Faced with the threat of our bombers, those who would challenge world peace have undertaken to make your tasks as hard as possible. They have hardened installations, buried them deep underground, made the vulnerable areas of them as small as possible. This is why just using devices of ever-increasing yield is no longer a viable approach. If the area of the target is halved in each of its dimensions and the same amount of material is used to build it, then that target will be four times harder. If the amount of material used to build it is doubled also, then that target will be 16 times harder to destroy, meaning the destructive force exerted upon it must be increased by the same proportion. Assuming that accuracy remains unchanged, that means the explosive power of our devices must be increased by a factor of more than four thousand. That means we would require devices that generate destructive power in the gigaton range. Obviously, this is not possible or desirable."

There was a certain level of disagreement about the last word. Kailie chose to ignore it. "If, however, we can ensure that our devices can hit these much smaller targets directly, then the problem goes away. No known structure can survive a direct hit from a 550 kiloton weapon. Who knows? One day we may even be able to drop such a device down a mineshaft or into an air conditioning duct on a building. That would give the occupants food for thought, would it not?"

For the first time Kailie was actually connecting with his audience. "So how do we do it?" It was one of the voices that had been barracking him earlier.

42

"In theory, the idea isn't new or particularly difficult. We've been using guided missiles for striking targets on the ground for many years. From an operational point of view, there's very little difference between hitting a target with a guided AGM-76 that can be dialed up to around 100 kilotons and with a gravity bomb that has a yield twice that. In fact, for many targets there's no difference at all and, as you know, we've been hitting strategic targets with defense-suppression AGM-76s for years. So, all we have to do is design what amounts to an engineless missile.

"The Navy has already been working along similar lines. They've come up with an idea that is essentially a glide bomb with an optically-guided system. The launch aircraft has a camera in its nose, the pilot or bombardier steers it so the image of the target is framed by the camera and that image is transmitted to the bomb. The bomb is then dropped and the guidance system senses when the target image is drifting away from the center of the frame and applies a correction so it stays in the center. This system will even compensate for the target moving, great for hitting ships. Now, your B-70s have a much better electro-optical camera system than anything the Navy has so this same device should be applicable to your nuclear devices. Note, by the way, that the guidance system actually gets more accurate as the bomb nears its target. Quite the reverse of the normal situation where accuracy decreases with range."

The hum around the room had changed from hostility to interest. Kailie decided to exploit the moment. "That's one approach; we've got another. How many of you have heard of a laser?"

A forest of hands shot up. SAC crewmembers tended to be very well-read. There was little else to do while sitting in the cockpits of their aircraft while on alert and the chosen reading matter tended to be scientific.

"That's very helpful. Well, we've designed a system that has two components. One is a pod that contains a stabilized laser hooked to the electro-optical camera in your aircraft. Using the pod and camera you can shine the laser on the target. The other is a receiver in the nose of the bomb that picks up the reflected laser light. Again, it keeps the source of reflected laser light centered and flies into the target. Again, the closer it is, the more accurate it gets. The big advantage of this system is that the aircraft dropping the bomb doesn't have to get anywhere near the target. It can just deliver the bomb into a position where it can see the reflected laser and then drop on the target."

"So we have to operate in pairs?" A thoughtful voice.

"Perhaps. Or one spotter aircraft can designate targets for several delivery aircraft. The RB-58s could do that for you. Or one aircraft can both designate and drop."

"How accurate?" Mike Yates spoke for the first time.

"The first system? The Navy can get accuracy of around 50 – 100 feet but that's much slower and lower. The laser system? Theoretically, we can get accuracies measured in inches. Also, you can drop several bombs sequentially and then designate targets while the bombs are on the way down. You don't have to drop one at a time the way the Navy do."

There was a surge of interest and Kailie was bombarded by questions from the interested air crews. After more than two hours of dealing with surprisingly detailed technical questions ranging from how the laser was cooled to where it could be mounted on the B-70, he was allowed to sit down. General Carson took his place.

"Gentlemen, four of our aircraft are to be fitted with an improved version of the Navy system, four with the new laser system. We will fly exercises to compare them and decide which, or whether both, are best suited to our needs. Thank you."

Yates left the conference room in a hurry. It was running late and he had to stop at the bank on the way home before he found out what his wife had in mind for their evening.

Puerto Belgrano Naval Base, Argentina

"Captain Astrid. How goes our operations?"

"Very well Admiral. We have made a number of our service families very happy by providing them with babies for adoption. I have given Major Mazza and his lady their new child. That was a little difficult for they are both fair-haired and blue-eyed. We were lucky we had that Swedish girl in custody."

"That may be a problem. The Swedish Embassy is asking after her again."

"There is no problem. She is no longer in our custody." Admiral Ruben Chamorro nodded quietly, understanding the euphemism that had been used. "And the Mazza's do not know?"

"They do not. They believe that the baby was born to a young woman who got pregnant by one of our sailors and was unable to care for the child." Viewed objectively, that statement was true enough. She had been made pregnant by one of the men in Astrid's command and a bullet in the head made the Swedish girl unable to care for anything.

"Very good. Now, Alberto, we have a different mission for you. One that will take much care and precision on your part."

"Another group of dissidents?"

"Not this time; well, perhaps, in a manner of speaking. You know of Operation Soberanía?"

"Of course, Sir."

"Well, there is a second phase to that operation that few outside the Navy know about. Even the government and the Army know little of it. It is called Operation Rosario and it involves an amphibious assault that will seize the Malvinas Islands, South Georgia and the South Sandwich Islands."

"That will mean war with the British." Astrid did not look upset by the suggestion.

44

"Indeed it will. That is the whole point. We have had our dispute with the British for more than one hundred and fifty years and they have treated us with nothing but contempt. We had to swallow our pride because they were strong and we were weak. But now the boot is on the other foot. The British are of no account now. They have never recovered from their defeat in 1940 and they will do anything to avoid another war. When we seize the islands, we will not only be recovering our territory, we will be establishing ourselves as the major power in the South Atlantic. First with Chile and its mineral wealth in our hands, then with the British possessions returned to our control, we will dominate the South American continent. The British still have the aura of a great power. By defeating them so easily, we will assume that mantle of power."

"And how do I fit into this?"

"You will take your unit of commandos to South Georgia. The island has no civilian population. The only people who live there are the British Government Officer, Deputy Postmaster, some scientists, and support staff from the British Antarctic Survey who maintain scientific bases at Bird Island, the capital, King Edward Point, and at Grytviken. You will find these people and you will kill them. There may be some women on the island. If there are, it will be up to your discretion whether they are killed there or brought back here for our adoption program. After you have secured the island, you will establish our own military base there and you will then secure the rest of the islands in the area."

Astrid nodded approvingly. It was a nice, neat and simple operation, well defined in scope and objectives. That was the sort of plan that he liked, not the endless chasing of dissidents in the darkness. "Very good, Sir. I will commence operational planning immediately."

"Good, Alberto. Very good."

Pan-American Sonic Clipper Clipper Fleetwing, *Final Approach, Washington International*

From her window, Branwen could see the forward canard flaps drop into the landing position and could sense the Sonic Clipper level out. From the films she had seen, she could imagine the nose visor dropping down to expose a conventional cockpit canopy. Barely more than two hours ago, the aircraft had taken off from Stockholm. Now it was heading in over Delaware to make its landing at Washington International.

"Are you comfortable Mrs. Sunderstrom?" Branwen turned to look at the woman who was sitting beside her. They had the only two seats this side of the central isle. The Sonic Clippers carried a maximum of 96 passengers, all first class. Despite the luxury of the flight, the woman's eyes were filled with pain. That was nothing to do with the experience of a triple-sonic airline flight. Her eyes were always like that.

"Yes, yes thank you. You've all been so very kind. There was no need for Mr. Loki to have gone to this expense. . . "

"I hope you don't expect me to fly on a people-hauler." Branwen put mock indignation into her voice. "Seven and a half hours with only a cheese sandwich to eat! And we'd have to *pay* for it. At least our fiskbullar i hummersås came with our tickets."

45

"It was very good. As good as we would find in a fine restaurant." Mrs Sunderstrom didn't notice, but one of the stewardesses was in earshot and smiled happily at that.

For a moment, Mrs Sunderstrom almost smiled. Watching her out of the corner of her eye, Branwen hoped that she might break through the loneliness that engulfed her. But the veil of sadness dropped down again. "You'd better fasten your seatbelt. We'll be landing very soon now."

Branwen expected the airliner to hit the ground hard and come to a halt on the runway amid a squeal of brakes and a cloud of dust and smoke, but the actual landing was smoother and gentler than the big people-haulers ever managed. The only unpleasant bit was the way the aircraft porpoised on the runway. That was a characteristic it had inherited from its B-70 ancestor. Loki had taken the trouble to get them seats that were in the middle of the cabin so the motion wasn't too pronounced. The aircraft even porpoised a couple of times at the unloading ramps before it finally came to a halt.

To Branwen's complete lack of surprise, it felt as if it took almost as long to get through immigration, baggage claim and out into the airport arrivals lounge as it had to fly over from Stockholm. It didn't, of course; the big hold up was immigration. She felt bitterly envious of Lillith, Naamah and the rest. When they travelled outside the United States, they did so on diplomatic passports and immigration was a barely noticed formality. But she was a commodities trader's secretary and Mrs. Sunderstrom was a housewife. They had to queue up like everybody else. Finally, though, her passport was stamped and the two of them could pass through the sliding doors that meant they had finally entered America.

As she did so, her face lit up. A youngish-looking man was waiting for them with their baggage already loaded on to a trolly. "Gusoyn! It's good to see you. Thank you for coming."

"It is a pleasure Branwen." The two exchanged hugs, then Gusoyn touched his hat to Mrs. Sunderstrom. "You too, ma'am. I have a limousine waiting outside, I guess you want to go to your hotel first and rest up. The Boss is expecting you tomorrow morning."

"The Boss?" Mrs Sunderstrom looked confused. "Loki said there was somebody here who might be able to help but…"

"The Seer." Gusoyn grinned at her. "Also known as the National Security Advisor. Your appointment is for 09:30 and you will have an hour. Take a word of advice and spend the evening rehearsing exactly what you want to say and do. He does not take kindly to people who waste his time dithering."

Branwen laughed. That was an understatement if ever she'd heard one. Gusoyn led his party out and loaded their luggage into the trunk of a stretch limousine that was parked in a restricted area. Branwen checked discretely; the car had US Federal Government plates. She also noted the bulge under Gusoyn's left arm where his gun nestled against his ribs. This was the American circle's ground and they played to different rules here.

"Which hotel are you staying at?"

"The Park Hyatt. Dupont Circle."

"Very good choice. I am surprised Loki knows the city that well."

"He doesn't." Branwen grinned again. She knew Loki looked on Washington as the sink of iniquity, not least because it was The Seer's home base. "Lillith booked it for us."

"I see." Gusoyn nodded. "I sense a conspiracy. It is an easy run this time of day; not least because the police will wave us through. I will have you there in 45 minutes. Sit back and enjoy the ride."

HMS Glowworm, *Bay of Biscay, Western Approaches*

The Bay of Biscay was always an uneasy stretch of water. The rollers coming in from the vastness of the Atlantic collided with the short chop of the coastal waters and the directed currents from the Channel. They produced a confusing maze of weather and water patterns. Even on a good day, when the sun was warm and the winds gentle, a ship could be hit by a sudden, complex wave formation that would have her dipping and rolling in a dangerously erratic manner. No seaman worthy of his salt took the Bay of Biscay lightly.

"Weather, Number One?"

"Just in Captain." Lieutenant Commander Simon Baxter turned his pad over and read the second sheet down. "Complex low Iceland 973 slow moving, deepening 969 by midday tomorrow. Warnings of gales, eight, in Viking, North Utsire, South Utsire, Forties, Cromarty, Shannon, Rockall, Malin, Hebrides, Bailey, Fair Isle, Faeroes and Southeast Iceland. Increasing to severe gales nine in Viking, North Utsire and Fair Isle. Our area forecasts for the next 24 hours, northerly 5 or 6 backing westerly 4 or 5. Very rough becoming rough. Drizzle. Visibility moderate or good. Fitzroy Sole, Westerly 4 or 5 backing southwesterly 5 to 7, veering north westerly later. Rough. Occasional rain. Visibility moderate or good."

Commander James Foster looked through the spinning discs embedded in the front of his bridge windows and out at the green water piling up over *Glowworm's* bows. Something about the wave pattern caught his eye. He picked up the telephone to the pilot house below. "Starboard wheel, 30 degrees."

Through the windows let into the curved face of the bridge, he could see his ship bring her bows around. Without warning there was a slam and a lurch. A freakishly large wave surged over the long bow that stretched out before him. The water rolled back along the forecastle until it piled up against the bridge. For a brief second, the world went green as the windows went underwater. Then the wave was clear and past.

"Nicely done Sir. One more like that and we'd qualify for our dolphins." Baxter's voice was filled with genuine admiration; one that was echoed by the rest of the bridge watch. The marvelous informality and companionship of a destroyer was one of the glories of serving at sea. It made those whose careers took them to larger ships yearn for their days on the Navy's smaller combatants. It also gave them a chance to learn seamanship and to read weather patterns that no mere classroom could ever begin to equal.

That last course change had been a classic example. If that wave had taken them on the beam, the ship would have rolled through a frightening arc. There were whispers of great waves. Waves so huge that they swallowed unwary ships whole; waves that arrived from nowhere with little warning. This hadn't been one of those legendary swells, but it had been big enough and Foster's last-minute turn had been finely calculated to catch it on *Glowworm's* bows.

"Slacken off to ten." Foster gave the helm order without outward sign of having heard the compliments passed by the watch crew. He did, however, appreciate the favorable comments of his peers. The Royal Navy had designed their post-war destroyers to remain operational in seas like this. They had enlarged hulls but vestigial superstructure. His bridge was one deck above the main deck and everything possible was moved inside the hull. There were no deckhouses; even the ship's boats were carried in hangars inside the hull and the missile launchers were buried vertical tubes amidships where the ship's motion was minimized. It had taken a long time to get the vertical launch system working properly but now it was a technology in which Britain led the world. Even the mighty American cruisers still used the more vulnerable and less flexible rail launchers. It was Foster's conceit that his 5,000 ton *Glowworm* could fire off her missiles in weather that had American cruisers five times her size rolling helplessly.

There was another reason for the design principles that lay behind *Glowworm*; the changing nature of war at sea. Back in the 1950s, the Royal Navy had taken a look at the way things were going and had decided that the days of formations of ships battering each other, with gunfire or with massed air strikes, were over. Naval battles would be decided by small numbers of nuclear weapons delivered by high-flying aircraft. If a ship took a direct hit, it was gone. There was no way it could survive. But, a near miss, that was different. The killing mechanism against ships would be blast and radiation. The better a ship could ride out those, the more likely she was to survive at all. So *Glowworm's* unusual design was intended to ensure that everything vital was protected from blast inside the hull. The ship herself was as low in the water as possible, so that blast had the smallest possible area to act upon. The clean design meant that her outsides could be washed down as quickly and as completely as possible before the fallout from a near miss could start its evil work. The Royal Navy had prided itself that its new generation of warships, designed after the humiliation of the 1940s had started to fade, were the first real atomic age ships built anywhere.

"Bad seas, Sir." Baxter watched the waves and saw how the runs were interlocking and anticipated a sudden turn to port.

"Port twenty." Foster gave the order almost as Baxter thought of it. *Glowworm* swung again to take the wave on her bows. That was another good thing about these ships. Resistance to blast also meant resistance to sea damage. Most other destroyers would have wrecked railings and topside damage from the battering of the storm. *Glowworm* didn't; there was nothing topsides to damage. There was a price to pay for that, of course, she ran without any of her crew outside the hull except on the most benign of weather conditions. Even the lookouts were inside, scanning the world through electro-optical periscopes built into the bridge. One of them showed the forward 4 inch 62-caliber Mark 24 gun, a weapon positioned above and behind the bridge in an arrangement that defied tradition and, apparently, common sense. The scanner showed the fallacy of 'common sense' though. Up where it was, the mount remained dry and clear of the waves and spray. "We'll be out of this in a day or so, Number One. Then a straight run to Bermuda and down to Jamaica.

You'd better get the Gun Team in training. The Jamaicans have challenged us to a Pack Gun Race when we get out there and they're tough opponents."

"Understood Sir." Baxter spoke with relish. It was traditional for a new destroyer on West Indies Station to take on the Jamaican team in a Pack Gun Race. How well the ship performed would have a lot of impact on her crew's status during her two year stay out there. The Commonwealth (and some of the ex-Commonwealth) civilians might have cricket but the services had Pack and Field Gun racing. Even some of the non-Commonwealth countries joined in occasionally although Baxter got the feeling that they didn't quite understand the spirit of the race. Once the American SEALs had been challenged to a Pack Gun Race and they'd accepted with alacrity. Only, on the day of the race, their challengers had found their gun had been mysteriously stolen overnight. Even in sports, the damned Septics never fought fair.

"I hope so. *Daring* lost their race. *Mermaid* won theirs, meaning we need to win ours so the Andrew can hold a lead. Starboard twenty."

Baxter nodded again as the destroyer swung to take another wave over the bows. It wasn't surprising *Daring* had lost her race. Even though the destroyers looked impressive with their quartette of four inch guns, they'd never really fitted into the Andrew and they were unpopular postings. They were cramped, uncomfortable and the standards for the enlisted men was well below those on other Royal Navy destroyers. It made matters worse that the officer's accommodation was well above normal standards. In the Andrew, as the Royal Navy was affectionately called by its members, that difference wasn't acceptable. They were only in the Royal Navy because they'd seemed to be a deal too good to turn down, but they would be gone soon and they wouldn't be missed much.

"I'll get the team training in the boat hangar, Sir. And on the flight deck when we're out of this clag." The Rotodyne deck aft was one of the few places on *Glowworm* where major exercises could take place while the ship was underway. He'd have to send around a message asking for volunteers. That wouldn't be a problem. Every seaman knew that the one sure way to get the favorable notice of a ship's captain was to be on his winning Pack Gun Race team.

Married Quarters, MacDill Air Force Base, Florida

Selma Hitchins-Yates applied a last touch to the garish make-up she was wearing, then stepped away to look the general effect in the full length mirror. Indecently short leather skirt, high-heeled boots, fishnet stockings and a blouse that was both microscopic and transparent. *Lord girl, you do make one mean-looking sidewalk stewardess.* She checked her appearance again, then glanced over to the "secret" cabinet built into her wardrobe that held her costumes. A police woman's uniform, a nurse's uniform, an Indian maiden's outfit (bought after her husband had become fascinated by the heroine of Ghostwalk), a western saloon girl's dress, a maid's outfit and even the orange coveralls worn by inhabitants of a state prison. Few others as well. The cabinet wasn't actually hidden, although it was arranged so its existence wasn't immediately obvious. Mike Yates kept the family guns in there as well. With young children in the house, a little care over things they weren't ready for was essential. She closed the door and reached in behind the front paneling to secure the lock. Then, ready, she started to think herself into character.

"I'm home darling. No visitors." Her husband's voice came from downstairs. She heard him close and lock the front door, then move around, closing the windows, pulling down the blinds and drawing the curtains. Selma picked up her bag, slung it over her shoulder and made her way downstairs with a practiced swing of her hips. Her husband was in the study, unloading papers on some new equipment.

"Hey, handsome, you want to buy a girl a drink?"

Yates looked at his wife and his eyebrows twitched slightly. "Err, yes, ma'am, what would you like?"

"Not so much of the ma'am handsome. I'm Sugar, Brown Sugar. And I drink Champagne."

"I don't think we have any." Yates looked suddenly disappointed.

"Wanna bet, handsome?" Selma jerked her head at the refrigerator. Her husband opened the door. Sure enough, there was a bottle of champagne chilling in an ice-bucket.

"Well what'ya know? Let me pour you a glass, Brown Sugar." The glasses were close at hand and Yates was a master at opening champagne bottles. The cork popped out with barely a plop and none of the wine was wasted fizzing out. "You want to party?"

"Sure thing handsome. You got the dough, we got the party." Selma was working hard to keep the sultry, seductive tone in her voice while the champagne bubbles went up her nose. She was suppressing the urge to laugh. *Did people actually fall for this routine,* she thought to herself. She supposed so; what amazed her was that her husband seemed to be doing just that.

"What's this going to cost me?" Yates asked the question straight-faced. Selma reached into her bag and produced a list of 'available services.' It was quite genuine. She'd got the details from a friend of hers in the local police, explaining that she needed it for a paper she had to write as part of her liberal studies requirement at university. Although, if her professors ever found what she was using her PhD studies as a cover for, they'd probably have heart failure.

Her husband was reading the list while his eyebrows went out of control. "You know, there are things on here I didn't think were possible."

"Been there done them all handsome. Now, you wanna party or do I find another catch?"

"Let's party. I want to try that." Yates indicated an item fairly far down the expensive end of the list.

"That'll be two hundred bucks handsome. Payable in advance." Selma looked at the item in question and felt her own eyebrows rise slightly. *That was unexpected*, she thought. Still, it was on the list so she'd have to go through with it. Then, she took the roll of notes and stuffed them in her bra. "Right, lover, let's party."

Several hours later, Selma quietly got up, leaving her husband snoring happily on their bed, went to her room and changed out of her costume. The family bank books were on her desk and she filled out a paying-in slip to put the two hundred dollars she'd just 'earned' into the kid's college fund. Then she cleaned off her make-up. By the time she got back, her husband had woken up.

"Oh, it's you. I thought it was 'Brown Sugar'."

"Perhaps another time, lover. You happy?"

"Yeah, Broke, but happy. Sellie, you fancy a trip to Cuba? I can grab a week's leave while the birds are in dock for the new tests."

"*Shield Maiden* in the test program then? We haven't had the work orders yet."

"We are. We're part of the laser test team. So, how about Cuba?"

"I've got leave coming up as well. We could take the kids as well; make it over Christmas?"

"Sounds good." Yates relaxed, his arm curled around his wife. "I hear Cuba's quieted down a lot since the old days. Had to happen I suppose. Once regular companies started investing lots of money, I guess the Mob ways didn't really work so well."

"Still pretty wild, and the Mob still run the place, in theory at least. We can book up in Disney's place there; the kids will love that. And if you're a real good boy, Brown Sugar might pay you another visit."

Government limousine, approaching the NSC Building.

"Is the traffic always this heavy?" Branwen was shocked by the congestion that was typical of Washington's rush hour. Geneva had nothing on this.

"This is not too bad. It will be worse in a month or two. All we need is half an inch of snow and Washington grinds to a halt." Mrs. Sunderstrom snorted slightly, Stockholm dealt with serious snow every winter without much fuss. Gusoyn edged into the right hand lane and then turned on to a down ramp that took them under one of the office buildings. He brought them to a halt behind a bright red Ferrari that was passing through the security checkpoint. Ahead of them, the candy-striped barrier rose and the Ferrari shot through. It dropped again and Gusoyn eased the government Packard up to the box.

"Don't tell me that Ferrari was a government vehicle?" Branwen sounded incredulous.

"No, that is Igrat. She is not really supposed to park it down here, but everybody gave up trying to stop her. One of her jobs is checking out security systems, so I suppose getting in came under the heading of work." Gusoyn lowered his window and fed a card into a slot. A number came up on the display and he punched another into the keyboard. Then, the barrier rose and he drove in.

"What would happen if I punched that number in?" Branwen was fascinated.

"If you were Igrat, as far as we can make out, you would get in. Otherwise, unless you hit lucky on literally a thousand to one shot, a steel barrier would come up behind us and Security would be down here in seconds." Gusoyn drove in and parked the car in a spot with its registration plate number painted on the blacktop. "Ladies, follow me please. This is a secure government building, so I am obliged to warn you not to take any photographs or look in any offices that might be open."

He led his charges to an elevator, ushered them inside, then pressed the button for the 14th floor. The elevator ride was smooth and swift. The dreadful elevator muzak that some buildings inflicted on their occupants was mercifully absent. The lift opened directly opposite the National Security Advisor's officer suite. Branwen looked around, a little furtively, comparing it to Loke's suite. It was less opulent; the style was modern rather than Loki's preferred classical, but there was no absence of modern technology. Her eye was drawn to a painting on the wall that separated the reception area from the Seer's office. It showed a B-36 on a runway with a B-70 taking off over it. She couldn't read the signature on it. Gusoyn read her thoughts "Leonard Vincent," he said quietly.

"Hi, Branwen. You must be Mrs. Sunderstrom? Thanks Gusoyn, I'll take it from here."

Lillith pressed the button on the communication box on her desk. "Boss, your oh-nine thirty is here."

"Trot them in." Branwen and Mrs. Sunderstrom headed for the Seer's office. Lillith scribbled something on her pad and grinned at Gusoyn. "This should be fun."

"I thought The Seer did not care for those things?" Gusoyn gestured at the communication box.

"He doesn't. That's why we don't have them on the Thirteenth Floor. But we do have them here."

The Seer's Office, NSC Building, Washington D.C.

"So, what can I do for you?" The Seer relaxed in his chair, looking at the two women sitting opposite him. The apparently older woman looked a little confused by the surroundings and apprehensive at being in the lair of the notorious targeteers.

"Sir, it's my daughter, Karyn. Two years ago she was at university in Stockholm when she met a young Argentine student. They fell in love, and a year ago she went to Argentina to be with him. About a month after she arrived, there was some sort of incident on the Buenos Aires university campus and a lot of students were arrested. One of them was Karyn's boyfriend. About two days later, some men came to the hostel she was staying in and bundled her into a car. That's the last we have heard of her. She has just vanished. I've been asking the Swedish Foreign Affairs Ministry and they've made inquiries but they get nothing."

"So, I ask again, what can we do for you? In this case, 'we' being the United States Government?"

"Nobody cares what Sweden says or does, but they do care what America does. So could you make the inquiries, make the Argentine government release my daughter? Or send your SEALs to get her?"

The Seer sighed and tapped his fingers. "Firstly, Mrs. Sunderstrom, I must ask you to be realistic about this. Argentina is notorious. People who oppose the regime in power there 'disappear.' None of those who have vanished have ever, say again, ever, reappeared. Your daughter has been missing for a year and I am deeply sorry to have to say that it is almost certain that she has been killed. She was probably dead within hours of being picked up." The Seer didn't voice the other thought that had run through his mind. *She had been picked up as a lever to make her boyfriend talk. In that case she might have lived longer, at least while she had that use, but there is no need to distress this woman with the implications of that.* "Also, none of the bodies have ever turned up. You must resign yourself to the certainty that you will never see your daughter again. The best you can hope for is to find out what happened to her.

"Now, as to what we can do, I am also very sorry to tell you that the answer again is 'very little.' The U.S. policy on Argentina, both under this administration and its predecessor, is that we regard their regime as deplorable and an affront to human dignity. We have as little to do with them as possible. We've cut off supplies of military equipment and do not support the systems that they do have. But, as far as your daughter is concerned, there is very little we can do. Since she is not a U.S. citizen, we have no right or duty to take any action on her behalf. Nor are there any other reasons that would give us cause to involve ourselves on her behalf. I'm afraid the only government that can take any action is the Swedish government. It would be different if an American citizen had been disappeared in this manner but the Argentine Junta has been clever enough not to do that. The worst they have done is put any of our people they don't like on a plane out of the country."

"But she's my daughter. If you'd lost children of your own....." In the background, Lillith, quietly taking notes of the meeting, winced. Both on her own behalf and on the Seer's.

"As it happens, Mrs. Sunderstrom, I do know exactly how you feel. That is why you are sitting here today. However, I cannot allow my personal feelings to affect the interests of the United States. We can't do anything, however much we might like to. We have been accused of trying to rule the world by terror, of using the threat of nuclear destruction to force people to obey our commands, but we don't do anything like that. We can't, couldn't even if we wanted to. We can't go sending troops into countries to rescue any and all people from the governments of those countries. Otherwise we would be doing exactly what our critics accuse us of doing."

Mrs. Sunderstrom nodded, slowly and unhappily, painfully aware that she had been one of those who, in days long past, had spoken out against the United States and its supposed nuclear-based tyranny. Now that the reality of the world had started hammering on her door, she had become painfully aware of the limits of power. The Seer, watching her, saw that reality strike home.

"We have certain vital interests that we must protect and every country in the world knows full well what those are. The prime one is, don't start wars of aggression. If a country really wants to fight a war, then it must keep it small, keep it restricted, fight decently and end it reasonably. Break those rules and we'll end the war by ending the aggressor. Another vital interest; don't abuse American citizens. If one of our citizens goes to a country and breaks their laws, that's their hard luck. As long as they get a fair trial and a punishment that's commensurate with the offense, then we're happy. But disappear one of our people and we'll get them back or exact a due, dispassionate and totally excessive revenge on their behalf. Now, can you tell me how committing U.S. forces and getting a lot of people killed on behalf of your daughter falls under those categories?"

Mrs. Sunderstrom shook her head, crying slightly. "But she's my baby. Is there nothing we can do for her?"

"I didn't quite say that. Can we do something now? No. Not officially any way. We can hang our ears out. We can search the winds for any mention of your daughter. We can try and find any reference to her in various places. Mrs. Sunderstrom, one thing I have learned in this job is that powers like Argentina eventually make mistakes and bring the wrath of the world down on their heads. When that happens, we may be in a position to ask the right questions, to get answers and to find out what will happen. That day may come much sooner than you think. When it does, Karyn Sunderstrom will be on the list of names we will be asking about. More than that, I cannot promise you."

Cabinet Room, 10 Downing Street, London, UK

"Cruisers are obsolete. Their inclusion in the proposed building program is simply old-fashioned admirals trying to hang on to the past. They'd be building battleships if we let them. The Treasury insists that these ships be cancelled and that the Royal Navy estimates be reduced accordingly." Derek Featherstone looked around the assembled Cabinet aggressively, defying anybody to disagree with his dictates.

"Admiral Gillespie, do you have an answer to that." The Prime Minister's voice was mild. Those who knew him detected an edge that threatened an unpleasant half hour for somebody.

"Yes, Sir. As you might expect, I disagree with the opinion expressed by the Chancellor of the Exchequer on many levels. The cruisers we have in our fleet perform a number of vital functions that cannot be duplicated by smaller ships. First and foremost is that of flagships. . . "

"Barges for admirals." Featherstone snorted the description with contempt.

"Derek, please do not interrupt the Admiral again." Prime Minister Newton's voice was still quiet but the edge was noticeably sharper. "Continue please, Admiral."

"As I was saying, the four cruisers we have in service fulfill the role of command ships excellently. They have the internal volume to contain the equipment for both long- and short-range communications. They have the accommodation for the staff. Their size makes them stable in bad weather and they have the electrical power generation needed to run the equipment on board. The last is something of a new factor but it's becoming very important. The role of flagship isn't just restricted to fleet operations. When we have been conducting joint missions with the Army, the cruisers have been invaluable forward command facilities."

54

General Howard raised a finger and the Prime Minister nodded. "I would like to support the comments made by the First Sea Lord concerning the value of the cruisers in joint operations. In that Sierra Leone business last year, they proved invaluable as command ships. Their six-inch guns came in useful as well."

"Arguably, the same facilities could be built into a destroyer-type ship, but the results would not be as satisfactory. The Australians went that route. They tried to build a version of their Wellington class destroyer with the required flagship facilities. Wellicruisers they called them. The class was unsuccessful and are considered failures on a number of points. An interesting thing is that the cruisers don't actually cost that much more than the destroyers. The majority of the cost of the ships is the electronics outfits and that's determined by the ship role, not by her size. We also believe that the new cruisers we are proposing will be significantly cheaper to run than the four existing ships. They were, after all, ordered in 1939 even though they weren't completed until 1960. They were radically modified while under construction and their layout isn't optimum. Given modern technology and starting from a clean sheet, we can get a much more efficient ship with a crew only slightly larger than that of a destroyer.

"As General Howard pointed out, the gun cruiser is by no means obsolete. I grant you that in the early 1960s it appeared that way, but the Battle of the Pescadores put that idea to rest. Guns still have a vital role to play both in naval engagements and in support of shore operations. The Tiger class have four six-inch guns each, their replacements will have eight. By the way, after their Wellicruiser experiment, the Australians are building a new class of cruiser with 7.5 inch guns, to supplement their large helicopter cruisers.

"The cruisers are also invaluable as station ships and for showing the flag. They have a presence that smaller ships lack. They are diplomatic tools as well as military ones; they allow negotiations to be carried out in secrecy while their communications equipment means those on board can refer issues to their home base. Sir, you remember how well that worked in the Tanganyika negotiations?"

The Prime Minister nodded. The delicate negotiations with South Africa over military operations in Tanganyika had been carried out on HMS *Leopard* and he remembered well the virtues of the ship. "Those are strong points, Admiral. The proposed building program contains four such cruisers. One-for-one replacements for the Tigers?"

"That is correct, Sir. To be followed by the three new aircraft carriers."

"I forbid this." Featherstone was almost spluttering with rage. "The Treasury demands large cuts in the Ministry of Defence's overall budget and the cancellation of these ships."

David Newton glanced around the assembled Cabinet. *Time to strike.* "Derek, it is not within the remit of the Treasury to set the budgets for the individual ministries. That is a decision to be taken by the Cabinet as a whole. We have been down this road before, when the Treasury took upon itself the duty of determining government spending on a ministry-by-ministry level. That led to 1939 and to the rise of That Man. We will not repeat the experience. The Treasury's responsibility is to determine options for overall government expenditure levels. It is the collective decision of the Cabinet to determine how that available pool of finance will be divided out and the role of the Secretary of State

55

for each ministry to decide how their allocated funding should best be spent. In the end, the voters will decide whether they approve or condemn the decisions we are making. You presume too much upon yourself, Derek. Now, General Howard, your funding requests?"

Howard stood facing the Cabinet table. By a historical quirk, only the professional heads of the Royal Navy and British Army had the dubious privilege of addressing Cabinet directly. As he looked around the Cabinet table, he sensed the effect the Prime Minister's comments were having. Now was not the time for inter-service rivalry. "Sir, at the moment, our top priority is converting a second brigade to Air-Mechanized configuration. We have our First AirMech brigade, consisting of First and Second Battalions, the Parachute Regiment and First Battalion, Royal Regiment of Marines, operational and exercises have proved it to be of great value. The second proposed brigade will consist of Third Battalion, the Parachute Regiment and Second and Third Battalions, Royal Regiment of Marines. We also need to replace the Cavalier tank, finalize the order for Boomslang tank destroyers and to purchase batteries of the Australian Kunchi long-range guns for our artillery park. The Ministry of Defence budget projections have provision for all these requirements in addition to those whose case was so ably made by the First Sea Lord."

"You support the naval construction program, General?" The Home Secretary sounded more than slightly surprised.

"I do, Sir. It will serve all three services and provide much-needed facilities for us all." *And that will get me some markers I can call in at a future date* he thought.

Prime Minister Newton looked around the table. It was dawning on the Cabinet that they had been given a chance to break the control the Treasury was establishing over their budgets. Even if they temporarily lost some of their budgets to Defence in the process, it was a price worth paying for the increased control over their own finances. "Admiral, I have one question. You stressed the value of the cruisers as station ships, a function whose value I can attest to from first hand. Would it not be more sensible to include six such cruisers in the program rather than four, using the extra pair of ships to replace the Daring class destroyers that can then be scrapped without replacement?"

"It would, Sir. The fleet would be the better for that change."

"Then I put it to Cabinet that the 1982-1987 medium term costings for the Royal Navy shall be amended to provide three new cruisers rather than two in 1982 and 1983, that the aircraft carriers should be funded at a rate of one each year in 1984, 1985 and 1986 and that the four Jupiter class destroyers planned for 1984 should be stricken from the program. That the other defense acquisition programs as laid out in the Ministry medium term costings shall be approved unchanged. Do I hear a second?"

"I second your motion, Prime Minister." The Home Secretary still couldn't believe the Army and Navy were actually agreeing on something.

"Then, I call for a vote. I vote Aye."

"Aye!" The Home Secretary wasted no time in getting his vote in and managed it just before the barrage of 'Ayes' went up around the table. The Chancellor of the Exchequer's 'Nay' was feeble-sounding by comparison.

"Very well. The vote is carried and the Ministry of Defense medium term estimates are approved as amended by Cabinet. Now, next subject. We have a proposal to construct to new prisons on the Isle of Wight for long-term prisoners convicted of heinous crimes. Home Secretary, any thoughts on this proposal?"

Sir Humphrey Appleday's Office, The Cabinet Office, Downing Street

"It's an outrage. Who do they think they are?" Derek Featherstone was purple-faced and almost apoplectic with rage.

"The elected representatives of the people, I think. Some may think they are politicians. A few may even believe they are the government, but they'll come around in the end." Sir Humphrey Appleday viewed his visitor with some concern. At seventy years old, Featherstone was by far the oldest member of the Cabinet and his condition caused Sir Humphrey to believe he was on the edge of a heart attack. He hoped not. Having somebody drop dead in one's office was tiresome and led to inordinate amounts of tedious paperwork. He looked at Featherstone from under his eyebrows, his eyes twinkling slightly. In the eternal game fought between departments and various civil service powerbases, this morning's debacle was worth its weight in gold.

"It was all decided; all agreed. Just who is responsible for this mess?"

"Well, Derek, if you are seeking a culprit, I suggest that you begin your investigations in the domains where munificence and good works on behalf of the deserving are usually regarded as having their best and most promising start."

"Eh?"

"Look in a mirror, Derek; look in a mirror." Sir Humphrey sighed to himself. He wasn't surprised by the turn events had taken over the last few hours. The confrontation had been building up ever since the new Prime Minister had taken office. It was the same old problem, one that had bedeviled the Civil Service for the last forty years. In the final analysis, it was split into three factions. There were the members who had either been abroad when the Halifax-Butler Coup had taken place and stayed there or who had subsequently left during the 1940-42 false peace. Then there were the ones who had stayed and joined the Resistance or Resistance fighters who had entered politics after the occupation had ended. Finally, there were the ones like Featherstone who had stayed on and tried to keep things running. Those were divisions that crossed party lines but one thing most agreed on was that there was a distinct whiff of collaborationist about the third group. In most cases it was unfair, but that was the way it was.

"You can't be serious. Blame me for this? If that fool in the Prime Minister's seat knew his job."

"Derek, please be aware that our present Prime Minister not only knows how to kill people with his bare hands, he has actually done so." *Including several collaborators* he thought. "And, what is more, he is actually quite competent. All the more so since he treats governing this country as an extension of his previous battle against 'occupying forces,' by whom he now means us. He was looking for an opportunity to win a victory against us and you threw this opportunity into his lap." *And, like a good resistance fighter,*

57

he seized on the hole in the defenses and exploited it for all he was worth. Sir Humphrey mentally nodded in appreciation of an opponent's achievement. Prime Minister Newton was the worthiest opponent he'd had for more years than many people would believe possible.

"But it was all decided..."

"But not by them. Look, Derek, you blundered badly. You let your dislike for the Navy get the better of you. You allowed yourself to be trapped into an argument on tactical and operational grounds which you were patently unable to justify and it made your opposition to the cruiser program appear petty and groundless. Even then, you had an opportunity to redeem yourself. You could have pronounced yourself convinced by the arguments and supported the proposal. We could always have obstructed it later, contract problems, funding difficulties, an unexpected economic crisis requiring a – purely temporary of course – delay. But now, all that isn't plausible; such machinations will be seen for what they are. You traded away our traditional program of judicious obstruction for a full frontal assault and walked into an ambush. Now, we have to live with the result."

And all because the Navy broke out in 1942 and you didn't. Sir Humphrey sighed again as the thought ran through his mind. Life would be so much easier when the divisions caused by the Occupation were a part of history.

"So what do we do?"

"Nothing, Derek. Nothing at all. What is done is done and that's the end of the matter. Tell me, on another matter entirely, how's your garden doing?"

Across the desk, Featherstone went dead white. "Not gardening leave, Humpty please, not that."

Cabinet War Room, 10 Downing Street, London.

"That went very well Prime Minister." Admiral Charles Gillespie was happier than he'd been for many years. Six cruisers when he'd been prepared to settle for two. Trading the Darings for the extra ships was no great loss, they were worn out and probably the most disliked ships in the fleet.

"Don't count on the carriers yet. We may have an election before they get to the order phase, and then you'll have to fight the whole battle over again. But, your cruisers should be safe, and we've started the process of cutting the Treasury down to size. Now, we have the room secured, how is the situation developing?"

"It certainly looks like war, David." General Pitcairn Howard spoke gravely. "The Cousins are convinced the Argies are going to have a go at the Chileans as soon as the weather clears, in as much as it ever does down there. Our Friends in Northumberland Avenue agree with them. The troop movements and ship deployments are quite definitive. The Cousins have shared their data with Chile and the Chilean Army is digging in all along the Andean frontier. If it comes to war, it'll be bloody. However, it may not come to that. SAC's taking a hand. We understand they'll be doing B-70 overflights of the whole area over the next few days. Just a gentle warning."

58

"Nothing gentle about it." Gillespie wasn't too fond of SAC's casual disregard for other people's aspirations to control their own airspace. "Pretty bloody direct, if you ask me."

"As long as it works, that's good enough."

"For Chile, perhaps. For us? I don't think so."

Newton looked surprised. "Why?"

"Look at it from the Argentine point of view. They're setting up to invade Chile. Grab some choice bits of it perhaps; annex the whole lot possibly. They'll be getting their people psyched up for a war, then SAC scares them off. They can't admit that, so they'll substitute something else." Gillespie went over to the map on the wall and tapped it with his finger. "Here, for example."

"The Falklands. Who the hell think's they're worth a war for?"

"A country that's falling apart, that's who. The truth is that the whole Falklands business was pretty ripe when one looks at it objectively. Argentina got muscled out and they never accepted it. They still maintain their claim to the Islands. The local people don't want to know, they're British and they want to stay that way."

"That settles it then."

"Not according to Argentina. They don't recognize any claimed rights of the local population. And remember, anybody who disagrees with them 'disappears.' In a nutshell, if the Argies get warned off Chile, they're quite likely to go for the Falklands and they've got enough justification to keep SAC from turning the country into a radioactive car park. Anyway, the Americans made it clear at the Pescadores that they'll accept fighting over a few islands as long as it stays contained. So we need to have a contingency plan." Howard snapped his fingers idly. "It'll be one hell of an operation."

Gillespie was staring at the map. "If we have to forward base out of Ascension, then it'll be an operation unequalled by any amphibious force, ever. An assault on defensive positions at the end of an eight thousand mile supply line. I don't think anybody's ever considered pulling something like that before."

"Which is why the Argies might think we'll just have to fold if they present us with a fait accomplice." Newton was thoughtful. "Can we do it?"

"Yes, Prime Minister."

HMS Furious, *Portsmouth Harbor, U.K.*

"How was the honeymoon, Jerry?"

Mullback grinned guiltily at the whistles as he entered the air group Mess. However, he was saved from making a response by the sound of a bell being rung. The Mess President looked around the gathering of naval pilots with displeasure. "There will

59

be no discussion of Ladies, Politics or Religion in the Mess. Sub-Lieutenant Craig will stand the Mess a round of port."

There was an eruption of cheering and the officers converged on the bar. Almost immediately the bell rang again. "And Lieutenant Commander Mullback will stand the mess another to take that smug grin off his face!"

"Everything go O.K., Jerry?" The question from Alasdair Baillie was quiet. He'd been best man at the wedding and confirming that the arrangements for the honeymoon had gone through smoothly marked the end of his responsibilities.

"Thanks   Jock; everything went fine." That had been an understatement. The arrangements had been perfect, even down to the fly-over by four Buccaneers from *Furious* and the small detachment of the ship's Royal Marines who'd 'dealt with' some photographers who'd been unduly intrusive. They'd had a photo-opportunity for the legitimate cameramen of course, one made memorable by Sam's enthusiastic rendition of 'All the nice girls love a sailor.' That, it was rumored, had caused a peak in recruiting the following week and earned Mullback brownie points at the Admiralty. "Sam says, anything she can arrange for you, just let her know."

"Perhaps one of her colleagues?" Baillie sounded unduly hopeful.

Mullback punched him on the arm. "You? Maeve would flay you alive when she found out and you know it. What's been happening round here anyway?"

"Many changes, Jerry. Strange and worrying omens have been seen. Ravens circling the foremast, seagulls gathering over the destroyer pens. And *Glorious's* cat has died."

Mullback looked at his friend sharply. "Are you serious?" He knew Baillie was superstitious, but this had a note of seriousness about it.

"About the cat? I am. The poor wee thing died last week, nobody quite knows how or why. It's got the Glories quite upset. And here's another thing for you. The fighter OCU has moved down here; they're flying out of Yeovilton for a while. There's rumors a flight of them will be joining us and the rest going to *Glorious*."

"Us carrying deck park?" Carrying aircraft on the flight deck was anathema to the Royal Navy. They believed that the airgroup should be kept securely in the carrier's hangar when it wasn't flying missions. But, with the old carriers carrying such a limited number of aircraft, even an extra four fighters would be useful. That would be about as many as the *Furious* could carry without obstructing the deck. Even then, it would be tight.

"That's right, old chum. You know what the dockies are doing right now? Fitting the two of us with outriggers so we can have that deck park. And you should see them working on *Courageous*. Like one of those old silent movies running double time."

"What's up? Any word?"

"The official line is that the financial year is ending and the Navy has unspent funds. If they're still unspent when the year does end, we'll not only lose them but our

60

budget for next year will be reduced by that amount. So, there's a drive on to spend the money and catch up on any overdue damage and defects repairs in one stroke. We're pretty much getting whatever we want."

"I suppose that could be it."

"Yeah, right. With all three carriers in port at the same time? And take a look over to Gosport. The trots are empty. *Dreadnought* pulled out three days ago and *Bellerophon* followed her last night. Something's up, Jerry. I've had whispers from the other ships; the same thing is happening all over the Navy. The fleet's like a swan, everything smooth and serene on the surface but paddling like mad underneath. There isn't a drydock without a ship in it having a scrape and clean."

Mullback looked over the water to where *Hood* was anchored. It was late evening and the last of the tourists would have left her by now. "I guess if we see her being recommissioned we'll know something is really serious."

"Doubt it. They've taken her screws off and the engine rooms have been opened up for tourists to gawp at. Now, if they commission the one behind her. . . "

Mullback laughed. The 'one behind her' was HMS *Victory*. "You're right there Jock. If they recommission her, we'll know times are desperate."

"I've got a feeling they already are, Jerry; we just haven't found out yet. You grab all the time with Sam you can, we'll cover for you." Baillie put on an effort to leer lecherously. "In exchange for copies of her better pictures, of course. . . "

HMS Hotspur, *Alongside, Vickers Fitting Out Basin, Barrow*

"She's a big one, that's for sure." Able Seaman Johnson and his companions looked up at the ship towering over him.

"Makes the old *Acorn* look tiny, she does." Leading Seaman Goldsteam was trying to spot his traditional station, starboard look-out, but the sleek superstructure didn't seem to have watch positions.

"Look at those guns. Six-inchers just like the cruisers. Not a four-inch pop-gun." Able Seaman Tunney was equally impressed, although he was trying not to show it. The rest of the draft from the old *Acorn* was spreading along the dockside to inspect their new home. Morale had been grim on the train up from Portsmouth. It always was when a crew were drafted from a decommissioning ship and had yet to reach their new home. Now, as their ship was before them, it was climbing again.

"I say, you chaps, stop dithering about down there. Fall in on the flight deck immediately." Sub-Lieutenant Hargreaves' voice echoed from the ship. In response, the draft picked up their sea bags and scurried up the gangplank that led to the rotodyne deck. To eyes accustomed to a tiny A-class destroyer that had never heard the beat of wings, the flight deck was a vast expanse, more than 60 feet across.

"Look at that Taffy." Johnson jogged his friend's elbow. "Two rotodynes."

61

"Aye, and what's the odds we'll have to sleep in them." Tunney grumbled. His pessimistic approach to everything had long ago earned him the nick-name 'Tragic,' but life on the cramped *Acorn* had led to her crew having few expectations of comfort.

"Quieten down you men." Hargreaves walked along the ranks of the draft, checking off each man on the roster to make sure that they were all present and accounted for. "Welcome to HMS *Hotspur*, the latest and finest addition to the fleet. We're still completing and won't commission for another six months, but that doesn't mean we'll have an easy time of it. The ship may be incomplete, but we have much work to do on board and we'll have to do it while the yard men are still installing equipment. So we'll need patience and tact as well as hard work. The mess decks are amongst those that still require additional work. . . "

"Told you we'd be sleeping in the hangar." 'Tragic' Tunney whispered lugubriously.

". . . but that doesn't mean we'll be sleeping in the hangar Able Seaman Tunney." Hargreaves carried on as smoothly as if he'd never heard the remark. "As the first draft of the crew, your accommodation is complete and ready for you to occupy. Leading Seaman Goldsteam? Take the following seven men and proceed to this compartment."

Hargreaves handed the Leading Seaman a compartment address and a list of seven names. Goldsteam was surprised to see Tunney, Johnson and five other seamen listed. All men on his watch and ones he got along well with. Hargreaves left him studying the list and picked out another Leading Seaman to receive a second list and compartment address. From the look on his face, he was pleased by the selection. It occurred to Goldsteam that somebody had been watching the draft on its way up and made out the lists according to the relationships between the men.

"Grab your kit, boys. Let's find our new home." Goldsteam lead the way into the hangar and down a deck. He could smell the distinctive "new ship" smell, a combination of fresh paint, raw metal and other odors that would, all too soon, be lost under the press of a crew living on board a warship. The ship was obviously incomplete. Cabling was hanging loose and there were timber structures every so often. He read the address again. The allocated compartment was forward but on this deck. Well, that didn't seem too bad. He made his way forward and quickly found the allocated compartment. The hatch was open and he looked inside.

"This can't be right." For once he matched Tunney for pessimism. His party pressed forward and then stopped dead. The compartment had eight bunks, each with its own locker and an overhead light. They were fitted with curtains so that a man inside could draw them and give himself a little privacy – or darkness to sleep in when the life of the ship meant that sleep had to come at unusual hours. There were chairs in the compartment, simple ones it was true, but chairs none the less. There was even a table that could be folded up against the bulkhead.

"This must be for the awficers. Ain't for the likes of us." Able Seaman Oswald, known as 'Orrible' Oswald after an incident in a Portsmouth public house that had gained *Acorn* fame around the fleet, looked at the palace and shook his head.

"Hurry up and unload your kit men." Hargreaves appeared behind them, checking that his men had found their compartment and were stowing their kit safely. "This is your little home from home now. I've doubt if you've eaten properly on the way up here so I've arranged for the messdeck to be open for the next hour. We have cafeteria-style messdecks here, so head along and get yourselves a good feed. It's straight down there."

Goldsteam watched the officer disappear through a watertight hatch on his way to another compartment. He'd misjudged the man. At first he'd thought he was an ineffectual fop but the way the men had been split up into groups that all got along well and then making sure hot meals were available for the hungry seamen proved that there was a good man beneath the pose. "Right lads, pick out your bunks, I'm claiming the lower one at the rear."

There was some good-natured rivalry over the bunks. There were two tiers of three, one on each side of the compartment and a two-high tier at the rear. Eventually, when they were all sorted and their gear stowed in the lockers, he led them out and followed Hargreaves directions. Sure enough there was a cafeteria-style mess three compartments forward. He closed his eyes and tried to place himself on the ship. As far as he could make out, they were under the forward edge of the aft superstructure; probably just aft of the vertical-launch Seadart battery.

The mess was as impressive as their berthing compartment. Very clean of course; it was still brand new, but well lit and bright. Wonder of wonders, there was a choice of food: sausages or a Cornish Pasty, chips or mash. And no less than three desserts: treacle pudding, figgy duff or jam rolly-polly. The men filled their trays and sat down at one of the tables. Goldsteam noted that it was big enough for eight so that all the occupants of a berth could eat together. A lot of thought had gone into designing this ship.

"This is good!" Johnson's comment came out mixed with sausage and mash, well lubricated with gravy.

"You should know Fatso." Johnson was indeed a well-built man but the Navy had long ago given up trying to slim him down. 'Orrible' took a bite of his Cornish Pasty, expecting the usual paste of unidentifiable meat-like substance inside. To his surprise, there were chunks of real beef and recognizable vegetables. To complete the shock, the chips weren't soggy. "You're right, this is good. We've just got to be in the wrong Navy."

"Can't be a Septic ship boys. An ice-cream machine is nowhere to be seen." It was an article of faith that no American ship went to sea unless its ice-cream machine had at least six flavors available.

There was a polite cough from behind the serving bar and one of the cooks pointed at a corner of the mess. Sure enough, there was an ice cream machine there. Small by the standards of an American ship perhaps, but none the less, an ice-cream machine.

"All right lads, we are in the Septic Navy somehow. Let's make the best of it."

The ratings finished their meal and cleared the table up, obeying the signs that told everybody to clear their tables and clean up after them. It was a small price to pay for a feast of this standard. On their way back to their berths, they met Sub-Lieutenant

63

Hargreaves. Goldsteam snapped out his best salute. "Sir, we'd like to get to work. Where to start?"

Hargreaves thought for a second. "Follow me, we need to get the watch keeping equipment set up." As he lead the way forward, he smiled to himself. *Nothing like a good berth and a good feed to keep Jack happy.*

HMS Collingwood, *At Sea, North Atlantic*

"All right men, settle down." Captain Gregory Hooper looked around the cramped compartment. The nuclear-powered submarines were big, much larger than the diesel-electric boats they replaced, but there was little enough space in them. The Royal Navy had only eight of them. Three were now at sea, heading for the South Atlantic. The interesting thing was that if anybody cared to check, all three boats were somewhere else according to whatever records people could find. In fact, they were anywhere else other than on route for the South Atlantic.

The men in the compartment were also officially anywhere else. They were an elite squad, part of the Royal Marine Special Boat Service. The SBS had started its life doing beach reconnaissance for the invasion of Europe back in '47, slipping ashore to gather sand samples, measure gradients, plot exit routes from the beaches, all the things that planners had to know before selecting the ground for an amphibious assault. They'd had another function as well; striking fear into the hearts of the Germans guarding those beaches. That also, they had done; leaving Germans with cut throats in the darkness of the night. Since that time, they'd become the tip of the spearhead, the leading edge of any cross-shore operation. This particular unit had been specifically trained for operations in the bitter cold of the Arctic winter.

"What's going on, Boss?"

"A very good question, Stokes, I didn't know myself until just a few minutes ago. I actually had sealed orders, only to be opened when we were three days out. Well, three days after we got underway to the very minute, I opened up the envelope and found we're on our way to South Georgia. Yippee, I thought, mint juleps, barbeques and southern belles all lusting after my body."

A series of catcalls went around the compartment accompanied by some lurid suggestions. "Err, Boss, that's Georgia. South Georgia is somewhere else."

"No it isn't, Sandy. I looked it up on the ship's charts. South Georgia is nowhere. And I mean nowhere; it's stuck out in the South Atlantic, so far from anywhere else that it doesn't even have its own tax collector. It's seriously nowhere. Its sole occupants are thirty-odd men from the British Antarctic Survey split between two stations and, get this, two women doing a television documentary on the island."

"Two women for thirty-odd men. If they're on the game, they'll be making a fortune."

"Shut up, Harry. One of those girls is the daughter of a belted Earl."

64

"That settles it then. She *is* on the game." The occupants of the compartment broke out into song.

> *"It nearly broke her father's heart*
> *When Lady Jane became a tart*
> *But blood is blood and race is race*
> *And so to save the family's face*
> *Her father bought her a cosy retreat*
> *On the shady side of Jermyn Street."*

"Quite. Now, let's get serious shall we? The fact is there could be as many as forty British citizens on South Georgia and they've got just about one shotgun and a carving knife to defend themselves with."

"Whose going to attack them, Boss?" The atmosphere had changed completely. Now, it was all business.

"We hope, nobody. We hope this could all be nothing. But, the Argies are on the move and it looks like their target is Chile. There's a problem about that. The Septics don't like people invading other people and they tend to get very nasty about it. Especially since they smile on Chile. So, Her Majesty's Government believes that the Septics will warn the Argies off. Very emphatically. To give you some idea how seriously they take it, they've moved *Ohio* and *North Dakota* into the area and they've started B-70 overflights of Argieland. That's warning off with a vengeance. Then, just to drive the point home, they've organized a naval regatta in Santiago with virtually every fleet in the world sending ships. So, do the math. You're the Argie government, you've got the population psyched up for a war and suddenly you get warned off by nuclear-armed bombers and you haven't got a friend in the world. What do you do?"

"Find somebody else to declare war on. Pronto. Somebody the Septics won't object to. Us."

"Right. The Pescadores business a few years back showed the Septics don't mind people fighting over islands as long as it stays contained. They've even got a reasonable cause for action in the Falklands, but if they go there, they'll go to South Georgia as well."

"So we're the South Georgia garrison." Harry's voice was thoughtful. "All, what, twenty of us?"

"All twenty of us."

"But why? The Argies will start a war with us because the Septics warned them off Chile? Doesn't make sense." Another of the Marines, Curly, was puzzled.

"Oh yes it does. What's every war about in the end? Money. Economics. Argieland is going broke big time. They need resources they can trade; that's why they want Chile. All that copper you see. Now, there's huge deposits of everything under Antarctica and, guess what guys, Antarctica is divided up between nations on the basis of how much of the surrounding ground they own. Specifically, how much of the baseline of the Antarctic Convergence they control. Argieland has a little slice, from its holding in Tierra del Fuego. Even occupying Chile won't really change that, But measuring from

65

those existing holdings to South Georgia puts a massive amount of Antarctica into their hands. And that's worth a lot of money."

"So, Argies attack us and we surrender. Where does that leave us?" The speaker's voice was resigned.

"This time, I don't think we will surrender." Hooper looked around. "Just remember, Prime Minister Newton killed RAB Butler. Did it himself in an ambush. He won't get caught out like poor old Winnie did. This time, we're going to fight. And our little bit of that fight is South Georgia. So now we get the maps out and work out how."

CHAPTER FOUR
MOVEMENT ORDERS

Headquarters, Transvaal Rifles, South African Border.

"Do you know how much trouble you two idiots have caused?"

Standing at attention in front of the General's desk, Captain Shumba Geldenhuys and Lieutenant Bastiaan van Huis exchanged glances. That was a question nobody could answer without hanging themselves. A studied silence was the only real option. Still, van Huis consoled himself, he was only a reservist and he still had his civilian career. Geldenhuys was different. He was a career officer and this affair could break him. Geldenhuys was a good man; he didn't deserve this. Van Huis had already made his mind up that, worst came to worst, he'd make sure his Captain got a good job in van Huis Engineering. Wouldn't be the same of course, but a man had to look after family.

"No excuses, Sir. My responsibility, my orders. Lieutenant van Huis was simply obeying my orders." Geldenhuys was emphatic on that point.

"So your report said. And the women riding on your vehicles?"

"Some were pregnant, Sir; some were sick. Only way to get them out before the militia came back."

"You shouldn't have been trying to get them out at all."

"Respectfully Sir, I disagree Sir. It was a matter of honor, Sir." Geldenhuys spoke but van Huis nodded emphatically.

General Brock shook his head. Secretly he sympathized with the two young officers. In their place he would have done the same thing. "I suppose you know there was trouble at the new village this morning?"

It felt like a punch to the stomach and van Huis almost visibly gasped. "Sir?"

"Some newspapermen went in there, got past the security fence somehow and tried to get the villagers to tell them how you had forced them to leave. The villagers attacked them, quite vigorously so I am told. It's lucky for you that the first newspaper reports caused the Irish to send an investigation committee on a 'fact finding mission'. If their members hadn't been there, it might have gone badly for the press. As it was, the Commissioners laid on the Irish charm and cooled the whole thing down. Lucky for you they did. By the way, their report tends to exonerate you two of any responsibility for the evacuation of the villagers. 'Best choice from a bad range of options' was their conclusion. You two can't stay on the border though. We'll have to find somewhere else for you."

There was a profound silence as their General's words sank in. At first relief that the inquiry was running in their favor, then a terrible suspicion as to what he had planned for them.

"Oh no, Sir. Not the International Zone Garrison." Van Huis got the dreaded words out. The International Zone, in what had once been Egypt, was a feared posting. Tiny, isolated cantonments in the Nile Valley around the antiquities and one in Gaza as a refugee staging point, surrounded by a hate-filled and resentful enemy that savored the chance of over-running what they regarded as abominations. Most communications were by tactical transport aircrafts, usually Australian Pelicans, although the Nile Valley garrisons were connected by rail and by truck convoys. The tiny zones were a perfect breeding ground for what the French had called "Le Cafard," the desert madness born of depression, boredom and loneliness. A place where there was nothing to do all day but try and fit bits of the Sphinx together. It was rumored that sometimes, South African units got out for short forays into Caliphate held territory but such penetrations were top secret and officially denied. Just as it was denied that some of those missions, if they had ever taken place of course, had failed to come back.

"You should appreciate the International Zone more." General Brock spoke chidingly, as if he was rebuking impertinent children. "An opportunity to steep oneself in the glories of ancient history, to see sights that have endured for millennia. To be responsible for the guardianship of the oldest treasures of mankind and receive the gratitude of the world. Not to mention the fact that we agreed to take the responsibility and, in payment, our Air Force now flies C-133 transport aircraft and F-110 Spectre fighters. Such great gains for such a small commitment. And what opportunities; why I'd go out there myself if it wasn't for this accursed allergy I have to dates."

Geldenhuys and van Huis were slowly going green as the horror of a two year tour of duty in the International Zone sank home. Veterans who had been there told of the excruciating boredom in areas so small that within ten minutes a man knew every stone by name. They had also told of the constant vigilance needed, and of the Caliphate tribal levies who always were waiting for a soldier who had dropped his guard. They'd also spoken, in hushed and sickened tones, of what had happened to those soldiers once they had been snatched away. Watching them, Brock decided that enough was enough.

68

"I really pity you, missing out on a magnificent opportunity like that." He shook his head and watched while Geldenhuys and van Huis tried to hide their relief. "I have another assignment for you, one that offers none of the pleasures of the International Zone. The British have signed an order for two hundred Boomslangs, but there are conditions."

"Offsets?" van Huis was very familiar with the way arms deals were put together. Being the son of the founder of one major armaments company and the son-in-law of another tended to do that for a man. In the closely-knit clan that comprised the McMullen-van Huis-Vermaak families, it was a standing joke that they could all negotiate international sales contracts before they could walk.

"Surprisingly no. The British didn't even ask for them. Just a straight cash purchase. But, as a part of the deal, they asked for two things. One was the right to use Simonstad as a base for their South Atlantic squadron, rent free."

Van Huis nodded. It made a lot of sense. The British got a first-class naval base whose operating costs were paid for by South Africa. "And?"

"They also want a South African Army team to help them incorporate the vehicles into the British Army, train their people, that sort of thing. Now, Lieutenant van Huis, your family makes the engine for the Boomslang and you, Geldenhuys, worked on the field trials team for the Mamba missile. So, you two get the job."

"When will we be leaving for Britain, Sir?"

"You won't. The British are sending their people here. Funny thing, the whole deal was conditional on them getting the first dozen vehicles off the production line. We, and the Indians, will have to wait. So you fly out tomorrow for Kaapstad. Of course, if you really want to go to the International Zone, I suppose I could pull some strings for you and arrange it. . . "

"That won't be necessary Sir." Geldenhuys almost tripped over his tongue trying to speak quickly enough. "The lieutenant and I will look after the Englanders. It's a dirty job, but somebody has to do it."

B-70 Shield Maiden, *MacDill Air Force Base, Florida*

"Canard flaps down." Yates gave the order as he held *Shield Maiden* on her brakes at the end of the runway. Her six great engines were barely idling over. "Fuel and weapons status?"

"Internal tanks one to seven topped off. Four 1,000 gallon underwing droptanks. Aft bay contains a fuel tank, forward bay, two AIM-47s, four AGM-76s, all nuclear. Bomb bay doors closed."

Yates nodded, absorbing the information. With the fuel load she was carrying, *Shield Maiden* could easily make it down to Buenos Aires and back. Still, there would be a tanker available if they ran short. After all, they might have a failure and be unable to use some or all of their external fuel. It had happened before.

"Did you hear about *Axe Lady* and *War Mistress*? They got sent to Santiago on a 'friendly visit.' Stayed there for three days, and more importantly three nights. The guys still go into a trance every time Chilean senoritas are mentioned."

"Yeah, and they were guests of honor every where they went. Even the cab drivers refused to take their money."

"When Casey and Donnette went to the Sergeant's Mess, every man there stood up and wouldn't sit until the ladies were properly seated. They've been a bit dream-like ever since as well."

"Hey Mike, we going to Chile soon?" Lieutenant Archie Gautreaux sounded hopeful and his question was met by a round of laughter from the flight deck.

"Not this time, Archie. Down the Andes on 168, swing to oh-nine-oh to Buenos Aires and then back up here. But, I have heard that we've got one more flight to do that will involve a four day layover in Santiago."

The laughter on the deck turned to cheers. Yates finished off his checklist and then advanced his throttles. The night ahead was black, the stars shining clearly, a good night for a high altitude run. He advanced the throttles, waited until the engines had spooled up to max and the released the brakes. *Shield Maiden* accelerated smoothly down the runway until she reached 200 knots. Then he rotated and climbed away from the runway feeling the bumps as the undercarriage retracted. MacDill had a shorter-than-desirable runway. The money to lengthen it had been held up under the Carter regime but work would start soon. He held the climb rate to 2,000 feet per minute, allowing his aircraft to gain altitude smoothly. At 40,000 feet, he would switch over to drop tanks, and then climb to 60,000 and hold speed at Mach 3.2. That would do fine until the tanks were empty and could be dropped. He settled back in his seat. It wasn't going to be that long a flight but it was still better to be comfortable.

Royal Australian Navy Submarine Rotorua*, Puerto de Valparaiso, Chile*

Entering a foreign port on a visit with the civilian population turned out to cheer the arriving warship is one of the great pleasures of Navy life. Nothing else quite generates the sheer delight experienced by the crew at the spectacle. And so it was with *Rotorua* as she entered Valparaiso Bay and made her turn to follow the sea lane into port. She was putting on a good show for herself. Her flat forward deck was ideally suited to manning the rails, something few other submarines could do well. The men were in dress whites, spaced out forward of the sail in a double line. On the after end of the bridge, the 'waving detail' was industriously returning the waves and salutes from the people lined up along the outer breakwater. Finally, on the deck aft of the sail was the submarine's band. It was not large but made up in vigor that which they lacked in numbers, as they thumped out "Waltzing Matilda".

It was, as Captain Steven Beecham had to admit, a pretty damned good show after the high-speed underwater run across the Pacific. Snorting was rough on the crew. All it took was a wave to shut the snort valve for the diesel engines, better known as the donks, to suck the air out of the engine compartment and then from the rest of the boat. The experience for the crew was unpleasantly similar to being sucked inside-out. Still, *Rotorua* had made her run in record time. For a diesel-electric that is.

"The Fleet's in Sir, no kidding." Lieutenant-Commander Cardew sounded impressed. "There's our old friend *Sacramento*." Cardew looked harder through one of the pairs of powerful navigational binoculars on the bridge. There was a long queue of people waiting to board the American cruiser, a line that seemed to terminate on the ship's huge flight deck. "Sir, I don't believe it. The Septics have got a *nuclear warhead* out on their flight deck and are lining people up to stroke it."

"I always said there was something unhealthy about the Septics and their fondness for nukes." Beecham spoke lightly but he knew there was more to it than that. The cruiser was here to show people that America smiled on Chile. The nuke was on open display as a message. "Who else is in?"

"Pommies have got a sloop; moored just in front of *Sacramento*. She's *Chessie*, Sir. I wonder how she got around here."

"Those sloops keep turning up wherever something interesting is going on. I think the Andrew has quietly discovered the secret of teleporting them around the world."

"Sir, you have to see this, inside the breakwater. It's *Vanguard*."

"What!" Beecham was genuinely shocked. *Vanguard* was the Royal Navy's latest nuclear-powered submarine and was supposed to be running trials in the North Atlantic. *How the devil had she got down here?*

"There she is Sir. No mistaking the curved front to her sail, she's *Vanguard* all right."

"My God, you think that's surprising? Take a look behind her."

Beecham looked where he was told and nearly dropped his binoculars. "It can't be. A Chimp nuke-boat? Here?"

"It is Sir, I-700 class hunter-killer by the look of her. Dear God, she's got her masts up as well. The spooks must be having a field day with cameras."

"Where is she. . . Where is she. . ." Navigating Officer Graeme Gavin known as 'Horsey' to the crew, was using the other pair of bridge binoculars to scan the shore.

"Inside the breakwater Navs. By *Sacramento*. It looks to me like the Chileans put the three nuclear-powered ships together."

"I think he's looking for his girlfriend, Sir." Cardew sounded almost despairing.

"Girlfriend? He's never been to Valparaiso before."

"That has never stopped Horsey before, Sir. Ah, there we are, I think he's spotted her."

Beecham swung his binoculars to where the Navigating Officer was looking with such diligence. There was a Corvette Fancy Free convertible parked on the headland with a girl standing on the seat, waving furiously. It didn't take much of an inspection to realize she was gorgeous.

"How does he do it, Sir?" Cardew was in despair.

"He'd better be careful. Chilean senoritas are known for being charming, beautiful, affectionate and warm-hearted but they also have affectionate, warm-hearted fathers with loaded shotguns. One step in the wrong direction and our Navigating Officer is likely to find himself emphatically married. We'd better confine him to the ship."

"With respect, Sir, bad idea, Sir. Shouldn't interfere with people's love lives. Cemeteries are full of people who tried to interfere with other people's love lives."

"That's true Number One. Europeans thought the Black Death was bubonic plague but it wasn't. It was the result of too many people interfering with other people's love lives. Ah, the Pilot's coming out. Stand by to receive."

As the pilot boat pulled alongside, *Rotorua* shuddered when a roar appeared to fill the sky. Overhead, a pair of B-70 Valkyries were taking off from Santiago and climbing away on their flight back to the United States. Beecham guessed they would be crossing Argentina on their way. After all, those who arranged this little naval fiesta had the Argentine government firmly in their sights.

Ministry of Defence, Whitehall, London

"Brigadier, good to see you. How are the Airmech brigades doing?" General Howard leaned back in his office seat. "Pull up a pew and have some tea."

"Thank you, Sir. Oh, Jaffa Cakes; good-oh." Strachan knew the MoD rules far better than anybody could possibly suspect. Plain rich tea biscuits were official issue, but chocolate ones came out of the host's private purse. The presence of Jaffa Cakes meant either the guest was being honored or asked to volunteer for something suicidally dangerous. Probably both. He munched for a second, savoring the blend of orange jelly, sponge cake and dark chocolate while using the interval to put his thoughts in order.

"First is up, running and ready to crack some heads, Sir. Fully equipped with vehicles, both Boarhound infantry carriers and Chevalier gun busses. The Paras and Marines have finished beating each other up and settled down to a wary truce. Second, well, Sir, it's only just formed up. They're short on everything. Vehicles, supplies, even the new unit insignia. Not short on fighting spirit though. They wrecked three pubs on Camberley High Street last night. God help a town with both brigades stationed near it."

Howard snorted with laughter at the thought. "I think that even if God himself declared a truce, the Paras and Marines would dispute it. They can fight each other; how about an enemy?"

Strachan thought for a few seconds more. Howard waited patiently for the answer. He preferred a man who thought his replies through before giving them to one who just galloped in.

"All the exercises we've run show that Airmech works, Sir. The great secret is to keep the operations close, to commit the troops so that the follow up forces can get to them fast. The way to do it is to use the Airmech units to grab the critical terrain and hold it so they form a corridor for the troops to advance through. Make sure the corridor isn't too long and is wide enough and it's a deadly tactic. Put the two brigades side by side and its perfect. Put them one behind the other for a long, thin corridor and they'll get massacred."

"And the Junglies?"

"They're a revolution, Sir. They're three times a helicopter. Three times faster, three times longer-ranged, carry three times the load. We've got them rigged with unguided rocket packs forward so that they can hose down the landing area as they come in. Others carry anti-tank missiles to pick of any heavy armor they see. There was a bit of a barney about that, Sir. Some thought giving them that much weaponry would tempt the pilots to go hunting instead of delivering their load. Well, that is a factor, but the benefits of coming in shooting outweigh it. They carry flares and chaff to handle anti-aircraft missiles and, of course, the range means we can plot safe routes in. It's the same as the troops really, Sir. Handle the operation properly, keep remembering that these units aren't the be-all and end-all of warfare and we do fine. Get a case of the God-like delusions and there's a disaster waiting."

"God-like delusions. Where have I heard that phrase before?" Howard spoke thoughtfully and Strachan cursed to himself. "Anyway, so the key to using one of these units is to use it properly. That's a very, very old story, Brigadier."

"And as true today as it ever was, sir. I bet Caesar heard the same thing when he was a cadet." *And I know for a fact that Alexander did, before the Granicus. And ignored the lesson.*

"Well, Brigadier, you're going to have a chance to prove an old adage. Effective as of January 1st, 1982, you will be gazetted to the command of the First AirMech Brigade. We believe you will have three months, possibly less, to get the brigade ready to move out."

"May I ask where to, Sir?"

Howard pressed a button on his intercom. "Please send the young lady in. The Cousins have been kind enough to send a bag of intelligence data over, one of their OSS couriers arrived with it a few minutes ago."

The door opened. A sultry-looking young woman with a waist-length mane of silky black hair walked in with a bag handcuffed to one wrist. She and Strachan knew each other very well, but neither of them gave a sign of that.

"Isn't that a bit melodramatic? And tempting fate?" Howard and Strachan had stood up as she came in and Strachan politely seated her.

"It's to make sure the bag and I don't get separated accidentally. I've got the key so there would be no need to cut my hand off. My name's Igrat Shafrid, by the way."

73

"Welcome to Whitehall, Miss Shafrid. I think I may have seen you around before."

"London's part of my regular run now, although usually I go to the Foreign Office. It's a convenient drop-off point on my way to Moscow. Anyway, my principal has asked me to deliver the latest intelligence scope on the Argentine build up. They're definitely on the move. Some of the material is imagery and we have intercepts as well. The Seer says, you had better watch your backs. Two things by the way. The Seer asks if you hear anything related to a young woman called Karyn Sunderstrom, he would regard it as a personal kindness if you would let him know the details in full."

"Karyn Sunderstrom. She's the Swedish girl who disappeared in Argentina a year or so back isn't she?"

"That's right. The Seer stresses that this is a personal interest of his. The other thing is. . ." Igrat reached into her bag and got out a photograph of a young Argentine naval officer. "This man is of considerable interest to a lot of people. His name is Captain Alberto Astrid. Every horror you can imagine, this man has performed. Every story you have read about him so far is true, and the worst of his deeds have yet to be revealed. The Seer says that if you get your hands on this man, whoever you hand him over to will owe you big-time. Don't waste the opportunity."

Howard and Strachan nodded. They looked at picture of the naval officer again. At first glance, he appeared a handsome and intelligent officer, but Strachan looked closely. Even in a photograph, the signs of madness could be seen behind the eyes. The sort of madness one saw in a rabid dog.

"Will you thank the Seer for his thoughts and assure him that we will be delighted to keep him advised of any news we hear on Karyn Sunderstrom?" Howard was in no doubt that his words would be transmitted back exactly as he has said them, down to the intonation and hesitations. Just as Igrat had repeated the messages from The Seer. That was a gift a skilled courier had, to transmit a spoken message perfectly. It was called 'the word' and was as important as the documents. Despite her appearance which, in honesty, Howard felt was just a little vulgar, this woman had the reputation of being one of the best couriers in the world.

"I will do that. Good afternoon, gentlemen." Igrat left and Strachan sighed with relief. If Igrat wanted to, she could create chaos.

"Three months, General?"

"Three months. There is a chance, how great a chance we do not know, that the Argentines will strike at the Falklands. We can't do anything obvious, not yet but the Prime Minister wants plans made and assets readied. You will do both with First AirMech."

"Transport?"

"You can rely on having either *Albion* or *Bulwark*. Possibly both."

"That's good. The helicopter assault ships are ideal AirMech platforms. Capacity is low though; if I'm going to go in as a single wave, we'll need both. We could really use *Centaur*."

General Howard grimaced. The helicopter assault ship *Centaur* had been on the 1969 request list but the then-government had cancelled her. Her loss had been a constant low-level problem ever since, causing the planning staff to juggle refits so that one ship would be available when needed. "Perhaps, if this mess really goes down, we'll get her in years to come. But, at the moment, plan on one of the assault transports."

Casa Rosada Presidential Palace, Buenos Aires, Argentina

The dull boom rattled windows, causing President Videla to look up from the report he was reading. "That is the second one today. The norteamericanos have become much more active recently."

"It means nothing." Defense Minister Galtieri was dismissive, both of the President's concerns and of the pair of Valkyries that had just flown overhead. "It is like everything they do these days, much noise but no teeth. They have lost whatever spirit they may have had."

Videla sighed. He had an unpleasant feeling that Galtieri was very wrong. "And this sudden spurt of visits to Chile? Valparaiso is full of warships and there are B-70s at Santiago's airport. Lined up by the passenger terminal where everybody can see them. Our man in Valparaiso says that there is a Chipanese submarine there which is unprecedented and some of their officers attended a party on the American cruiser which is far more than just unheard-of."

"Posturing, just posturing. The bombers will flee fast enough when we take out the airport and the ships will have to take their chances when we do the same to the port." Galtieri stared at the President. He was beginning to feel that Videla was too soft, too cautious to lead the country. Perhaps it was time for a change.

"Are we ready to do more than posture?" Videla knew exactly what Galtieri was thinking and wondered again if the man understood what the world was like outside his narrow, focused little clique.

"We are. The two assault cruisers are finishing their yard maintenance now. Both will be assigned to the attacks on Picton, Nueva und Lennox islands. The *Veinticinco de Mayo* is also finishing her refit." Galtieri was careful not to mention that it had only been possible to refit her by stripping her sister, the *Neuve de Julio* for spare parts. Technically, the latter carrier was in dock for a long reconstruction. The truth was, she lay in the yard like a gutted fish. "And the amphibious groups are ready. If the Chileans resist, our cruisers will make them rue the day they decided to do something so rash."

It wouldn't be so rash if the Chileans got their air force off the ground. The Argentine fleet was weak on air defenses; they had always thought to rely on the fighters based from the two carriers. But, now one carrier was gone. Even by merging the air groups, the *Veinticinco de Mayo* could only just make up a full air group, 36 fighters and 24 bombers. That would have to be enough. It just had to be.

Pack Gun Race Course, Kingston, Jamaica

"GLOWWORM! GLOWWORM! GLOWWORM!"

"JAMAICA, JAMAICA, JAMAICA!"

The roars echoed across the race ground, battling to drown each other out, for this was a special match, one that was the ultimate prize in Pack Gun racing. A team might win the Diamond Cup or the Hood Holdfast, they might rack up a record time on the King of the Kopje ascent, but they would never be considered a real Pack Gun racing team until, win lose or draw, they had faced the Jamaican Team on their home ground. The Jamaican Navy might be a few small patrol craft. The Jamaican Army might be a single (albeit well-regarded) battalion. The Jamaican Air Force might still be flying F-63 Kingcobras left over from World War II. The Pack Gun team fielded by the consolidated armed forces of Jamaica was an entity to be feared. On their home ground, with the crowd to urge them to greater efforts and the jangling music of the steel drum bands to stir their hearts, they dominated the Pack Gun racing community.

Their racing ground was a tribute to the pride the Islanders had in their team. The run out consisted of two long strips of grass, a wall half way down each. By tradition, the teams tossed a coin for the choice of strip. Really serious teams, which was every one that competed here, had been studying the grass, the weather and the 'form' of teams that had competed earlier. The *Glowworm* team had won the toss and they'd chosen the portside track. The *Glowworm* Team Captain, the "Gunny" in the language of the Pack Gun Race had run the results of every Pack Gun Race held here through the ship's computers. He'd noticed there was a slight tendency for the home team to chose Portside when they run the toss. Working on the basis they knew something he didn't, he'd taken Portside himself when given the chance.

There wasn't much in it, but Captain Foster thought his Glowworms had just the slightest of leads when it came to manhandling their gun over the Wall. That was the first obstacle, five feet high. It was no great feat for a man normally, but for a team of ten dragging a 3.7" Pack Howitzer No.2 it was a feat worth noting. He couldn't help noticing that the steel drum band had done this before. They had the timing of their music worked out to the split second. Their drum roll for the run up to the wall was perfect; the crescendo coming as the barrel was swung over the obstacle and down to the other side. Then the two teams were off again and if one of them had a lead over the other, Foster couldn't see it.

Up ahead of the teams was 'the mountain.' A square pyramid sat fifteen feet high, two of the sides were smooth ramps, the other pair made of three 'steps,' each five feet high. The smooth ramps came first. The teams had to scramble up them, no easy task dragging the load of the pack howitzer. Going up was the easy part compared with turning the gun around on the small platform at the top then rolling it down the slope with only their strength and the grip of their boots to brake its roll. Then they had to climb up on to the first step, prepare their gun and fire off three rounds at low elevation 'to engage the enemy.' To Foster's amusement the band had their music perfectly synchronized with the artillery fire. The chanting of the crowd blended with the drums and the smoke drifting from the guns to create a spectacle unmatched elsewhere. *It would be a man who lacked any soul,* thought Foster, *who could watch a Pack Gun Race and not be stirred by the sight.*

The teams were hard at work. They stripped their guns into twelve parts, 14 with the two boxes of ammunition; the heaviest of which weighed 250lb. They then threw the parts up to their team-mates who had formed a human chain to get the dissembled gun over the crest of the ridge and down to the first step on the other side. There the gun would be assembled and fired at high angle for a three round 'defiance of the enemy.' Then, it would have to be dropped down to the ground again for the run home. Foster held his breath. It was so easy in the urgency of the race to forget one of the ammunition boxes and leave it on the steps of the mountain. That was a disaster; one of the team would have to run back and get it, costing his team irrecoverable seconds and giving the crowd a chance to shout a barrage of ribald, if good-natured, advice. He relaxed. His team had both their ammunition boxes and they were starting the run home. Just the run left: down the track again, over the wall and back to the starting line where they would bring their guns "home." The team to get the muzzle of its gun past the finishing line first was the winner. Foster couldn't honestly tell who that was. To his eyes, the two guns had crossed the line together.

After the roaring of the crowd, the deafening music and the crash of the guns, the silence around the sports ground was eerie. The umpires and stewards were gathering around the guns. It was obvious the issue was so close that it would come down to the photographs taken on the finishing line to decide. Both teams were lined up in perfect order, trying not to gasp for breath too obviously and equally trying not to watch the umpires too keenly. Finally, a steward came out with the pictures and handed them to the Head Umpire. He studied them intently, nodded and spoke to the other Umpires who also nodded. The die was cast.

"Ladies and Gentlemen. In today's Pack Gun Race between the Home Team, the representatives of the Jamaica Defense Forces. . . " There was a surge of cheers from the local supporters. ". . . and the Visitors, the representatives of HMS *Glowworm*. . . " There was another surge of cheers from the ship's company.

"The time for the Home Team is four minutes, twelve point nine seconds. The time for the Visitors is four minutes, twelve point three seconds." There was a moment's silence as the crowd took in the figures. "I therefore declare the Visitors to have won today's Pack Gun Race!"

There was a wild burst of cheering as the crowd saluted the victors. In some places, in some sports, the supporters of the losing team might have booed the winners but this was a Pack Gun Race. Anyway, the Jamaican people were made of finer stuff than that, and would consider displaying such a lack of sportsmanship despicable. The Jamaican Defense Forces team broke ranks and ran over to the Glowworms, pumping their hands and slapping them on the back to congratulate them on their win. It was a sight and a sound that made the heart feel good.

"Well done Captain." A grinning Jamaican patrol boat commander grabbed Foster's hand and pumped it enthusiastically. "That's a race that will be headlines on the news tonight!"

"Thank you, Commander. Your men ran a damned fine race; there couldn't have been more than a hair in it."

"Point six of a second, a result that close does credit to both teams, Sir. Better to lose a well-run race than to win one unfairly run."

Foster knew exactly what the Jamaican Commander was referring to: the notorious race where the American SEALs had stolen their opponent's gun. They may have thought it was amusing, but it still rankled a Jamaica where sportsmanship and 'playing the game' were still regarded as high virtues. The Americans had had their fun and made their point, but they'd left a residue of ill-feeling behind them. It was so typical of them, gaining a short-term point at the expense of longer-term interests. And yet, that brought him back to the question that was quietly debated in political science circles, one that was called The Septic Paradox. The Americans frequently took actions that only benefitted them in the short term and harmed their long term position, yet behind all that there was a consistency and purpose to American actions that spoke of long-term planning. A paradox indeed.

"I was admiring *Glowworm* as we came in Captain. Fine looking ship, first time we've had a G Class out here. You've still got the low bridge on her though."

"We're the last; the other three Batch Ones have all been refitted with the raised bow and enlarged superstructure. We'll be getting the same rebuild when we return from this commission. I'll be sorry to see the old bridge gone though; down low like that we got a real feel for the sea."

"Out for two years Jimmy?" The voice was familiar and Foster turned slightly to welcome an old friend to the group. "Mickey, how are you. Still driving *Mermaid* around in a cloud of diesel smoke?"

Commander Michael Blaise grabbed Foster's hand and pumped it. "We may be a bit slow, Jimmy, but we'll still be thumping along when you gas turbine types are wallowing round looking for fuel. Have you met Alice?"

"I've not yet had that honor. Mrs. Blaise, pleased to meet you." One of the benefits of serving on the sloops was that the crews were allowed to bring their wives and families out with them. The sloops had been built with extra accommodation, so it was no great problem fitting in the crew's families on the run out and the three-year tour of duty on foreign station made bringing out the families a popular policy. It also allowed the families to see what their husbands and fathers actually did for a living. Sometimes, the families had even joined in, helping out when needed. On her way out to station, *Mermaid* had stopped at a small island called Tristan da Cuhna to evacuate islanders threatened by a volcanic eruption. The ship's small medical staff had been aided by the families on board for the journey down and that had made a major difference. The sloops were happy ships and their crews were quick to defend their virtues from aspersions cast by the more glamorous members of the fleet.

"Pleased to meet you, Captain Foster, Commander Quigley. Congratulations to both your teams, that was a good race. The children were shouting themselves hoarse."

"Well, we'll have to get them some tea, won't we." Commander Quigley knew his duty as a host and offered his arm to Alice Blaise.

As they set off, Blaise and Foster dropped back slightly. "You got the word too?" Foster didn't know if the quiet message that was going around the fleet had reached here yet.

"We most surely did. We're getting *Mermaid* ready now. Nothing too obvious but we've been asked to do a fast run down to South Georgia. There's people down there and we're supposed to get them out. I've heard…" Blaise dropped his voice still lower, "that the Booties have put some people in there as a garrison in case we can't get there in time. They'll be coming out with us as well if we are. Once the civilians are out, I hear there'll be a proper garrison put in place."

"This is serious Mickey. I've got a feeling we're going to be earning our salaries sooner than we think."

Flight Deck, USS Sacramento *CGN-169, Puerto de Valparaiso, Chile*

This was a strange meeting by any standards. The arrangements were eminently sensible, the Americans and Australians had set up barbeques on the downwind side of the rotodyne deck and their cooks were busily competing to turn out the best food. Over on the other side, the crew of the Imperial Japanese Navy (everybody had been cautioned not to refer to the force as Chipanese) submarine had set up tables loaded with sushi, sashimi and tempura, to be washed down with copious drafts of sake. Finally, on the broad fantail, the British had set up a fairly authentic-looking Pub bar and had even found a buxom barmaid to hand out beer and single-malt whisky with a generous hand. The *Sacramento* had managed to put together a good band and they were on a stand in front of the hangars, playing a miscellany that varied from romantic favorites to good old Dixieland Jazz for the members of the ships' companies who were dancing with their wives or local guests. With the sun setting over the hills that lay between the harbor and the open sea and the lights on the ships twinkling in the growing twilight, it was a magical setting.

"Anyway, so there we were, minding our own business, when suddenly this Australian submarine pops up in the middle of our formation and asks for directions to Chile." Captain Ernesto Karposi, commanding officer of the *Sacramento*, shook his head sadly.

"Actually, it wasn't *quite* like that. We knew you were on your way here but you were heading west not east, so we asked if *you* knew the way to Chile." Beecham sounded almost apologetic as he delicately inserted the barb. He took a bite of the sashimi on his plate and sighed softly with delight. "This is really excellent. Captain Sazuko, how did you manage to get fish this fresh?"

"A single pulse from the bow sonar and we had all the fish we needed." It was a sign of the informality of the party that the Japanese officers had actually unfastened the collars of their tunics. The Japanese submarine skipper looked around innocently at his audience, then chuckled. "In truth, yesterday, we saw some of the Chilean fishermen and told them of our needs. They made a special trip out this afternoon for us and brought the fish back alive to make sure it stayed fresh. We offered to pay them, but they would accept nothing but a few bottles of sake."

Which probably had much to do with the fact that the yen was worthless, thought Karposi. Still, it was true that the Chileans were going out of their way to make the foreign warships in their ports welcome. There was no doubt that this really was a unique occasion. All week, ships had been pulling in to Valparaiso, some staying only a few hours, others for the full week. And yet, for all the festivities of what was apparently an impromptu international fleet review, there was an increasing edginess, a tension in the atmosphere that

79

was growing daily. The Argentine presence along the border was still growing. Their units were still moving up into position in a threat display that was obviously deadly serious. They were being monitored by space-based assets and by the now-continuous American over-flights but the Argentine military government was showing little inclination to be deterred by that fact. Quite the reverse, in fact. Looking around the party being held on the fantail of his ship, Captain Karposi had the unpleasant feeling that he was watching the band playing on the deck of the *Titanic*.

From high overhead, the dull thump of sonic booms momentarily interrupted the band and rattled the glasses behind the Royal Navy's bar. Karposi looked up at the dark blue bombers, almost invisible in the darkening sky.

"Your Vigilantes I think." Captain Sazuko was also staring skywards. "On their way to watch our friends over the border. From *North Dakota*?"

"Probably." Karposi was slightly guarded. Despite the current situation, Chipan and American interests were rarely aligned and one had to be careful what was said. "*North Dakota* is still officially running trials so she's getting in all the air operations she can." There was more to it than that of course. With two carriers out there, somewhere, one was carrying out the offensive operations, the other was riding guard. Even now, 35 years after the sinking of the *Shiloh*, the U.S. Navy was still cautious about protecting its carriers.

"*Vanguard* also ran her trials on her way down here. You know she came under the ice?" Sazuko was impressed. A transit from the Atlantic to the Pacific by way of going under the Arctic ice was a remarkable feat for a newly-built submarine. "She is very modern." The Japanese captain sounded almost wistful. His country's navy was falling further and further behind world standards as the economic crisis back home slowly bit deeper. He'd been almost embarrassed to conduct the foreign skippers around his boat when his turn had come to return the invitations extended to him.

"She is indeed. The British have come a long way in a few years."

"And soon they will be tested, yes?" Sazuko blinked. "Oh, it must come. If the Argentines are deterred by our little show here, then they will have to turn on the British to satisfy the expectations they have raised in their own people. And if they are not, and war starts, then they will attack the British as a natural extension of that war. Either way, in a few weeks, the British will have to fight and then we will see how well they have rebuilt themselves."

Themselves; not their navy. Karposi noted the expression carefully. For all his apparent openness and joviality, the Japanese skipper would not be here if he wasn't both absolutely trusted and the very cream of the crop. He was right too, what was on test here was more than the ability of the Royal Navy to fight. It was the willingness of the British to do so. They'd had plenty of good ships in 1940 as well, but Halifax had done for them then. *Was there a Halifax in the wings today?*

"At least they have one advantage." Sazuko was almost laughing. "At least their ships are all Navy. There is an agreement in our country that the long-range bombers and cruise missiles are Navy but the ballistic missiles belong to the Army. So, on our ballistic missile submarines, we run the ship but the missile compartment amidships is run by the Army. The Army actually puts armed guards on the hatches leading from our part of the

80

ship to theirs and our sailors need special passes to cross through those hatches. That is why our ballistic missile submarines have long tubes that join the weapons and command sections forward and the machinery section aft. Just so our sailors do not have to pass through Army country. Madness."

Now why did he tell me that? Karposi thought while he filed away the information for transmission back to the Naval Intelligence Department. *Always remember the first rule. When given information, ask why the person giving it away is doing so. He is never doing it in your interests, always in his.*

"Thank heavens we never had that problem." Karposi's voice was devout. "We scrapped our ballistic missile submarine designs the day President LeMay cancelled all the strategic missile programs. If it fights at sea, it's Navy. If it fights on land, it's Army. If it's Strategic, it's Air Force. All nice and simple. And, since we don't do fighting on land, the Army keeps out of everybody's way."

Karposi, Sazuko and several other Navy officers who had been politely listening to the conversation on behalf of their naval intelligence services all burst out laughing. "But Monsieur Captain," the Captain of a French corvette anchored in the auxiliary port a mile or two down the way contained his laughter for a second, "is not the Air Force just long range artillery for the Army? After all, in Algeria, the Valkyries saved our Army from destruction by the Blackpox Plague."

There was a split second of uneasy silence as people remembered the terror of Blackpox and the bombing that had wiped out the factories that gave it birth. They also noted a French officer giving credit to the Americans for their action. It was of such little things that shifts in international politics were made. There were eleven navies whose intelligence operations would be receiving confidential reports on tonight's party and every one of them would mention that small but significant statement – as the French officer who had made it had known they would. Then the silence was broken by the sight of an Australian officer dancing past with a gloriously beautiful Chilean woman whose evening dress was the height of Rome fashion.

"I hope he's aware of the custom out here that flirting is one thing, but attempting anything more serious is tantamount to a proposal of marriage?" The Captain of HMS *Vanguard* had just joined the group.

"If he isn't, he'll soon find out." Karposi mentally shrugged his shoulders. The complications of a run ashore didn't just end with making contact reports on interesting conversations and, anyway, the officer didn't come from his ship.

Conference Room, White House, Washington D.C.

"Hours, Sir; not days. Our satellite imagery and our reconnaissance flights show the Argentine units are moving to their jump-off positions. Their Air Force units are also readying. My guess is dawn tomorrow."

"So the naval demonstration didn't deter them." President Regan sounded disappointed. "I really had hopes that might work. We even had the Chipanese taking part. Lord knows why, but they came on-board."

81

"Because this is a war that nobody wants, Sir. It has the potential to cause entirely disproportionate damage, especially if the Argentines go nuclear, and it won't do anybody, even Argentina, any good at all. The Chipanese are just as keen to see things kept peaceful as anybody else; a message that got sent to us via the back door before we started arranging things." The Seer hesitated slightly; he was keen not to mention which back door had been used primarily because he still didn't quite know what to make of it himself. "Anyway, I wouldn't write the exercise off as a failure. In fact, it's done a lot of good, Sir. Quite apart from the various navies getting to know each other a little better, it also showed the Argentines that they are truly on their own. Their nerves must have been shaken by that. When we make an example of the first forces to get in our way, it'll be much more effective."

"Perhaps there is something in this international cooperation business after all." Reagan didn't really believe that but he was interested to see what his National Security Advisor would say in return.

"Oh there is, Sir, As long as we're in charge. The problem comes when everybody at the top thinks they are either running things or have an equal say in running them. Then everybody talks and nothing gets done. Then while that circus is going on, somebody picks them off one by one."

"Tomorrow at dawn. A traditional time."

"With good reason, although I prefer three in the morning myself. Dawn is so traditional that people tend to have alerts then. They'll probably be slipping their path finder units over the border a bit earlier. But, their main thrust will be in daylight, either at dawn or a couple of hours later. That can work as well. People go on alert at dawn but then relax when nothing happens. Then, in the first early brightness of morning when everything seems cheerful, they get the hammer dropped on them. One thing we do know, Sir; their objective is annexation. They're going for broke, grab the whole country."

An aide quietly entered and gave a message to the President who read it and passed it to The Seer. "I think that makes it final."

The Seer read the note quickly. "Cruiser *Pueyrredon*, assault cruiser *Almirante Brown* and two destroyers heading south towards the Beagle Channel. The assault cruiser is carrying Argentine Marines. That does make it final, Sir. The grab's starting."

"We can't allow it to succeed. And we will not. We have a strike plan I assume?"

"Of course, Sir. 35th and 448th Bomb Groups. Both B-70 formations."

"Order them to full readiness."

CHAPTER FIVE
ENHANCED DETERRENCE

Captain's Cabin, HMAS Rotorua, *Puerto de Valparaiso, Chile*

"Are we ready to move?"

"Yes Sir. Donks are warmed up, batteries are fully charged, everybody is on board. We can be under way in five minutes."

Beecham nodded. An alert had come through during the night; a war-warning. He happened to know that all the other ships in port had received similar warnings from their governments. During the time this international naval display had been in progress, an efficient unofficial communications system had grown up.

"Good. Now we can deal with this." He fingered the card in his hand and read it again. "The Veracruz Family invite the officers and men of HMAS *Rotorua* to attend the wedding of their daughter Emilia Consuelez to Lieutenant Graeme Gavin."

He looked balefully at his Navigating Officer. "Well Lieutenant, what have you got to say for yourself?"

"Sir, I haven't proposed, honestly."

"Gavin, you got the briefing before you went ashore. Chilean girls flirt with their male acquaintances and their men are expected to flirt back. It is a pleasant pastime that means nothing. However, anything more than flirting starts to have meaning. Petting is a declaration of serious intent; attempted seduction is a proposal of marriage. If the girl allows the seduction to succeed, she's accepted your proposal. Which is, I understand, the situation here."

"But Sir, it was just a run ashore."

"You may call it a run ashore Gavin. Here, when a man seduces a woman and doesn't follow through, it's called 'ruining a virgin' and it's taken very seriously. Even in our country, not so very long ago Gavin, an officer who was accused of such an offense would find himself being given a bottle of whisky and a revolver with one bullet in the cylinder. Avoiding disgrace to the ship or regiment, you see. In some countries, the brothers of the wronged woman might kill her to save the family honor. Here in Chile, they are much more civilized than that. Her brothers will kill the man who seduced her instead. So, what do you propose to do?"

Gavin gulped and looked desperate. *It was*, Beecham thought, *not a productive course of action.*

"Sir, we'll be setting sail soon."

"We will. However, that won't solve the problem. The Veracruz family are very rich, very powerful, very influential. By the way, I went to see the pater familias as soon as this card arrived. A most pleasant, extremely reasonable man who is deeply fond of his daughter and, by the way, actually quite approves of you. In his eyes, his daughter has made a very good catch. I have also spoken with the young lady in question and there is no doubt she is deeply fond of you. I might say that you appear to have made a good catch as well, one that will be of great help to you in your future career. If you live to have one."

Gavin gulped. Then he started to think a little more clearly. Emilia was indeed beautiful, wealthy and he was aware that she did love him. In fact, he was suddenly sure of the fact that he was inordinately fond of her himself. "But Sir, we're due to set sail and if we go down south, you'll need me."

"Well, that's an odd thing. We are indeed going south, to the Antarctic in fact, to see how this class of submarine performs in extreme cold and very rough weather. Based on those trials, a Chilean Navy order may well be forthcoming. However, due to the navigational problems down there, we will be embarking a Chilean Navy navigating officer. In making those arrangements, I met with our naval attaché here and it appears he needs an assistant and the post has been approved by Canberra. It's yours for the asking. It would mean a two-year tour of duty in Santiago, of course."

Gavin made up his mind. He suddenly realized that fortunate was actually smiling on him, although she was, perhaps, hiding the smile behind a tactful hand. "Sir, that would be a wonderful start to my marriage. How do I go about this?"

"You have to go and see the pater familias, Ernesto Veracruz and ask for his daughter's hand but that's a formality. Her family will take it from there. He's expecting you at 10:30. And Graeme, if I may say so, you have made a very wise decision." Beecham was about to say more, but he was interrupted by sirens wailing on shore and from the *Sacramento*.

F13F-4 Tomcat Kittykat, *Flight Deck, USS* North Dakota *CVN-79, 250 miles West of Chile*

"All Raptor aircraft, ready for launch." The message was a little superfluous; the red flare arching skywards from the bridge had made the fact quite clear, but it never hurt to be sure. Ahead of *Kittykat*, the long slot of the catapult was already leaking steam as it built up power to hurl the fighter airborne. Captain Paul Flower advanced the throttles, watching the needles on his instrument panel edge up towards the red zones as his twin J-93 engines built up power. Each of the four catapults on the *North Dakota* had a Tomcat sitting on it. Far away to port, almost over the horizon, the *Ohio* had the same number of fighters ready to go. In total, the eight fighters made up Raptor Flight. It was the fast-response group that would take action if Argentina actually decided to go through with its assault. Each aircraft carried four nuclear-tipped AIM-54C Phoenix missiles, two conventional warhead AIM-54Bs backed up by four heat-seeking AIM-9 Sidewinders. Between them, the eight fighters could take on a fair-sized air force all by themselves.

Ahead of him, the launch captain lifted his green flag up high, signaling that launch was imminent. He spiraled it above his head to ensure that *Kittykat* had her engines pooled up to full, then dropped it. Flower felt the slam in his back as the catapult kicked in. His aircraft was hurled down the forward flight deck towards the bows that seemed terrifyingly close. *Kittykat* dipped as she left the catapult track. She briefly dropped below the level of *North Dakota's* flight deck before soaring skywards, accelerating quickly as her nose lifted towards the dawn sky. Flower angled his fighter around until he could see *North Dakota* underneath him. Her deck lights were still twinkling in the dawn nautical twilight.

Kittykat swept her wings back a little to match the increasing speed of her climb. For a moment, Flower regretted the loss of his beloved F9U *Rosie*. Even with only one engine, she had climb and turn rates that put *Kittykat* to shame. He held speed at Mach 0.7 with a 15 degree climb, watching the altimeter spiraling upwards as the other seven members of Raptor flight joined him. When he hit 25,000 feet, he leveled off and added throttle, accelerating his fighter up to Mach 1.25. That would carry him upwards to the next staging point at 45,000 feet. There, he would level off again and accelerate to Mach 2.5 before the final climb to 70,000 feet and Mach 3.2.

By the time *Kittykat* had completed her climb, *North Dakota* was far behind her. Her AWG-9 radar was scanning for the inbound Argentine formation that had started the alert. The eight aircraft of Raptor Flight were spread out in a long line, each barely visible from the next. The days when aircraft had flown in close formations were long gone. The nuclear-tipped air-to-air missiles in *Kittykat's* belly that had seen to that. It was the same way that nuclear-tipped anti-ship missiles had finished off traditional navy formations. An amateur might have expected to see the two American carriers inside a ring of escorts just like the publicity pictures showed. That was a formation that was only used for publicity shots though.

"Got them, Raptor-One." Raptor-Seven called in the radar sighting. The bearing and range information followed quickly. There were two Argentine formations inbound; one heading for the military airfields around Santiago, the other for the naval base at Puerto de Valparaiso.

Flower accelerated slightly and his formation swung so that they were on an intercept course with the Argentine aircraft. The Tomcats were almost 30,000 feet higher than they were and were moving two whole Mach numbers faster. "Raptor Two, Three and Four, join me taking the southerly group. Raptor Five, Six, Seven and Eight take the north formation. Each Raptor aircraft fire two conventional AIM-54B. Say again, AIM-54 Bravo. Fire on my command. Acknowledge."

The acknowledgements came in. Flower designated the center of the hostile formation as his center of aim and selected his pair of AIM-54Bs. Behind him, he felt the

85

whir and vibration as the triple revolving racks rotated to that the missiles he had selected were in position to fire. "All Raptor aircraft. Open fire."

The sixteen AIM-54Bs fired almost simultaneously. Flower saw them split into two groups as they hurtled out in front of the Tomcats and started to climb upwards. They'd arch upwards, climbing to almost 125,000 feet before turning down and diving on their prey underneath. Even at Mach 6, it would take almost two and a half minutes for them to cover the distance to their targets. Flower watched with almost grim amusement as the Argentine aircraft, *they were probably Macchi Ciclones*, he thought, swept onwards. Then, suddenly, the Argentine pilots realized what was happening. *Probably their radar warners had picked up the AIM-54 homing heads switching on.* The neat formations shattered in panic as the pilots scattered to avoid what they assumed was a salvo of nuclear-tipped missiles descending on them.

There is only one defense against a nuclear initiation. Don't be there when it happens. The Argentine strike pilots swerved away, attempting to get as far away from the inbound missiles as they could in the few seconds possible. They were helped by one thing, the AIM-54 Phoenix was a large and clumsy missile. It was a modified and much-improved version of the older AIM-47 Falcon, but it was too fast and too large to be very agile. In fairness, it had never needed to be particularly maneuverable; it was designed to deliver a nuclear warhead that spread destruction over a wide area. In a way it had brought about its own obsolescence; its warhead had made formations of aircraft a means of multiplying kills from a single shot. These days, pilots flew far enough apart to give them a chance of escaping the missile's fire. There was a new missile coming, the AIM-120 Harpy that was much smaller, much more maneuverable and longer ranged but it wasn't available yet.

For all that, the AIM-54Bs did well. As the Argentine pilots headed away from the kill zone, jettisoning their bombs in a frantic effort to survive, the Phoenix missiles dived on them and blotted seven of them from the sky. The other nine missed their targets, thrown off by jamming and last-minute maneuvers that took years off the airframe life of the Ciclones. The pilots of those aircraft saw the conventional explosions and heaved sighs of relief. Then, they headed for home. With their bombs gone, there was no point in continuing the mission. Their part of this attack had failed.

High overhead, Flower looked down on the retreating Argentine formation and reduced speed. His Tomcats held station about eighty miles behind and 30,000 feet above the surviving bombers. His Raptor Flight aircraft kept the Ciclones illuminated with their radars, *just to keep them honest* Flower thought, *but there is no doubt, they are heading home.*

"Raptor-Five here. They're going home, Raptor-One. Sensible fellows."

"Affirmative Raptor-Five. All Raptor Aircraft, hold station on them. Let's be gentlemen and see our guests safely home.

Sail, HMAS Rotorua, *Puerto de Valparaiso, Chile*

Captain Beecham had made it to the conning position on the sail of *Rotorua* in record time. He made it fast enough to see the rails of the Talos launcher on the fantail of *Sacramento* slam to horizontal. Then two of the long blue missiles slid out from their hangar under the flight deck onto the launch rails. Within seconds, the loaded launcher was rotating skywards and turning to the engagement arc. Beecham swept his binoculars along the length of the cruiser. The Terrier launchers forward were also loaded and waiting.

That was when a movement on the Chipanese submarine caught his eye. Two clamshell doors were opening just aft of the sail and a twin-rail launcher was elevating from the hull. It also had missiles loaded. Beecham recognized them as Keibo anti-aircraft missiles; a new weapon and one that Australian intelligence knew very little about. Beside him, Cardew already had the ship's camera out and he photographed the missiles as rapidly as he could roll the film and press the shutter.

"Now that's a surprise." Beecham was fascinated by the installation.

"Signal, Sir, by lamp from *I-709* to USS *Sacramento*. Message reads. 'Do not worry; we will protect you.' Message ends." The signalman had a delighted smirk on his face.

A chuckle ran around the bridge, one that turned into a full-bellied laugh as the signal broke the tension that had been building up. Cardew wiped his eyes and shook his head. "You know, I really like Captain Sazuko. I bet Captain Karposi is jumping on his hat up there."

"No doubt, although I don't think he'll be on the bridge." Beecham knew American doctrine. The Captain would go to the Combat Direction Center when the alert sounded, not the navigating bridge. "Anything word?"

"Inbound hostiles, Sir. Aircraft from *Ohio* and *North Dakota* are intercepting."

The minutes seemed to crawl past. Beecham was fascinated to see that the Talos launcher on *Sacramento* was constantly making tiny movements, presumably to ensure that its missiles were on a perfect intercept course for the inbound Argentine aircraft. One thing he did know; the American cruiser couldn't be using her radars at full power. If she had, the paint would be peeling off the walls of the dockside houses with the power output. Presumably, she was targeting using information downloaded from one of the carriers airborne command and control aircraft.

"Intercept, Sir. The Tomcats are claiming nine aircraft shot down. The rest have turned back after jettisoning their bombs. The Argie aircraft were Ciclones, so the 'cats are claiming."

"Makes sense." The Italian-built swing-wing Ciclone was the standard Argentine strike aircraft. Macchi claimed it was the equal of the Chipanese Nakajima B10N Shuka and it had certainly sold a lot better. Macchi's reputation for supporting its products helped there. Of course it wouldn't help the aircraft that had just been shot down. That brought a quick thought into Beecham's head. "Any radiation traces?"

"No Sir. Septics used conventional warheads as a warning. Kept the nukes for the next salvo. Anyway, they're following the Argies home just to make sure the message was received and understood."

The wail of the all-clear sirens brought about a quick fall in the tension. Beecham sighed with relief. It seemed like the effort to deter war was beginning to work.

"Aircraft pre-flighted, prepped and ready Sir. Check lists for your inspection." Master Sergeant Hichins-Yates saluted smartly and handed them over to her husband. He returned her salute equally smartly and without a trace of humor at the situation. Here, on this side of the base gates, for all practical purposes, they weren't married. Each morning, they drove together up to the main gates and he got out of the car. A quick good-bye kiss and Selma would drive inside while he would either walk through the gates or be picked up by another member of the duty shift. Relationships were off-base only. It was a policy that had been instituted when women had started to serve in SAC and it had avoided a lot of problems. Breaking it meant that both partners would be assigned to other bases, ones that were a long, long way apart. In Mike Yates' case, the fact he was an officer married to an enlisted airwoman was an added complication.

So, here, now, he was Major Mike Yates speaking to Master Sergeant Selma Yates. The fact they had the same surname was a meaningless coincidence. He ran his eyes down the long lists of data on the clipboard, checking the readings and technical data. "Oil sample readings seem a bit high?"

"Filters are well within spec Sir. *Shield Maiden* is due for a major overhaul after this run, we'll put new filters in then." *Shield Maiden* had been doing a large number of relatively short flights over the last few weeks testing out the new guided bomb equipment. That put a greater strain on her systems than the normal missions.

"No metal contamination?"

"No, Sir. We'd have pulled them if we'd found any. They're holding up well. I'd say they've sixty percent life left."

Yates nodded. Normally the oil filters would be pulled and replaced at fifty percent remaining life. "No carbon?" The oil in the B-70s hydraulics operated at the temperature of a deep fat fryer and carbon contamination was a problem.

"None we could find, Sir."

"That's good." Yates read the rest of the sheet and signed the bottom before turning to the next. There was nothing exceptionable there so that signature followed quickly. "Right, Sergeant, the aircraft appears in order, I accept her as mission-ready." The words were formal and were followed by a last signature. Another exchange of salutes and *Shield Maiden's* crew took delivery of their aircraft from her ground crew.

On board, Mike Yates eased into the pilot's seat and started fastening his harness. This was very close to being an operational mission. *Shield Maiden* had 2,000 gallon drop tanks on all four underwing hardpoints and her belly was stuffed with real nuclear weapons: missiles for her own defense, gravity bombs for eliminating ground targets. All seven fuselage fuel tanks were filled to capacity, as were her overload wing tanks. Yates checked the weight manifest again, *Shield Maiden* was right up against the maximum allowable weight limit for MacDill. Soon, she would be heading south, ready to orbit her fail-safe point over the Atlantic, east of the Argentine coast. A point that put her just twenty minutes from her targets.

"Ready to go, guys. Begin pre-take off checklists." Each member of the crew started reading through their own station's checklist. Another strict rule. Checklists were always read, never recited from memory, even though the crews knew them by heart. At last, the formalities were complete. Yates gave the orders to start up the six J-93 engines.

"Tower gives us clearance to taxi, Mike. The contractors have been told to stop work on the runway extension and clear the work area while the bombers take off."

"Very good." Yates listened to the aircraft and to the sounds from the undercarriage as they taxied out towards the runway. "Entering 71 taxiway now."

"Turn on to crossway Tango and hold." The word from the tower came over the earphones. Yates acknowledged briefly. It was hardly out of his mouth before he got clearance to move on to the main runway. Ahead of him, the long strip of concrete seemed to shimmer in the morning sun.

"*Shield Maiden* ready for take-off. Canard flaps down."

"Cleared, *Shield Maiden*. Good luck and Fly High."

Yates advanced the throttles on the Valkyrie's engines and felt *Shield Maiden* shudder as the thrust built up. As the needles hit 100 percent, he released the brakes. His bomber rolled down the runway, picking up speed as she did so.

At the end of the runway, the Canada geese that lived there were annoyed and nervous. They had long before come to an agreement, so they thought, with the great white screaming birds that lived here as well. They would avoid each other and that suited the geese well. But now things had changed. There were nasty, noisy, smelly things that had come into their home and were digging it up. They'd crushed the nests and destroyed the eggs that were carefully laid there. Their home was being destroyed and the geese were very frightened. So, when one of the giant screaming birds started its approach, the geese panicked. They tried to escape the only way they knew how. By flying.

Yates eased back on the control column.*Shield Maiden's* nose lifted as her rotation started. She was doing almost 200 knots, beyond the point of lift-off but also getting dangerously close to the red lights that marked the end of the runway. "Sure going to be glad when the extension is finished." The words were almost drowned out by the sound of the take-off. The wheels lifted clear and that made the noise and vibration drop sharply.

"Gear up. Canard flaps up."

"Acknowledged."

Yates heard the thump as the wheels twisted around and retracted into their bays. Then, the whole aircraft was shaken by a terrible crashing noise; one that made the Valkyrie shudder in mid-air. Yates saw the sky rearing and lurching around him as *Shield Maiden* went out of control. He heard the desperate yell from his copilot. "Flameout! Engines one, two, three and five are gone. Power on four fluctuating."

Shield Maiden was losing power and speed at the one point where she couldn't afford it. Yates was still struggling with the controls, trying to get the aircraft under control but her nose was already rearing up past the critical point that ended any hope of saving her. There was only one priority left at that point. Yates took it, activating the system that dumped the nuclear weapons so they would be as far from the crash site as possible. Helplessly, Yates felt the great aircraft stall. The voice recorder in the cockpit caught the last words from the flight deck as she dropped from the sky. "Oh SHIT!!"

Selma Hitchins had stepped out of the hangar just as *Shield Maiden* made her take-off run down the runway. She heard the Valkyrie lifting off the runway. She was watching the undercarriage retract when she saw the great gouts of flame exploding from the six-pack of engines. She, and everybody on the base was already starting to run towards the end of the runway when *Shield Maiden* plowed into the ground. Her belly slammed down hard, the impact causing the structure to fragment. Even at that distance, she felt the heat on her face from the fireball. More than a quarter of a million pounds of exploding JP-6 created a roaring inferno to mark where *Shield Maiden* had just died.

Casa Rosada Presidential Palace, Buenos Aires, Argentina

"They did what?" President Jorge Videla was stunned by the news.

"They broke off the attacks, Sir. They had no choice. They were under fire from American carrier fighters. They had to jettison their bombs in order to evade the missiles. If they hadn't, they would have been wiped out. And with their bombs gone, there was no point in continuing with the mission."

And no real desire to, Videla thought to himself. A good officer knew when his men's hearts weren't in their work. Ever since planning for Operation Soberanía had started, he'd had a feeling that enthusiasm for the plan didn't extend far beyond those who had planned it. On the other hand, the bomber pilots hadn't really had a choice. If they had been under fire from American fighters, they were lucky not to have been incinerated in mid-air by nuclear bursts.

"What about their fighter escort? They did have one, I suppose?"

"They did, but the Americans fired from far outside their range. There was nothing anybody could have done."

No plan survives contact with the enemy. "So the attacks on the military airfields around Santiago and the naval base at Valparaiso failed. What of the rest?"

"They did better, Sir, although not as well as we hoped. The naval bases at Punta Arenas and Porto Williams was hit as we planned, We struck at Chabunco as well." There was something in the aide's voice that seized Videla's attention.

"What went wrong?"

"They were waiting for us, Sir. Our pilots think it was the Americans again. They saw the aircraft taking off on their radar and alerted the Chilean Air Force. There was fighting: our pilots held their own at least but the airfields were empty. They cratered the

90

runways, but you know how quickly they can be fixed. The naval bases were empty as well."

Videla felt the same way a boxer feels when he delivers a perfect punch only to have it connect with nothing but air. "How many aircraft did we lose?"

"Around thirty Sir, and we scored about forty kills. No Americans, of course."

That meant around a dozen Chilean planes had gone down, Videla thought grimly. The losses weren't actually as heavy as projected but they had been calculated on the basis of catching the Chilean aircraft on the ground. "Anything else?"

"Yes, Sir. The *La Argentina* amphibious group has spotted a Chilean force closing on it. They're staying behind a weather front, but they'll be intercepting our ships this afternoon."

Videla was about to say something but he was interrupted by an aide entering his office in a state of great urgency. "Sir, the television news; you must see this." He flicked the television set in the corner on in time to catch the tail end of the news bulletin.

"And so, back to the main item on the news tonight. A Valkyrie bomber of Strategic Air Command has crashed on take-off from its airbase in Florida, killing its crew of four. A Strategic Air Command spokesman has confirmed that the aircraft was carrying nuclear weapons and was on an operational mission." The newsreader's voice had dropped on the last two words and their significance was ricocheting around the world. "It is reported there is significant radioactive contamination at the site of the crash and decontamination crews are already at work clearing up the wreckage. Asked if the aircraft's mission had anything to do with the scattered fighting reported between Argentina and Chile, the spokesman declined to answer. However, our correspondent in Cuba has reported that large numbers of Valkyrie bombers have been seen heading south. And now, over to our weather office for the 24-hour forecast. George?"

"Well Anna, I guess our forecast for Buenos Aires is going to have to include extreme heat and strong winds. Now, for the London Area. . . "

The aide shut the television off. The other occupants of the room stared at it with the same fascination they'd have for a poisonous snake. The mood was broken by the telephone on Videla's desk ringing. Another aide answered it. "Sir, the American Ambassador is here. He wants to see you. Now."

"Send him in."

The American Ambassador must have been just outside the door. The words were barely out of Videla's mouth when the Ambassador pushed the door open and sprawled out in a chair in front of Videla's desk.

"Mister President, you are so screwed."

"Ambassador Jordan?" Videla was very much on his dignity when faced with this undiplomatic invasion of his office.

"Look, President, if you're going to start a war, don't screw it up this bad. I guess you've heard the Valks are on their way down. That gives you one hour to stop this mess. They won't be here for four but I want at least three hours to get clear of the target zones. Once I leave Buenos Aires, the bombers won't be turning back. If you move fast, I can get word to the Chileans and they can call Washington and then, the Valks will hold at their fail-safe points. The Chile government has agreed to write this morning's fun and games off as a regrettable misunderstanding and say no more about it. Provided you publically give up your territorial claims in the Beagle Channel of course. You'll pull your troops and ships back and drop this crazy Operation Soberanía nonsense. Be good, peaceful little international citizens."

"Or what? There is always an 'or else'." Videla was furious at what he was hearing but in his stomach there was a cold pit of dread. In reply, Ambassador Jordan got up and walked over to the window. He stuck his index finger in his mouth to wet it and held it up in the air. "Just what are you doing?"

"Checking wind direction. We don't want fall-out landing on our friends."

The cold pit in Videla's stomach suddenly jumped up a notch in size. The Americans were committed. They couldn't change their minds now, not after losing one of their bombers so publicly. If this war went ahead, Argentina would cease to exist. Already, the war hadn't gone well and it would only get worse. *How many more bombers were heading south with the names of Argentine targets written into their navigation systems?*

"One hundred." Ambassador Jordan's voice was dead neutral, dead level, devoid of intonation. The menace in it was chilling. "You were wondering how many bombers were heading this way weren't you? The aircraft that crashed has already been replaced by a back-up. To do the maths for you, that means there are 1,400 more ready to come down if you continue annoying us."

Videla made his mind up. Operation Soberanía had been checkmated, any attempt to proceed with it would result in a national catastrophe. "Very well, Mister Ambassador, America gets its way, again. One day, one day, you will pay for the things you have done in this world." He turned to his aides. "Get the words out to the Army; stand down. Discontinue air operations. Order the fleet back to base." He looked at the clock on his wall. It was just six hours until the assault cruisers and other amphibious ships had been scheduled to start their assault.

Ambassador Jordan nodded and started to leave. As he did so, he heard Videla repeat his words. "One day, you Americans will stand where we do now."

"Not if SAC has anything to do with it."

Maintenance Operations Center, MacDill Air Force Base, Florida

"I have the records for *Shield Maiden* here sir." Selma Hitchens-Yates voice was dead flat and eerily cold. Almost robotic. "The ground crew who prepped her for the mission have been isolated and are awaiting debriefing."

General Bennett took the pile of documents from her hands, noting their cold, clammy feel and lack of response. Outside, at the end of the runway, a great pyre of black smoke still marked the spot where *Shield Maiden* and her crew had died. Even though her wreckage was still burning, the investigation had started. Everything was being done by the book. The maintenance records had been sequestered and would be put under lock and key until technical experts could go over them. All the people who had worked on the Valkyrie had been separated and kept in isolation until they could be debriefed. There would be no opportunity for them to get their stories straight and agree what was to be said and what was not. Bennett was distracted by the telephone ringing. He picked it up and listened to the report from the commander of the decontamination crews.

"That was decon. They've found the five gravity devices, all intact, on the edge of the fire area. Looks like the last thing the crew did was to dump their weapons before going in."

"There'll be ten more, Sir. Four AIM-54s and six AGM-76s, all nuclear-tipped of course. The Frisbees on board are explosive. Not nuclear."

"I know tha . . ." Bennett stopped himself, remembering this woman had just watched her husband die. *Just what in hell was she still doing here anyway?* "Thank you Sergeant. You're dismissed, you need to go home to your family."

"Sir, there's too much to do here. We need to get the investigation. . ."

"Into the hands of investigators. You've done your share, Sergeant Yates; done it above and beyond the call of duty under the circumstances. Now go home to your family, they need you. Don't make me have you carried out."

A fleeting grin crossed Selma's face; a reflex to a General joking, nothing more. "That won't be necessary, Sir." She saluted and left.

"She shouldn't drive in that condition." The General spoke to Colonel Carson, the most senior of the pilots still on the base.

"She won't have to Sir. Three of the guys are standing by waiting for her. They'll stay with her while they pick up her kids from school. Fortunately, her parents and one of her in-laws are close by. They've already been told."

"Her car be big enough for the family?"

"No Sir, but they're taking your limousine."

"Nice of me to have offered it." The sarcasm was interrupted by another telephone call. Bennett listened again, his face grim.

"Right people, we have contamination. The smoke plume is hot; not very, but enough to cause problems. Get the emergency procedures started. The wind is taking it out to sea and a Navy P6M is monitoring it, but we can't take chances. Move."

Outside, Selma was walking dumbly towards the way out. Unobtrusively she was joined by three pilots from her husband's squadron. They gently but firmly steered her to the waiting limousine. "One of the boys is picking your car up, Sellie." The words were as quiet as all the other actions.

"Red Studebaker Eclipse. Sorry, you all know that." Her voice was flat and neutral, as gray and washed out as her skin color. The men with her exchanged glances, it was obvious that Selma was in a state of severe shock. The only thing they couldn't understand was how she was keeping going.

"We'll go to the school first, pick up your children. They don't know yet. Do you want us to tell them what's happened?"

"No, no. I'll do that. They'll know a Valkyrie's gone in; everybody for miles around can see that smoke and know what it is. They'll be worrying and fretting. We have to tell them soon. Have our parents been told?"

"Yes, the base chaplain called on them. It was fortunate your parents were staying with Mike's father. He's staying with them now. Where to?"

"School first. Then can you take us all to my father-in-law's house? The kids can stay there. I'll go over to our quarters later."

"No, Sellie, you won't. Kit Carson was quite firm about it. We stay with you all the time, drive you around, whatever it takes. When our shift finishes, you'll have a couple more of us to stay with you and the kids. We were told to make sure you take at least 72 hours leave; more if you need it. Look, that's your car isn't it? Better be because Kennie's driving it. He'll tail us over."

Four hours later, Selma was in her married quarters. One of her companions sat in the car outside. The teachers guessed what was happening when the official limousine had pulled into the car park and Selma had been escorted into the building. The principal had given her his office to tell the children and she'd hugged them while she'd told them that their father wouldn't ever be coming back. They were with their grandparents now; the enormity of what happened still hadn't sunk in. Then, she'd been driven back to the quarters she'd shared with her husband. She knew the drill. With her husband dead, she had to vacate these quarters within 30 days. The waiting list for married quarters was too long to allow any exceptions. She'd checked her husband's desk for any material there that should be returned to his squadron and started the process of clearing up.

Now, she was carefully packing the contents of the hidden compartment in her wardrobe into a suitcase. All her costumes, including the 1920s 'gangster's moll' dress she'd bought on their holiday in Cuba. She'd worn them to please her husband; now she would never wear them for anybody else. She closed the case, locked it and took it downstairs. Then, in what had once been their living room, she sank to her knees and started a long wailing scream.

Casa Rosada Presidential Palace, Buenos Aires, Argentina

President Videla sat at his desk, watching the shadows lengthen as dusk fell. The Argentine Army was pulling back from the borders, the Air Force was on its bases and licking its wounds while the Navy was heading for port. The country's air defense radars had picked up more than a hundred American bombers orbiting points surrounding the country. If the publications were true, they were one thousand miles from their targets. Or, put another way, 23 minutes from whatever it was they had been assigned to destroy.

A hundred bombers; a tiny fraction of the aerial might SAC could throw at its intended targets. The Americans had been serious. Whatever that bumbling fool Carter might have said or wanted, the iron fist was still there, still clutching its thunderbolts. All it had ever needed was a President with the will to use the power that iron fist provided. Galtieri had been wrong. He had made a mistake that all too many others had made when dealing with the Americans but Videla knew *he* would pay the price for the other man's blunders.

There was a crash outside his office, shouting, the sound of people running. Videla sighed. He had guessed this was coming so the crackle of rifle and machine carbine fire came as no great surprise. It was a little sooner than he had expected but perhaps Galtieri had had this planned all along. Just as a contingency of course. The gunfire came closer then ceased. There was a brief period of silence, a few seconds, no more than that. Then there was another crash as his doors were kicked open.

The men who strode in, covering him with their machine carbines were naval troops. *Probably some of Astrid's swimmer-commandos. They had the look; the hint of mad dog in their eyes.* They made a point of 'clearing' the room, throwing open doors and checking cabinets, presumably looking for hidden guards or concealed exits. Or, perhaps, just throwing their weight around. Behind them, Galtieri made his entrance with all the unnecessary flamboyance that was a part of his nature.

"You sniveling worm." Galtieri's voice was an odd mixture of triumph and loathing. "You sold out our men."

"No, I saved our country. Operation Soberanía was dead the moment the Americans decided to move. Would you rather see those Valkyries making their bombing runs on our cities?"

"Soberanía is not dead. With your treason out of the way, we can move again." The voice had changed. There was now anger in it; anger mixed with a good dose of insanity.

"You might think so, but nobody else will. Everybody knows those bombers are just waiting for a show of bad faith on our part. The Americans may even be hoping for it, so they can show their desire for a peaceful world, as they define it anyway, is unchanged and still has its teeth. In any case, Operation Soberanía was based on us achieving tactical and strategic surprise. That has gone. The Chilean Army is guarding the passes. Their Air Force, backed by American carrier aircraft, is on full alert and their Navy is at sea. A war now will be long and bloody and that our economy cannot stand. We will not win that war. Operation Soberanía is dead, Galtieri. Accept it."

Galtieri waved to his men. They moved to the President and nudged him with their guns. He stood and smiled sadly at Galtieri: in a strange way Videla was relieved that he didn't have to deal with this situation any more.

95

As the men took him out, Galtieri slipped behind the desk Videla had once occupied and gave his first order as the new President of Argentina. "Do it in the courtyard. We don't want the inside walls damaged."

The commandos nodded and left. Galtieri looked around at his new office then picked up the telephone to the Operations Room. "Operations, cancel all remaining troop and aircraft movements. Operation Soberanía is defunct. Say again, Operation Soberanía is over, abandoned. Prepare to execute Operation Rosario in its place."

PART TWO

ROSARIO

CHAPTER ONE
SECOND CHANCES

King Edward Point, South Georgia

HMS *Collingwood* rocked gently against the wooden wharf. The roller at the end of the brow rubbed against the rubber anechoic coating with a peculiar squeaking noise that put Captain Gregory Hooper in mind of his days at school long before he had joined the Royal Marines. Blackboards, and the sound of erasers being drawn across them. Looking ashore, the sight of the party of nine men who had gathered to greet them reinforced the memories. There was something about academics that never changed, even though their surroundings might rather drastically. Hooper was even tempted to look around for some old bomb sites for a quick game of "Resistance and Collaborators" but he restrained himself. In any case, if the situation blew the way everybody was expecting it to, there would be bomb sites enough in the not far distant future. Every time *Collingwood* had popped her satcom mast up, the situation had got worse.

"Pleased to see you and your men here Captain, although I'm not sure why you have made the trip down to this forgotten end of the world." The man who appeared to be leading the party sounded as if the arrival of the Marines was a serious imposition.

"Just a precaution Sir. You are?"

"James Walsingham. I'm the Postmaster here and, in the absence of anybody else qualified, unfortunate enough to be in charge of this settlement. The Commissioner has been away for some weeks now."

Hooper frowned, he hadn't been aware of that. "Away Mister Walsingham? I didn't know that."

"He took ill about three weeks ago. There are twenty of your men here? I hope you brought supplies with you. We're only fitted up to look after the British Antarctic Survey base here. Nine of them you know. We just don't have the resources to look after all of your people. Especially since the rest of the Antarctic Survey team will be coming in when winter closes down. How long you staying here for?"

Hooper's feelings deepened. He'd seen enough fouled-up situations in his time and this had all the hall-marks of being a real classic. "We've got some supplies with us, more will be coming in soon. *Mermaid* is on her way down to pick you all up and she'll drop off everything we'll need."

"Pick us up? Why should we leave here? Just what's going on?"

"We hope, nothing. But there's a chance the Argentines will try to make a grab for this place and we want to make sure they get a suitably hot reception."

"Ridiculous; absolutely ridiculous. I know the Argies here; damned fine group of people. Very friendly. Make a grab for the place you say? Stuff and nonsense!"

"Argies, here?" Hooper snapped on to the words, giving them the shaking and mauling that a rottweiler would have been proud of. "What Argies? How many? Where? How long?"

"Arrived about a month ago. Scrap merchants, come to dismantle the old whaling station at Leigh Harbour. Don't know how many of them. What do you expect? We should have sent somebody to count them?"

"Actually, yes." Hooper's calm voice gave no outward sign of his feelings, most of which involved strangling the postmaster. "That would have been a good idea. And you didn't tell anybody about their arrival?"

"Why should we? They wouldn't have come here unless everything as in order. Just what is going on?" Walsingham was becoming belligerent, beginning to understand the true dimensions of the affair and just how negligent his own behavior had been.

"What is going on, Mister Walsingham, is that a full-scale war is about to start. We had hoped, although we've been planning contingencies, to avoid getting caught out. Our presence here is one of those contingency plans. Only from what you've been telling us, any hope that we could sit this out has been dead for more than a month. These Argentines, did they arrive after the Commissioner left sick?"

"Of course not. When Will Durand, he's the Commissioner you know, got sick, the Argentines had just arrived. They had a doctor with them, well a medic they called him, and he said it was appendicitis. We all thought it was a gyppy tummy, but he was the doctor. So, they offered to fly him out. The trawler they came in on had a helicopter, you see."

"Oh, I see all right." Hooper was trying to absorb the situation and decide what to do. From what he could see, he was in the classic situation of not many options, all of them bad. "Stokes, get back on board the submarine, fast. Get the skipper to tell London what's going on down here. We've got Argies already on the island and that the Commissioner is missing, presumed dead."

"What!" Walsingham went bright red and appeared to be gulping for air.

100

"You don't seriously think they took him to hospital do you? If he's very lucky, he's locked up in a store-room somewhere. More likely, they took him out on their helicopter and dropped him into the sea as soon as they were out of sight of here. For your information, civilian scrap merchants don't have medics. They have doctors. Military units have medics." Hooper thought for a second. His next priority made him feel cold. "According to our information, there are two women here. Where are they and please don't tell me the Argentines took them away as well."

"Those two? No. They're off in the hills somewhere. Claim to be making a documentary film about the birds or something."

"Did they leave a movement schedule?"

"I think so. . ."

"Didn't you look at it?" Hooper almost screamed in frustration.

"No, I thought. . ."

"Dear God, that'll be a first. They left that schedule so you'd know where they were and then. That way, if they got into trouble, people would know where to start looking. And you never even looked at it?"

"Look, I'm just the postmaster here. I can't be expected to. . . "

"You were quick enough to claim the leadership though weren't you? Get me that schedule now. MOVE! Harry, get our stuff ashore. We've stepped right into the middle of a situation here. Curly, pick four of the boys; get started on your way to Leith Harbor and do a scouting job. Assume the opposition are Argentine Marines until we learn different. Dusty, get another four, then set off after those women as soon as we've found their schedule. What happens then, that's up to you and what goes on here. Either come back in or go into hiding out there. That leaves us with ten of us here. Lofty, start working out how to defend this place."

"Defend, Boss?"

"We've lost the initiative already. We have to assume they'll hit us first, especially if they've got a spotter out there and see us arriving." Behind him, an elephant seal on the beach roared its annoyance at the disturbance. Hooper could see his point.

Washington International Airport, Washington DC, USA

Supersonic airliners had made more of a difference to international politics than anybody might have suspected. It took a Fairey Aviation Concord just three and a quarter hours to fly from London to Washington; that made it possible for the Prime Minister to make this emergency trip over and return within a single working day. With the Anglo-Argentine confrontation rapidly reaching boiling point, that ability was of inestimable value. *Exactly why that was so would be*, the Prime Minister thought, *an unexpected surprise to the Americans.* Whether they would be relieved or concerned at the development would be an interesting question.

101

The sleek airliner was already parked in the VIP reception area, far removed from the big terminals where passengers were poured on to the waiting people-haulers. There were several other aircraft in the area including two of the new VC-170s, the military version of the North American-Boeing 3707. One of them sported the blue-and-white paint scheme of the aircraft allocated to the President; the other was an Air Force VC-170A, presumably to move key staff around. The NAB-3707 had been one of the weapons used against the Fairey Concord in the bitter campaign waged to have the aircraft cancelled. After all, as the critics of the British program had pointed out, it was two thirds of the American aircraft at three quarters of the price. On paper that was true enough. It carried 120 passengers against 180, cruised at Mach 2.05 instead of Mach 3.15 and had a range of 4,500 miles as opposed to 5,750. What those numbers didn't say was that the British aircraft also had a running cost that was also two thirds of its American rival. On lower-density routes, where an airline could find 120 passengers per aircraft but not 180, that meant it generated more profits. The Concord had done well on those shorter, lower density traffic patterns, vindicating Fairey's faith in their design.

Newton reflected that it hadn't been the first time Fairey had had to fight a determined campaign against those who wanted to shut one of their projects down. The memory of an older fight came back to him, one that had done much to shape the European aircraft industry. It was keyed by the Presidential Rotodyne that was already spooling up its engines. The VC-138 would fly him direct from the airport to the White House. There had been a grimly determined effort by parts of the British establishment to kill the whole Rotodyne project. What might have happened if it had succeeded chilled Newton, Fairey had fought off the attack and turned their concept into a spectacularly successful military and civil aircraft. It was hard to imagine a world without Rotodynes. How else would people get from their homes in the centers of cities and towns to the airports that lay well beyond the city limits?

Unlike the transports used by airlines and armies, the VC-138 had no rear ramp. Instead, it was fitted with large side doors that were served by retractable stairways. The British delegation filed on board and settled down in the well-upholstered seats. The doors slammed shut and the sound from outside diminished abruptly, even though the Kuznetsov turboprops that powered the Rotodyne were already reaching maximum power. With the odd whistling whine that was its characteristic trademark, the VC-138 took off and headed for the White House.

A helicopter would have taken 20 minutes to make the flight from Washington International to the city center; the Rotodyne made it in ten. It touched down on the landing pad just behind the White House and the doors hissed as they opened. It was another quick transit for the party before they were out of the early morning chill and inside the comforting warmth of the White House. *It wasn't bad going* Newton thought, *Breakfast at home in Britain, Brunch in Washington, back home in Britain for dinner.* An eight hour day, six hours travelling and two hours deciding the fate of the world between meals.

"David, welcome to the White House. It's a pleasure to see you. We have a briefing on the latest intelligence from the South Atlantic all waiting for you." President Reagan's warmth at seeing his visitor was, on one level, quite genuine. A gregarious and sociable man, he was always pleased to have visitors to the White House. On another level, the warmth was highly deceptive. He was a man who drew a sharp distinction between his personal feelings and his official duties. The phrase "a man who would do things in his professional capacity that he would view with disgust in his private capacity" might have

102

been written for him. His genuine friendliness towards the representatives of a country would not affect a decision to destroy that country should it become necessary.

The conference room was set up and waiting. The National Security Advisor was already behind the podium, arranging papers and checking that the graphics up on the display screen were fully updated. Newton looked around, recognizing the familiar figures of the Secretary of Defense, Chief of Naval Operations and the Head of Strategic Aerospace Command. Newton also saw the less-familiar but still distinctive figure of the President's Executive Assistant, quietly making sure that the briefing booklets were distributed and folders of supporting documentation given to those present. Newton reflected that she'd had enough practice at such meetings. Naamah Sammale had served as Executive Assistant to four Presidents. Her distinctive red hair was streaked with gray now and she had crow's feet around her eyes and mouth. Even so, twenty years of responsibility had been kind to her. Newton smiled and accepted the package of documents from her hands, then sat down in the front row, beside President Reagan.

"Mr. President, Prime Minister. . . ." The briefing had started and Newton stared at the material he had been given. The theme was quite simple. The effort made to scare off the Argentine attack on Chile had been successful; the invasion had been aborted with the loss of a dozen or so Chilean and Argentine aircraft. It had been dismissed as an unfortunate incident, one that was of no great consequence. It was better to downplay the whole thing that risk further escalation. Profuse diplomatic apologies had been exchanged; threatening troop concentrations had dispersed. Peace was descending on the Chilean-Argentine border. The Chileans were relieved, the Argentines furious, but the storm had blown over.

"And that is where the problem lies. Argentina has been defeated, we know it, they know it, but they can't let their population know it. All the intelligence we have, imagery, communications intercepts and overflight data, points to the fact that they are switching their attention to the Falkland Islands and South Georgia. Their naval movements are already heading in that direction. Their argument, we expect, will be that this is simply their attempt to remove an illegal occupation of their territory. We anticipate they will draw parallels with the Chipanese-Indian confrontation over the Southern Pescadores ten years ago. They will define that conflict closely and they will argue that since the Chipanese action to expel the Indians was tolerated, so also should their attempt to expel British forces."

"Thank you, Seer." Reagan turned to his guest. "Now, David, the question is this. War over the Falklands appears to be inevitable. How do you see the position of the United States in this eventuality?"

Newton braced himself slightly for the shock his answer would cause. "Mr. President, the parallels with the South China Sea fighting a decade ago are, as the National Security Advisor has pointed out, compelling. They emphasize that this is a problem Britain must face and we must do so from our own resources. In this conflict, our traditional friendship with the United States means much and your guarantee against a nuclear dimension to any hostilities is most welcome to us. But this is a battle Britain must fight and one that she must fight alone if we are to have any future claim to being a nation of consequent. We have rebuilt our economy from the dregs of ruin. We have reconstructed our armed forces from the debris of destruction. We have rescued our nation from the shame of defeat. Now, we must show that we can stand on our own feet, that we are no longer the emaciated survivor of a cataclysm. The British Lion must be resurgent, Mister President, or it will never again be able to hold up its head."

Up on the podium, the Seer blinked. He'd been expecting a British request for support; logistic at least, possibly even the commitment of combat forces. The blunt announcement that the British would handle this alone had shaken him. Then he thought the situation over. Newton was right; there was no doubt about that. If Britain was to have any claim to having recovered from the disaster of the Second World War, they had to show that they could defend their own interests against incursion. This crisis was the opportunity they had to do it.

In the audience, Reagan also nodded. "Very well, Prime Minister. We will, of course, comply with your wishes in this matter. And we wish the men and women in your armed forces good fortune in the days and weeks to come."

Karoo Desert, South Africa

The line of fourteen Boomslang tank destroyers was an impressive sight but Bastiaan van Huis couldn't help but feel the dark green and black camouflage used by the British looked odd to eyes used to the grey-yellow used by the South African Army. He also had the feeling that these vehicles should have been in South African camouflage and their sale to Britain had been at the expense of South African security. On the other hand, the money earned from exports financed further developments. Perhaps it all evened out.

Around him, the British crews were looking into the rear compartment of the Boomslang, taking in details of the magazine arrangements contained in there. "As you can see jongmens, the magazine is automated. There are two separate twelve-round feeding rings. Each one feeds rounds to the launcher in the cylinder mounted in front of it. Both magazine and launcher pairs are completely independent, so if one gets knocked out, the other can still function. In an emergency, both rings can be removed and then this compartment can be used for other purposes. That is for emergency only; we do not recommend it as a standard practice."

"How reliable is the magazine system?" Lieutenant Conrad Cross made the question sound tentative, as if he wasn't quite certain whether it should be asked or not. Van Huis looked at him carefully. He'd read the files on the men he would be training and this Cross had an impressive record for a man who had never seen a shot fired in anger. It was interesting that the British were giving their new tank destroyers to the infantry, not the cavalry units.

"A very good question." Van Huis looked around. "The honest answer is better than it could be, not as reliable as we would like it to be. The main problem is a jam caused by the tube in the launch cylinder not being properly aligned with the loading ring. That is a maintenance issue, of course. We urge that a crew check alignment before taking their vehicle out. This is why removing the magazine system is not recommended except in an emergency. It is easy to take out but the devil's own work to get it back in and properly aligned."

"What happens if there is a fire back there, Sir?" One of the sergeants had spoken up. Three of the four vehicles in each platoon of the company would be commanded by Sergeants.

"Bail out. All of you." There was a ripple of laughter around the audience. "There is an automatic fire suppression system in the rear compartment. A sensor detects a fire and drenches the compartment with inert gas. That is very well but rocket fuel has its own oxidizer and burns without need for air. If the fire has spread to that, nothing will put it out. So get out of there and watch from a safe distance. If the fire has not spread to the missiles, the suppression system will deal with it. If it has, then nothing can save the vehicle. Either way, you being in it will do nothing. So get out of there."

"Why such a complex suspension, Sir?" It was Cross again. "Surely the missiles don't need to be aimed precisely?"

"They do not jongmens, but the suspension has other uses. Watch this." Van Huis waved and the Boomslang in front of him started up its diesel. It rumbled quietly for a moment, then there was a hiss and the vehicle dropped nearly three feet as its suspension contracted. In its new position, the Boomslang's belly was almost touching the ground. "See, jongmens, the first armored vehicle that can duck!"

This time the laughter that went around the group was much louder. Van Huis took a mental bow, then picked up where he had left off. "You must remember that the Boomslang is a tank destroyer, not a tank. It fights from ambush, picking off its enemies at long range. It stresses speed and agility, not armor. It is designed to fight from concealment. Later, when we work with the Mamba missile we will show you how that can help to do so. But, for now, it is enough to know that the Boomslang can get behind cover and duck so it is invisible. The missile gunners can dismount and take positions up to 100 meters from the vehicle. So, the Boomslang can sit behind a berm, completely invisible and fire its missiles over the ground between." Behind him, there was another hiss and the front of the tank lifted so that the vehicle was sitting at an angle of over 20 degrees. "The driver can also use the suspension to correct for irregularities in the ground. Remember that the Boomslang is armed with missiles, not a gun. Missiles drop when they are fired and the launch position must compensate for that. A line of sight does not mean a line of fire."

"Sir, what is a jongmens?" A corporal had asked the question.

"A jongmens is somebody who has just joined a unit. One that has not yet seen blood spilled. Once he has seen his first action, he is no longer a jongmens. He becomes a broer, a brother within the unit."

The man nodded and seemed thoughtful. Van Huis knew why; the entire British Army consisted of jongmens. It had been rebuilt, reconstructed and reformed. Its ancient heritage had been repolished and the stains of defeat removed but it was untried, untested. Worst of all, its officers were inexperienced and unseasoned. Cross was a good example. He was a man with an exemplary record and well-regarded by his superiors. Yet, he had never fired a shot in anger. Compared with van Huis and his veterans, he was indeed a jongmens. There was another problem. It was significant there were only eleven crews here for the 14 vehicles in the tank destroyer company. They were the three four-vehicle platoons, two of which still lacked a commanding officer. The Company headquarters section still had not arrived. *Did that mean the British were finding it hard to decide on suitable candidates?* van Huis did not know. But, without the headquarters section it would be hard to exercise the new unit the way it would have to perform in the field.

"Any more questions? No? Then come to the next vehicle. We will show you how to reload the missile magazine. Note that this can be done at any time; it is not necessary to wait until the magazine rings are empty. We start by opening the doors at the rear of the vehicle. There is a trick to this, one not in the manuals. Watch closely, jongmens."

A hard six hours of work later, Bastiaan van Huis treated himself to a cold beer in the Officer's mess. It cut through the gritty dust that lined his throat perfectly, and led him to contemplate the virtues of a second. The old principle "one to cut the dust, one to wet the throat" kept creeping into his mind.

"And how are our Britse friends doing?" van Huis jumped as the question cut into his train of thought. Captain Shumba Geldenhuis was standing behind him with a beer in hand.

"Very well Sir. They are keen and smart, just very inexperienced. And we are still short of men for the whole unit."

"And will remain so. There is a war coming for the British. The Argentines, angry and humiliated from their fiasco in Chile, will pick on them next. The Britse know it and are already moving their forces south. There are few enough as it is and those they have are not needed in a training unit." Geldenhuis narrowed his eyes as he thought over the situation. "And yet our Boomslangs could be of great use to them. It is a pity the unit is not complete."

"It is not so far from being so." Van Huis had his eyes narrowed as well and he was sure that he and Geldenhuis were thinking along the same lines. "They just need a company commander and two platoon commanders."

"A pair of lieutenants and a captain in fact." The narrowed eyes had become a grin. "and some veterans to give the new unit a backbone."

"My thoughts exactly, Captain."

"I am pleased to hear it, Lieutenant." The two men smiled broadly at each other and touched their glasses. "Now I will make some discrete inquiries and see what our much-loved superiors have in mind."

HMS Hotspur, *Alongside, Vickers Fitting Out Basin, Barrow*

"At ease." Hargreaves looked at the men assembled on the ship's hangar deck. "There have been some rumors of late that we will be cutting short our fitting out period and sailing for parts unspecified very shortly. Well, just for once, the rumor mill is right. We will be setting sail within 48 hours and our destination is, as stated in the rumors, unspecified. Of course, we've all been reading the newspapers and it doesn't take much to guess where parts unspecified are likely to be. That means we have 48 hours of really hard work ahead of us. Everything that needs dockyard equipment to complete either gets done in the next two days or it doesn't get done at all. We'll be taking on stores and equipment at the same time. That means no rest for anybody. All watches will be on duty all the time for the next two days, no exceptions.

"Also, I'm pleased to say that many of the dockyard staff have volunteered to sail with us and they will be continuing to work on the ship once we have put to sea. You old hands, remember these men are dockyard workers, not sailors. They won't have a clue about shipboard routine so help them out.

"Finally, another two drafts are on their way up and they will complete our crew. Again, help them out. They won't know their way around and they'll have to learn fast. No pranks and practical jokes; we just don't have time. We'll be getting our two Rotodynes fairly shortly as well. I'm told that a full load-out of Sea Dart and Sea Wolf missiles are already on their way up to us. So our teeth are coming.

"That's it men. This is the real thing, I believe we all know that. The Septics saw the Argies off from Chile but they don't care what happens to us, so we'll have to show them we can look after ourselves. *Hotspur* might be incomplete and missing a few important parts but I think we're already the finest ship and crew in the Navy. Now, we have a chance to prove we're the finest in the world. Dismissed."

Hargreaves watched the men disperse back to their work stations. There was an urgency in their steps, a sense of purpose. He hoped it would keep them going for the next two days. Then he turned and set off for the ship's galley. He had to strip it of all unnecessary manpower so the stores and equipment arriving would be loaded and stowed. But, he also had to make sure that enough men were left to provide hot food for the crew. Then there was the problem of finding somewhere for the dockyard workers to sleep. He shook his head. Compressing six months work into two days was going to be hard enough. Getting the crew ready was going to be even harder.

King Edward Point, South Georgia

The pile of parcels, suitcases and steamer trunks on the jetty was growing steadily. Captain Hooper looked at the mess with almost bewildered disbelief. *What part of 'hand luggage only' did these people fail to understand?* For an insane moment, he had a suspicion that King Kong himself was hidden away somewhere in the settlement and was being used as the standard for 'hand-carried.' "Mister Walsingham, a moment of your time please."

Beside the growing pile, Postmaster Walsingham pretended not to hear the call. Since the arrival of the Special Boat Service team, he had been carefully nurturing his sense of outrage and injustice at the slights he believed they had poured on his head. Making the officer come over to him was a small but, to him, significant first step in evening up the score.

"Officer calling you, Sir." Sergeant Wharton kept his voice quiet and polite.

"Can't you see I'm busy?" Walsingham spat the words out. Being slighted by an officer was bad enough. Having an ranker doing the same was intolerable.

"Yes, Sir, but getting a bruised arse won't help with your work, will it?"

"How dare you. . . . ."

"And arses do tend to get bruised when people bounce off them while being hurried to answer my officer's request. So, if you really are busy, I'd suggest you see what Captain Hooper wants. Pronto."

Walsingham wattled furiously, but took a discrete look at the marine Sergeant and decided not to press the point. Instead he stalked over to Hooper. His mind greedily added this latest exchange to his already overflowing mental file of complaints and grievances.

"Captain Hooper, your sergeant just . . . "

"I'll speak to him about it. We have more important matters to address. Did I not advise you that the nine members of your party should prepare to embark upon HMS *Mermaid* as soon as she arrived? And the nine members of the British Antarctic Survey Team should do the same? With hand baggage only? So where are they and what is the meaning of this pile of cases?"

"The ship's not here yet, and we have official property here, most valuable official property."

"Mister Walsingham. We believe that Argentine ships are closing on South Georgia. Exactly how far away, we are not quite sure but the margin between the arrival of HMS *Mermaid* and the Argentine ships will be very small. Perhaps only a few hours. There is a grave danger that if her stay here is extended beyond the minimum possible, she may get caught in port by the arriving Argentine forces. We have to get the civilians here on board as quickly as possible and get her back to sea with the minimum of delay."

"That's not my responsibility. It's more than my job's worth to allow any of this material to be left here."

"Mister Walsingham. Frankly Sir, I do not care in the slightest what you think your job is worth. What I do care about is getting the civilians on this island out of here before the Argentine invasion force lands and the fighting starts. I will do whatever is necessary to achieve that end. If that includes having you locked up in a temporary cell, then so be it. *Mermaid* will not be docking at this jetty for more than a few minutes. So, decide which of these bags you love the most and the rest go into the sea. Got it?"

Walsingham said nothing. Instead he stomped off and started rooting through the pile of bags. Hooper was amused to note that the bag he finally selected was his own personal property, not one of the 'official' crates he had expressed so much concern about.

Field Exploration Camp, Penguin River, South Georgia

"Ohh, look, Cynthia. The brutal and licentious soldiery have arrived."

"At last. After six lonely months on this island we're going to be brutally ravished."

"That is as may be ma'am, were we soldiers. But we're not, we're Marines. You ladies are, I take it, Cynthia Paine-Williams and Georgina Harcourt?"

"We are." Cynthia looked at the five Marines and dropped the dumb blonde act on the spot. "Something's wrong, isn't it? Badly wrong, Sergeant?"

"Sergeant Bill Miller, ma'am. Dusty for short. And yes, things have gone very wrong indeed. Have you been listening to the radio up here?"

"We tried but our set is out. Georgy here is a whiz with radios, but she couldn't fix it."

"Ham. Ranked as expert by the British Amateur Radio Association. Daddy was a radio operator in the Resistance and he taught me himself." Georgina flipped her hair back and her smile faded as quickly as her friend's had done. "But I lost contact with King Edward Point and Grytviken about three weeks ago. When I saw you, I thought Bill Durand had sent you up to find us. I'm going to give him a right telling-off, you see if I don't. The agreement was, if we went off the air for 72 hours, he'd send a team up to find us. We'd left our movement schedule at the base and we stuck to it religiously. So he's in trouble."

"More than you can possibly know. Why didn't you try to get back when your radio went down?" Miller was curious.

"We're about ten miles out as the crow flies, not that any do down here, but it's more like twenty when we go around the bay. And the weather has been frightful. So, we thought we would stay here where there is shelter and plenty of food."

"We've done this kind of expedition before, Dusty." Cynthia seemed on the defensive. "We're not amateurs. First rule in a situation like this is to stay put where we can be found. But Bill let us down."

"Quite right, ladies. But the situation has changed now. While you've been up here, there's been a near-war in Chile with the Argies. Got to shooting it did, but the Septics stepped in and banged heads together. Now, we think the Argies will come here. They may have already started. The reason why nobody came to check on you is Bill Durand got sick and a bunch of Argie troops disguised as scrap metal merchants took him away to 'treat' him. Walsingham took over and my guess is that Durand isn't breathing any more. So we need to get you out. Excuse me, Jacko, got the radio set up?"

"We have, Sarge. Got the Boss loud and clear. He's not happy."

"Ah. I was afraid of that. Gimme the set. Sir? Dusty here. We've got the girls, they're safe and sound. Put on a bit of a dolly-bird act when we got here, but turned out there's a couple of hard heads buried under the fluff. . . . . . Twenty miles back the girls reckon. 24 hours?" Cynthia shook her head vigorously and traced an x in the air followed by two fingers held up. "Wait one, the girls disagree."

"Allow for two days. It's ice-covered rocks all the way and Georgy and I will slow you down. You might make it in 36 without us."

"48 hours, Sir. Yeah, I understand. Wait one."

"How much food have you got here?"

109

Georgina laughed. "We provisioned for six months and we've been here five weeks. You brought some food as well of course."

"Seven days for us. So we're OK for what, another five weeks?"

"Easily."

"Here's the thing. The Argies are due in less than 24 hours and there'll be a hell of a firefight when they land. The sloop picking you up will have to be here and gone in that time. We can try to hoof it back to the Point and risk getting caught in the open or hole up here. How many people know where you are?"

"Only Bill Durand and anybody who read our movement schedule."

"So we can hole up here then. We'll get picked up before the food runs out. If not, we can always shoot a few penguins."

"No!" Georgina was horrified. "We're here to study them, not eat them."

"I wouldn't say that ma'am. Roasted King Penguin is very tasty. Season the penguin breasts well with salt and pepper and dip each piece in melted fat. Roll in flour and fry to seal the meat. When each side is crisp, put the breasts in a tray and pour over the fat from the frying pan. Sprinkle with dried onion from a ration pack and roast until tender. If you want gravy, just stir a teaspoon of flour into the cooking fat then add a spoon-full of gravy granules, also from a ration pack, and sufficient water to thicken." Miller had been through the Arctic Warfare survival cookery course.

"Anyway, we'll talk about that later. Sir? Right, we can stay holed up here then. . . Sir? . . . Better we stay put. . . . We've got food for five weeks and we can stretch that if we need to. Hut is pretty well hidden already and we can improve on that a lot. Yeah, that's assuming Durand didn't talk. Just come and get us ASAP, Sir."

"So we're staying here." Cynthia sounded scared. "And you think they tortured Bill to find out where everybody is?"

"Oh no." Georgina was nearly in tears. "And we were saying such nasty things about him. The poor man."

"With your radio out, there's no way you could have known. Let's get settled down and see what we can do to make this place less obvious."

Whaling Station, Leigh Harbour, South Georgia

"Scrap merchants." Sergeant 'Curly' Carter loaded the words with contempt. "Sir, they're flying the Argentine flag here. They have vehicles on-site. They look like Sno-Cats. I don't think they're armored. No sign of artillery. Estimated number is between 35 and 40. That makes them a platoon or so. I think they're one of the Argentine Navy APCA swimmer-commando outfits."

110

"Nasty bunch by all accounts." Marine Patterson looked disgusted. In his eyes the behavior of the APCA units in Argentina was a stain on the reputation of every Marine unit everywhere.

"Very nasty. Is base on the line?"

"Here, Sarge."

Carter took the microphone. "Sir, if they're scrap merchants, I'm the flying Dutchman. We have a count of forty maximum and eight Sno-Cats. . . No, Sir, I don't think they're military Sno-Cats. They don't seem to be armed. Swimmer-Commando unit we think. Yeah, if we get the chance, we'd be doing the world a favor. Wait one."

"Sarg, there's something going on down there. Take a look."

Carter took the binoculars and watched the activity. "Sir, they're fuelling the Sno-Cats. Definitely not military Sno-Cats for all they're camouflaged. They're using petrol not diesel. From 55 gallon drums. They're coming your way, we can be sure of that. Looks like six of the 'cats will be carrying the unit, the other two supplies. . . That would make sense, wouldn't it, Sir. Landing force from the ships, these boys close the back door to stop us escaping into the island. . . We'll do what we can, Sir."

Carter closed the button on the microphone. "Boss wants us to set up an ambush, try and slow the Argies down a bit."

There was a sound of teeth being sucked. Patterson voiced the collective opinion. "Going to be rough Sarge. We've got one rocket launcher and four rounds for eight 'cats. And no machine gun."

"We've got rifles and grenades. They'll have to do. Whoa, what's going on down there?"

"Just carrying on with the fuelling up Sarg. Take a look."

Through the binoculars, Carter saw a pair of men rolling out another 55 gallon drum of gasoline. The angle of the sun, the position of the heavy cloud banks that marked the storm approaching from the east and the surface of the rocks all combined to give what appeared to be a snail-trail behind the drum the men were rolling on the ground. Then, Carter realized it wasn't a trick of the light and shadow. There really was a trail of shining liquid behind the drum. It barely had time to register before fire streaked along the trail. The fuel drum exploded. A ball of smoky black flame engulfed the two men rolling the drum. They ran out of the fireball, alight from head to foot; their screams audible even at this distance. Behind them, the building that was obviously the fuel store was also burning. The fire had ignited the drums within and sent them through the air, trailing fire as the drums burst and the contents burned.

Carter watched in awe as the fire spread to engulf two of the Sno-Cats. The men surrounding them ran clear as the vehicles erupted into flames. The base was in chaos. Men ran with fire extinguishers; a hopeless gesture if ever there had been one. Others were trying to tend to the burned men. There were at least four on the ground and who knew who else had been inside the fuel store? Watching the scene, Carter imagined he could almost feel the heat of the fire on his face. The scene at the base had the same terrible fascination as a railroad wreck. He found it very hard to tear his eyes away from the sight. Carter forced himself to turn away and picked up the radio again.

"Sir, change in situation here. They've just had an accident down there. Bad one. Rolling a fuel drum and it caught light. Flashed forward to two of the 'cats and back to the fuel store. Looks like they've got four badly burned down there. . . . . I guess sparks from a hobnailed boot set off the petrol vapor. Bad stuff petrol fumes. Only needs a slight spark to set them off."

Carter was laying it on thick. Who knew who else might be listening to this and he didn't want to voice his real thoughts. Because, to him, it had seemed as if the fuel store had exploded first and the fire flashed forward along the liquid trail to the men rolling the drum. There had been something odd about the whole incident. Professional units did not make mistakes as clumsy as the one he had just watched. He shook his head, dismissing the feeling there was more to the incident than met the eye. "That's right, Sir. They won't be moving from here for a day or so; not with their fuel gone."

Carter put down the radio and looked at the scene below. Then, he scanned the low hills that overlooked the derelict whaling station. Suddenly, they didn't seem as forbidding as they had before.

King Edward Point, South Georgia

"Lofty, we've heard from Dusty and Curly. Dusty's staying put with the girls, they can't get back here for a couple of days and we can't afford to wait. We got a real break though, according to Curly. There's an Argie unit at Leith Harbor right enough and they were getting ready to move over and shut the back door. Only they had some kind of fuelling accident with their Sno-Cats and they won't be moving for hours."

"A fuelling accident. Now that's very convenient." Sergeant Shorthouse spoke carefully and thoughtfully. "I wonder if we've got some friends on this island?"

There was a long, pregnant pause. Both men were thinking the same thing. *Did the fabled Auxiliary Units really exist?* The legends about them were always denied. The official explanation was that they were disinformation put out by the Government-in-Exile in Canada during World War Two. Part of an effort to get some of the German attention off the Resistance. That was the official line. *There are no such things as the Auxiliary Units and there never have been. The stories are partly World War Two disinformation and partly the overheated imagination of tabloid journalists. And that is the end of the matter.*

But a sudden, unexpected and completely deniable 'accident' that took out the fuel reserves of the most threatening Argentine unit sounded just the sort of thing that they might have pulled off. The German policy of massive reprisals against civilians had taught the resistance to disguise their attacks as deniable accidents, and taught them well. *If the Auxiliary Units existed of course.* Hooper shook his head. If they did, they certainly weren't part of the armed forces. Anybody who tried to make inquiries about joining them found themselves the subject of career-ending ridicule. They'd get painted as gullible fools who got taken in by modern-day fairy tales and they'd end up in backwater postings where they had nothing to do and nowhere to go.

112

Hooper shook his head. Accidents happened. It was a mark of how desperate he was that he even took the legends half-way seriously. He had ten men left to defend South Georgia against a whole Argentine naval landing force. If *Mermaid* didn't turn up in time, the situation was far beyond critical. It was no wonder he was seeking help from myths and shadows. Just where was *Mermaid*?

HMS Mermaid, *North of South Georgia*

"This bloody storm is slowing us down." Saying the obvious was sometimes a cathartic release. This wasn't one of those times. Instead, vocalizing the problem seemed to make it more pressing and dire. The storm was slowing *Mermaid* down sure enough. Every minute it did so cut into the margin of time she had available to get into South Georgia, lift out the civilians and get clear. Somewhere out there, lost in the storm front, was an Argentine task group whose orders were to land troops on South Georgia. What they planned to do with the civilians there wasn't known. Given their behavior in their own country, it probably wasn't good.

It wasn't as bad as it could have been. *Mermaid* was a sloop; her hull was designed to deal with bad seas. She wasn't fast, the book said 24 knots but that was on a good day with a smooth hull. Two years out of Britain, on a day that was far from good, she could make 22 at best. With this storm, she was down to 18 and had been for almost 24 hours. That put her almost a hundred miles behind her planned position. A destroyer or frigate, with its hull optimized for speed, would have been slowed down much more. The storm was easing at last. That was one good thing, but the damage had already been done. If it passed now and she strained her diesels, it would take her at least ten hours to get to her destination. Did she have that time?

Commander Michael Blaise knew that the answer to that question was unknown. It depended on too many variables, too much on what the Argentines had decided to do and how fast they could move. Reports were that a small assault group had been scheduled to carry out the attack on South Georgia; two destroyers, two frigates and a landing ship. A small assault group to be sure but one entirely adequate for the task at hand. *Mermaid* could put up a decent fight against one of the frigates, probably. Two would be desperate odds. Against the destroyers, she would need a miracle. "Anything on radar?" He was desperately hoping that the answer would be negative.

It was. Blaise sighed in relief. No news really was good news. That was when the electronic warfare systems operator called the bridge.

"Captain, we are picking up multiple search radars. D-band and E-band. We have the D-band set isolated as a Septic SPS-40. The E-band set we're not sure of but we think it's an Italian RAN-10S. Two of each Sir, and we're picking up flashes of a Decca navigation radar, commercial type."

"Number One, get our own radar offline now. I want full emcon, immediately."

"Yes Sir." Lieutenant Keighley rattled the orders out and *Mermaid's* radar and communications systems shut down. "The Argies, Sir?"

113

"Two Septic radars, two Eye-tie jobs. That sounds like two destroyers and two frigates doesn't it? And the civvy job, she'd be the transport. Sparky, got a bearing and track on those contacts."

"Got bearing Sir. Abbey Hill gives us 180 degrees, almost exactly due south of us. No range data yet."

Blaise drummed his fingers on the bridge console. Abbey Hill was the standard British electronic surveillance system. In his opinion, it was as good as any in the world and better than most. Its array of receivers wrapped around his foremast gave a fine directional cut. Against a stationary transmitter, he could get move a few miles to establish a baseline, get a cross bearing and pin down that transmitter accurately enough to engage it. But against radars on ships, it was much harder to get range data. It could be done, given time and luck, but Blaise had a nasty feeling he had just run out of both. That 180 degree contact bearing put the contacts directly between him and South Georgia.

"Sparky, any idea on range at all?"

"No, Sir. Well, in these conditions there's only a limited chance of significant ducting. So, that would put them within radar horizon range. Less than 50 nautical miles certainly. Probably less than twenty. Signal strength is still below detection threshold but it's climbing."

"Close, Sir."

"Too close, Number One. Bring her around to oh-eight-oh. Let's stretch the distance a bit and get over the radar horizon before this clag starts to clear up." Blaise guessed that it was only radar interference caused by the storm, the clag as the radar community called it, that had stopped the Argentine ships spotting him. They were in the trailing edge of the storm. The clag was dispersing slowly and the radars would be gaining in range and precision.

"South Georgia, Sir?" Keighley put the question as quietly as possible.

"The Argies are ahead of us. They'll get there first now. Our best bet is to slip away, head east and then try to come in at night. The Argies have a base camp at Leith Harbour. It's just possible they'll go there. If they do, we can slide into King Edwards, pick up the civvies and run before they wise up. If they decide to go for Gyrtviken first, then we're bollixed. We'll have to slide off somewhere and ask for orders."

"Sir, bearings on Abbey Hill changing. SPS-40s, now designated as Bandit-Able, are still on bearing one-eight-zero. RAN-10S and Deccas, now designated as Bandit-Baker, are on bearing one-seven-five. It's within the error margin of the system but I think Bandit formation has split Sir. And Bandit-Able is coming straight at us."

Blaise thought carefully despite doing so at frantic speed. Abbey Hill wasn't accurate to within five degrees by any manner of measurement; twenty would be closer. On the other hand, a good EW operator would see things on the scanner that he shouldn't be able to. It wasn't just the contacts, but how they moved and changed that gave the clues. "On the other hand, Number One, we could be bollixed anyway. Hit action stations. Close up for surface engagement."

114

"Radar contact Sir. Nothing solid, could be atmospheric shadowing. In a storm like this. . . "

Captain Isaac Leonardi acknowledged the report by nodding his head briefly. Fleeting contacts were all too common in a South Atlantic storm. "Keep watching the bearing. If it appears again, alert me immediately."

"Sir, communications report message from *La Plata* by signal lamp. Message reads 'Transient radar contact bearing zero degrees.' That's all, Sir."

Leonardi looked out of his bridge windows into the gloom that pervaded everything outside. The clouds were iron-colored; a blue-black shield against the light. Rain from them was lashing down across his ship, streaming off the decks and swirling as it made its way into the areas inside. The Italian-built destroyers had been designed for the Mediterranean, not the rigors of a South Atlantic that was almost in the Antarctic and had storms no other sea could match. Oh, other storms could be vicious, have stronger winds and heavier rain, but they passed. Here, in the South Atlantic, a good blow could last for weeks and was accompanied by a bitter, chilling cold. Leonardi corrected himself; by a bitter, killing cold. Go into the sea down here and a man could expect barely few minutes of life.

Over to starboard, Leonardi watched *Catamarca's* sister-ship *La Plata* dig her bows into a great wave. The green water flowed over her bows up to her 'A' turret before breaking and flowing off down the ship's side. For all their size, the two destroyers were making heavier weather of the storm than the two frigates behind them. *Catamarca* and *La Plata* might be very large destroyers, after all, they had started life as light cruisers, but they were old. They'd started life before the Second World War and the years of fighting while the Allies had tried to batter their convoys through to Murmansk and Archangel had taught designers much about designing ships for those conditions. Leonardi thought about Archangel for a second and shuddered; even the thought made his bridge seem warmer by comparison. The two frigates, *Querandi* and *Punta Alta*, were able to handle much heavier seas than the destroyers.

"One, not two." Leonardi was reflective. "It is unlikely that two radar sets would see the same ghost?"

In fact, it wasn't. Winds could whip clouds and rain into a tall spiral, a larger-than normal wave could crest above the rest and the result would be a radar contact, solid and substantial until it dispersed as if it had never been. Lieutenant Brian Martin was an electronics specialist, one of the few top men in his field that the Argentine Navy had. He knew radars and he knew how contacts behaved. He'd seen the blip on the SPS-40 display and it hadn't faded away like a ghost. He wouldn't bet his life on it, but he would consider it an excellent hand for a poker game.

"Sir, I think there is a ship out there."

"And, therefore, not one of ours. It is not a Yanqui by any chance?" Every officer in the Argentine Navy was terrified of the possibility they might fire on an American warship by accident. They all knew the tiny margin that had separated Argentina

115

from nuclear destruction – and knew that reducing the margin to such tiny proportions had cost the Americans one of their precious bombers. And its crew. One ill-judged shot and that margin could vanish.

"No, Sir. But we believe, our intelligence tells us. . ." Leonardi listened to that differential. Intelligence was dominated by the army and he didn't trust what they said at all. "The British have sent a sloop down to remove their civilians from South Georgia. Probably the one from West Indies Station. I believe she is *Mermaid*."

"If she is West Indies Station, then yes, she is *Mermaid*. An elegant ship." Leonardi had been in Kingston with *Catamarca* once and he had seen the sloop anchored the other side of the port. "If she is coming to extract the civilians, then we should let her pass. Having them out of the way would be a good thing."

"No it would not." Captain Alberto Astrid almost snarled the words. "If the British have landed troops on the island, we can use the civilians as hostages. Tell them that we will shoot one every hour until they surrender."
"Hijo de puta." Martin hissed the words under his breath.

"You said?" Astrid swung his bulk off the bridge chair and moved threateningly towards the Lieutenant, his hand dropping to the pistol at his waist. Behind him, the Master at Arms and a particularly burly sailor seconded from the engine rooms also started to move. Leonardi ordering their presence on the bridge had not been a coincidence or an afterthought. He was a religious man who believed in the existence of pure, undiluted evil. When he had first met Astrid, he had recognized the marks of that evil on him. It left a stain somehow on the face and in the eyes. And he had kept strong, loyal seamen on his bridge ever since.

"I will call the flotilla commandante." Astrid's head snapped around. The expression in his eyes changing from anticipation to fear when he saw the two seamen much closer to him than he had expected. "He must make this decision. Signals, patch me through to *Bahia Thetis*."

The storm was making radio reception difficult, but the connection was made. "Commandante Romero? Sir, Captain Leonardi. We have a radar contact, very vague but due north. No more than that. We believe it may be a British sloop, possibly the *Mermaid*. We think she may be heading for South Georgia to remove the civilians."

"A sloop." The voice on the radio was tired and shaky. "Yes, she might be doing that. But she could also have a couple of hundred marines on board. We cannot chance that. One humiliation however carefully hidden, is enough. Take *La Plata* with you, find that ship and sink her. Or at least hunt until it is proved she is not there."

"Very good, Sir."

"And Captain Leonardi, remember you are a seaman." The radio connection broke.

"Helm, come to course oh-oh-oh. Make maximum speed, crew come to battle stations."

Simonstad Naval Base, South Africa.

"One day the oerwoud, the next the ocean. It's a man's life in the Republic's Army, eh Randlehoff?'

"Just what the devil is the oerwoud?" Lieutenant Cross was almost desperate to learn everything he could from the South Africans who had suddenly turned up to complete his tank destroyer company. The trouble was that he couldn't understand half of what they were saying.

Lieutenant Zander Randlehoff, his officer's pips still so new they had a wholly undesirable shine on them, looked at the British officer with amusement. He reminded the South African of a young puppy, anxious to please but not quite knowing how to do it. "Oerwoud is forest, jongmens. Not as dense as true jungle, but tough to get through. Down here in the Republic, we have the plains and the grass but go north and the trees close in."

Cross nodded and stored the information away. Randlehoff looked at the commander of the unit. "Captain Geldenhuys, we have authorization to join these men now?"

"Not yet. Lieutenant van Huis is at the signals office waiting for it. It will come soon. Taylor, I wish you to join me in company headquarters. Van Huis can take command of the first platoon. Cross, you will take second. Randlehoff can take third." There were enough South Africans to provide one officer for the platoons and one crew member per tank destroyer. Geldenhuys was hoping that enough experience would rub off on the British jongmens to give them a fighting chance.

"Very good, Sir."

"A very professional sounding reply." Geldenhuys sounded amused. "You come from a British military family?"

"No Sir. My father served in the 29th Panzer Grenadiers."

"Ahh, German."

"With respect, Sir, no Sir. My father was German, but there is no Germany now. After it was destroyed, Britain took him in, looked after him and protected him. Now, I repay that debt for him. I am British."

Geldenhuys laughed and clapped him on the back, sending the young officer staggering. "Well said, jongmens. My family, we are Griqua, you know what that is?"

Cross shook his head. "No, Sir."

"Griqua is what the British called us because they did not like our real name. We are the descendents of the original colonists here and native women. So we call ourselves Baastaards." Geldenhuys laughed at the expression on Cross's face. "And if you write that in a letter to your girl, remember, four letter a, two and two."

"The Griqua are great fighters." Randlehoff spoke quietly to Cross. "And the Captain is a very good soldier. You are most fortunate."

"I know. I just hope we can learn enough."

"You know you must learn. That is the first and greatest step of all. Wait, I think we have word."

Van Huis's sports car barreled through the base and skidded to a halt near the line of Boomslangs. He hauled himself out of the driving seat and ran over to the Captain, waving papers in his hand.

"We have our orders. We are to remain with the British unit. The story is we are assigned to McMullen Industries as technical advisors and they are sending us with the unit to help them get their vehicles ready. And, of course, if attacked, we must defend ourselves." He wagged a finger at Cross. "So if you shoot at us, we will shoot back."

"Then I will try and avoid doing so." Cross gave the reply gravely and for a second time, a clap on the back sent him staggering.

"I also have a movement order for you jongmens. In two days, no more, a vehicle transport will be arriving here. We will load the Boomslangs on her for transport. If the world stays calm, she will head for England and we will train you on the way. And stay with you for a few weeks until you can stand on your own feet. But if the world does not stay calm, then we will not be heading for England. And then, we will be doing much more than just training."

HMS Mermaid, *North of South Georgia*

"The cut isn't good enough to tell." The report from the ESM station didn't ease Captain Blaise's mind at all. He needed to know whether the Argentine landing force was heading for King Edward and Grytviken or Leith Harbour. A lot depended on that simple piece of information.

"Where are they?"

"Bandit-Baker is still due south of us, course is for South Georgia. Their estimated time of arrival is about four hours in this weather. Bandit-Able is south west of us. They're still heading on an intercept with our original course, so we should be gradually gaining range on them. I can't confirm that of course."

It was an interesting tactical situation Blaise thought. *We're in a dark basement and being hunted by two men with shotguns and flashlights. All we're doing is trying to work out what's happening by watching the flashlights.* "We're not going to make our pick-up from South Georgia. Even if we break clear now, the Argies will beat us in. We can't assume they'll do anything other than head for Grytviken; that's where everybody is. We've got to warn the SBS boys down there that we won't be coming."

"As soon as we do, Sir, we'll tip Bandit-Able off to our course change. They'll have a good fix on our position." Number One gave his advice quietly but firmly.

118

"I know. We're just going to have to be sneaky. We'll swing south. That'll put us on a reciprocal to Bandit-Able but about 18 miles east of them. We'll send out a burst transmission and then head north at maximum speed. With luck the Argies won't be able to read the code, so they'll assume it's a 'get ready we're coming' message and we'll be heading south. By the time they realize we're not there, they'll be twenty or thirty miles behind us and too far out to catch us. Then we swing east again, wait until we're well clear and make for the southern coast of South Georgia. We can hide in the fjords and inlets down there."

Keighley shook his head. It was all very well to criticize but to come up with an alternative plan was much more difficult. "We've got to let them know. I can't think of anything that gives us a better chance."

"We'll make it so then. Sparks, what's the signal strength on Bandit-Able?"

"Well below detection threshold, Sir. They were getting odd anomalous spikes earlier. That's probably how they spotted us, but we haven't seen one of them for a while. I think they've lost us."

"Very well. Helm, bring us around to one-eight-zero. Sparks, ready a Kourier burst transmission to the SBS team. Message reads 'Regret chased from party by gate crashers. More of same coming your way. Suggest you leave by back door with other guests.' Code it and repeat it three times. Alert me the moment the transmission is complete."

Blaise paced his bridge and looked outside, as if by doing so he could will the transmission on its way. "Remember when we were in London for Navy Day, Number One? And the woman from the Sea Scouts wanted to bring deck chairs on the bridge. Her troop really told her off, didn't they?"

"That they did, Sir." The bridge crew laughed at the memory of a stout, middle-aged woman being told off by her charges.

"Signal transmitted, Sir. And acknowledged."

"Very good. Helm, course zero-zero-zero. Engines, get those diesels cranking out every revolution they can generate. Ignore the gauges and the book."

King Edward Point, South Georgia

"Sir, message from *Mermaid*. She's been intercepted by hostile forces and won't be able to pick us up. There's more hostiles coming in fast. They suggest we evacuate the area and hole up somewhere on the Island."

"Thanks, Mickey. Damn." Hooper thought for a second. "Get the British Antarctic Survey Team people out. They can take the other civilians inland. I want their team leader here now." The man arrived before Hooper had a chance to turn around. "Mister Duncan?"

"Captain?"

119

"*Mermaid* isn't coming and the Argies are on our doorstep. I want you to get the civilians out the back, into the hills. Is there a base camp you can hide in out there?"

"A small one, yes. It's about two days out though. I'm not sure the civilians can make it."

"Take as many as you can. Any who want to stay here and take their chances with the Argies can do that. But warn them, there's going to be a hell of a fight."
"Captain, why don't you come . . ." Robert Duncan's voice trailed away.

"We gave up and got occupied once and it's taken us more than thirty years to recover. We roll over now and we might as well have handed the keys to the jerries in '47 and done ourselves in. We can't stop the Argies taking this port, but by God, we'll make sure they know they've been in a fight. Now get moving."

"Sir, we got on the set to Dusty and his boys and girls. Told them hope of any pick-up's gone pear-shaped and they're going to have to hole up. They didn't seem too upset about it."

"Nor would I. By all accounts, the girls up there are quite tasty. And they weren't expecting to get out anyway. Oh God, what does he want?" Hooper had seen Walsingham running up the quayside to see him.

"Mister Hooper, Sir. What's this I hear about *Mermaid* not picking us up?"

"That's right, Mister Walsingham. We've had word that she's been intercepted out there and can't get to us. So, the BAST team are taking the civilians out while we have the chance."

"Well, you listen to me." Walsingham had seen how Hooper had looked at him when he had salvaged his own bag from the pile on the quay and he wasn't going to repeat the experience. "That is the Queen's mail and I am the Queen's postmaster. I will not abandon it to a bunch of Argies."

Hooper lost control of his eyebrows for a brief second then managed to retrieve them from his hairline. "Those civilians who wish to remain here and take their chances may do so. There is going to be one hell of a fight though."

"I will not abandon the mail. It's more than my job's worth.' Walsingham had his jaw set. He had made himself look foolish twice; he was not going to do so again.

"Very good, Sir. But I suggest you take cover. What do you want us to do with the mail when the Argies arrive?"

"Burn it."

Hooper nodded. That made sense; there could be valuable information in there. "Curly, get some thermite charges and rig the mail to burn. Postmaster Walsingham doesn't wish it to fall into enemy hands. He'll be staying with us to make sure it doesn't."

CHAPTER TWO
FIRST SHOTS

ARA Catamarca, *North of South Georgia*

"There's nothing out here, Sir. Radar is completely clear. Whatever the contact was, it's gone."

Captain Leonardi scanned the gray mass of fog, rain, clouds and sea. It was very hard to tell which was which. Almost anything could be hidden in this mass of foulness that passed for weather in the South Atlantic.

"They're out here. I can feel it." Leonardi spoke the truth. He could sense another ship out here somewhere not so very far away.

"Woman's intuition?" Astrid's voice was sneering and derisive. He took some satisfaction from the stir of anger that ran around the bridge crew.

"A sailor's sense." Leonardi spoke absently, willing himself to ignore the evil presence on his bridge. *If I ignore it on my bridge, isn't it just what we have all done when we ignore these people in our country*. He didn't like that train of thought at all. Another one also ran through his mind *all that is necessary for evil to triumph is for good men to do nothing*. That stirred his conscience. Like everybody else, he had assumed the tales he had heard were wild exaggerations; stories of cartoon villainy that were intended to blacken the name of the armed forces. If he'd taken them seriously, he would have expected Astrid to board his ship, twirling his moustache in comic-opera style. He hadn't. He'd appeared a normal, personable young officer. Only when Leonardi had looked into his eyes had he known the truth and realized the stories he had heard were, if anything, a pale reflection of reality.

"That sloop has to be around here somewhere." He looked again, as if expecting to see his target emerge from the gray morass. *Which could*, he reflected *easily happen*. "If she had held course we would have seen her," *or run into her* "a few minutes ago."

"Sir, we have an intercept, a burst radio transmission. From east of us."

121

"East?" Leonardi thought about that one, and then light dawned. "Abbey Hill. She picked our radars up and changed course." The name of the British electronic surveillance system was almost a curse. It was well known that the sloops had very good electronic intelligence equipment, but he'd forgotten all about it. "How far east?"

"Getting a cross reference from *La Plata* now." There was some frantic measuring on the charts. "The baseline is very short, but a minimum of 25 kilometers and a maximum of fifty."

"She must have turned as soon as she picked up our radars." Martin looked at the chart, computing distances in his mind. "Her message will have been to warn the troops ashore that she was coming in and get ready to embark. She'll be heading south at maximum speed."

Leonardi shook his head. "No. The pick-up must have been pre-arranged. She wouldn't have taken a chance on transmitting just to confirm it. No, the message must have been to tell them she was not coming in. She will be heading north, trying to get clear."

Martin nodded. "Then we should make course oh-four-five to intercept."

"Very good. Only we need to spread our net. We will make oh-four-five, *La Plata* should make oh-five-oh until we are twenty kilometers apart. Then we will parallel each other. Make to *La Plata* accordingly."

Headquarters, First AirMech Brigade, Aldershot, UK

"Strachan here." The answer on the telephone was curt. Anybody in the Headquarters Building, in this brigade or any other could sense the tension that filled the whole Army. A war was coming, everybody knew it and everybody sensed that much more depended on this that just the ownership of a few islands nobody had ever heard of. "That's marvelous news, Sir. We'll amend our plans accordingly."

"Sergeant Harper? Good news, we're getting *Albion* and *Bulwark*. The Incredible Bulk finished her yard period in record time. Spread the word; an O-group immediately, every officer to the conference room on the double."

The second assault ship being ready was a miracle. For four weeks, Strachan had been trying to work out how to pare down his AirMech brigade so it would fit into a single assault ship. Anyway he cut it, the result was a unit that sacrificed too much of its fighting power for comfort. Now, with both ships, the unit could go to war the way that the Gods and the War Office had intended.

He paused and picked up his secure telephone and dialed a number, one known to very few people. The receiver the other end rang and he heard Sir Humphrey Appleday's voice, "Piccadilly Circus."

"Strachan here, Humpty. We've got both assault ships, the whole Brigade is going down."

122

"I know that." Appleday was slightly irritated. The strain was telling on him as well.

"Well, it means we're going to have to change our plans slightly. Can you tell me how long we've got?"

There was a long silence on the end of the line. "It's starting now. Literally now. Don't count on more than 24 hours. Just get the equipment on the ships. We can sort it out later. Oh, and Brigadier, as our friend over in Washington might say, come back carrying your shield or carried on it."

"That's Spartan, not Macedonian." Appleday wasn't the only one who had a classical education. He and Strachan were two of the much smaller number who knew how wrong some of that classical history was.

"In the great scheme of things, the difference made by the geographical minutia of the post-Alexandrine geopolitical gestalt is of very little consequence. Brigadier, we've turned down American assistance on this one. We're on our own. That's our choice and it has to be this way if we are ever to rise again as an independent nation. So, carrying your shield, or carried on it, because everything we have ever worked for depends on you now."

The telephone clicked and Strachan looked at it. It had been a very different call from the usual chat with the urbane and loquacious Sir Humphrey Appleday. The last time Strachan had heard him speak that way was when That Man had pulled his coup and taken Britain out of the War.

"Sir, officers assembling in the Conference Room." Sergeant Harper looked solemn. "A word from the Squids Sir. The Ozwalds are offering to take over Indian Ocean Station, put a destroyer and a couple of frigates in so the Andrew can pull its ships out for the coming excitement. South Africans are reputed to be putting in some discrete help as well. And the Canucks, they're offering their C-133s to help supply Ascension. Commonwealth pulling together, gathering around the mother country and all that."

"The Canadians don't operate C-133s." Strachan objected.

"They do now, Sir. Funny that isn't it."

Strachan laughed. The Senior NCO circuit in the British armed forces worked extremely well. He strode down the corridor to the Conference Room, overtaking the last straggling officers as he did so. Some were muddy and had obviously come straight off the training ranges. Once everybody was inside, he banged on the desk to quieten the room.

"Gentlemen. . . I am sorry, Ladies and Gentlemen, I have two urgent pieces of news for you. One is that I have just been informed that we will be allocated both *Albion* and *Bulwark* for our journey south. We will, therefore, have enough lift capacity for the entire Brigade. We can forget our plans to strip the unit. The word I have is just to throw everything and everybody on to the ships and we'll sort things out on the way down.

"The second piece of news is that the situation is coming to a head right now. We can expect a movement order literally any minute. Get your units ready to move out accordingly. Do not pass this word to anybody outside the unit, not even your families."

Strachan noted that some of the women in the medical and communications units looked uncomfortable with that.

"Another word. There has been some talk about us receiving help and assistance in the upcoming campaign. Don't believe any of it. Her Majesty's Government has refused an offer of American assistance so the objective will not be glowing in the dark when we get there. A few of the Commonwealth and ex-Commonwealth countries are providing support assistance but the fighting forces will all be ours. I was given a very unambiguous message on this. I was told to come back carrying our shield or carried on it. I think that applies to us all. This is it, Ladies and Gentlemen. This is our chance to expunge the blot on our national name caused by That Man. Let us not falter, let us not weaken. Let us show the world, we are back as a power to be reckoned with."

HMS Mermaid, *North of South Georgia*

"Bad news, Sir. The Argies have made us. Their track is showing they swung north just after we did. They're on an intercept course. If we hold present course and speed, they'll literally hit us."

"Hmm, Italian-built destroyer hitting a British-built sloop. I wonder who would come off worst in that collision?"

"Italian-built, Sir? It could be one of the Gearing DDEs or DDKs the Septics sold them a few years back."

"They've got SPS-37, not -40. These are the Cordoba class, you can bet your gold sovereigns on it." A nervous laugh ran around the bridge at that comment. It was technically illegal for British subjects to hold gold, whether as bullion or coin, but the occupation years had taught the population much about hiding things away and keeping quiet about them. Despite the prohibition on owning gold coins and guns, every Government since the ban had been imposed in 1950 had sadly accepted the fact that probably every family in the land had a few of both hidden away.

"Cordobas. With those 5.3-inch guns, they'll shoot us to pieces." Keighley sounded mournful. The Italian 5.3-inch gun was a very effective weapon. Even the old versions carried on the Cordobas were fast-firing and their shells had a lot of punch. Much more so than the twin four inch gun mount that was *Mermaid's* only real armament.

"Of course. Although it won't be as easy as they think. We're a better shooting platform than they are and I bet their forward turrets are washed out." Blaise was thinking carefully. "That'll buy us a little time. Helm, bring us around to oh-nine-oh. We'll try and put them north and behind us. As soon as they cross our old track, we'll come around to two-two-five. We'll keep heading for the worst weather we can find."

Keighley nodded. It made sense. In the foul seas they had to handle now, Mermaid's sea-kindly hull meant that the Argentine destroyers were barely, if at all, faster than she was. But, if the seas improved the difference would grow quickly. The Cordobas were the fastest destroyers out there, every one of them had run trials at over 40 knots in smooth water. Given their heads, they could run *Mermaid* down easily. So, it made sense to head for the worst weather and the roughest seas.

Blaise felt his ship's movement change as she swung around to oh-nine-oh. Quietly, he knew he was running out of options.

ARA Catamarca, *North of South Georgia*

"There's still nothing out here, Sir."

Leonardi thought it over. *What would I do if I was commanding that British sloop?* The answer was obvious, he'd use his electronic surveillance system to track the destroyers and move away from them. *That being so, where would I be, right now?* Suddenly, a light switched on in Leonardi's head. "Make to *La Plata*. Tell her to maintain course oh-four-five for thirty minutes, then come around to two-oh-five. We'll come around to one-three-five and make twenty five knots. And shut down all our radars, every one of them. We'll make this run blind." He hesitated. Twenty five knots in these conditions was driving his ship hard. She would have damage, perhaps just guard rails buckled and deck fittings lost but more likely cracks and flooding.

"*La Plata* Sir? Her radars?"

"Full power transmission. All of them. Surface search, air search, navigation. I want her to make so much noise that sloop will think we're both up there. That sloop is tracking us with her passive surveillance equipment so *La Plata* can keep her focused while we do a silent run in to a new position. With luck, she'll walk right into us."

Royal Australian Navy Submarine Rotorua, *Leaving Puerto de Valparaiso, Chile*

"Message Sir. From *I-709*. Message reads 'Goodbye and good hunting.' It's from Captain Sazuko himself."

"Make return message. 'Farewell. Wish you fair seas and a smooth voyage.' Sign it from me personally. I wonder what he meant by 'good hunting'?"

"I guess he's assuming we'll be helping the Andrew out. We're heading south after all. Lieutenant Elorreaga, you have found your cabin and everything you need?"

"I have indeed, Sir. Your officers were most helpful. I took the liberty of bringing some bottles of wine from my family vineyards on board. I hope it would be in order for me to donate them to the wardroom?"

"Lieutenant, I can think of no way to make yourself more welcome on this submarine. We'll be diving in about an hour, as soon as we're clear of the shipping lanes."

"Very good, Sir." The Chilean officer looked around the bridge. "This submarine is much larger than any I have served on before."

"You were assigned to an old V-boat, weren't you?"

"That is correct, Sir. The *Simpson*. Only four tubes forward and very small inside. Very handy and quick though. Sir, how does *Rotorua* handle?"

125

Captain Beecham reminded himself that this was also a sales trip and this personable young Lieutenant would be making a full report on his experiences. "A lot better than the French and Italian boats, especially on the surface. They use the cylindrical hull like the American and Chipanese nuclear boats. Great for underwater but very poor on the surface. Running surfaced, they can barely make eight knots, ten in a smooth sea. Underwater they can make twenty five as long as they don't mind running their batteries flat in less than an hour. Now, our oval hull makes us a lot more seaworthy. Even in a blow we can hold twenty plus knots on the surface. More importantly, we can have people out on deck while on the surface, something the French and Italian boats could only dream about. That can come in pretty useful if we want to put people ashore; a special forces team for example."

"This is a large boat, more than four times the displacement of my *Simpson*. Doesn't she take time to dive?"

"Not really. We can't get down as fast as a V-boat of course, but we can dive pretty damned quick. The hull planes forward and the beavertail aft mean we can drive ourselves underwater. We'll beat our rivals underwater and once down, we're a lot quieter. No blade beat you see. The screws are outside the turbulence from the sail."

Elorreaga nodded, carefully filing the information away. "*Simpson* is noisy, that is for certain. No rafting on the machinery, blade beat and lots of flow noise. A good boat for forty years ago, but time has passed her by. We don't even have a missile launcher."

Captain Beecham laughed. "That was a surprise wasn't it. Almost as surprising as the fact they let us see it. A twin-rail launcher like that, I wonder why they did. It would have been a nasty surprise for a sub-hunting bird. We don't have anything like it. We've got missile launch tubes down there, beside the sail. You can see the hatches from here. But they're for land attack missiles only."

"Perhaps them being a nasty surprise is why they showed that launcher to us, Sir?" Cardew spoke slowly. "There was something odd about the whole business of that sub turning up. A Chimp hunter-killer with a friendly Captain almost tripping over himself to show us his boat. Almost as if he was under orders to be as accommodating and unthreatening as possible."

"I got that impression as well, Number One. The Chimps were playing a deep game, that's for sure. Remember Sazuko going out of his way to tell us that the Navy and Army were at daggers drawn? There's politics there, Steven, politics deep and dire. Somebody in Japan is trying to tell us something."

"Japan, not Chipan?" Cardew thought about that. Although everybody in the rest of the world referred to the the Japanese and occupied China as Chipan, the official name was still the Empire of Japan and that was where real power still remained. *Or did it?* The internal politics of the Empire were almost as mysterious as those of the Caliphate. *Was somebody in Japan trying to open a window to the West?* "Strange though. We've always thought of the Chimps as being a faceless, threatening horde. It was odd meeting Sazuko and his group of bandits. They reminded me of us."

126

"Except we cook our fish, of course. Lieutenant . . . " Beecham fumbled for the Chilean officer's first name. He had the man's file of course, but in the urgency of getting out and to sea, he hadn't had a chance to read it yet.

"Marcello, Sir. Marco for short"

"Thank you. Marco, we need to get far south as quickly as possible. Our snorting speed is four knots. Our speed and battery drain rates are down in the chartroom. Remember, we've got a lot of battery, twice as much as the French boats and four times your old V-boat. So, make me a course and speed that gets us to the Beagle Channel soonest." *And that should convince you just how good a submarine* Rotorua *is. Not as mobile as a nuclear boat perhaps, but faster and longer-ranged than any other diesel-electric.*

"Very good, Sir." Marcello Elorreaga lowered himself through the hatch and vanished.

"Seems like a good man, Sir." Cardew spoke quietly.

"We'll see. But he does shape well. I wonder how Gavin is getting on with his wedding preparations back in Valparaiso?"

"He looked a bit like a stunned fish last time I saw him."

"I don't doubt it." Beecham hesitated slightly. "Chris, get a group of torpedomen together. Inspect every torpedo we have and check everything about them. Fuzes, engines, depth keeping system, homing system, the lot. Take nothing for granted. Sazuko was right. Once we're down south, anything can happen. After all, this is a sales cruise. But . . . "

"Submarines are nobody's friends and if attacked we may have to defend ourselves. We're on it, Sir."

ARA Catamarca, *North of South Georgia*

"We're at the target point, Sir." Leonardi nodded. "Switch on main search radar."

"Yes Sir." There was an agonizingly long pause while the SPS-40 mounted on the foremast resumed its search. "Got her!" The surge of triumph that went around the bridge was unmistakeable. "Range less than twenty kilometers; bearing oh-nine-oh. We could open fire with our guns, using radar fire control."

"At this range and in this weather?" Leonardi's voice was stern but inwardly he appreciated the officer's enthusiasm. "I think not."

"Use the anti-ship missiles. At once." Astrid's voice echoed across the bridge from his seat in one corner.

"Again, I think not. We only have four and there is a war coming. There are no reloads for us, not one. You and your army friends never allocated the money to buying reserve stocks, remember. Now, we must conserve our missiles and close to use gunfire.

"Where the hell did she come from?" Sparks was stunned by the sudden appearance of the radar transmissions dead ahead of *Mermaid*. Then bad news turned to worse. "She's got us. Received signal is well over threshold value."

"Range?"

"Very close. I'd say if it wasn't for the clag, we could see her."

Blaise banged his first. "Too late for hide-and-seek. Sparks, main search radar on. We need to know exactly where she is. Helm, bring our bows around, back to oh-nine-oh. We'll give her a tail chase."

"Radar contact, Sir, range approximately eleven nautical miles out. Bearing two-seven-zero. Battle stations. Close up all gun crews. If we can't get away, our only chance will be to get the first shots in and hit hard."

"Sir, radar contact, now designated Bandit-Charlie, has turned to follow us. Speed estimated at 24 knots. Sir, Bandit-Baker up north has turned to close on us as well. Range thirty nautical miles, speed, 25 knots, bearing three-five-five."

"Charlie has reported finding us. That rules out us heading north again. Hold on oh-nine-oh. Engines, we need everything, absolutely everything you've got down there." Blaise felt the rumble of the diesels under his feet but he knew it wasn't anywhere near enough.

"Visibility range is about three miles, maximum, Sir."

"Bandit-Charlie will have a visual sighting in less than two hours. When the range is down to five miles, we'll turn and engage."

"The rules of engagement are that we can't fire the first shot, Sir." Number One was doing his job, reminding his Captain of the details where, notoriously, the devil hid out.

"I know. We'll just have to hope that the shot in question misses."

NSC Building, Washington D.C.

The two men were in civilian clothes but it was obvious that they were accustomed to being in uniform. They crossed the reception area, nodding briefly to the statue that dominated the area and strode up to the reception desk. It could be said that they ignored everybody else in the area, but that would have been untrue. They showed no sign of even being aware that other people existed.

"I wonder if they are even aware that we have an appointment with the National Security Advisor." The older man snapped the words out to the younger man with him.

"That would require a level of administrative efficiency on their part." The younger man sounded reluctant, as if he couldn't quite conceive of anybody meeting his standards of competence.

The receptionist bit back her irritation and looked down the printed list of authorized visitors. She had met some very strange people since starting this job, but these two were weird even by the standards of the NSC Building. To make matters even more interesting, these two appeared to be Chipanese. "Mister Takeda? We have your appointment listed. Miss Bonney will take you up to the Advisor's offices."

"Gentlemen? If you would come with me please?" Anne Bonney had made a private bet with herself that the two guests in the building would turn up on time to the fraction of a second. She had won and promised herself some chocolate ice cream in payment. "Please display these visitor security badges prominently."

"I wonder what would happen if we refused?" The younger man spoke to the elder, ignoring Anne completely.

"The last people to walk about this building without authorization never got out alive." Anne spoke equally idly. As it happened the comment was true, but the circumstances had been very unusual. She moved her body so the control panel on the lift was masked, then pressed a combination of buttons before selecting the 14th floor. Although there would be no indication of the fact inside the lift, it would now stop at the 13th floor. One that did not, officially, exist. When it did open, Nefertiti Adams was waiting outside the doors.

"Shingen-Sama, Katsuyori-San, welcome to the NSC Building. The Seer is waiting for you in our conference room."

The two Japanese men showed no sign of having heard the comment. Nefertiti glanced at Anne Bonney and raised one eyebrow. Dealing with representatives from the Kempetai could be wearing and the fastidious Nefertiti always felt an urgent need to wash her hands afterwards. Nevertheless, she took her guests into one of the conference rooms where the Seer was reading through a file full of papers.

"Ah, they've turned up at last, have they?" The Seer's expression didn't change. "Sit them down please. I suppose they'd like some tea. Could you organize that, honey?"

Nefertiti left the room, allowing herself to smile as soon as she closed the door behind her. The two Japanese Kempetai officers weren't the only ones who could play games.

HMS Mermaid, *North of South Georgia*

"Bring her around to two-seven-zero. Weaps, prepare for surface action; guns ready to fire on command. Sparks, prepare to get the following message out: 'Am under attack by Argentine warships. Enemy ships have fired upon us. Am returning fire. Issue is in doubt.' Once you start, keep transmitting until we get acknowledgement or the ship sinks under us. Or both. Engines, if we weren't at full power before, get the diesels running red-zoned. Burning them out isn't going to matter too much anyway."

Keighley looked grim. "No chance of us getting away?" As if to answer him, there was an express-train roar overhead and two shells splashed into the water ahead of them. "Sorry I spoke."

"Sparks get that message out and keep transmitting. Weaps, you have radar fire control solution. Return fire." The Gunnery Officer's finger must have been poised over the switch because *Mermaid's* two four inch guns cracked out their shots almost instantly. "Helm, bring her around to two-two-five."

Mermaid's hull lurched as she turned abruptly to chase the shells that had missed her. Keighley grabbed a bridge rail as she rolled. "Think those were warnings or intended to hit us?"

"Hard to tell in this." Blaise was interrupted by another express-train roar. This time three shells that fell in a straight line, two short, one over. They were well aft though, thrown by *Mermaid's* change in course. "Right, well that answers the question doesn't it. First pair were warnings; that one was a ranging ladder, meant for business."

"Starboard look-out here Sir. Enemy ship, bearing two-seven-zero. Range eight thousand yards. She's firing."

"She's a Cordoba all right. Look at her digging her bows in." The dark gray destroyer had white water piled up around her foremost turret and the mount was obviously incapable of firing. "Weaps, hit her with something please."

Mermaid's four inch twin mount cracked again. The shots were good for line but both fell well short. Up forward, under the shield of the Mark XIX mounting, the gun crews were reloading as fast as the aged design of their guns and the atrocious weather allowed. Across the sea, Blaise saw the three turrets on the destroyer that weren't flooded out suddenly masked by the orange flare of muzzle-flash. First the port gun in each turret, then the starboard gun. "Helm, three-three-five."

Mermaid swerved again. The two three-round ladders scythed into the water beside her. First ladder was two short and one over; the second two over and one short. Both were perfect for line. The Argentine destroyer had her range and Blaise guessed that her Captain would be ordering a 'fire-for-effect' with all six guns he had operational. "You know, Number One, I wish I was commanding an Indian destroyer right now."

Keighley laughed at the thought. If *Mermaid* had been an Indian destroyer with her eight rapid-fire 4.5s, there would be a solid line of shells joining her to her target and the Argentine destroyer would be well on the way to being reduced to a heap of scrap metal. Then, reality was restored. The Argentine destroyer's turrets flashed again, this time a six-gun salvo. "For what we are about to receive, may we be truly thankful." The old prayer was lost in the crash as the salvo crashed home.

The dispersion on the salvo was much larger than it should have been, the dreadful weather saw to that. Three of the shots landed in the water too far out to do any harm. Two more landed close alongside. One raked the hull over the screws with splinters, the other repeated the process the other side, further forward. One of the 5.3 inch shells scored a direct hit on the ship's cutter, blowing the wooden small craft to fragments.

"Damage?"

"Coming in, Sir. Minor flooding aft, crew spaces by splinters. Helicopter support area badly damaged. Nothing important." Keighley was interrupted by a cheer on the bridge. There had been a brilliant flash amidships on the enemy destroyer. One of the four-inch shells had struck home. The belch of black smoke from the hit was clearly visible. "That's got to hurt."

"Back to two-two-five." Blaise knew the hit had probably done next to no damage but at least *Mermaid* had drawn some blood. He was barely able to see the flash as the next Argentine salvo was fired before everything dissolved into chaos.

"What happened?" He was barely able to think. The first thing that struck him was the bitter cold. One of the seamen on the bridge was wrapping a greatcoat around him.

"Mister Keighley's bought it, Sir. Argie shell hit deck down from us."

Blaise looked around, his eyes focussing again. The bridge was torn open. The windows were smashed and the sides riddled with fragments. Most of them had come through from the deck below. He didn't want to look at the red stains and debris that marked his bridge crew. "Damage?"

The voice came up from below. "Three direct hits, Sir. Bridge you know about. Engine room is hit. One of the diesels is gone, the other is hurt. We're down to ten knots maximum. Aft mast is hit and the shell took the two aft Bofors guns with them. We're taking in water amidships and aft."

Across the sea, the Argentine destroyer fired again. Grimly Blaise noted she wasn't even trying to fire at her maximum rate. She was pacing herself, firing shots as her guns came to bear. The crack of *Mermaid's* four inch guns was lost in the explosions as more Argentine shells struck the crippled sloop. Blaise waited for the smoke to clear. It didn't. Instead, the thick oily cloud that enveloped the bridge told him his ship was burning. In a moment of detachment, he was quite surprised the fires hadn't started sooner. "What's happening?"

"Machinery has gone, Sir. We're dead in the water and we have oil-fed fires where the engine rooms used to be. Four inch mount is gone, direct hit. We've just got the forward Bofors working. The crew tried a few shots but the Argie is out of effective range. We're flooding and listing. Pumps are out, we're trying to rig emergency power now. No perimeter, we've got fragment holes all over the ship."

Blaise looked forward, seeing the cratered ruin of his forecastle where the four inch twin mount had been. The deck was torn up; the bodies of the gun crew scattered all over the area. As he watched, green water washed over the bows, sweeping the human wreckage away. Blaise knew that water had to be surging below, weighing down the bows. Then the ship shook again as a single 5.3-inch shell slammed into the waterline forward. *Mermaid* rolled and her bows started to dip deeper.

"Damage here, Sir. We're done. That last hit's opened up our bows. We can't get pumps working. The fire amidships is out of control."

"Understood Ronnie." Blaise sighed and looked over at the destroyer. She hadn't fired again. He guessed her Captain realized *Mermaid* was finished and was holding fire to allow her crew to escape. A man of honor. "All hands, abandon ship. Repeat, all hands, abandon ship."

ARA Catamarca, *North of South Georgia*

"Why have you ceased fire?" Astrid almost bellowed the question.

Leonardi didn't even bother to look at him or answer the question. "Lieutenant, bring us in close to *Mermaid*. Prepare to pick up the survivors. Pass word around for volunteers to man the seaboats to help the rescue. We can't order men to take the boats out in this storm."

"Yes, Sir."

"Rescue survivors? What nonsense is this? This ship is needed at South Georgia. I order you to leave them and make maximum speed for Grytviken."

Remember you are a seaman. The last words of Commandante Romero echoed in Leonardi's mind. He hadn't needed the reminder, but it gave him the official cover for what he was about to do. "Astrid, shut up. If you had any right to wear that uniform or respect for it stands for, you would know why we must do what we must do. Now, be silent and leave my bridge or I will have you confined in the ship's brig."

"You will. . ." Astrid lunged forward. His movement was assisted by a sudden lurch as *Catamarca* rolled with the seas. There was a dull thud and he measured his length on the deck. Behind him, the Master at Arms patted the heavy flashlight he carried fondly.

"Sorry, Sir. Our guest appears to have hit his head on the ducting."

"Very well Master at Arms. Take him to his cabin. And lock the door, he might have a concussion and wander around.

Ahead of *Catamarca*, the British sloop was already in her death-throes. She had rolled over to where her decks were almost perpendicular to the seas. Her bows had already vanished into the waves. Leonardi could see the crew scrambling off the ship, into the icy waters that were swallowing her. *She hadn't taken much to sink*, Leonardi thought, *but then she had never been designed to fight a proper warship.* She'd done enough to save her honor though. Her four inch guns had hit *Catamarca* twice. One shell had blown up the potato locker, the other knocked out the aft search radar. "Bring us right alongside, get nets over the ship's side."

Leonardi looked aft and saw that his orders had been obeyed before he had even given them. There were scrambling nets being laid and the amidships area of the destroyer was already crowded with men. Some were throwing lifebelts with ropes attached to the sailors struggling in the water; others were climbing down the nets themselves to help the survivors climb to safety. Both his whalers were in the water, moving out to groups of men who were separated from the rest. The crews were in grave difficulties. The swell caused the small craft to ship water and roll, but they still managed to start pulling the men they were hunting out of the water.

132

Back on his ship, the first of the British survivors were already on the main deck. Each man was being wrapped in blankets and given a steaming mug of hot cocoa before being rushed below decks. The whalers were already on their way back; getting them in was going to be a difficult job in this swell. Then, Leonardi saw the men on the nets looking around; some of the British survivors were obviously wounded and losing strength in the bitterly cold water. Some of the Argentine sailors jumped from the nets, swam over to them and started to pull them back to the waiting men hanging on the nets. They handed the rescued sailors up before catching a helping hand to safety themselves.

Eventually, everybody who could be saved was on board. *Mermaid's* wreck was slipping fast. She slid under the water at an increasing speed as the flooding dragged her down. Soon, just a small triangle of her stern was left. As it too vanished from sight, *Catamarca's* siren blasted a long mournful note of farewell. Then, the sloop was gone.

Several minutes later, Leonardi was writing up the action in his long when there was a tactful cough at the hatchway leading on to his bridge. "Sir, Captain Blaise wishes to speak with you."

"Captain Blaise?"

"Sir, I wanted to think you for your rescue effort. Your men were very brave and my casualties would have been much higher had it not been for their chivalry. Could you tell me how many of my men were rescued?"

Leonardi looked at the tally. "We have picked up seventy seven survivors. Of these ten are injured and two are not expected to survive their wounds."

"Thirty six men lost, including those two." Blaise's voice shook slightly but Leonardi pretended not to notice. "May I ask what your current plans for us are?"

Leonardi thought carefully; the picture of the madness in Astrid's eyes in his mind. "I propose to keep you and your crew on board until I can find a safe place to put you. Now is the time when I could really use a neutral merchant ship. Captain, there is madness loose in my country, I am responsible for you and your men and I will not place you in harm's way by exposing you to it."

Conference Room, NSC Building, Washington D.C.

"The Spirit Warriors are fools." Takeda Shingen spoke the words with utter contempt. "They have taken our warrior code and turned it into a suicide cult."

"Spirit Warriors?" The Seer hadn't heard the phrase before.

"Those who believe that Japan's divine destiny is to rule over the whole world. They see Japan's lack of resources and weak industry make challenging the world a losing proposition. So what do they do? They make themselves believe that there is a divine spirit in Japan that will triumph over all material considerations. They believe in war and death for its own sake, not as a means to an end. They demand absolute unqualified obedience from those they command, yet they throw their lives away as if they are of no account. They teach those who follow them that defeat and surrender are unthinkable, that it is better

133

to be wiped out to the last man than to suffer the ignominy of defeat. You see where this insanity will lead?"

"I do and so does the rest of the U.S. Government."

"Who do you speak for now, Seer? The United States Government?"

"Of course. Shingen-sama, the Japanese empire is doomed. It will fall within ten years or twenty at the most. These men, the ones you call Spirit Warriors, when the ruin of their dreams of Empire stares them in the face, they will lash out at the rest of the world, in one last great surge of anger and spite. They will fire their nuclear weapons at everybody, bring the whole world down with them. Oh, we here will ride it out. We'll lose the West Coast for a certainty but nothing much beyond that. But the disaster will be appalling. Somehow, we must aim for a soft landing."

Takeda drummed his fingers on the table. "I agree. Our primary aim is to make sure Japan survives the fall of the Spirit Warriors."

That may be your primary aim, it isn't mine. My aim is to make sure the rest of the world survives the fall of your Spirit Warriors. If that means taking out Japan with a pre-emptive strike, so be it. Let's just hope we don't get to that point. "We have made a good first step in that direction, I believe. The naval demonstration in Chile wasn't a complete success in its public purpose but it's real role was achieved quite well. Some of your Navy people met some of ours and found that everybody could get along quite well. It isn't much, but it's a start. There's a little bit of understanding now that wasn't there before. It gives us a foundation to build on at least. We must hold more such unofficial meetings, help our people build confidence in each other."

"Ha." Takeda sounded slightly scornful. "And what will confidence be worth?"

"One day, when those inside Japan face off against your Spirit Warriors and seize power back from them, it will mean that our people can trust the new government to try and put things right, not just to continue the same old policies under a different name. That will be of the greatest possible importance. Excuse me; what's up, honey?"

"Boss, a message has just come through from the National Reconnaissance Office. It appears that the Argentine Navy has just sunk a British frigate north of South Georgia. The war is on out there." Lillith shook her head. "Anyway, the White House and the Chiefs of Staff are holding a meeting in thirty minutes. Obviously, you're invited."

"Oh well; we knew it was coming. What are the British up to?"

"Emergency session of Parliament. Formal declaration of war I believe."

"Over some small bits of frozen rock?" Takeda was contemptuous.

"More than that. Argentina is caving in economically and the aborted attack on Chile has made things much worse. This is their last chance at surviving as a functioning state. For Britain? It's their chance to show the world that they are back as a functioning state. There's a lot more here than just a few frozen rocks."

House of Commons, Parliament, London, U.K.

"And so it is, with great reluctance and with a heavy heart that I am forced to support my Right Honorable Friend's motion that, with immediate effect, a state of war be declared between the Republic of Argentina and the United Kingdom." The leader of the Labour Party acknowledged the thunderous roll of applause and sat down. Dennis Skimmer, unaffectionately known as 'The Beast of Bolsover' and regarded as probably the best reason why the Labour Party had lost the last election, sat down.

"The House recognizes the Honorable Member for Linlithgow."

"Mister Speaker, I cannot agree with the sentiments expressed by my Right Honorable Friend and leader of our party. I will resist a war with every sinew in my body. Why must we ask young men to die for the possession of a few ice-covered rocks in the desolate South Atlantic? If another nation wants them so badly, let them have the things. They are not worth the life of a single human being."

Skimmer jumped up. "Must we listen to That Man again?" There was a stunned silence in the house at the invocation of Lord Halifax; the one name that, by convention, was never spoken in the House of Commons.

The Speaker banged his staff on the floor. "I would remind the Right Honorable member for Bolsover that unparliamentary language is not permitted in this House and ask him to retract his statement."

"Mister Speaker, you are right. My apologies, my feelings overcame me and I will retract the word 'man'." An explosion of laughter ran around the chamber.

The Speaker shook his head. "That isn't what I meant and you know it. Out you go." Skimmer rose to his feet and limped out of the Chamber to a thunder of applause that the Speaker's efforts couldn't quell. He shook off an attempt to help him. The fact that he had been the youngest member of the resistance to survive a Gestapo interrogation, albeit one that had left both his legs broken, was a major part of his parliamentary persona.

After that, the debate was an anti-climax. The Government motion was passed with only one vote against.

Ernest Mullback's Home, Yeovil, UK.

"Leave it." The sleepy protest from his wife, and the implicit promise in it, almost made Lieutenant-Commander Ernest Mullback ignore the telephone that was ringing so urgently. It really was a most uncivilized time to call. It was eleven PM, he and Sam had only got to bed a few minutes earlier.

"Can't do that, darling. Nobody will call here unless it's an emergency and Lord knows, we're expecting one." It was true. Mullback's squadron mates had been united behind an effort to make sure he was disturbed as little as possible during the brief time he and his wife were likely to have available. So, he picked up the phone, knocking it off the nightstand in the process. "Mullback here."

"Jerry? Alastair. Everything has just dropped in the pot. The Argies went and sank *Mermaid* a couple of hours ago. Now the booties on South Georgia are under attack. Government declared war five minutes ago. *Furious* is out in the Solent right now; she needs her air group ASAP. Air Group Commander asks you to get to Yeovilton and bring down XT-279 right away. It'll be a night landing I'm afraid. Alex is already on his way over. Jerry, be careful. We're loading more aircraft than the book says. It's not just the four extra fighters we heard about. We've got four additional Bananas on board as well. So, the deck's already crowded. Got to run, there's the rest of the squadron to alert."

"War?" Sam was sitting up in bed, her eyes wide. Expecting something didn't make it any the less shocking when it actually happened.

"War. The Argies went and . . ." Mullback was interrupted by the telephone ringing again. He picked it up. "Mullback. Oh, right. Hold one."

"Darling, it's for you. Features desk."

Sam mouthed an 'oh' and took the telephone while Mullback scrambled into his kit. By the time he got back, she was dressing. "I'm on call. Photosession tomorrow morning at six. The fleet's putting to sea and the desk want shots of me on the foreland waving good-bye to you."

"They'll be lucky. Fury is already out in the Solent. I'm flying down to her right now."

"*Glorious* is leaving port at six and I'll wave her good-bye. Nobody else will know the difference."

"Easy to tell. *Furious* has three HF antennas forward of her island; *Glorious* has four."

Sam threw a pillow at him. "And who knows that but you? Get dressed, we'll take my car and I'll drop you off at the base on the way down."

HMS Hotspur, *Alongside, Vickers Fitting Out Basin, Barrow*

The whistle blast pierced every compartment of the ship, bringing the banging and clattering of work to an abrupt standstill. "Attention all hands. Effective as of 2300 tonight, a state of war exists between Great Britain and the Republic of Argentina. We will be putting to sea in two hours time for a run down to the Channel where we will be meeting with the rest of the task force. All hands will darken ship and we will be at action stations on the way down. Civilian workers, you will remain with us and we will put you ashore at Ascension Island for a free flight back to Blighty. Now, the Padre wishes to speak to you."

The voice was grave and solemn. "I fear I must confirm what many of you may already have heard on the grapevine. The *Mermaid* was sunk by an Argentine destroyer earlier today. We have no word as yet of the casualties but given the sea and weather conditions, we must presume they were heavy. Please will you join me in a moment's prayer for the safety of our fellow seamen who are now in enemy hands and to ask God's blessing on those who are now in his."

There was a long two-minute silence throughout the ship. Then the sound of work resumed with renewed frenzy.

"You hear that." Able Seaman Tunney sounded mournful. "Darken ship and run at action stations all the way down. There's Argie submarines waiting to pick us off as soon as we stick our nose out of port, you mark my words."

"In which case, you'll be glad you're sleeping in the hangar tonight, won't you Tunney?" Sub-Lieutenant Hargreaves' voice cut across the clamor.

"Right there. . . . Eh what? Sorry Sir, didn't see you there. Sleep in the hangar Sir?"

"Not tonight, Tunney. The rotodynes are arriving at dawn. Very special birds so I'm told; crews are instructors from the training establishment. Nothing but the best of the best for *Hotspur*. Captain Lanchester is having us at action stations so we can work out any bugs there while we're still in home waters. No submarines around here, not hostile ones anyway. So, get this ship ready and we'll start paying the Argies back for poor old *Mermaid*." Hargreaves ambled off, apparently nonchalantly, but actually keeping a careful eye on his men. At times like this, an encouraging word went a long way.

Simonstad Naval Base, South Africa.

"Up, up jongmens! The kaffirs have risen and are storming the gates. Every rifle needed on the wall." Randlehoff bounced into the barracks displaying an unhealthy amount of zeal.

"It's started?" Cross rubbed the sleep out of his eyes. He and his men had been working on the Boomslangs all day, trying to get a handle on its systems and keep them working.

"War has been declared and your transport ship is here. We must get the Boomies on board without delay. Get your men to the docks now; mine are already on their way." He swept out again, leaving the British officer exhausted but awake.

Cross ran his hand over his chin and decided to take a few seconds to shave. It never hurt to look calm and collected, even when everything imaginable had just dropped into the pot.

HMS Glowworm, *Kingston, Jamaica*

"How did she take it, Sir?"

"Alice? Very calm, very quiet. She'd made a pot of tea and was just sitting there. I suppose she's lucky being here with the kids and all. All the *Mermaid* families are the same I think. They're keeping together, but she's Mrs. Captain and has got to be the tower of strength. Apart from that, they're all just waiting to hear the worst. Like the rest of us I suppose."

HMS *Glowworm* was edging out of Kingston Harbor, Port Royal off to port, the lights of the airport twinkling in the night. The airport was busy tonight. Three BOAC Fairey Airbus airlines hurriedly drafted into military service had landed at dusk, bring out personnel. Foster thought they were men on leave or drafts to fill out depleted crews. A little later a Concord had arrived. Its sonic boom had sent seagulls scattering into the air. More personnel; this time of the VIP variety. The big surprise had been a Canadian Air Force C-133 touching down. Foster had a nasty feeling that the paint on its maple leaf roundels was still wet. That aircraft was not bringing personnel. Instead, long boxes had been unloaded from its belly and hurried off to the munitions dumps. A few minutes later, he'd received an urgent call; were his vertical launch systems full? He'd acknowledged the call and confirmed that he had a full load of Seadart and Seawolf missiles. That probably explained what those long crates had contained.

"What was the word, Sir? South for Saint Vincent and out?"

"No, Simon. The brass has too much mistrust of the people that way. Nobody likes the Argies but they're worried about Latin American solidarity and all that. We don't want too much word of our location getting out. Once we're clear, we're to head east, rounding the south of Cuba and then down to Ascension. We'll be meeting the rest of the fleet there. We'll be screening the carriers."

"Makes sense, I suppose. Who's going to be looking after the Station while we're gone?"

"The Cuban Navy?" Foster offered the possibility and caused a laugh to run around the bridge. The 'Cuban Navy' had precisely one ship, an Italian-built light frigate that spent its time taking tourists out to sea so they could fire the ship's guns. For a fee, of course. It was probably the only navy in the world that ran at a profit.

"Seriously, Sir. The Canucks?"

"Possibly. They've got some frigates they could send down here. Take over the station the way the Ozwalds have taken over Indian Ocean Station. We'll see. Full ahead both; we've a long way to go.

Headquarters, First AirMech Brigade, Aldershot, UK

The curiously whistling whine of the rotodynes was drowning out much of the noise caused by the brigade moving out. Vehicles were lining up to drive into the holds of the Junglie assault rotodynes while men seethed around the slung loads that would be carried by others. Fortunately, Strachan had got much of the heavy equipment and supplies down to the two ships waiting in Devonport earlier in the day. That eased the burden on the aircraft, but getting everything needed down to the two assault carriers was still a major undertaking.

"Oh-six-hundred." Harper yelled the latest word into Strachan's ear. "They'll be pulling out then."

"We'll have time beyond that." Strachan yelled back over the whine turning to a roar as another Junglie took off and headed for the ships waiting at Devonport. "We can shift more kit down to them as they go down the Channel. We'll be able to get two more ferry runs into each before we have to jack it in. We'll make it."

138

Harper looked doubtful at that. There were chains of men passing crates down the line and stowing them in the rotodynes as fast as the laws of physics allowed, but the loading work was slowly falling behind schedule. Nothing major had gone wrong; just the usual plethora of small problems that added to the time needed.

Strachan caught the look. "Don't worry Harper. There's a Plan B. Anything we can't get aboard now will be flown to Ascension and we'll pick it up there."

"Ascension." Harper sounded concerned. "Everything depends on Ascension doesn't it?"

"Almost. We have Simonstad as well. But Ascension is the key."

Personnel Office, MacDill Air Force Base, Florida

"There's a vacancy for a senior maintenance NCO at the 100th, up at Kozlowski. You started your career up there, didn't you?" It was late evening; the meeting was being held after duty hours.

"I did, Sir. But, respectfully Sir, I would prefer to stay down here. Mike's father lives here and my parents will be coming down often. They'll help with the kids."

The detailer grunted. It was preferred policy to get the dependents of aircrew killed in an accident off-base as quickly as possible. This was a different situation though. "How are you settling in?"

"Pretty good, Sir." Selma Hitchins-Yates had found a new apartment off-base for herself and her children remarkably quickly. She didn't know, and never would, that another family had actually outbid her for the place. They'd stepped back when they'd learned she and her children were the family of one of the dead Valkyrie crewmembers. All she knew was that she had secured an apartment in a good part of town. It was large enough for the three of them and had amenities that made it suitable for her children to grow up in.

"Bird ingestion. Nothing anybody could have done." The detailer was still tapping his pencil, trying to make a decision. "Going back to Kozlowski would be good for your career you know."

"Yes Sir, but there's SAC-funded post-graduate work going on at University of Florida. I'd like to apply for that. One of their projects is related to some stuff I did with the 100th, applying it to the Dynasoars and the hypersonics."

"Ah yes, the electronic warfare problems on the Valkyrie." The detailer came to a decision. "Very well, why don't you stay at your present posting until your application for the post-grad work is finalized? Then, if you are in, that's sorted; if your application is turned down, then we'll find another place for you. The 100th vacancy will be gone by then of course, so you'll have to take your chances on what's available. Might not be such a favorable opportunity."

"I understand that Sir. But the University program leads me into the space program and I want to go that way if I can."

"Understood. Well, best of luck and I hope you make it."

Outside, Selma Hitchins-Yates looked across at the expanse of MacDill Air Force Base. Even with the sunset, the massive black scar that disfigured the end of the main runway was still painfully obvious. The wreckage had been cleared away; the radioactive contamination cleaned, from the base at least. The plume from the fire had stretched across the county and that was still being remedied. A new B-70 and a new crew had already arrived to take *Shield Maiden's* place. A new family had already moved into the married quarters she and her husband had once lived in. Life at SAC went on; they'd absorbed the loss, closed ranks and moved on.

She got into her Studebaker Eclipse and turned on the car radio. She'd just caught the end of the evening news and heard the somber tones of the news-reader. "And so, the main point of the news again. Following the sinking of the British battleship the HMS *Mermaid* by Argentine forces, Great Britain has declared war on the Republic of Argentina. Sources close to the Ministry of Defence in Britain say that a task force is being prepared and will be sailing for the area soon."

Selma sighed. She wondered if, somewhere in England a service wife had just seen her detailer about a new posting since her husband was dead.

Ten Downing Street, London, UK

Prime Minister David Newton stared out of the window, across at Horseguards. It was done. War was declared. Now all that remained was to see whether the forces that had been so carefully rebuilt would be adequate for the task they faced. One thing they would not have to face was the danger of a stab in the back. The old system of Conservative Party leadership selection that had been so ably exploited by That Man had been swept away. Now, a new party leader had to be voted in by all the sitting MPs of the party. If that made him Prime Minister, he would face an immediate, automatic, vote of "No Confidence" in the House. If he lost that, then an election would follow. That was one line of defense against That Man's actions being copied.

There was another line. One that did not exist. Men and women who did not exist, whose real names appeared nowhere in the vast records of British bureaucracy. Their units did not exist. Their headquarters did not exist. Their lines of command did not exist. They were myth and legend. There was, quite literally, no way their reality could be confirmed. If they had existed, which they didn't of course, they might have had several responsibilities. One of them might be making sure that what had happened in June 1940 never, ever happened again. For a second, Newton remembered his youth in the Resistance and his anti-tank rocket slamming into the car carrying Richard Austen Butler. Hitting right beside him so that his body was consumed by the explosion from the rocket. No, what had happened in June 1940 wouldn't happen again. With that thought, Newton went to bed and slept soundly.

CHAPTER THREE
ZERO HOUR

ARA Punta Alta *Approaching King Edward Point, South Georgia*

The procession of ships approaching Grytviken was supposed to be imposing. The frigate *Punta Alta* was in the lead as they rounded King Edward Point; the transport *Bahia Thetis* was three cables behind her. The frigate *Querandi* brought up the rear. The two big destroyers would have made it a really imposing demonstration but they were still to the north. They were closing in as fast as they could but weather, time and approaching night were against them. It was already dusk in South Georgia. Captain Fabian Torres didn't like approaching a poorly-charted harbor in the tricky light conditions.

"Bring her down to three knots; prepare to back on the starboard screw." He should have had a pilot on the bridge for this operations but no Argentine pilot knew these waters and if there was a British pilot here, he would probably put the ship aground. Torres had a nasty feeling that this operation wasn't going to be as easy as its supporters had claimed. "Any movement on shore?"

"No Sir." The navigating officer was busy taking fixes as the frigate moved inshore. "We're almost dead center on the deep water channel to quayside. Separation is 100 meters."

For a brief fraction of a second, Torres believed that his ship had been struck by a sudden, violent rain squall. There was the same drumming noise, the same hammering of multiple strikes on the thin metal of his ship. The illusion was convincing but was quickly disrupted by the sight of the bridge windows. They starred and shattered as bullets smacked into them. Almost paralyzed with disbelief, Torres realized that his ship was under heavy, close-range small-arms fire.

"Where is the fire coming from?" His yell was drowned out by one of the windows blowing out completely. The navigating officer went down; his head distorted by a bullet wound that appeared to have removed most of one side of his skull. *Whoever is firing on us has a heavy-caliber sniper's rifle. Bullets from normal rifles might not penetrate the bridge but those would.* Torres heard ricochets inside his bridge, the heavy bullet that had killed his navigating officer had opened the way for the smaller rifle and machine gun fire. "I said, where are these damned bullets coming from?"

141

"Can't see. They're not using tracer." The gunnery officer was interrupted by another crash. The sniper ashore had started methodically shooting out the bridge windows.

"Then take out anything that might give them cover!" Torres shouted the order. The storm of bullets had started shattering the instruments and equipment on the bridge. *Just who the blazes is laying down this volume of fire? There were supposed to be civilians only on this benighted island.* The sound of the gunfire was drowned out by the four-rounds-per-second firing of his beam 47mm guns. They were targeted on a stone building at the base of the quay. Their effect was dramatic. Fragments of stone flew into the air with the impacts as the two-kilogram shells struck with all the force that the 70-caliber barrels could give them. The 47mm was a good gun, probably the best of its class in the world. Its sheer power turned the stone building into a blazing shambles.

"That's it. Use the 76mm to take out any other buildings down there."

"The forward 76mm is gone Sir. Not answering commands. The aft mount can't be brought to bear."

Torres chanced a look over the sill of the bridge windows. He ignored the rattling of bullets striking the metal structure. The 76mm forward was out of action all right. Its fiberglass gunshield had been shredded by the volume of machine gun fire. Its all-too delicate mechanism was jammed by multiple bullet strikes. Torres noted that the hail of bullets striking the bridge had slackened dramatically but the bursts of fire from the 47mm twin mount had stopped also. He guessed that the mounting had just received the same treatment as his 76mm. As that realization sank in, he felt his ship lurch heavily. A grating sound rang through the structure.

"We're aground!" The helmsman was trying to handle the ship's wheel while laying on the deck. Obviously, it hadn't worked too well, but Torres couldn't blame him. To have stood up while the bridge had been under that volume of fire would have been suicidal.

The words were half drowned out by another crash, this time obviously an explosion. "Anti-tank missile, Sir. It's hit us amidships." The surface combat officer was nearly in a panic, the thin sides of the frigate weren't intended to keep out missiles capable of knocking out tanks.

"All power, full astern. We've got to get out of here." Torres gave the order and felt the engines trying to pull *Punta Alta* off whatever it was she had hit. She rolled and lurched again as another missile struck her, this time well forward.

"They're trying for the magazines." The voice was getting nearer to a full-blooded panic.

"Of course they are. Wouldn't you? Now control yourself. We must be able to see where those missiles came from."

There was a pause while the Surface Warfare Officer steadied himself. "Those wrecked ships, off to port. The last missile came from there." He paused. "Aft 76mm mount. Derelict ships bearing red oh-nine-oh. Engage." The aft 76mm would be on the extreme edge of its firing arc but it was better than nothing. It started firing and the heavy crash shook the grounded frigate. Perhaps that might have broken the suction that was holding her in place because she lurched backwards and then started crabbing awkwardly.

"Steady her, back her up, get us out of this." Torres kept his own voice calm and thoughtful. *Enough bad examples have been set this day.* "Get me through to Commandante Romero. Commandante? We have been hit by intense small-arms fire and two anti-tank missiles. We've lost our forward 76mm and port 47mms. We've taken out the missile launcher but we can't see where the small arms fire is coming from. We're just taking out anywhere that might give them cover. . . Thank you, Sir."

On the quayside, a large pile of crates suddenly erupted into flame. The hot white fire caused strange shadows to dance in the gathering dusk. As if it had been a signal, a splash erupted between the *Punta Alta* and the quay. A brief pause then another splash, further from the quay, closer to the frigate. It was mortar fire. Whoever was using the weapon was walking his fire on to the ship. The third round dropped alongside; the fourth was slightly over. Both lashed the frigate's side with fragments. The fifth exploded on the helicopter deck aft.

Overhead, Torres saw a dark shape sweep over. Streams of tracer from its side lashed down at somewhere in Grytviken. *Querandi* had launched her helicopter and the Agosta was using its door guns against whoever was firing the mortar at *Punta Alta*. "Sir, *Querandi* reports her helicopter got the mortar man."

One man? Torres asked himself. *Just what was going on here?* His reflection was broken by a streak of white light that leaped up from Grytviken. It ended in an orange flash as the Agosta helicopter finished its run. The bird seemed to crumple in mid-air with the blast. It dropped out of the sky, into the bay. "and they got it." His reply to the SWO spoke volumes. He'd been tempted to think this was some foolish civilians putting up a fight, but civilians didn't have anti-tank and anti-aircraft missiles. There were troops here; very well-trained ones.

Out to sea, *Querandi* was firing both her 76mm guns and her 47mm twin at the area the surface-to-air missile had come from. *There were old, cylindrical storage tanks there, once used for holding whale oil? Or fuel for the whalers?* Torres didn't know, but they were shredded by the rapid-fire guns.

The firing had stopped. Torres stood up slowly, the rest of his bridge crew followed suite. He guessed the machine guns and rifles had run out of ammunition at last. Or burned their barrels out given the hail of fire they had generated. The ambush was over. *Punta Alta* had paid dearly for her lead into South Georgia. In the darkening gloom, *Bahia Thetis* sailed past her and started to land the troops she had on board. They would be spreading out through the town, trying to hunt down the men who had staged the assault on the frigate. Torres guessed that they would be long gone by now. As if to chastise him for the thought, there was another crack. A single shot. The surface warfare officer slumped to the deck. He had been shot in the head. He was the only officer on the bridge who was still wearing his cap and had probably been mistaken for the Captain.

"Sir, Commandante Romero asks your status." The communications officer handed over the microphone. It was a wonder the radio was still working.

"Sir, forward 76mm and port 47mm mounts out of action. Damage and flooding forward from grounding and a missile hit." He paused for a second as a piece of paper was pushed in front of him. "Hangar is damaged by shell and missile hits. We have hundreds of bullet strikes on the superstructure; some of which were armor-piercing and penetrated the hull plating. Minor flooding amidships and aft. So far two officers and seven enlisted men known dead; twenty wounded. We need to dock, Sir so we can do a more thorough survey. Very good, Sir."

Torres turned around and sighed. This was not going to look well on his fitness report. "We're to dock as soon as the Marines have cleared the quayside area. All damage control teams, start sealing off the flooded areas and get the pumps going."

Moody Brook Barracks, Near Stanley, Falkland Islands

"Men in position Sergeant?" Major Charles Pettigrew had moved his men out more than three hours earlier, as soon as word of the *Mermaid* sinking had been received. He had guessed that the Marine garrison barracks at Moody Brook would be the first target of the Argentine strike group.

"That they are, Sir. Covering Yorke Bay and Mullet Creek."

"Radar showed two groups of ships approaching. Big one heading for Yorke Bay, smaller one for . . . . Here we go."

The train-like roar overhead told its own story. Pettigrew watched as his barracks erupted into fireballs as the eight-inch rounds from the cruisers and assault ships offshore slammed into the empty structure. The building collapsed almost instantly into burning ruins. The big shells continued to pound the area where the Marine garrison had been quartered.

"They weren't playing games were they, Sir?"

"Batting for keeps I would say, Sergeant. Well, every shell they fire at the old place is one less they'll fire at us. And the barracks has done us a real favor. With a little luck, we'll catch the landing force off guard."

There was a final salvo of shells. The bombardment was over. What had once been the Marine barracks was now utterly destroyed. Pettigrew heard a more distant rumble from over by Stanley. The Argentine cruisers had shifted their fire to the airport.

Lake Cove, Falkland Islands

"Here they come. Like lambs to the slaughter." Lieutenant Hallam was watching the cruisers offshore through night-vision binoculars. There were four ships out there. One a conventional heavy cruiser, the other one of the Argentine Navy's odd 'assault cruisers.' He knew the details of both ships. They'd both started life as American Baltimore class ships with nine eight inch guns each. One had been sold to Argentina in that configuration but the Septics had converted the other into an early missile cruiser. Not very successfully by all accounts. The converted ship, with her six eight inch guns forward still in place but her stern gutted, had also been sold to Argentina. The Argentines had rebuilt the ship again. The stern was now equipped with a helicopter landing pad and hangar and facilities for handling landing craft. She was launching her troops now. The four landing craft were already on their way to the beach while the amphibious personnel carriers were forming up behind them. Hallam counted ten of them. *A reinforced company. How reinforced depended on what was in the landing craft of course.*

The landing craft were taking their time coming in, waiting for the amphibious carriers to join up with them. Behind them, four medium-sized assault helicopters were taking off from the assault cruiser.

"Now that's appropriate." Hallam had looked at the assault cruiser carefully.

"Sir?" Sergeant Fox was also watching the approaching invasion group.

"The assault cruiser. She's the *La Argentina*, I can see the extra long-range communication antenna between her masts."

"Nice to know, Sir." Fox's family name had once been Fuchs. His father wasn't quite able to grasp the relationship that existed between British NCOs and their officers.

"I think so, Sergeant. The regimental history will demand details like that. Ah, the amtracks are coming in first, the landing craft behind them. What's the betting that there's a tank platoon coming ashore?"

"Sounds likely, Sir. One here and two around at Yorke Bay? With the helicopter boys to hold the road between. Talking of which. . . "

The four helicopters had formed up and were heading towards the beach. Hallam recognized what was happening easily enough. It was a typical Septic-style vertical envelopment assault. The tanks and amphibious infantry carriers, the amtracks, would attack over the beach while the helicopters landed troops behind the defenses to take them in the rear. Before the Americans had taken a dislike to the Argentines, they'd sold their forces a lot of American kit and trained their officers. So it wasn't surprising the Argentine assault was strictly American-pattern.

The problem was that the helicopters were slow and clumsy. Hallam recognized them, *Agosta Pumas. Probably carried a reinforced platoon between them.* With a marine company and a tank platoon heading for the beach and a platoon hitting them from the rear, Hallam's platoon was seriously overmatched. On the other hand, he'd known that before he'd moved into position. He had a good chance of wearing down the opposing force while it was still making its way to the beach. A little bit, anyway,

It was really a question of timing. Each of his three squads had a single man-portable anti-aircraft missile launcher and a pair of anti-tank rocket launchers. His weapon squad had an anti-tank missile launcher and two tripod-mounted machine guns. Now, if he could fit all of those together properly, he had a chance to inflict a serious hurt. *Enough to make them back off? Probably not, but it was a chance.*

The helicopters came first. Three missiles streaked up from the rock fields that lined the bay, towards the Pumas. The reaction was immediate. The helos tried to maneuver out of their way, while spitting out flares and chaff. Hallam couldn't quite understand why they were kicking out chaff. Everybody knew the British Kestrel SAM wasn't radar homing. Perhaps the aircraft threat warning system was programmed to fire both regardless of the threat. For one of the helicopters, neither chaff nor flares were able to save the situation. The missile exploded under the tail boom and took out the tail rotor. Without its counteracting force, the Puma span out of control and fell out of the sky. It crashed offshore in a spray of greenish-white. A second helicopter took a hit high up on its fuselage, right by its twin engines. It staggered in the air but kept flying, turning back to the assault cruiser offshore. The third missile missed completely. That left just two helicopters to dump their infantry behind the defensive line on the beach.

Out to sea, Hallam saw the orange-red cloud that marked the heavy cruiser firing. The shells screamed over his head and impacted on the hills behind the beach. The Argentines had got that broadside wrong; not by much but they had made a mistake. They didn't repeat it. The second salvo of shells landed right on the beach itself. Out of the corner of his eye, he saw the brilliant white line of an anti-tank missile heading across the water towards the amphibious carriers. It hit one. The orange-red flash of its warhead silhouetted the bulky shape of the carrier. The amphibious personnel carrier was hit hard. Hallam could see its bows rear up as it sank. He wondered if anybody inside had actually managed to escape from the sinking vehicle.

It didn't really matter. Another carrier was hit by a rocket as it hauled itself out of the water. It stopped, burning, but the tail ramp dropped down and the infantry inside bailed out. They started to move towards the rocks that bordered the small strip of sand. Hallam's men fired on them. Some of the Argentines fell, but the armored carriers used their machine guns to spray the defensive positions. His defenses had already been badly disrupted by the eight-inch shells from the cruiser and his platoon lost its cohesion. By the time the landing craft reached the shoreline and dropped their ramps, the situation for the defenders was already critical.

It was the tanks that made the difference. Each of the landing craft carried a single American-made M92 light tank armed with a 76mm semi-automatic gun. The combination of rate of fire with close range was a disaster for the defense. One tank took a pair of anti-tank rockets and burned. The other three hosed down the positions with cannon and machine gun fire. By this time, Hallam had more than enough of his own to do without trying to understand what was happening across the whole bay. His little command group was under direct attack by a dismounted squad of Argentine Marines who had their amtrack in support. In the darkness and confusion of the assault he managed to disengage and fall back towards the agreed rendezvous point. He was dreadfully aware that few of his men would be joining him there.

Back on the beach, the Argentine Marines who had lost their vehicles on the way in were mopping up the last instances of British resistance. The rest of the invasion force, the three light tanks and seven of the ten amtracks were already forming up and starting to move along the road to Stanley. They were the left-hand prong of a two-stage envelopment. The rest of the force was coming ashore at Yorke Bay.

ARA Almirante Brown, *Yorke Bay, Falkland Islands*

The eight-inch guns forward were firing steadily. The vibration from the shots caused the tightly-packed LVTP-7 amtracks in the *Almirante Brown's* vehicle hangar to shudder. Major Facundo Caceres felt the shock through his commander's seat in the lead LVTP. He didn't object. To him, the more shells that were poured into the beach defenses the better. Word had already come in that the attack on Lake Cove had run into much heavier opposition that had been expected. It hadn't helped matters that the assault here at Yorke Bay had been delayed by navigational problems. All the marker buoys had been removed and the ships had had to pick their way in very carefully. The delay had meant that the assault on Lake Cove had gone in first and the defenses would be thoroughly alerted.

"Prepare to land the landing force." The time-honored order that had been a Navy standard since the days of the Spanish Armada echoed through the vehicle hangar. When the cruiser had first been built, decades ago, it had been a spacious aircraft hangar, supposedly capable of housing four seaplanes. In the early 1950s, the U.S. Navy had converted her to a missile cruiser. When better-designed conversions had become available, they'd stripped the missile systems out and sold what was left of the ship to Argentina. The stern half of the ship had been gutted when Argentina took delivery. So, the ship had been rebuilt as an assault cruiser, a hybrid ship that was heavy cruiser forward and amphibious landing ship aft. What had been the floatplane hangar had been extended to give capacity for ten LVTP-7s. A flight deck and helicopter hangar had been constructed where the aft eight-inch guns had once been. Davits amidships carried four LCTs, each capable of landing a single light tank. All-in-all, a useful ship; one the Argentine Navy was proud of.

The vehicle hangar shook again. This time the cause wasn't gunfire; it was the aft doors opening. As they slid sideways, a ramp started to lower. It allowed the LVTPs to drive down from the hangar to the sea. It was a narrow ramp, wide enough for a single amtrack to use at a time. Caceres gave the order. His amtrack started to move forward, its bows dipped as it descended the ramp then levelled off as the vehicle entered the water. In front of him, the water started to pile up as his vehicle picked up speed. The swell was causing the amtrack to roll. Momentarily, he felt sorry for the troops in the back. The infantry compartment in the LVTP-7 was bad enough at the best of times; when full of sea-sick Marines, it was hideous.

Over to Caceres's left, the destroyer *Entre Rios* was lobbing shells from her 5.3-inch guns towards Port Stanley Airfield. This was a carefully-planned exercise. The airfield was Caceres's primary objective and the gunfire was calculated to suppress any defenses without destroying the facility completely. The Argentine Air Force was already preparing a squadron of its Ciclone attack aircraft for transfer to the airport. They would be a key part of the defense if the British actually tried to retake the islands. A key part that wouldn't be there if the airport was destroyed by eight-inch gunfire.

The LVTP company Caceres commanded wasn't the only part of the landing force coming ashore at Yorke Bay. The landing ship *Candido de Lasala* had her well deck flooded and more LVTPs were sailing out of the docking area and forming up before heading out The white sand of the beach that glittered so enticingly ahead of the invaders. Once ashore, they would be heading for Port Stanley itself, to join up with the column that was already ashore and advancing from Lake Cove.

Caceres watched the four helicopters from the *Almirante Brown* lumber overhead. Their job was to seize a bridge about a mile behind the landing beach. That bridge was also a key point. It would provide the armored column with access to Port Stanley. If it went down, the LVTP-7s could swim across, but the M92 light tanks would be stuck until a temporary replacement could be built. So, the platoon of infantry on the Pumas would seize the bridge, remove any demolition charges and hold it until they were relieved

147

by the advancing armor. That part of the plan was already beginning to go wrong. As the Pumas crossed the coast, they were greeted by a barrage of gunfire and the streaks of surface-to-air missiles being fired.

The effects were catastrophic for the helicopters. One blew up in mid-air as it tried to cross the beach. The streak of light connecting it to the ground told Caceres that one of the British Kestrel missiles had claimed the kill. Another was in bad trouble. It was attempting to make a crash landing on the beach itself; probably in autorotation after its engines had been hit. It might have made it, but an anti-tank missile forestalled the landing and the helicopter slammed into the ground and burned. The remaining two helicopters were the victims of machine gun fire. Too slow and clumsy to evade the hail of fire, they staggered out of the ambush and tried to make it back to the *Almirante Brown*. One made it. The other made a forced landing in the sea half way between the beach and the cruiser. *It was not,* Caceres thought, *an auspicious start to the landing.*

He had his own problems. Those facing the main body of the landing force were theirs to be concerned over. His own target was a small sub-bay to the north of Gypsy Cove; one flanked by rocky outcrops. They possibly barred the way to the inviting white sand. As his LVTP-7 plowed through the water towards the beach, he was waiting for the blast of gunfire and rockets that would mark his group being caught in a vicious crossfire. He stooped down in his turret; trying to gain some comfort from the armored protection, but also painfully aware that the armor was paper-thin and wouldn't stop an armor-piercing bullet from a rifle. The expected hail of fire never came and Caceres felt the bow of his amtrack lift as the treads gripped sand instead of water.

Slightly surprised at his own survival, he glanced over to his right. The explanation for his good fortune was immediately apparent. The main body landing in Gypsy Cove was in chaos. Obviously, the British had expected that to be the main beach. After all, the good road to Stanley lay just behind it and the beach itself was near-perfect for a landing. He could see at least three amtracks and a M92 light tank burning on the water's edge. The beach was being raked with gunfire from the headland that lay on its west and the small island that Caceres had passed on the way in. Grimly, he realized the troops there must have let him pass, waiting for the greater game to come. More fire was hosing the main body from inland, pinning the troops on the beach. The main body was almost surrounded. Caceres saw another red ball rise in the night sky as an Amtrack exploded just inshore from the water's edge.

Behind him, the landing craft had dropped their ramps and the M92 tanks surged out, on to the white sand. Their odd shape made them look like beetles that had somehow found their way into this chaos. Caceres picked up the microphone of his radio and got himself patched through to his battalion commander. "Sir, Delfina group is ashore without casualties. Beach is quiet; say again beach is quiet."

There was a crackle on the radio. He could hear the hammering of gunfire in the background. A lot of gunfire. "We are pinned down here, the beach is mined and there were at least two companies of English marines waiting for us." The next words were drowned out by the roar of explosions. The cause was obvious. The two cruisers had moved closer inshore and were firing on the rocky outcrops that were allowing the defenders to fire into the Argentine rear. The mix of eight inch and five inch shells were drowning the rock piles in the orange-red balls of explosions. The firing from them ceased.

148

"Sir, we can swing west and take the defenses in the rear."

"Negative, Delfina. Say again negative. We'll look after ourselves here. You carry on with your assigned task. Seize that airfield. Jasmine out."

Well, orders were orders and that had been made clear enough. Caceres switched from the battalion command net to his company net. "All Delfina units move out. Delfina-One will lead, four will follow, two and three will bring up the rear." That put his own amtrack and the three of first platoon in the lead, then the platoon of four M92s and the two remaining platoons of infantry at the rear. As his LVTP-7 lurched forward, the driver carefully picked his way through the icy rock field. Caceres was studying his map. Just 300 meters in the road to the airfield should open up. Another 700 meters beyond that and he should be on the airfield itself. Behind him, the beach shook again as the two cruisers offshore hurled more shells into the British defenses at Gypsy Cove.

Headquarters Section, NP8901, Gypsy Cove, Falkland Islands

"Those bloody cruisers are chewing us up." Sergeant Jordan was of the opinion that stating the obvious was never a bad idea when speaking to an officer. The damage being done by the two cruisers was very obvious. Their blanket of fire from eight-inch and five-inch guns had silenced both the outposts that had done so much damage to the Argentine force. They had sunk at least two LVTPs with rocket hits and their machine gun fire had raked the troops on the beach in a murderous crossfire. The Argentine Marines were trying to take cover using dips in the white sand. That was only a temporary relief. NP8901's two 50mm mortars were already at work, dropping their bombs into the knots of trapped troops.

"We can write off second platoon." Captain James Fitzhugh carefully kept the guilt out of his voice. He had known the chance of the platoon's survival was virtually nil when he'd sent two of its three squads out to hold the two rocky points. The third squad was his reserve and was about to be committed. On the other hand, the chance of first platoon surviving wasn't much higher. The reports from Lake Cove suggested that third platoon was already gone. This mission had always been a forlorn hope; the islands couldn't support a large enough defense force to make an invasion impossible. NP8901 was a force small enough to be supported for an indefinite period, large enough to make any invasion force bleed badly so that sovereignty had been defended, small enough that its inevitable loss wouldn't matter too much. *A fine balance*, Fitzhugh thought, *I just wish that I wasn't one of the elements being balanced.*

"They're moving behind us on our right, Sergeant. Take third squad and refuse the right flank. Prevent their armor getting behind us. We'll disengage from here and fall back to Lady Elizabeth Bay with your squad acting as rearguard. From there, we'll get over the bridge and blow it behind us." *Those of us who survive, which won't be many.* Fitzhugh thought gently to himself. "That'll buy us a little time."

"Very good, Sir." Jordan slipped off. Fitzhugh took another careful look at the beach through his night-vision binoculars. The Argentines were already organizing themselves and starting to assault his beach defense positions. Some of the groups laid down suppressive fire while others slowly moved up the beach. His left flank was already beginning to crumble under the pressure while his center and right were still holding. Now

149

was the time to pull back, while he still could. Once the troops were locked into a firefight, he would have to stand here. That was a bad idea with those cruisers shelling the beach.

"Order all three squads to fall back, towards Lady Elizabeth Bay. We've done all we can here."

Major Caceres's Column, Approaching Port Stanley Airfield

Every so often, things did work out the way they were supposed to. The road, such as it was, had been where the map showed it to be. It was only gravel with two thin tire tracks the width of a landrover apart. The 'heavy' armor was tearing it apart, spraying the small stones to either side in shotgun blasts. For all that, it was better than nothing. The map also showed the road making a long curve before straightening up for the run into the airfield. Caceres saw the curve approaching. That's when things stopped working the way they were supposed to.

Three rockets streaked out from a rocky outcrop on his right. Two shot harmlessly overhead. The third hit the second of his four M92 tanks. The tank exploded; immediately dissolving in a fireball as its ammunition cooked off. Light tanks did not take well to getting hit. The response from the Argentine column was instantaneous. They had rehearsed this often enough and had performed the maneuver for real when ambushed by insurgents. The three surviving M92s peeled away from the column followed by the second platoon of three LVTP-7s. They headed straight for the source of the rockets. The semi-automatic 76mm guns on the tanks were firing steadily. Most of the shots went wild as the vehicles lurched on the rock-covered ground. That wasn't the point. They, and the streams of machine gun fire from the sub-turrets on the M92s and the LVTP-7s, were intended to force the ambushers to take cover. Killing them would come just a little later.

Back on the road, the seven LVTP-7s accelerated. Standard ambush procedure; the nearest forces attacked the ambush while the rest cleared the killing zone as quickly as possible. Caceres didn't worry about what was happening at the ambush site. He had competent officers; they knew what they had to do and they could be trusted to do it. Instead, he concentrated on commanding his reduced force as it swept around the curve in the road and accelerated along the straight stretch of road towards the airfield. He could see it now. The lights in the control tower gleaming yellow in the darkness. His amtrack vibrated and shook from the gravel as it surged forward. Behind him, the firing from the ambush site reached a crescendo, then abruptly stopped.

Third Squad, Second Platoon, NP8901

There were a dozen machine guns at least, most of them .50-calibers, firing on the squad position. They saturated the area with fire. Sergeant Jordan was already down to three men. He'd lost two when a 76mm shell had plowed into their position. That shell had also cost him one of his two remaining anti-tank rockets. He had the other and he was waiting for the opportune moment to use it. That would be soon; he was all too aware that there weren't very many moments left. The three LVTP-7s had already dropped their ramps. The infantry inside were deploying, covered by the never-ending hail of machine gun fire. Almost forty Argentines, three tanks and three APCs against a sergeant and three men.

The tanks had stopped moving. Now they picked their shots with deliberation. The remainder of his squad were firing on the vehicles, but their rifles just didn't have the hitting power to penetrate the armor. They scratched and scarred it but they did no real damage to the vehicles it protected or the men who sheltered by them. The muzzle flashes from their rifles were different. They revealed the position of the British marines to the M92s. The flat cracks of the 76mm guns quickly ended the gunfire.

That was what gave Jordan his chance. While the tanks dealt with the three survivors of his squad, he took careful aim with his rocket launcher. The nearest of the three LVTP-7s had three radio antennas, not two. That suggested it was a command vehicle. That sealed its fate. Jordan fired his rocket carefully into its side. Shooting at amtracks with small rocket launchers was a dicey proposition at best since the flotation tanks and bulky hull shielded most of the vehicle's vital parts. There were only a few areas where the rocket launcher could actually hurt. Jordan's rocket hit one of them. The LVTP-7 exploded into flame, its crew leaping out of the top hatches and out of the rear.

By the time return fire arrived, Jordan had grabbed his rifle and was away, squirming through the rocks as he made his escape. He was off to Lady Elizabeth Bay. Before that he needed to know what the Argentine column was up to. The group on the road had already reached the outskirts of the airfield and were about to turn on to the taxiway. The group that had wiped out his ambush were starting to move out, paralleling the road. Jordan guessed they were heading for the end of the runway so they could advance down it. That made sense. With the information filed away, he started to head for the rest of NP8901.

Control Tower, Port Stanley Airfield, Falkland Islands.

"Come on lads, put some muscle into it. Thump it, don't tap it!"

His words were rewarded by a redoubled effort. The noise of destruction increased exponentially. His two "lads" were furiously wielding heavy axes as they smashed in the radar displays and communications equipment. Warrant Officer Truscott had a 20-pound sledgehammer that he swung with all the berserk enthusiasm of a medieval bishop swinging a mace at the ungodly. He hated being stationed in the Falklands instead of the West Indies or Ascension. He hated the equipment he had to work with here and he hated his job in general. So, the opportunity to wreck everything in sight was a precious one. He meant to take every advantage of it. Outside, the runway lights were going out one-by-one as the third of his "lads" took them out with the other 20 pound sledge. The lad had always liked running. Now he was getting the chance.

There was a hammering on the steps outside. The door to the air traffic control center crashed open. A sweating Argentine Major stepped through, his pistol drawn and his presence backed up by armed men. Men with the Argentine FAS rifles; weapons that looked almost absurdly large compared with stubby British L1A2. "Drop those weapons." The major snapped out the order in perfect English.

"Do it, lads." Truscott kept his voice calm and even as he let the sledgehammer fall from his hands. Only a fool took on a 7.65mm Argentine FAS with a sledge. Or an axe. Truscott heard the axes hit the wooden floor with relief. He'd been afraid one of his lads would get carried away with testosterone and try something stupid.

The Argentine officer was looking around at the wreckage of the control tower, struggling not to laugh at the devastation. "You three must really hate the Malvinas."

"Not a prime posting, the Falklands." Truscott said agreeably, making sure his hands stayed in sight. "Give us a few more minutes and we'll finish the job off if you like."

"That will not be necessary." The major's voice was theatrically grave. "You have another man out there smashing the lights? Stop him please."

Truscott picked up the microphone that fed the Tannoy System. "Give it up Jimmy. The Argies are here. Drop the sledge and walk back to the control tower with your hands raised."

"Thank you. I am Major Caceres, Argentine Marine Corps. This airfield is now under our control. You are our prisoners and under our protection." There was an emphasis on the last three words that Truscott didn't quite understand.

"Warrant Officer Winston Truscott, Sir. These are my lads, Leading Aircraftman Steven Handley and Leading Aircraftman William Scott. The lad outside is Aircraftman Jimmy Fish. All Royal Air Force."

"Very good. My men will take charge of you. I hope you do not mind riding in an Amtrack back to the beach. I need to get you on to a ship as quickly as possible. Warrant Officer, have you set demo . . ."

Caceres was interrupted by a massive orange fireball rising into the sky from the outskirts of the airfield. A split second later, the dull boom of the explosion set the control tower rattling.

"Ahh, the fuel dump. Of course." Caceres looked at Truscott with curiosity. The Warrant Officer was standing with his mouth hanging open in shock. "Why the surprise? Surely you knew what a fuel explosion would look like."

"Of course, just a bit sooner than I expected, that's all. Damned time fuses."

Caceres nodded understandingly. His demolition men also had problems with the erratic performance of time fuses. He gestured, and three of the marines took the RAF team down the steps, outside the control tower and over to a waiting LVTP-7. As they took their seats inside, Scott whispered very quietly. "Mister Truscott, we didn't rig the fuel dump to blow."

"I know lad; I know."

Headquarters Section, NP8901, Lady Elizabeth Bay Bridge, Falkland Islands

The wreckage of the bridge had joined the old rusting hulks that littered the Bay. The number of discarded hulks around Port Stanley were hardly tribute to British stewardship of the Island. They had the ironic nickname of the "Port Stanley Yacht Club," but in reality, they were nothing but eyesores. A few pounds of C-4 had sent the bridge into the water with them. It was now just another twisted blemish on the water.

152

"Think that will hold them?" Fitzhugh started at the unfamiliar voice. The long-familiar tones of Sergeant Jordan had gone. Fitzhugh was sadly certain he would not hear them again.

"For a little while, Sergeant. The rest will depend on us. Men in position?"

"Sir. But it's a thin front, Sir."

Fitzhugh nodded. Of the two platoons, eighty men, who had held Yorke Bay, only nineteen had survived to fall back to this position. He had no idea yet how many wounded had been taken prisoner by the Argentines, but the hammering from the eight-inch guns on the Argentine cruisers hadn't left him hopeful that there would be very many. His men had lost most of their heavy weapons in the hurried retreat from Yorke Bay. He had two machine guns and a single rocket launcher with two rounds left.

"It'll have to do. The bridge being down will slow the Argies up a bit. The M92s they've got aren't amphibious."

"They won't have to be, Sir. Look across the bay."

Fitzhugh swung the night vision binoculars across the front and looked past the rusting wreck of the *Lady Elizabeth*. The heat signatures of a group of LVTP-7s were easily seen against the bitterly cold water. At least six and possibly more were swimming the bay, heading parallel to the coast. Fitzhugh guessed what their commander had in mind. They would swing south soon and come ashore eight or nine hundred yards behind what little was left of his command. He sighed. This had been a good position but the enemy would be coming up the road behind him. That meant it was already lost. The only real option left was to try and disengage again and move to engage the Amtracks behind him. That way the blown bridge would be guarding his rear, not pinning the enemy in his planned kill-zone. That was better than nothing.

He wouldn't even get that. Before he could issue the orders, brilliant flashes split the night in front of him. 76mm shells started tearing into the ground his side of the creek. The semi-automatic guns on the M92s fired fast and the gunners were good. They were picking out the obvious defensive positions and pummeling them hard. The chance of actually killing some of his men wasn't high. The 76mm was designed as a tank-killer, not an infantry support weapon, but the barrage of fire was stopping him disengaging to handle the amtracks. It was a classic maneuver, hammer and anvil. The tanks and the creek were the anvil and the Amtracks crossing behind him were the hammer. Fitzhugh became uneasily aware that his gonads were exposed to the two converging slabs of steel.

Major Caceres's Column, Port Stanley Airfield

"Delfina, is the airfield secure?"

"Delfina-Actual here, Sir. The airfield is secure but the control tower and landing lights have been thoroughly wrecked. The fuel dump has been blown up as we expected. I would recommend we check the runway for mines before anybody lands here."

"There will be some engineers on the way as soon as they've finished clearing the beach and the access roads. The Anglos laid a lot of mines at Yorke Bay. The place is thick with them. How many prisoners have you?"

"Four, Sir. They're in an Amtrack on its way back to the *Almirante Brown*. All RAF enlisted personnel. I made getting them out a priority."

"Good man. It is essential we don't allow the political people anywhere near any prisoners we take. God knows, this will cause our country enough problems without that. Secure the airfield, guard it with a platoon and bring the rest of your force along the Surf Bay Road."

"Sir, we had to fight through an ambush on the way down. I can bring over three tanks and four Amtracks."

"That will do. Move fast, Delfina. We want this operation over by dawn."

Headquarters Section, NP8901,Lady Elizabeth Bay Bridge, Falkland Islands

"Sir, Sergeant Jordan on the radio."

That's a relief. Fitzhugh grabbed the speaker. "Jordan, what's happening your side of the island?"

"Nothing good Sir. We knocked out a tank and an amtrack but the rest of our squad bought it. The Argies have the airfield. There's a platoon dispersing round it. The crabs did well, they bashed in most of the lights and blew up the fuel dump. The real nausea is that the rest of the column is already pulling out. They're heading along the Surf Bay Road and that'll take them straight on to your right flank. Three M92s, four amtracks. You're outflanked, Sir. They'll be on your right in ten minutes or so."

"On both sides, Sergeant. Another group of Argie amtracks swam Lady Elizabeth Bay and they're coming ashore on our left. Jordan, evade and hold out if you can, otherwise surrender. This will be all over here as soon as the jaws close."

"Understood, Sir." The radio went off the air.

Another salvo of 76mm rounds slammed into the defensive positions. The Argentine M92s were moving slowly forward as their fire neutralized any obvious defenses. Now, they were close enough for their .50 machine guns to hose down the ground near the wrecked bridge. Fitzhugh watched them spraying the old rusty wrecks offshore as well and admired the thoroughness. He'd have used those wrecks for cover if he'd had enough men to do so. The men he could have used were dead or prisoners and that thought made him cringe. No matter how long he lived, he knew he would never forget the fighting this night.

Viewed objectively, it was a beautiful sight. The criss-crossing lines of tracer and the brilliant red streaks of the 76mm shells reminded him of a really good November 5th party. The problem was, they also were defining just how small the area his troops held was. The definition was improved by the increasing amount of gunfire coming from his left. The amtracks were ashore. It seemed like the Argentines were advancing dismounted, using the LVTP-7s as support. Underneath the crash of the 76mms and the thudding of the .50s, he could hear the crackle of the British L1A2s and the deeper bark of the Argentine FAS rifles.

"Sergeant Macy on the left, Sir. He says he can't hold. He's got three men down."

Out of six Fitzhugh thought. Before he could reply, another blast of gunfire came out of the darkness on his right. The column from the airfield had arrived. Jordan's report had suggested a reinforced infantry platoon with M92s in support. There was no way he could hold that as well.

"Tell Sergeant Macy to give it up. We've done all we can here."

"Sir." The radio message went out and Fitzhugh felt sick. Giving it up now seemed to put him on a par with That Man. But, with tanks on two sides of him and closing in on his flanks and rear, he really had no choice.

"Smash the radio and give me the antenna."

There was a crash as the radio was broken up. Fitzhugh took the antenna, hung a handkerchief over the end and squirmed through the rocks to his right. Then he held it up and started to wave. It took what seemed like hours for it to be noticed, but the firing from his right stopped. A few seconds later, the attack on his left and the shelling from the tanks over the creek followed.

Major Caceres's Column, Port Stanley

Caceres saw the British officer waving his flag through the thermal sight on his amtrack. He passed the news to the other units and heard the barrage of fire from the Argentine units peter out. Once the night was silent, he climbed out and walked across to the man with the flag.

"I am Captain Fitzhugh, Naval Party 8901, Falkland Islands garrison. Major, I recognize that our position here is hopeless and request terms."

"Major Caceres, Argentine Marine Corps. Captain, your men have fought well but your position is indeed hopeless. I must advise you that our forces have also made a successful landing at Lake Cove and are approaching from the east. I have already been authorized to offer you an honorable surrender. Your men may walk out bearing their arms and pile them by my Amtracks. They will be treated as prisoners of war and the Red Cross in Geneva will be informed of their capture. I must inform you that we already have some of your men as prisoners and others have been wounded. If you will provide identification of your men, we will also advise the Red Cross of the dead and wounded."

Fitzhugh nodded. The Argentine Marines were offering terms that were indeed honorable and proper. "Very well, I will give the necessary orders. Major Caceres, I have wounded; may I request the services of your medics?"

"I only have the platoon Medic here but we will get your wounded to the cruisers where there are decent medical facilities." Caceres dropped his voice. "A quiet word

155

Captain. Tell your men to keep their mouths shut. There are political officers in our force who only look for an excuse to do things no honorable soldier would stomach. The less your men say, the better it will be for them."

Terminal Three, Heathrow Airport, United Kingdom

"Heather, how are you?" Igrat had swept out of the diplomatic arrivals channel with Henry McCarty and Achillea in tow. That alone suggested how much things had changed in the last few hours. Normally, she made the London trip alone. With a war on, her usual bodyguards were with her. She seized and hugged Heather Watson, holding the hug just long enough to make the rigidly heterosexual Heather distinctly uncomfortable. "and the rest of the Circus?"

"I'm fine thank you." Heather disengaged herself, feeling her ears turn pink as she did so. "As for the Circus, well, all the boys in the services are either heading south or getting ready to do so. I'll tell you more in the car; there's one waiting just outside."

"Not a Rotodyne?" Achillea sounded slightly resentful.

Heather shook her head. "Not tonight and not for a hop this short. The civilian rotodynes have all been impounded for military use. Anyway, we're not going to London; we're going to Windsor. The Castle, to be specific. In any case, all but a limited number of flights are closed down this evening. There's military air movements all over the place and air traffic control are afraid of collisions. Your Machliner was one of the few civilian flights allowed in, I think that was probably because you were on it." Heather seemed suddenly sad. "I wish I had your job, Igrat; travelling all over the world the way you do. It sounds so exciting."

"It's not all fun, Heather. Remember a few years ago I got picked up by an opposition group and they beat me into a bloody mess. If Henry and Achillea hadn't been on the ball, I would have died. As it was, it took me a year to recover. And that wasn't the first time."

"Thank Branwen." Henry sounded friendly but the keen eyes never stopped scanning the semi-deserted terminal. It had the strange atmosphere of a deserted amusement arcade after dark. "She's the one who thought to put a backstop tail on you. Is this our car?"

"It is indeed." Heather grinned impishly. It was ostentatiously parked in a no-parking area. Three traffic wardens stared furiously at it. Igrat was reminded of horror movies where a group of vampires were being held at bay by a crucifix. This time the traffic wardens were being foiled by a simple badge in the car's window. It was a crown, a greyhound and the letters OHMS. *On Her Majesty's Service* Igrat mentally translated them. Heather noted her glance. "That certainly works doesn't it? I've got something for you, Igrat."

She handed over a slim, black wallet. Inside was a golden version of the same crown-and-greyhound crest opposite Igrat's picture. "You're a Royal Courier now, Igrat. For the duration anyway. That means you can go anywhere in the world and walk into the British Embassy there unchallenged. Show that badge and even the Ambassador himself has to do what you want."

156

"Oh goody." Igrat managed to inject a remarkable amount of lechery into two words.

"In a professional context, of course." Heather tried to speak severely but gave up. Igrat's reputation made the effort pointless. "Oh, get in the car."

The Rolls-Royce looked and smelt luxurious. Igrat sank into the soft leather upholstery with a sigh. "Let me guess. From the Royal Garage?"

"That's right. I've wanted to drive one of these all my life. Before we get to the Castle, any private messages for us?"

"Not this trip. To be honest, the Boss has been too busy getting the other aspects of this war sorted out. Hey, how come we haven't hit a red light since we left the airport?"

"Car's equipped with a gizmo that turns the lights to green as we approach them. All Royal Garage cars have one. Can't have Her Majesty waiting at traffic lights.

"I want one for my Ferrari."

"Sorry Igrat. It's illegal to have one installed on anything other than a Royal vehicle." Heather made a mental note to have all the cars in the Royal Garage checked when Igrat left to make sure they still had their traffic light override system. She had an uncomfortable feeling that the check would show one was missing.

St Georges Hall, Windsor Castle

Heather Watson paid her respects to the Queen then stepped unobtrusively to one side. A part of her rather maliciously expected to see Igrat slapped down by the Queen who was known for her dislike of vulgarity. As a matter of fact, Heather felt slightly guilty about the malice but knew she was not alone in that. Igrat had many male friends but very few women liked or trusted her. Outside the confines of her immediate circle, feelings towards her ran from mild distaste to outright loathing. It didn't occur to Heather that a womans' instinctive dislike for Igrat was inversely proportional to how well she knew her.

To Heather's surprise, the woman who followed her through the doors of St George's Hall was quite different from the flamboyant figure she'd met at Heathrow airport. It wasn't the clothes or the jewelry, both of which were unchanged, but the bearing. Somehow, at some point in the walk from the car to the Hall, Igrat had picked up the persona of a princess. She approached the throne and made a formal curtsey, dipping her head in the prescribed manner as she did so. "Your Majesty does me great honor."

"Welcome to Windsor. You have material to deliver to us?"

"Communications intercepts and satellite imagery, Your Majesty." Igrat hesitated. "I am commanded to place them in the hands of the Prime Minister or Minister of Defence only."

"And you always obey your commands to the letter." The Queen spoke approvingly. "When you were selected as a courier, your employer picked well. Proceed with the meeting."

157

"Prime Minister? I have words that go with the material in the case." Igrat's voice adopted the flat tones of The Seer. "The C-133Bs taken out of storage in Arizona have been delivered to the Canadian Air Force on lease. By a clerical error on our part, the agreement was back-dated a year. We have heard from the Government of Uruguay. They have offered to provide neutral ground for the detention of prisoners of war and the treatment of the wounded."

"Aren't they afraid that Galtieri will attack them? Uruguay has been the subject of Argentine ambitions for many years." The Foreign Secretary sounded concerned. If this war started to expand, its end would be explosive.

"No, Sir. They have a powerful and very supportive Uncle." A ripple of amusement went around the room. "The Uruguayan Navy is painting a naval transport in hospital ship colors so that they can collect the prisoners and wounded but they require the agreement of both sides that the ship's immunity will be respected and that any prisoners taken will be submitted to their care."

"That could be a great burden for a small nation." Prime Minister Newton was thoughtful. "Certainly we agree to their proposal and will announce our declaration to that effect immediately."

"The United States has agreed to reimburse Uruguay for the costs it will incur. In the interests of peace and international amity of course. I am also tasked to request whether Her Majesty's Government will be declaring a combat zone around the Falkland Islands and South Georgia."

Newton nodded. "Two hundred nautical miles around each, the two circles joined to form an oval. Any hostile ship in that region will be attacked and sunk. Please tell The Seer that we already have nuclear-powered submarines in that area to enforce that declaration. Ships outside that area may be attacked but only if their operations appear to be posing a direct threat."

Igrat nodded, her eyes almost blank as she mentally recorded the message. Then she clicked back to the meeting. "General Dyess, the new Commander of SAC, has included a message with the imagery we have included in this package. He says that we did an SR-71 overflight of the combat area late last night. It appears that organized resistance on both South Georgia and the Falkland Islands has ceased and Argentine forces had surrounded the Governor's house. We expect that he will have surrendered formally by the time this meeting is held."

"The last communication we had from the Governor was that his house was in process of being surrounded. No word since then." The Foreign Secretary spoke grimly. As a non-military man, he had entertained hopes that the reinforced garrison might actually have held out against the Argentine onslaught.

"We also have a communications intercept from one of the Argentine destroyers. She reports having sunk HMS *Mermaid* and picked up the survivors. She included a long list of those she had picked up. The message was transmitted in clear and on international distress frequencies. The presumption at the National Reconnaissance Office is that we were intended to intercept that message and that your people might do well to ponder upon its implications." Igrat dropped her facsimile of The Seer's voice and reverted to her own. "Those are all the words I am carrying."

"We will retire now and allow you to continue with your deliberations undisturbed." The Queen paused for a second. "Igrat, you have received your appointment as a temporary Royal Courier?"

"I have indeed, Your Majesty, and am honored by the confidence shown in me."

"Deserved by all reports. But tell us, if you were to receive orders from us that contradicted those given to you by The Seer, who would you obey?"

"The Seer of course, Your Majesty."

"And why is that?"

"Because he is my father."

"And as a hereditary monarch, we cannot disagree with you there. Igrat, would you take a very late high tea with us?"

"It would be an honor, Your Majesty."

Heather watched the Queen leave with Igrat in tow. "Well, that was a surprise." She thought she had said the words under her breath, but she realized that Henry McCarty had overheard her.

"That Igrat didn't get squelched?" McCarty was amused. Not just that Heather had been disappointed, but that British security had slipped up. They'd taken his Colt revolvers and Achillea's Model 50 pistol plus all three of her knives. They'd even had to walk through a metal detector afterwards. For all that, they'd missed the tiny knife hidden in Igrat's hair. When metal detectors had started becoming commonplace, she'd replaced the tiny metal knife she'd carried for so long with one of the new ceramic blades. It was no bigger than her old knife but was wickedly sharp. Just touching the blade could cause it to slice deep into a careless finger. In this case, it was a harmless lapse. McCarty was in two minds over whether to tip off the security people to the loophole.

"Heather, Igrat is a chameleon. She adapts to whatever the circumstances around her demand. On the street, she's a street-girl; in a Royal Palace, she's a princess. She doesn't do it deliberately. It just happens. Just like a chameleon."

"So what is she really like? When she is in private and just herself?" Heather Watson was confused by the change.

"I don't know. I think Igrat's original personality was shattered at an early age and has never put itself back together again. Her childhood was the sort of nightmare we can only imagine. Subconsciously, she created whatever personalities she needed to protect herself. Even after The Seer found and adopted her, the pattern continued. I don't think even Igrat knows who she really is or what she might have been like under normal circumstances."

Field Exploration Camp, Penguin River, South Georgia

Georgina Harcourt moved slightly in the rocks and scanned again with her binoculars. She and Cynthia had changed a lot since the Marines had arrived to protect them. Their bright orange high-visibility clothes had been put away. Now they wore white and gray camouflaged overalls. Instead of walking around openly, they now kept down, moved carefully and kept in the rocks as much as they could. Behind her, their hut had changed as well. Rocks had been placed around and on top of it to break up its outline. It had been painted to match the blend of white snow and gray rocks that surrounded it. It was very hard to see but that posed dangers all of its own. She very much doubted whether she would be able to find it again if she got lost.

She jumped as a hand touched her foot. It was one of the Marines, the one the others called Jocko. Keeping noise to a minimum was another lesson that had been absorbed over the last few days. It was in a near-whisper that Jocko asked her what was happening.

"Nothing now. It's all gone quiet down there." Her voice matched his. "After all that gunfire earlier, everything is quiet now. There's two big ships out to sea, though."

She handed the night vision binoculars over to the Marine and he stared out to where she had indicated. "Destroyers, Georgy, big ones. They're probably waiting for dawn to come in. I wouldn't want to bring a big ship in here at night."

"Any word from your Captain, Jocko?"

"None. No word at all. We don't think he and the rest of the boys got out of Grytviken. They didn't expect to, that's for sure."

"That's terrible."

"Comes with the job description, Georgy. Comes a time when taking down a decent honor guard is the only way left to go. Anyway, enough of that. Meal's ready."

The two slid back off the rocky rim and made their way back into the hut. Once inside, the smell of a hot meal was a delight to Georgy. There had been a strong wind blowing that night, so Sergeant Miller had taken the chance of cooking a hot meal for the group. The wind would disperse the smell and not lead any Argentine search parties this way. Previously, the air had been too still and the group had made do with cold food.

"Ohh, this is nice." Georgina climbed out of her cold-weather equipment and hastened over to the table. There was a filet of meat with onion gravy and some vegetables on her plate. The meat was a bit fatty, tough and had a fishy flavor. It was still a relief from the canned meat they'd eaten cold.

"Made a pudding as well, Ma'am. A nice jam rolypoly. Even got some custard made from powdered milk and flour.

"Dusty, you'll make a marvelous husband for some lucky lady some day. You know my father's got oodles of land everywhere, don't you?" Cynthia fluttered her eyelashes at him and inserted a hopeful note into the banter. While she did so, two of the Marines slipped out and took over guard duty.

"Already spoken for, Ma'am. And three kids." Miller went over to the radio set up in one corner. Earlier, he had recorded a situation report that included as much information as he knew on the battle at Grytviken. That message had been run through a system that compressed it into a single burst of less than a second. Once the schedule came up, that burst would be transmitted on a tight beam to a satellite and then rebroadcast to London. There, it would be decompressed and taken to the war room in Downing Street and its equivalent in St George's Hall.

Outside there was a sudden uproar from the penguins. The marines tensed but the two women remained calm. "It's just the penguins. They do that now and then when the weather is bad. We think it's a way of encouraging them all to huddle closer together against the cold. Sometimes it's a lot worse, there are a hundred thousand Emperor Penguins out there you know.

Sergeant Miller looked at his plate and grinned. *Ninety nine thousand, nine hundred and ninety nine,* he said to himself.

King Edward Point, South Georgia

Captain Alberto Astrid strode down the gangplank joining the destroyer *Catamarca* to the shore in the foulest of tempers. His head throbbed and there was a lump the size of a pigeon's egg over his right ear. He knew what had caused it; a flashlight swung with considerable force. Oh, he would never be able to prove it. The official story was that he had lost his footing on the deck as a result of inordinately rough seas and the concussion of the guns firing. In doing so, his head had struck some overhead ducting hard enough to render him unconscious. That's what all the bridge crew had said anyway. Astrid knew what had happened. The ship's Master at Arms had a family; one that doubtless contained female relatives. He contented himself with the promise that they would be pulled in and would disappear. One day, then, the Master at Arms would get a film of how they had died. Then he could live with the results of his action.

The quay at King Edward Point was chaotic. It was barely large enough to accommodate the *Catamarca*, forcing the *La Plata* to anchor in mid-bay. Over by Grytviken, the frigate *Punta Alta* was moored at a quay but was listing badly. She was blackened and battered, her forward gun obviously knocked out of action. The town behind her wasn't in particularly good shape either. Rapid-fire naval guns at close range tended to do that. The transport *Bahia Thetis* and the other frigate were also anchored in mid-bay.

The Marines landed from the *Bahia Thetis* were working their way through Grytviken, securing the buildings and trying to find the bodies of the men who had shot up the *Punta Alta*. So far, six bodies in British uniform had been located. It seemed incredible that just six men could have created the destruction that had scarred *Punta Alta* so cruelly. But, six men were all that could be found. The search had to be completed, but it seemed unlikely that there would be any more.

The bodies of the dead Marines were not the only things the Argentine search teams had found. Three civilians had been found in the town. Just three. Two were in

Grytviken itself and they'd been quite honest about what had happened. Some Marines had come to evacuate them. The ship that was supposed to take them away had never arrived, so the civilians had evacuated inland while the Marines stayed to fight. The third man was at King Edward Point. He had also told of how the civilians had left to go inland. Asked why he had stayed, he had replied that he was the Queen's Postmaster and he would not abandon his post office. That had rather impressed the Argentine Marines and they had treated him quite cordially.

The news that the civilians had gone inland had not pleased Astrid. His swimmer-commando unit had been supposed to prevent that from happening, but they had failed to be in position on time. He'd heard the story without much sympathy. A fuelling accident had knocked out two of the sno-cats. Then a trail had been blocked by an avalanche; another cut by a recently-opened crevasse. He hadn't accepted any of the excuses and made it quite clear that the unit commander would answer for his failure. The maneuvering necessary to ensure that the man on the spot suffered without any blame transferring to Astrid was one of the things that had led to his present ill-humor.

Astrid's attention was drawn by a large pile of ashes in the middle of the quay. It was already spreading as the debris was blown around by the steady wind,. The core of what had obviously been a substantial fire was distinct and still slightly warm. He looked at this curiously. "What was here?"

"The Queen's mail. Burned to prevent its capture." The voice was slightly high-pitched and querulous.

"And who are you?"

"James Walsingham, I'm the Postmaster here and, in the absence of the appointed Commissioner, in charge of this settlement."

Astrid stared at the man. He knew the Commissioner wasn't here. The man had been taken away and quietly dropped into the sea like so many others whose continued existence the swimmer-commando units had found inconvenient. "Take off your hat when you speak to an Argentine officer."

"I am the Queen's Postmaster and I will not bow down to you. . . . Sir." The late timing of the word 'sir' was a masterpiece.

Astrid's face flared bright red. He took one pace forward and swung his fist, knocking Walsingham's hat off. The Postmaster caught it as it fell and he rammed it back on his head, his jaw thrust out pugnaciously. Walsingham himself wasn't quite sure why he was making an issue of the point. He did know he'd been pushed around and ridiculed for days and it was going to stop.

Astrid couldn't believe it. *Who was this pathetic man to defy him?* He swung his hand again, this time not just striking the Postmaster but removing the hat from his head. The trilby clutched in his hand, Astrid strode to the quayside and threw the hat into the water. It spun through the air, struck the side of the *Catamarca* and fell into the sea. As it did so, Astrid caught the ripple of derision from the ship and the Marines. He knew it was aimed at him.

As he turned around, he saw that Walsingham had a handkerchief in his hands and his fingers were working quickly. He took one step towards the Postmaster and then stopped in surprise. Walsingham had tied four knots, one in each corner of his handkerchief. Now he defiantly rammed it on to his head. It was a very poor imitation of a hat, but the act was symbolic and everybody knew it. He stood there, handkerchief on his head and a supercilious grin on his face. Another ripple of laughter went across the side of *Catamarca*, mixed with applause and even a few cheers. This time, Astrid knew that the sounds were certainly not directed at him. One of the Marines even gave the Postmaster a quick salute.

That pushed Astrid over the edge. His face brilliant crimson with rage, he stepped forward and swung his foot in a savage arc. The kick caught Walsingham squarely in the groin. The man dropped to his knees with a howl of pain. He crouched down, rocking from side to side and clutching himself. Astrid took a single pace forward so he was standing over his victim. Then he drew his pistol and shot Walsingham in the back of the head. The Postmaster lurched forward and fell; his head surrounded by a spreading pool of crimson blood.

For a second, there was a stunned silence. Then a tide of rage spread from the ships and the Marines. Several of the latter started forward in fury at the murder, only to be restrained by the more realistic of their comrades. It was not the time or the place to start a fight with Astrid and his men. Anyway, all the Marines had family back in Argentina. Up on the ship, a hiss of sheer rage spread all along the decks, mixed with cat-calls and derisive whistles. Amidst it all, the ship's siren sounded a long blast; a tribute to the cantankerous, officious man who now lay dead on the quayside.

Bridge, ARA Catamarca, *King Edward Point, South Georgia*

"That was murder. Pure, cold-blooded murder." Commander Michael Blaise was white-faced with shock and his voice was strained with fury. He'd been born too late to experience the Occupation and that meant he'd never seen a man summarily executed before.

"I will not argue that." Captain Leonardi knew that such things were commonplace when the swimmer-commando units were around. *This and much more.* "Commander, I will ask you to do me a kindness. Please write up what you have just seen, in your own words, over your signature. When you have done so, I will insert it in my ship's log along with my account of that brutal act. It will be a first step, just a first step, but one I hope that, one day, it will bring that monster to justice."

Blaise was silent, staring at the pathetic body stretched out on the quayside. Astrid was walking way, down the quay towards some buildings at the extreme end of the settlement. *If I was you, I would be seriously worried about an 'accidental discharge' at this point* Blaise thought.

Quietly, a group of sailors from the destroyer made their way down the gangplank and placed the body on a stretcher. As they returned with it, Blaise heard the distinctive sound of it being "piped" on board.

"We will bury him at sea." Leonardi spoke quietly. "With full honors, as befits a courageous man."

Governor's House. Port Stanley, Falklands Islands

"Just blow the building down and have done with it." Major Patricio Dowling yelled the words at the slab-sided LVTP-7 amtrack.

Inside, Major Facundo Caceres raised his eyebrows in mock-comic despair. He was tired, dirty and wanted to get this job finished with the minimum of problems. He was also growing increasingly exasperated with the military police major outside who was emitting sounds that sounded suspiciously like a cow giving birth. It hadn't escaped his notice that while his men had come ashore loaded down with weapons and ammunition, Dowling had arrived carrying a list of local islanders who were believed to be particularly anti-Argentine. He sighed wearily and climbed back up into the cupola of his amtrack.

"You said something Major?"

"I said, just blow the building down and have done with it." Caceres lifted an eyebrow, forcing a reluctant "Sir" out of Dowling Despite their equivalent rank, Caceres had seniority; a lot of it.

Caceres had what was left of his command, his three M92s and seven LVTP-7s, lined up in front of the Governor's mansion. He deliberately had left the back way open. The occupants could escape if they wished. The battle for the island was over and there was no point in anybody else getting killed. If the defenders wanted to leave, they could.

"I don't think so, Major. It's a pretty building and our Governor will want to stay there when he arrives. Anyway, it's got the only long-range communication system on the Island. He'll need that to speak with Buenos Aires."

Dowling growled and stomped away. As he did so, there was a bang from inside the Governor's mansion. It was followed by a whine as the bullet bounced off the armor of an amtrack.

"Have they hit anybody yet?" Caceres wanted that information immediately. It would have a profound effect on how he handled the situation.

"No, Sir. They're not trying to. I think there's four men with rifles in there and somebody with a pistol."

"That'll be the Governor." Caceres was thinking over his options. "Is there anything behind the house?"

"Only scrub, Sir. If there is anybody up there, it'll be plain bad luck on their part."

"Then fire a burst from a .50 over the house. Short burst, we don't want to waste ammunition." The cupola-mounted machine gun on one of the amtracks snapped out a quick burst, the tracers just clearing the roofline. "Mount up, we'll take the amtracks over the circular lawn up to the flower bed that divides it from the rectangular one. If anybody fires a shot, fire a burst over the house. If they hit somebody, then we take the gloves off. Spray the windows before taking the house by storm. But, I want to avoid that and talk these people out. Understood?"

164

"Yes, Sir." The amtracks lurched as the Marines bordered them, then the bulky vehicles moved forward. The flower garden surrounding the circular lawn was crushed and the grass itself ruined by the tracked vehicles. By the time the LVTP-7s had stopped, they were barely twenty meters from the house. Dowling was nowhere to be seen, which didn't surprise Caceres in the slightest.

"Governor, the position here is hopeless. Your Marines have surrendered and are being well cared for. There is no organized opposition on the island so please, lay down your arms. Further loss of life will be quite pointless."

"I am not authorized to surrender my post except under duress." The call came from inside the house and was quite indignant.

Caceres grinned to himself. He could understand the Governor's position easily. "Governor, I have three M92 tanks, each with a 76mm high-velocity gun. Using them, I could chop out the ground floor of the house, causing it to collapse on those inside. You have no anti-tank weapons and have no way of stopping me from doing just that."

"Ah." There was a long pause. "That is, of course, different. My people here will be well-treated?"

"You and your staff will be transported aboard our cruiser to meet with a Uruguayan ship. You will be held in neutral territory until this . . . . this matter . . . . is concluded. Along with the survivors of your Marine garrison and from HMS *Mermaid*"

"Very well. We will come out."

Governor Hunt left the mansion with his wife beside him. He walked up to Caceres and handed over his pistol, an antique .455 Webley. Caceres took it, broke the action open and dropped the rounds on the grass. Three had been fired; there were three left. "You want to keep those rounds of ammunition Major. They're the real thing from before the First World War. We found the pistol and a box of ammo in the safe. It will be a good memento for your family."

"Thank you, Governor, and thank you for not making me fire upon your house."

"Well, it wouldn't have done any good, would it? I told my people to be sure nobody got hurt. But we had to put up a good show."

Caceres took the Governor and his entourage to an amtrack and saw them on board. Behind him, one of his Marines had picked up the discarded cartridges and brass. They would be given to Caceres later. Caceres himself was thoughtful. According to the plan, this affair was all over. The islands were back under Argentine control; the British would accept it. Only, he had a nasty feeling that this was where the whole plan was about to become unstuck.

Goofer's Gallery, HMS Furious, *Atlantic*

"Glory is in position. We've got our full escort now." The voice came from behind Mullback. He was enjoying a few minutes of peace on the Goofers Gallery before heading down to the ready room. He could see HMS *Glorious* just over a mile away,

165

running parallel with *Furious*. The destroyers were further out: six of the G-class ships. He took another look at her then turned around. *Heaven be praised, another Lieutenant Commander*. Not one he knew though.

"Hi. Mullback, Ernest Mullback."

"Ah yes, I saw your wedding pictures in the papers. A Banana driver, aren't you?"

"That I am for my sins."

"Sea Mirage F2 here. Name's Pope by the way, Nigel Pope. We just got on board."

"Ah yes, the extra fighter detachment. Good to have you along. Have they found you a home yet?"

"Not yet, CAG was muttering about having us sleep in your bomb bay last I heard."

"Attention all hands. Darken ship. Say again, darken ship." The announcement came over the loudspeakers with a tangible urgency.

"We'd better get inside." The two pilots left the island wing and made certain the hatch was dogged tight and the blackout curtain in place. "The brass are deadly serious about this aren't they?"

"You can say that again. The amphibs are thumping along behind us and the cruiser squadron's out there, well, somewhere. We're all supposed to be meeting at Ascension Island in ten days time." Mullback shook his head. "And do we have some sorting out to do first. By the end of the day, we were just throwing stuff into piles instead of stowing it. If it hadn't been for the rotodynes, we'd never have got it all on board."

"Or got it all off." Pope spoke carefully.

"Sorry?"

"Our nukes. They've all gone. The Faireys took them on their return trips. Not a nuke in the fleet so I've heard. Septics put their foot down, so people say. Made some blood-curdling threats so everybody thought we'd be better off without them on board. Now, what's on the Mess menu tonight . . . . . Ahh, sausages."

Field Exploration Camp, Penguin River, South Georgia

"Two destroyers, two frigates, one transport." Sergeant Miller spoke the words quietly to himself as he wrote down the status report. The Field Exploration Camp had proved remarkably well-sited as an observation point. The hut itself was tucked in a dip and had no direct line of sight from the bay around Grytviken. However, a few minutes scramble in the rocks allowed a watcher to gain an almost perfect view of the settlement. Even better, it was close enough to allow infra-red binoculars to see the heat pictures of the ships. That gave a good indication of their operational status.

166

The three ships anchored in the bay were cold and dark. Oh, there were traces of green that probably indicated moored power provided by a donkey boiler or diesel generator but their main machinery spaces were definitely not working. In the case of the frigate that would make little difference. The ship was diesel-powered and could get under way very quickly. The destroyer and the transport were steam-powered. It would take both ships time to get up steam and move out. That was a point worth including in his report.

Miller turned his attention to the other destroyer, the one anchored alongside at King Edward Point. Her engine rooms showed a dull green that indicated she was in the process of raising steam. Why was a good guess, but she looked as if the plan was for her to leave at dawn. *Well, that made sense.* The remaining ship was the damaged frigate alongside at Grytviken. Miller looked at her carefully, trying to assess how much work was being done to her. Quietly, he was proud of the job Hooper and the rest of the boys had done on her. They'd shot her up a real treat. They'd paid for it though. He hadn't had any word from his captain but by the way the Argies had raked the town with gunfire, they hadn't stood much of a chance.

Suddenly his binoculars showed a shower of brilliant white up by the funnel. Miller recognized the characteristic signature of a welding torch. Obviously, work was being done on the frigate, probably patching her up so she could head back for Argentina and a proper repair yard. He looked at the frigate more carefully. There was some additional evidence of work being done on her. The hangar looked slightly green, suggesting warmth there. Perhaps that was the workshop where the repairs were being supported? Miller noted down the efforts at repairs and slid out of his watch position. Time to get back inside and into the warm.

Inside the hut, a cup of cocoa was waiting for him. He drank it down, feeling the warmth spreading through his chilled body. A cup of cocoa was a prize for those who had to stay outside on guard; one that was valued for its morale as well as its warming effects. Miller had been expecting his men to assume all the burdens of protecting the two women in this isolated research station. He had been pleasantly surprised when the girls had insisted on taking their turns. It had made organizing a guard roster so much easier.

A rumbling explosion shook the hut taking him completely by surprise. He pushed through the blackout curtain and the door, then ran back up to the rim of the dip. Snow had already drifted to fill the patch where he had been laying just a few minutes earlier. He also saw a red glow from over the rockline that hinted of a serious fire somewhere. When he was back in his watch position, he didn't need his binoculars to see where that fire was. It was alongside at Grytviken. The frigate Greg Hooper and his boys had shot up was blazing, her stern enveloped in an orange ball of fire. It was too far away for Miller to see what the Argies were doing about it, but from the look of this fire, they had to be in a terminal nausea about fighting it.

ARA Punta Alta *Grytviken Harbor, South Georgia*

The *Punta Alta* was in a sorry state. Bullets had torn through the thin aluminum plating of the superstructure, disfiguring what Sub-Officer First Class Lucas Fernández regarded as the most beautiful ship afloat. He was a fair enough man to admit that he was prejudiced in the matter. He had been a plank-owner on *Punta Alta* when he had been a lowly seaman and had returned to her as an exalted Sub-Officer First Class a year ago. Tonight, he was in charge of the ship's guard, responsible for maintaining the watch in a port that he still regarded as hostile. To a true sailorman with long experience of foreign ports, each had a character of its own. Some were friendly, some neutral, some hostile. Some harbors seemed to welcome visitors in and sorry to see them leave. Others exuded an air of resentment that others had dared to interrupt their slumber. Some were peaceful, others threatening. This one was hostile. Fernández turned around and peered into the shadows that surrounded his ship. He had the uneasy, creeping sensation that he was being followed by unseen eyes. It was the port, of course. It was as unfriendly as any he had ever been in.

Shaking off the sensation that he was being watched, Fernández continued to pace his rounds on the main deck. He passed the 14-inch torpedo tubes that constituted the ship's primary anti-submarine armament and went aft to the hangar. The helicopter inside, an Agosta Panther, was too small for serious ASW work. Its primary role was spotting targets for the battery of four anti-ship missiles forward. There was always a slight smell of aviation fuel in this area; enough to tell a crewman that he was leaving the naval part of the ship and moving into flight crew territory. Still, the flight deck that filled the stern was useful for sports and exercises even if clearing it of foreign objects was a task that needed painstaking care. Then Fernández stopped. There always was a smell of aviation fuel here but tonight it seemed stronger than most.

Strong enough to need investigating. He opened the hatch into the compartments that formed the side of the hangar. The first one was for the general stores needed for the routine operations of flying the helicopter. The smell of fuel was much stronger here and Fernández was suddenly a very worried man. There was another hatch in front of him. He undogged it. Then, he stopped in sheer shock at what was in front of him.

The Panther was riddled with bullets. That wasn't surprising. The hangar was a big target and the fusillade of small arms it had taken would have damaged most things. Given time and a major maintenance facility, it could be repaired. Short of such capability, it was grounded. What had stunned him was that the deck of the hangar was swimming in aviation fuel, at least a centimeter deep. The smell was strong enough to make his eyes water. The only thing he could think of was that in the chaos of the battle, nobody had thought to defuel the ship's helicopter. Then, the damage from the rifle and machine gun fire had caused a fuel line to break or a fuel tank to fail and the whole helicopter-load of fuel had been spilled on the deck. It could only have happened a few minutes before. Whenever the failure had happened, it had produced a desperate emergency.

Fernández nearly slammed the fire alarm switch but he stopped himself just in time. All it needed here was one spark and the whole hangar deck would burn. He stepped out of the hangar, closing the hatch behind him. It was an agonizing choice. *Leave the hatches open so that at least some of the fuel vapor would disperse or close it so it wouldn't cause the vapor to spread within the ship?* He ran out on to the main deck and then forward to an emergency telephone that was clear of the deadly vapor building up in the hangar.

"Captain Torres Sir. It's Fernández. We have a major fuel leak in our hangar,. The deck is awash with the stuff."

"Dear God." Torres had sounded sleepy at first but the damage report woke him immediately. Fernández could hear his Captain coming to life on the other end of the telephone. "I ordered the helicopter defuelled."

"Sir, I went in the hangar myself. There's fuel everywhere. The scavenging system must have failed as well. Probably, it was damaged in the fight." The full enormity of the situation began to dawn on Fernández. The hangar had become a floating bomb, one that could quite easily destroy the ship. He heard the bang as the telephone was dropped and the ship's communications system sounded an alert. Then, he headed aft again, trying to work out the best way of dealing with the fuel flood without endangering the ship. In his mind was the lesson of the German aircraft carrier *Oswald Boelcke*. She had suffered a major fuel leak. One wrong move had spread the vapor through the ship. It had needed just one spark to set it off. When that happened, there had been no survivors. The only reason why anybody knew what had happened was the German Admiral in charge of the German carrier group had survived to tell the tale.

Just how in the name of God had this happened? Fernández asked himself over and over. There were a dozen reasons why things like this shouldn't happen. There were purging and draining systems built into the hangar itself. There were procedures laid down for defuelling and securing the ship's helicopters. Everybody knew that the helicopter had been badly damaged by gunfire, but nobody had reported a fuel leak of this magnitude. As his mind worried away at the questions, he was summoning the damage control teams and starting the process of making the hangar safe.

"Get the hangar door open." Torres cut in on the stream of orders. "Manually. Don't use the motors. All it will need is one spark in there. We've got to get the vapor out. What happened to the venting system?"

"It's not working, Sir." One of the seamen was unrolling firefighting hoses and had overheard the Captain's question. "The fans just won't start up. Electrician's mate is checking it now. He thinks rifle bullets must have cut the power cables somewhere."

"Pumps are out too." Another seaman cut in. "We've got no high pressure water."

"I've got portable generators on the way over, Sir." Fernández added. "They'll set up a bit forward, away from the worst of the vapor." He was interrupted by the rattle as some seamen began to work the emergency chain hoist that opened the hangar door. Once that was done, they could get rid of the accumulated fuel and fuel vapor in the hangar.

The damage control teams never got the chance. As soon as the hangar door started to roll upwards, there was an explosion. A flare of brilliant white light was quickly drowned out by the roaring fireball of a fuel-air explosion. The whole aft of the ship erupted into flame. The fire spread quickly as burning fuel flooded through bullet holes and opened hatches to engulf the compartments surrounding the aviation facilities. Fernández picked himself up from the deck, noting that it was already beginning to heat up with the intensity of the fires underneath. He didn't remember being thrown down by the blast but he knew that there was only a limited amount of time to prevent the fire taking hold.

"Wash the burning fuel over the side." He rapped out the orders while grabbing a hose and playing it on the fire that was already spreading along the aft superstructure. "Get the foam generators working."

The crew of the *Punta Alta* were already running to the scene of the fire. Captain Torres was assembling them into damage control teams as they arrived, but Fernández already had a bad feeling about the fire. It was spreading too fast, overcoming efforts to set a perimeter for the blaze. The hangar was already on the verge of collapsing as the heat melted the aluminum. Sickly, Fernández realized that the fire had to be claiming its first victims. The men who had tried to open the hangar door hadn't stood a chance. Others would be trapped below decks by the fire and would either be burned or asphyxiated according to their luck.

"Flood the magazine." Torres gave the order. The aft 76mm gun was mounted above and in front of the hangar. Its magazine was above the main deck and formed part of the aft superstructure. It wasn't safely buried in the lowest areas of the hull the way older ships were arranged. Already the fire had spread to surround the turret and had made the glass-fibre shield start bubbling and cracking with the heat.

"There's no water pressure!" The voice from the work gangs sounded almost desperate. Fernández knew why. The torpedo storage area was only a little bit forward of the aft 76mm magazine.When the latter cooked off it would take the former with it. Together, the two blasts would devastate *Punta Alta*. They would also massacre the crew if they were in the way.

"Order all the men to abandon ship." Torres gave the order with a sinking heart. Without water pressure to flood the magazines, they would explode. It was only a question of when. "Fire and rescue teams, we will fight the fire from dockside until the danger of explosion is past."

By which you mean, when everything that can explode has exploded. Fernández thought. He grabbed the shoulders of his damage control team and pushed them forward, away from the fires. The only way off the ship was either forward and around the bridge or over the side into the water. It was a measure of how fast the situation was deteriorating that he seriously considered the latter option. The bitter cold would be fatal in just a few minutes but it was a better choice than burning. Anything was better than being soaked in aviation fuel and turned into a living torch. He shuddered at the thought and tried to remove it from his mind. The first job was to save the ship. To do that, he had to save as many of the crew as possible.

He and his men had just made it past the 47mm mounts. They were shielded by the mount trunking when the aft magazine exploded. He saw the fire turn from red to white, saw the great trails of flame as the cartridges cooked off, then heard the rolling thunder of the explosion. The ship's masts and superstructure were silhouetted by the intense white glow for a few seconds, then the fire began to return to normal. Only for a few seconds. As Fernández had expected, the torpedo storage followed a few seconds later. This was more of an explosion, less of an enhanced fire. He saw the vicious arc of fragments, steel from the hull, aluminum from the superstructure, scythe into the water. When the blasts had subsided, he risked looking past the 47mm mounting. The aft of the ship was tangled wreckage but the fire was still spreading forward.

ARA Catamarca *Grytviken Harbor, South Georgia*

"Get under way now. All search and rescue teams ready; damage control parties to midships. Engine room, we will need every bit of power we can get. Use the emergency generators, everything. All power to the pumps when we're alongside *Punta Alta*." Captain Leonardi was pleased that his ship had originally been designed as a cruiser for the Italian Navy. She had been built to proper Navy standards with tight subdivision and proper

170

damage control facilities. That meant powerful pumps and strong hoses. For all their elegance, the Ushuaia class frigates were export designs. Their cost had been kept to a minimum. That meant the minimum standards had been applied to every part of their design.

Catamarca was still raising steam but she had enough power to ease away from her berth at King Edward and start crossing the bay to the inferno that marked the spot *Punta Alta* had been moored. Leonardi could feel the heat from the fire through the open hatch that led to his bridge wing. He honestly doubted whether she could be saved. Even with *Catamarca* lending her help and her pumps to the battle, the frigate was already far gone. The funnel was surrounded by fire and that meant the machinery spaces underneath were already compromised.

"Captain, permission to enter the bridge?" Blaise's voice cut through Leonardi's contemplation of the disaster that had struck so unexpectedly.

"Granted. Commander Blaise, this is not a good time."

"Sir, I would like to volunteer the services of my men to help treat the wounded off that frigate. We have our ship's poiso . . . . the ship's surgeon and all the crewmen are trained in first aid. We cannot help you fight the fire, but we can help save the wounded."

"Thank you, God knows, there will be enough wounded waiting for treatment." Leonardi winced as another explosion racked the burning frigate. The 47mm magazines? he thought. *If they were cooking off, then the ship was finished.* Then, he turned his mind to bringing the *Catamarca* alongside the *Punta Alta*. As soon as he had the ships close, the jets of water started to arch over the gap, pounding down at the fires.

"Captain, Sir, message from ashore. The crew of *Punta Alta* are trying to fight the fires from quayside. They ask you to try and sweep the fire aft, at least to try and keep the forecastle deck clear." The signals officer pushed the message into his Captain's hands, but his eyes were riveted on the scene where *Punta Alta* was dying.

Leonardi nodded. The frigate was already settling in the water. The sea hissed and steamed as *Punta Alta* sank deeper. Given the depths shown on the charts and size of the ship, he guessed she would sink to main deck level before coming to rest on the bottom. Whether she would ever move from there or be scrapped where she lay was entirely another matter.

There was another brilliant white flare as an additional section of superstructure collapsed. The sight made Leonardi shake his head sadly. Building the upperworks of a ship out of aluminum had seemed such a good idea when it had first been proposed. It saved weight and that was an important thing in a generation of ships that had their superstructures enlarged to carry modern radars while the introduction of gas turbines meant they had also lost the weight of boilers and steam turbines deep in the ship. Now, looking at the sight of *Punta Alta*, Leonardi was very glad that his *Catamarca* was solid steel.

The power of his hoses was driving the fires back a little, but in his heart, Leonardi knew that the task was hopeless. The fires had spread too far, too fast. All he was doing was buying time for the remainder of the crew to abandon the doomed warship.

Field Exploration Camp, Penguin River, South Georgia

Even from ten miles away, it was obvious that the Argentine frigate was finished. Night vision goggles weren't that useful any more. The intense light from the burning ship swamped the systems. It didn't matter, even normal binoculars showed enough detail to make it clear that she was sinking. The big destroyer from King Edward Point had pulled alongside her and was dousing her with water, but it was too little, too late. It was a gutsy thing to do, though. Miller saluted the unknown Argentine commander who had risked his ship to aid another.

It was useless. That frigate was doomed. She would burn for hours and her wreck would be too hot to enter for days. She would settle on the bottom and the jagged rocks would finish what was left of her structure. Miller shook his head and dug out the status report he had yet to send. Carefully, he amended it.

"Two destroyers, one frigate, one transport."

PART THREE

CORPORATE

CHAPTER ONE
STRIKING BACK

Darwin Road, Port Stanley, Falkland Islands

The fact it was obvious what had happened didn't make the sight any less mournful. The truck had careered off the road at the start of the acute right-hand bend and hit the line of rocks that marked the start of the dip to the peat march below. The impact with those rocks had ruptured its fuel tank and caused the wreckage to be soaked with diesel fuel. The truck had ended its ride down the slope with its nose in the peat. There, the spilled diesel had ignited. Somehow, it had caught fire.

That was a bit of a mystery right there. Diesel fuel wasn't supposed to burn like that. A mystery? Major Patricio Dowling sneered to himself at the suggestion. He was rapidly coming to the conclusion that petroleum-based fuels and the Argentine armed forces didn't mix very well. The three weeks that had elapsed since the invasion had been one long litany of accidents a good majority of which involved the negligent handling of fuel. Leaking fuel drums, ruptured pipelines, careless spills igniting; one incident after another. He looked up at the glowering bulk of Sapper's Hill that overlooked the scene of the wreck. It was strange how even the landscape here seemed to be hostile.

"Any survivors?" Dowling snarled the question at a mud-soaked soldier who was struggling up the slope with a litter. The sheet on it covered the burned corpse of a soldier. He'd been found a few meters from the main burn site.

"No, Sir. The peat marsh stopped the men on board running away from the wreck fast enough. They all got caught when the truck burst into flames. This one got the furthest, poor devil. All it did for him was make sure it took him a little longer to burn."

"The driver?"

"Still in the cab. Charred." The two soldiers with the litter hurried off, before the notorious Major Dowling could develop more of an interest in them.

That made it fourteen dead. The two men driving the truck and the twelve in the back. Useless conscripts. Dowling had opposed the withdrawal of the Marines from the island while there were still British Royal Marines on the loose. They had started a guerilla war in the inner regions of the island and were proving disturbingly good at it. The Army conscripts who had replaced the Marines weren't even in the same league. The rash of accidents wasn't helping. It seemed as soon as the Army tried to push beyond its established perimeters, their ability to drive safely fell apart. As a result, the Argentine forces hadn't even managed to push deep into the islands yet, let alone try and bring those areas under their control. With the exception of the big Air Force base at Goose Green and the armored units around Teal Inlet, the rest of East Falkland was still largely British.

"Your report?" Dowling snarled at the lieutenant who was scribbling notes on his pad.

"Routine accident, Sir. The driver hit the slope far too fast and lost control of the vehicle when he had to make the curve. He hit the rocks, rolled over and that was that. Going by the marks on the road, I'd guess he was doing at least 80 kilometers per hour when he started down. With the roads wet like this and all the mud, he'd had it from there."

Dowling nodded. It was the most likely explanation. Poor driving skills shown by an inadequately-trained conscript. Only this one had taken an entire patrol with him. He looked again at the burned-out wreck of the truck. If the survivors of the British Marines out in the hills weren't bad enough. Dowling was not a superstitious man, but he had suddenly had an uneasy feeling that there were ghosts on the island. Malignant, vengeful ghosts. He shook himself and angrily dismissed the thought before looking around for somebody to shout at. Above him, Sapper Hill glowered down.

Field Exploration Camp, Penguin River, South Georgia

What had started off as being something of an adventure had long ago turned into a frustrating and miserable endurance trial. Cynthia Paine-Williams hadn't been able to wash properly for almost two weeks. Her hair had been cut down to a short stubble and her make-up had run out over a week before. She didn't just look like a tramp; she was painfully aware that she smelled like one. The only consolation was that everybody else was in the same boat. There was another difference as well. She was carrying an L1 rifle and knew how to use it. As much as anybody could without actually firing it. She found the stubby 7mm bullpup rifle remarkably easy to carry. Of that, she was glad. Hiding out from the Argies wasn't a game after all; it was deadly serious.

She was the guard, watching the ground around them while Jocko ran his check on the port in the distance. The burned out frigate was still in its place, listing and half submerged with a small trawler-like merchant ship next to it. The big merchant ship was out in the middle of the bay with the other frigate and one of the very large destroyers anchored at Grytviken.

"The other destroyer's not back then?" She kept her voice down to a very low whisper.

"Nope, no sign of it. Been away two weeks now. She'd be back by now if she was coming. Right, the radar station is still up on the hill over King Edward Point. They haven't moved that yet." He paused for a second. "Now that's new."

"What we got?"

"They've taken the anti-ship missiles off that burned-out frigate and set them up as a shore battery."

"Where are they?"

Jocko handed her the binoculars and took over her job of scanning the hills for trouble. "See those long, red-roofed buildings on King Edward Point? Follow them across the water to the other shore. Now, up a touch and there they are. See them? Sort of buried in a square of rocks? That's called a revetment. Where they are, they can take down any ship that tries to come through the harbor entrance."

"That's awful. You'll tell London, won't you?"

"Of course, Cyn, but it's worse than you think. The position shows the Argies are working their way along this shore. Sooner or later, they'll look at this outcrop and think what a wonderful place it would be for an observation point."

"Oh." Suddenly, being on the island was even less of a game than it had been before. "How long do you think it'll be before they find us?"

"Depends on them really. We've had a pretty good run so far. They could start moving towards us any time. I just hope the Navy gets its finger out and gets us away from here."

Civilian Camp, Deep Inside South Georgia

"All I can say is, thank God for bureaucracy." Sergeant Harry Wharton spoke with fervor. The refuge was supposed to have been stocked with food to last ten people for ten days. Somehow, the paperwork had been fouled up. The food supply here was enough to last those ten people for one hundred days. It was a minimal diet for the climate and, oddly, most of it was Royal Navy survival rations that appeared to have been brought quite recently. Still, the food was better than nothing for there were fourteen people in the refuge; seven civilians, the two surviving SBS men from Grytviken and the five SBS who had been scouting Leith Harbor.

"Any word from Dusty over with the girls?" Wharton was *de facto* commander of the SBS unit survivors after Captain Hooper had been killed at Grytviken.

"Not directly, Sergeant, no. But the flash messages tell us something. Somebody's keeping a regular watch on Grytviken and if it isn't them, then who?"

"A good question indeed, Lofty. We can but hope the Argies can't do decent intercepts, or if they can, they can't read our codes. Because if they can, they'll have come to the same conclusion and they'll run some patrols along that coastline."

"Foot? Or helo?"

"Could be either. They've got a helo. The book says they had one each on the frigates and one on the transport. Greg got one before the Argies killed him; the other must

177

have burned out when the frigate blew up. So, they've got one left, probably a troop-carrying Puma. Bit surprising we haven't seen it looking for us yet."

"That's Argies being smart, I reckon. We're no threat to them out here. All they have to do is wait for our food to run out and we have to come in. They couldn't know supply cocked things up and left ten times as much food as we can eat."

"You're wrong there, old son. Us being here is damned important just as the others loose on East Falkland are important. As long as we're here, Blighty still has continuity of occupation and that's a big thing when determining sovereignty. The Argies might not have come to mop us up yet, but they will. You can bet your own private coalmine on that, Lofty my boy. They'll be coming out after us unless the Andrew turns up first."

HMS Furious, *Off South Georgia*

"And now, fellow Furies, we have a special request from our colleagues over in the *Grimy Glory*. It's that old Elvis Presley favorite

Are you lonesome tonight,
Do you miss me tonight?
Are you sorry we drifted apart?"

It was unlikely, Mullback thought, *that Glorious actually has made a special request for Furious's on-board 'radio' station.* The two carriers had separated days earlier and had been maintaining absolute radio silence ever since. *Furious* had been pounding south as fast as her aging engines would allow, bringing her air group to support the amphibious assault force that was to recapture South Georgia. Or, as the ship's orders were dogmatic in phrasing it, 'to relieve the forces holding out in South Georgia and defeat the Argentine invading forces'. The fact that, as far as anybody knew, the forces holding out in South Georgia were five SBS men and two civilian women was a matter of supreme unconcern to anybody. International law had been swallowing elephants and straining at gnats for centuries.

Mullback opened a hatch, stepped through and dogged it behind him. Maintaining watertight integrity was a real pain, but nobody knew where the Argentine submarines were or what orders they might have. Knocking out one of the two available carriers at this early stage in the game would be a crippling blow. *Courageous* was working up in the UK after coming out of her accelerated refit, but it would be at least two weeks before she set sail south to join her sisters. That was too long and the brief campaigning season would be close to gone by then. So, the carriers were maintaining watertight integrity and radio silence. They were also thoroughly blacked out.

"Hi Jerry. What's come over the radio people? Putting that blasted septic dirge on. Now, a quick blast of the pipes, that's what we need at a time like this."

The problem, Mullback reflected, *is that Alasdair is right. A quick blast of martial music from the pipes would have gone down well right now.* "Aye, you're Jock. Presley was never the same after he did his stint in SAC. I think the high altitude ruined his vocal chords."

178

"Nah, it was spending all that time going around backwards. Bound to affect a man's sense of values."

Baillie and Mullback both nodded wisely at that. Elvis Presley had spent a much-publicized three-year tour of duty in SAC, technically as the rear-gunner on an RB-52. In fact they both knew full well that the tail gunner on an RB-52 did not sit in the tail, but they had also noted how the star seemed to have spent most of his time on public relations opportunities. That could affect a man's sense of values as well.

Another hatch, this one to the pilot's briefing room. Mullback stepped in and heard Baillie dogging the door behind him. A number of the pilots were already in their places. The two Buccaneer drivers joined them. A quick count showed that this was a big raid; there were twelve Buccaneer crews and four Sea Mirage F.2 pilots waiting to find out what was happening. The final attendees appeared and the hatch was dogged shut again.

"Welcome to this briefing, gentlemen." Commander Frances looked at the assembled group. "I am pleased to inform you that the target for tomorrow morning is the Argentine invasion force currently in Grytviken. This strike will be the opening act in Operation Parakeet, the relief of the forces currently holding out in South Georgia."

Frances threw back the sheet that was covering the map that dominated his end of the briefing room. "There are three primary targets. First will be the radar station here above King Edward Point. This will be the target for the first formation of Buccaneers. They will be flown by our four guests from the Yeovilton Operational Conversion Unit flying aircraft armed with ARMAT anti-radar missiles and 1,000 pound retarded bombs.

"Second formation will consist of Mullback, Baillie, Johnson and Canfield. You are the four highest-scoring Highball crews in the air group. There are three ships in the bay. A frigate here, a destroyer behind her and a transport in the middle. Mullback, you take the destroyer, Baillie, you get the frigate. Whatever you do, don't hit the frigate at the front of the line. She caught fire and is a burned-out wreck.. Johnson, you take the transport. Canfield, you hang back and if anything goes wrong with the first three, fill in the gap.

"Third formation will consist of Carter, Kingsman, Williams and Tweed. Your aircraft will be armed with eight one thousand pound retarded bombs each. Your target is this battery of anti-ship missiles here. They'll be hard to see and even harder to hit but you'll have to do your best. I suggest you attack in two waves so that the second group can correct for any errors made by the first. That way, if the first wave gets the missiles, the second pair can bomb targets of opportunity.

"You'll be escorted by four Mirages. Pilots Adams, Pickering, Hawkings and Snell. We don't anticipate any hostile aircraft, but you'll be there and loaded for bear just in case. Three radar homers and four heat-seekers each. There is reported to be a single Argentine helicopter in South Georgia. If you see it flying, discourage it from doing so again. If you spot it on the ground, make sure it stays there.

"We have detailed maps and the latest photographs available. Each team will inspect them and make up their attack plans accordingly. Any questions?"

"Flak, Sir?"

179

"Off the ships. Assuming they're alongside and the destruction of the radar station gives them warning, count of three twin 47mms under radar control. We know of no missiles there. The infantry may have some shoulder-fired stuff, but that's all."

Baillie stuck his hand up. "Sir, what about the rest of the aircraft on board?"

"We'll be holding eight Mirage F2s for combat air patrol. The remaining four Mirages and four Bananas will be maintained as an emergency anti-shipping strike. If they are available that is. If any of the other aircraft are unserviceable, we'll draw down on them to keep the strike groups up to strength. As far as we know, there's nothing dangerous around here and we have *Glorious* to the west between us and the Argentine Navy. She's our long range screen for this operation."

"What happens after we've bombed the place, Sir?" Kingsman sounded slightly nervous.

"That doesn't really concern you but you can assume there will be a follow up to your operation. One thing; if any of your aircraft are hit, try to get them back here where we can fix them. We're desperately short of aircraft as you know. If you are shot down, escape and evade, we will come and pick you up. Any more questions?"

A general negative mumble travelled around the room. Frances looked around the room. "Very well gentlemen; get a good night's sleep. We launch at dawn."

The Caledonian Club, Belgravia, London, UK

"I'm sorry Madam, but ladies are only allowed in the dining room as a guest of a member."

Igrat looked at the Club Steward and was severely tempted to be outrageous. However, she was a guest here and that meant she had obligations to her host. One of them was not to embarrass him. Also, the poor steward was only doing his job and she had an instinctive sympathy for those at the bottom of the social heap who had to do the dirty work for those at the top. So, Igrat gave him a friendly smile. "I am sorry, I should have introduced myself. My name is Igrat Shafrid and I am a guest of Sir Robert Byrnes."

"Thank you, Madam." The steward privately breathed a sigh of relief and checked a book on a podium by the door to the members area of the club. "Miss Shafrid, of course. Sir Robert has you listed as his guest for dinner this evening. If you would like to take a seat, Madam, Sir Robert will be down to escort you momentarily. Actually, my apologies, Madam. Sir Robert is here now. Enjoy your evening with us."

"Prompt to the minute, Igrat. T'is a rare virtue these days. Welcome to the Caledonian Club."

"Sir Robert, thank you for the invitation."

"Please Igrat, call me Robbie. It's a great joke here at the Burns Night supper." The two exchanged grins at the shared private joke-within-a-joke. "With your permission, I'll escort ye in to the Bar and Restaurant. Would ye like a drink before dinner? We have the finest selection of single malts in Britain here."

Byrnes circumspectly eyed Igrat. When he'd issued the invitation, he'd sent her some information on the club and hoped she'd read the bit on the dress code. She obviously had. She was wearing an Italian designer black watered silk suit and white blouse, both discretely expensive and in perfect taste. Her outfit was an ideal complement to his own evening suit. What he hadn't expected was how small she was. He guessed she was only an inch or two over five feet. She was hiding it with the stiletto heels she was wearing, but somehow he'd expected her to be taller.

"You're most kind. I would greatly enjoy a single malt, Robbie."

"Then let us awa' to the Bar where the product of many years of skilled industry await our pleasure." He took her arm and led her through the double doors and towards the bar. "Now, what would ye wish to try? We do offer a Highland Tour, distillery by distillery, but I would na recommend it."

Twenty minutes later, they were sitting at their table with Igrat trying to understand a menu that appeared to be written in some unknown tongue. In the end, she gave up and decided to take a chance. "Robbie, this place is wonderful. How long have you been a member here?"

"About twenty years or so." He dropped his voice slightly. "To have a good gentlemen's club is a problem for us ye know. Times are when I think we should start our own."

"Well, you can help a girl out then. What do you recommend?"

Byrnes laughed. "If ye like really strong flavors, then the Arbroath Smokie pate with a horseradish dressing is very fine. To follow, the carving table here is without equal. I'd recommend the venison. They serve it with a juniper berry and whisky sauce that ye won't find bettered anywhere I know of."

"That sounds perfect, I'll have that please. A carving table, they'll have somebody to do the carving I suppose."

"They do," Byrnes dropped his voice again. "But I heard ye were an artiste with a knife."

Igrat dropped her voice to match. "I am, especially close in, at body-contact range. Although Achillea is the one who is a real bladeswoman under any conditions. But those are skills we both prefer to keep well concealed."

"Aye. With ye it would be a shock I warrant. But one look at Achillea, and a wise man feels a chill run down his spine. There's no soul behind those eyes. Where are your friends by the way?"

"Around. Events like this, they stay in the background but they're around." Igrat hesitated and then was relieved to see the waiter approaching . "Ohh, look, my broached smoky is coming."

"Arbroath smokie. It's a very special kind of smoked haddock. I did warn ye it was strongly flavored."

"You did, Robbie, and you weren't joking. This reminds me of way back when, times when smoked fish was the only kind we had."

"Aye, smoked or salted. Youngsters don't know how lucky they are." Once again, they shared a conspiratorial grin. "Smoked herring is a rare thing these days. The North Sea and Baltic still haven't recovered. What there is gets imported from the Atlantic. I have na' had a kipper for breakfast these many years. Just Finnan Haddie"

"Poor Robbie. Doesn't Heather get you one now and then?" Igrat stared at her host and Byrnes got a disturbing sensation that those heavy-lidded sleepy eyes were looking straight through him. Her next words confirmed that impression. "Does she know I am here with you by the way?"

Byrnes decided honesty was the best policy. In any case, he was reasonably certain Igrat could spot a man lying to her at fifty paces. "No, that she does na'. I'll be honest with ye, she is scared of ye. She thinks ye are trying to seduce her."

"Perhaps I am." Igrat smiled at the thought and glanced around to make sure they couldn't be overheard. The way the dining room was laid out, privacy was guaranteed. She guessed that was absolutely essential. The deals struck in this room would shake the establishment to its foundations if word of them ever got out. Idly, she thought of Gusoyn and how his net of informants amongst the Washington limousine drivers kept the Seer better informed than any regular intelligence service. *Did one of the waiters here serve the same role for Sir Humphrey?* "Why, Robbie, would you want to watch us?"

To her delight Byrnes spluttered slightly and flushed. "Igrat, ye will be the death of me. Be kind to Heather though. She was born when conventions were different and she has na' shaken off the prejudices of that time yet. Even being a man's partner rather than a wife is hard for her to accept. The idea of another woman, t'is shocking for her."

One of Igrat's eyebrows lifted slightly. Looking at how carefully it had been shaped, Byrnes realized how much care Igrat took over her appearance. It was slightly humbling and he felt quite ridiculously flattered by it. "Robbie, tell her not to worry. I only go gay for pay or when I need to so I can do my job. I just like the people around me to be a little off-balance, that's all. Ah, the carving trolley is coming. You were right; that looks incredible."

Trolley was a misuse of words. The carving trolley was huge and required two people to push it into place. Igrat fought hard to stop herself drooling at the joints arrayed before her. She spoke quietly to the carving waiter. Her hands moved quickly but discretely as she specified the cut she wanted. As she did so, the waiter's expression turned to respect. Then, his knife moved deftly and the slices Igrat had specified found their way on to her plate. Byrnes asked for his favorite Beef Wellington.

"What are these, Robbie?" Igrat nodded at the dishes of vegetables that were arriving.

"Those are champit tatties and bashit neeps. That means just creamed potato and mashed swede. Then we have tarragon mashed mushrooms, baked onions in a cream sauce

182

and the little bowl is the sauce for your meat. If you would be a true Scot, you should dip each piece of meat you cut in the sauce, nay pour it over your plate. Your health my dear."

"Slainte Mhor."

"So ye know the Scottish toast do you? And what would that be where your home was?" Byrnes was very careful not to say where and when that was.

"Vashi nush." Igrat smiled nostalgically. "It means 'be at one with your food'. But there are few who speak the language these days. Even back then we used Attic Greek most of the time. After I learned it of course."

To Byrnes's surprise Igrat managed to put away a repeat slice of the venison before they both finished. Much less surprisingly, she seemed to have become the carving waiter's favorite guest. However, by the time Igrat had finished her cranachan, even she had to admit defeat and leave the cheese plate unsampled. The Caledonian Club had filled her to bursting point.

"Robbie, that was the finest meal I've had in as many years as I can remember. Tell me something. When I read the information you sent me, I noticed they had rooms for the members here." Igrat looked across the table at Byrnes who was also unable to contemplate eating anything else but whose eyes suddenly opened at the implication of her question.

"Aye, that we do. And very fine ones they are. But I had'na reserved one. It would ha'been presumptious."

"Well, next time, you'll have to remedy that oversight. I would like there to be a next time, Robbie. If you want to of course. Just make sure Heather doesn't find out."

Byrnes nodded happily. "It would be my honor to entertain you here again Igrat. And to be sure, Heather will not find out from me. It took her months to forgive me for the time I once called her Jean by mistake."

The account mysteriously materialized under his hand and he signed it with a flourish. "Igrat, you should be here for Burns Night. It's January 25th each year. You'd be a natural to make the reply to the Lassies Toast."

"Robbie, remember where I come from. I haven't got a drop of Scottish blood in my veins, although after the meal here tonight, I'm beginning to understand what I've been missing out on. But, if I'm still doing runs here next year, I'd love to take you up on the invitation."

"That's fine to know Igrat, but don't count on the war going on that long. Between us, for your ears and those of your father, one way or the other this war will finish fast. If it goes the way the Service Chiefs think, it'll be over in days once we strike back. If it doesn't, then we're gone as a power worthy of the name."

Igrat lifted her after-dinner glass of Laphroig. "Then, we had better lift our glasses to the forces down south hadn't we?" Though she hadn't apparently raised her voice, for the first time her husky tones carried around the room. Byrnes was not the only man there who lifted his glass in response.

Military Transport Drakensburg *South Atlantic.*

"So there we have the basic plan. The air-mech brigades land across the island, seizing the dominant points of terrain here, here and here. The key ones are the base here, at Goose Green, and the heights above Stanley. The former guards the southern flank while the ones here mean that Stanley itself will be under direct artillery fire. Our function, gentlemen, is to land here at San Carlos. The beaches are suitable for armor. In fact they are the only beaches suitable for armor except for those around Stanley itself. For obvious reasons we do not want to conduct a direct assault on Stanley. Naval Party 8901 suffered almost a hundred and twenty dead and wounded out of one hundred and sixty. Argentine casualties were proportional, we're fairly certain they had more than three hundred dead, nobody knows how many wounded. Their Marine Regiment was so badly chewed up it had to be pulled back to the mainland."

Lieutenant Colonel Rigsby looked around. "So, a direct assault in Stanley is out. Instead, our brigade will be landing at San Carlos and advancing along the line of airmech units, relieving each one in turn. However, there is a danger. There are armored units stationed here at Teal Inlet that are perfectly positioned to strike into the flank of our advance. Countering that threat will be the job of an armored task force supported by the company of tank destroyers carried on this transport. Any questions?"

"Armored units, Sir. Tanks?"

"The technical description is, I believe, armored cavalry. Regimental strength. Light tanks and armored personnel carriers. Their mobility won't be too good but they'll still be a menace sitting there. The tanks are American M92s. 76mm high velocity semi-automatic. Armored carriers are a locally built design. A suitcase on wheels armed with a 7.65 or 13.2 mm machine gun. No threat to your Boomslangs, eh, Shumba?"

Shumba Geldenhuys believed that answering that question would be tempting fate. Instead, he looked at the pictures pinned up on the bulkheads. "These are very good pictures jongmens. If we had these, our work on the border would be much easier."

"We can thank the Septics for them. They're doing overflights of the area daily."

"You said an armored task force; how many battalions?" Geldenhuys was already lost in the terrain, trying to work out the character of the battle he would be fighting.

"Four squadrons. Two with Cavalier tanks; two with Bulldog APCs. And your Boomslangs, of course."

"So we are outnumbered two or three to one?" Geldenhuys sucked his teeth.

"A bit more than that. If it wasn't for you and your men, this would be looking bad. But, your tank destroyers even things up for us."

184

"Sir, air and artillery support?" Cross had heard stories from his father about how devastating air support could be.

"Air support will come from the carriers. We'll have to hope the Bananas will be around enough to do the job. Artillery, we have the towed guns. Lightweight 25 pounders, with the Airmech units and the 105mms we'll be landing. The Argies have American-supplied 105s. Not many of them so I understand and they are short on ammunition. They haven't been able to get a major supply ship in since the invasion."

"Thank you sir." Cross sat down again, his mind chewing over the information. One thing suddenly seemed clear to him, this counter-invasion was being fought on a shoe-string.

"Sir, what's happening over in South Georgia?" Another voice from the group of officers present at the briefing.

"The relief of the garrison there is under way as we speak. Troops are already being inserted into the interior of South Georgia to pick up the civilians and the survivors of the SBS garrison force. Others will be landed after airstrikes take out the ships there and pound the Argie shore positions. The only real question there is how long the Argies will hold out. They are not real soldiers; they're a swimmer-commando unit. Very brave when it comes to shooting a helpless man in the head."

A hiss went around the room; the resistance of Post Master Walsingham and his subsequent brutal murder had made newspaper headlines worldwide. Idly, Rigsby realized just how bad the catastrophic Argentine propaganda error of releasing the prisoners from the sinking of the *Mermaid* had been. Even though they were now living in a detention center in Uruguay, they had been interviewed by the press. The image of the old postmaster refusing to take off his hat to an invader and being shot dead for it had become iconic for the war in general.

"What about prisoners, Sir?" Another unidentified voice from the audience.

The question was met with a derisive jeer. Rigsby slammed the flat of his hand down on the table very hard. The sound echoed around the room, silencing the crowd as effectively as a pistol shot. "We'll have none of that. Let's make this quite clear right now. Word from Brigadier Strachan: this is not the Kola Peninsula. That was then, this is now. It is becoming increasingly obvious that the Argentine forces are split right down the middle. We have murderous thugs like the swimmer-commando types on one side and the regular Argentine forces on the other. Do I have to remind you of the way their sailors went into the water to rescue the survivors from *Mermaid*? A lot more British wives would be widows today if it hadn't been for them. And the survivors from NP8901? The Argie Marines went out of their way to keep them away from the political types and get them to safety. So we play this one strictly by the book. If Argies get killed, well, we all take that risk. That's what we get paid for. But there will be no, repeat no, unofficial settling of accounts or quiet payback. Any allegations of such events will be investigated and will, if substantiated, result in the perpetrators being court-martialed on a charge of murder. Is that quite clear?"

Rigsby waited until the murmuring faded. "It's not just that we have to hold the moral high ground here. We have to think what will be happening after the war. If the

185

present mob stay in power over in Argieland, we'll be doing this whole thing over again some ten or twenty years down the line. But, we play the game, show people that doing the right thing is the proper way to go and brings its own rewards, then we might just see a change over there. That could resolve the problem for good.

"Another thing. We have to remember the Septic's attitude on this. They'll allow small wars, to let people blow off steam, provided they stay small and the people fighting them behave decently. The Chimps set the pattern there. They treated their Indian PoWs well and stuck by the book. We can't do any less. If we do, we'll lose Septic support. Amongst other things that will mean no more nice reconnaissance pictures. So its Geneva and Hague conventions all the way. One final thing; those swimmer-commando bastards didn't just kill a lot of their own. They 'disappeared' people from a number of countries. Any prisoners we take might be the only means of getting an accounting for those victims. If we do manage to wrap up a few of those cases, then not only do we give their relatives some closure, we also earn our government a few brownie points where it counts. So play it by the book or we'll want to know the reason why. And on that note, gentlemen, get some sleep and make sure your men do the same."

Field Exploration Camp, Penguin River, South Georgia

For a brief moment, Georgina Harcourt thought that the island itself was wailing in protest at having to wake up. The glow from the sun was just lighting the horizon. The disk itself wasn't even visible yet but already the light was enough to bring the first signs of life to the island. Or, more significantly, the harbor across the bay. "Can you see anything Tiny?"

Her whisper was almost drowned out by the cacophonous noise of the penguins down nearer the sea. Marine "Tiny" Stroud caught the whisper though and nodded his head. "Down there, on the airstrip. The Argies are warming their Puma up. It looks like they're going to be moving some troops with it." His voice was frustrated. This was the bad time for an observation post; too much light for using night vision equipment but not enough to make visual observation effective.

"You think they plan to come up here?" Georgina didn't like that idea at all.

"To early to tell but we'd better let Dusty know." He started to shuffle back and then froze. Two brilliant white streaks, tinged orange-yellow with the light from the rising sun flashed quickly across the sky, so fast that he never got a chance to remark upon them. A split second later they impacted on the ground near the radar station, masking its position with rolling red-laced black clouds. It seemed as if the explosions remained silent for an eternity. The ground shook first, then the shattering crack of the missile impacts rang off the rocks. Beneath the observers, the penguins went into a flat panic, waddling round in almost comical desperation. In their eyes, the situation was anything but comical. First some of the number had started mysteriously disappearing. Now there was this terrible new event for them to worry about. The entire flock went into collective hysterics.

"Tiny, what was that?"

"Anti-radar missiles at a guess. I think the radar station must have spotted them and turned off just in time. That means the Andrew has arrived, or its aircraft have at any rate. Look out!" Two more missiles tore across the sky and crashed into the rocks. They

186

missed by more than the first pair. "The pilots are firing them to make sure that radar stays off. Georgy, get back to the hut fast and tell everybody to get down. If the Andrew has gone Septic, this place is going to get a nuke tossed at it within seconds."

Stroud looked again at the radar station again. It had survived the four missiles that had arrived so far. The next pair were even further off target. He guessed that wouldn't matter though. The purpose of the missiles was just to keep the radars turned off so they couldn't give the base any specific warning of what was coming. Of course, the missiles themselves told the Argies something was on the way. As long as the radars remained down, they didn't know what. Or from where. Stroud found himself admiring the warship crews down there though. It had been less than twenty seconds since the first pair of missiles had exploded and already their ships were blasting the alert on their sirens. The sound carried clearly across the water in the still air of dawn.

So did something else; the scream of jet engines pushed to their maximum and beyond. Stroud saw four shapes skimming only a few feet above the sea; the shock-wave of their passing threw a huge rooster tail high into the sky behind them. The jets lifted slightly, then howled directly over the radar station. The explosions that followed in their wake dwarfed those of the missiles. The radar set and the prefabricated buildings around it vanished in the mass of bomb blasts and secondary explosions. Stroud tried to count them but couldn't. He had to give up at twenty. Too many, too fast, too big. One thing he was sure of. The radar station was history.

The four Buccaneers turned away. They'd managed to get in and out clean; a perfect air defense suppression mission. Stroud felt something beside him and glanced quickly sideways. Sergeant Miller had just appeared. "What's going on, Tiny?"

"I could be wrong, Sarge, but I think the Navy is here."

Blackburn Buccaneer S4H XT-279, Approaching Grytviken, South Georgia.

XT-279 shuddered from the thumps caused by fast, low-altitude flight and shook from Spey engines that were being pushed well beyond the manufacturer's warning notices. *This was it, this was the real thing.* Lieutenant-Commander Ernest Mullback couldn't help feeling the sheer exhilaration of the flight. It had been carefully planned. The twelve Buccaneers had come in from exactly due west, using the 1,200 foot mountains behind Godthul Anchorage as a screen. It had made for a round-about flight, but the sheer element of surprise had been worth it. Three formations of four aircraft had crested the ridge, clearing it by barely a hundred feet, leaving them only seven miles from their targets. The rippling salvoes of anti-radar missiles had silenced the enemy radar as effectively as direct hits would have done. Then the four Buccaneers plastered the site with retarded bombs. It vanished in a hail of primary and secondary explosions that spoke of a job well done.

Mullback knew he was just 45 seconds out from his target. He could see the ships ahead of him in the gloomy light of the dawn nautical twilight, their positions ingrained in his mind. The three ships formed a equilateral triangle. Its point was the transport in the middle of the bay closest to him; the destroyer and frigate at the dockside forming the baseline. He was very consciously, very deliberately slowing his breathing down to a steady, regular rhythm, as his the bomb bay door rotated opened. He watched the green lines on the head-up display already edging in towards his target's hull. Now was the

187

time for patience. Tthe years of practice paid off as the Highball installation spun its two bombs up to speed.

The movements needed were very precise; very delicate ones that shifted the big destroyer to the center of the display panel. As soon as the green lines touched the bow and stern of the Argie warship Mullback thumbed the release. Beneath his aircraft, the two spherical Highballs dropped clear, skipping in the long flat arc that ended with another impact and another skip that took them closer still to their prey.

To some extent, now that they were on their way, Mullback had lost interest in them. They were launched. They would either hit or miss and nothing he could do would change that. He was much more concerned about the black blots of smoke that had started to erupt around him just before XT-279 streaked over the destroyer. He felt the thuds as something, presumably fragments from the 47mm shells, struck his aircraft. Whatever they were, they'd done nothing serious. The Buccaneer slashed over Grytviken, then soared skywards as he pulled the stick back. Shoulder-fired missiles were only effective up to around 8,000 feet and he needed to get out of that range bracket as fast as possible.

"Look at that, Jerry! Have you ever seen anything like it?" In the back seat, Alex Peters had lost control of his voice, letting it rise into an astonished squeak.

Mullback glanced over his shoulder. The two Highballs he had dropped had full charges, of course. That gave them each more than twice the explosive power of a World War Two torpedo. Both had exploded between the keel of the destroyer and the seabed no more than ten feet underneath it. As a result, the explosive force of the Highballs had been directed straight up. The disintegrating destroyer was perched on top of two seething balls of water. For a brief second, Mullback actually saw the seabed underneath the ship where the water had been blown clear. Then, the wrecked destroyer crashed back down into the rocks and the water towers collapsed on to her, burying her from sight in a mass of white foam.

The freighter anchored in the middle of the bay was the last to be hit. Mullback saw two great white circles of white foam surrounding her as the Highballs exploded underneath her. She was in deeper water so the effects weren't immediately so spectacular as those that had blown the destroyer literally out of the water. The circles of water boiled up, joining to form a white figure-of-eight in the black sea of the bay. The center of the freighter was lifted with them. Her back snapped as her bow and stern sagged downwards. Then, suddenly, the lifted center was sucked viciously downwards as the underwater bubbles formed by the explosions collapsed. For a moment, the stricken ship was poised, her bow and stern pointing upwards. Then, the collapse of the gas bubbles under her keel formed a great water jet that tore upwards through her hull. Mullback saw her bridge and superstructure ripped away from the hull and tossed into the air. Then, the sight was gone as his Buccaneer skimmed over King Edward Point and headed back out to sea.

Mullback felt drained as he reached for the transmit button on his mask. "Highball, highball, highball. Say again. Highball, highball, highball."

Field Exploration Camp, Penguin River, South Georgia

"You're right, Tiny; the Navy has arrived." Miller shifted slightly to get a better view as four more Buccaneers made their attack runs. Three miles away, the missile battery they'd reported two days earlier vanished under a hail of bombs. "Well, if the Argies don't realize we're up here and tipped the Andrew off now, they never will."

"Might not matter Sarge." Stroud pointed at the pyre of black smoke rising from the helicopter pad south of Grytviken. In the distance, two Mirage F2s were climbing away. One trailed a thin stream of black and white smoke as it did so. "I think one of the Argies got him with a spiral. Hope he makes it back."

"Yeah. Hell's teeth, the Bananas made a mess down there. Didn't just hit the three ships, they blew them to hell and back. They're gone."

He took another look at the harbor. The freighter had already sunk; just the twisted wreckage of her capsized bows pointing upwards. The dockside was chaos. The blast from the exploding Highballs had done far more damage that just wrecking the two warships. The wash from the explosions had swept ashore and destroyed the clusters of derelict huts that had made up most of the harbor installation. The water was still surging backwards and forwards, eddying round the wrecked hulks that littered the Grytviken waterfront. Now there were two more. It was as certain as anything could be that the destroyer and the frigate would never leave the quayside again. As Miller had so grimly said, they were blown to hell.

"That clears us anyway. Without their helicopter, it'll take more than a day for the Argies to send troops around here. By then, the navy will be here and it'll all be over."

"You really think so, Sarge?" Take a look over there." Stroud pointed over at a rockpile inland. There were a dozen or so figures clustered around it, watching the aftermath of the sudden strike that had devastated the naval force in Grytviken.

Miller swept his binoculars around and looked at the men. There was enough light now to make them out clearly. They were Argentine swimmer-commandos. He watched them for a few seconds as they took in the scene down in the harbor, then they started to clamber through the field of ice-covered rocks on the way to the promontory that housed the Field Exploration Camp. *About eight hundred yards away*, he thought. *At least two hours, maybe three.* He slid out of his position and led the way back to the concealed hut. Once inside, he looked around at the team gathered there.

"We got company coming. At least a dozen swimmer-commandos. Georgie, Cynthia, you two head up into the rocks behind this place. You're the last line of defense here."

"We want to stay with you."

"Don't recommend that. It's five of us against twelve of them. We need to know you two are here guarding our backs. We'll give you a grenade each. It's up to you how you use them if you have to, but those swimmer-commando characters are not nice people. If you can bug out, do. Look, as far as we know, we're the only Brits left on South Georgia. As long as you two are outside, this place is still British. Above all of that, I wasn't joking when I said you'd be guarding our backs. As long as they're in front of us, we can pin them down for hours. If they get behind us, it's all over."

"All right." The two women had accepted the inevitable, just barely.

"They must have been moving up during the night. So, we'll have to make sure they regret that, won't we?"

Blackburn Buccaneer S4H XT-279, Approaching HMS Furious, *Off South Georgia*

Two Buccaneers and a Mirage F2 were circling the carrier, waiting for the rest of the aircraft to land. Mullback's Buccaneer had damage to its flaps and would be coming in faster than normal. XT-287 still had its two Highballs on board and would also be coming in fast. One of the Mirage F2 escorts had taken a spiral hit in one engine and was coming in on the other. She would be landing last. It was a cruel decision, but a logical one. The aircraft were being landed so that the intact aircraft were safe. That way, of one of the damaged birds cracked up and blocked the deck, no serviceable aircraft would be lost.

"XT-287, make your landing approach now." The carrier-controlled approach message came over the earphones. Loaded landings weren't pleasant, but they weren't that difficult either and the Buccaneers were low on fuel. Mullback watched while Canfield dropped into the "groove," the mythical path through the air that would lead his Buccaneer safely back to the carrier deck. The gray-painted Buccaneer seemed to be heading in very fast. When it hit the deck, Mullback could swear he saw puffs of smoke from the tires. Then, the aircraft caught a wire and swung to a halt. Much further forward than usual, but a safe halt none the less.

"XT-279, make your approach now."

"Roger Control. XT-287 make it?"

"Blew her nosewheel tires, but otherwise Canfield's fine. Out."

So he had seen puffs of black smoke from the tires. Mullback swung XT-279 around and started his approach run. He could see the angled deck stretching before him, the carrier island off to his right, the brilliant lights of the mirror landing sight lined up properly. Not quite properly though, the bars showed he was a little too high. He dropped slightly, bringing the bars into alignment, but the reduction in speed caused his Buccaneer to start shaking. He reached down to give increased flaps. The cure was worse than the disease. What had been shaking turned into a serious flutter problem. He hastily pulled the flaps up again.

"Control. Hot landing, no flaps."

"Understood XT-279." The voice was unemotional.

Ahead of him the flight deck grew terrifyingly fast. Mullback was aware that he was sweating with sheer stress as he concentrated on the sweet spot between the stern round-down and the first wire of the arrester array. At the last second, he realized he was slightly too high and too fast but it was too late to abort and go around. He cut power and felt his Banana drop onto the flight deck, throwing him against his straps. For all the unconventionality of the landing, the sturdy Blackburn structure took the impact although the bounce caused him to miss the first wire. He hooked the second and that brought him to a halt, a few feet from the end of the angled deck. Behind him, her heard the squee noise as the wire was pulled back to its proper position.

190

The tractor was already hooking up and Mullback felt his aircraft being towed clear of the deck. "XT-279, confirm you have fragment damage to your flaps. Good landing, all things considered."

CCA shut off and Mullback knew he had been forgotten. They were concentrating on the damaged Mirage. It was crabbing badly, the black smoke from its wrecked engine increasing in volume as the pilot neared safely. Mullback watched the wing on that side of the aircraft start to drop. The pilot didn't seem to catch it but a few feet from the fantail, he surged power on his remaining good engine. The added speed straightened the damaged aircraft up and lifted the drooping wing. The speed bled away again almost instantly but by then the Sea Mirage was on the deck and catching the first wire. Incredibly, it had been a near-perfect landing.

Once towed off the angled deck, the cockpit on the Sea Mirage opened up and Mullback saw the pilot, Lieutenant Adams start to climb out. As he did, a burst of applause rang out from the Goofers Gallery. That caused him to stop and he made a theatrical bow from the steps to his cockpit.

The deck crews were already at work, striking the damaged aircraft down to the hangar for repair while undamaged birds were kept on deck. The maintenance crew would be working hard to repair the three aircraft that had serious damage to them.

Something caught Mullback's eye. Over to his left he could see a signal lamp flickering from HMS *Griffin*. Instinctively, he read the message. ". . . . core? Query are all safe."

The bridge replied quickly. "Clean Sweep. All aircraft safe. We counted them all out, and we counted them all back."

Casa Rosada Presidential Palace, Buenos Aires, Argentina

"Are you completely incompetent or simply in league with the British?" President Leopoldo Galtieri read the report in from South Georgia with near-disbelief. Two warships and a civilian auxiliary sunk by British air attack and the defensive positions on the Island bombed. To make it worse, there were still British troops loose on South Georgia. That threw the whole plan off-balance.

"We needed those ships to support the next phase of the operation, extending our grip southwards into the South Sandwich Islands." Admiral Jorge Anaya wattled furiously at Galtieri's gibes. "Need I remind you that we were to leave a garrison in place on South Georgia and establish another on Thule Island?"

"I know that. Do you think I forget details of these plans?"

"Then you must also understand that our troops cannot walk on water. They needed ships to take them south. Warships might be able to carry the men, but equipment to set up a permanent base needed a freighter. We were told there were a handful of civilians on South Georgia. Unarmed civilians we could round up and dispose of. Instead there were dozens of heavily-armed troops in the town. Their presence has meant that our troops have been hard-put to secure Grytviken and Leith Harbor. Only in the last few days have they started to get on top of the problems the British troops there are causing. So the

191

ships were stuck in harbor waiting. It didn't matter, so we thought. After all, you were the one who was so sure the British could do nothing while the Americans would do nothing. No resistance, you told us. We could execute the plans at our leisure."

Galtieri slammed his hand on the table. "I will not tolerate such defeatism. Dozens of heavily armed troops? Not according to the reports your own men have made. There was one submarine came in and that was all. A dozen or so men at most. Your excuses are as feeble as the performance of your commandos. Since the British are on the move, we can be grateful we have good army troops in the Malvinas. They might be conscripts but they know their duty. We will concentrate our defenses there."

"And what about the troops on South Georgia? With the ships we had stationed there sunk, they can't get back."

"Then they can do what they should have done right from the start. They can fight. To the last man and the last bullet."

Anaya settled back and thought about that. Given how much Astrid knew, his unit fighting to the last man and the last bullet could solve a lot of problems.

Control Room, HMS Collingwood. *145 nautical miles south of the Falkland Islands*

"She's a freighter, Sir. Heading is one-three five; direct course from Port Ushuaia to Stanley."

"Any identification?"

"No, Sir. We're picking up sound signature for two diesels and two screws but that could make her anything or anybody's."

Captain Paul Wicklow nodded. There was only so much an acoustic signature could tell a lurking submarine. "No sign of an escort?"

"No sound signature of one, Sir. That freighter is all alone out there."

"Cheeky bastards. I suppose they thought we wouldn't really sink a freighter." Wicklow paused, his thumbs were prickling fiercely. "I don't like this. Beware Greeks bearing gifts and all that. Load a Mark Two into tube one, three Mark 22s into tubes two, three and four and squitters into five and six."

"A Mark Two, Sir?" Mark Two was a British-built 22.4 inch electric straight runner. It had replaced the older Mark One when British submarines had shifted from 21-inch tubes to 22.4s. It might be unguided but it had a ferociously heavy warhead. Ideal for killing a merchant ship from ambush. Since it was merely an enlarged and improved version of the old German G7e, that was hardly surprising.

"When that eel goes, I want it out and on its way. There's something out here; I can feel it. Bring the boat up to periscope depth."

Collingwood angled upwards, her decks tilting with the movement. She was moving very slowly, keeping her sound signature to an absolute minimum. Wicklow took a deep breath. "Up scope."

What followed next was a virtuoso demonstration of how to use a periscope. The mast broke surface, the slow speed and rough water combined to make the feather hard to spot. Wicklow knew exactly where to look and what to look for. He didn't need the bow identification number to confirm his opinion but everything came in useful. "Argentine flag, bow number B4."

He snapped the words out while he did a quick scan. "No other contacts." The scope was down less than ten seconds after breaking surface.

"Argentine naval auxiliary *Bahia San Blas*."

"Right, we have an Argentine naval ship well inside the exclusion zone and on course for Stanley. That makes her a legitimate target. I can't see how the Septics could complain about this. Plot, prepare firing solution and enter into the computer."

There was a delay while the fire control system took in the target course and speed, compared them with the characteristics of Torpedo, 22.4 inch Mark Two and came up with a solution that would put both together at the same time and place.

"Solution set, Sir."

"Well done, Weaps. Fire One."

There was a pause while the fire control computer made a minor adjustment, then *Collingwood* rocked slightly as the torpedo left the tube. It was wakeless, so the only warning the target was likely to get would be the initial uplift as the eel exploded under her keel.

"Impact in five . . . . . four . . . . . three . . . . . two . . . . . . one . . . ."

There was a pause that seemed to have taken hours, then the rumble of an explosion echoed through the boat.

"Periscope up."

Wicklow seized the scope and focused on the target. He had missed the spectacular under-the-keel explosion itself but its effects were obvious. The freighter had broken in half. Her bow section was already rolling over while the stern was sinking fast. Worst of all, the ship was under a pyre of black smoke, the sea around her in flames.

"Down scope."

"We get her, Sir?"

The question was verged on the redundant but Wicklow's nod of answer still caused a cheer that stopped suddenly with the comment that followed it. "She must have

193

been carrying fuel. She's burning like a torch out there. So is the sea around her; the crew must have had it."

The control room was silent. The men there were trying to imagine the efforts of the survivors trying to abandon ship in a world where everything was burning. "Anything we can do, Sir?"

Wicklow shook his head. He was about to speak when the sonar room cut in. "Sir, we have a contact; something stirring. Slow revs, single screw, very low frequency machinery noise, 50 hertz. I think we have a diesel-electric boat on our tail."

"Damn, I knew this was too good to be true." It was a well-put together ambush. A juicy target to make the submarine expose herself, a diesel-electric lurking to take the shot. "Any bearing on that threat?"

"Due west Sir. My guess is she was behind the freighter and below the layer."

"Make oh-nine-oh. Speed six knots." That was *Collinwood's* creep speed, the maximum speed she could make before her noise levels started to rise. "Single screw. An Italian-built Manta class?"

"I think so Sir. The CBs say she's got an average passive sonar set but is very quiet. Small too; designed for the Med."

"She knows we're here, that's for certain. Bearing still two-seven-zero?"

"Yes, Sir. Sir, we're losing her. I think we picked her up as she came through the layer, now we've lost her again."

Wicklow drummed his fingers. "We'll separate. Make speed 32 knots. Give her a tailchase. She can make 20 knots, but that'll run her batteries flat in a few minutes. Ready all decoy systems in case she tries for a shot."

Collingwood lurched slightly as her screw bit into the water. The three members of her class were known as the Ferraris of the fleet, fast and loud. The problem was at that speed, her sonar coverage was very poor.

"Sir, we have torpedo launch. Two torpedoes coming in fast from astern. American, Mark 37s."

"Full left rudder, take her down. Launch bubble decoys and fire a squitter. Reload tube with same."

The "squitter," more formally known as Decoy Mark 27, was basically a torpedo loaded with the electronics necessary to simulate the sound signature of a submarine. *Collingwood* was turning hard and diving to create a knuckle in the water that would block sonar pulses. Two foam generators had been planted in that knuckle to improve the effect. The squitter was running ahead. Hopefully the Mark 37s would track it and ignore the submarine that was already far down and out of their tracking cone.

"We're through the layer, Sir."

194

"Slow down to six knots. Lurk and listen." Separating from the diesel electric hadn't worked too well. It had to be a gutsy skipper in that diesel-electric to chance two torpedoes on a tail chase against a nuke boat.

The seconds ticked by and turned into minutes. Eventually the sonar operator shook his head. "I think he's out there, Sir. Can't pick him up. There's just little hints."

"He can't be getting anything better. Come back to oh-nine-oh and we'll do a creepy-creepy away."

Collingwood had barely started her turn when her hull rang with the pulse of an active sonar system. "She's got us, Sir. That was way above threshold value."

"Give a bow pulse." *Collingwood's* own bow sonar slammed out its signal and a bright contact light exploded on to one of the sonar displays. "Launch two Mark 22s as soon as the target is dialed in."

It was a race against time to get their torpedoes off. *Collingwood* won, just barely. Her Mark 22s were swim-out launched, another advantage of the larger-than-usual size of her torpedo tubes. That made the launch as near silent as made no difference. It didn't hide the torpedoes themselves as they started their run towards the Argentine submarine. They were well on their way when the report from the sonar room came in. "She's fired again, Sir. Two Mark 37s, coming straight at us."

"Fire all decoys, take her down, turn and go to maximum revs." The Mark 37 was a lot faster than the Australian Mark 22. Wicklow watched the two lines speeding out from the sonar contacts. Each represented a pair of torpedoes hunting their prey. *Collingwood* had the advantage of launching first; it paid off. The trace of the Argentine submarine vanished in a blaze of light on the display. He could picture what was happening; the Argentine boat had probably been hit on or near the bows. The Manta only had one watertight bulkhead in the whole submarine. It was unlikely that would save her. Her nose opened up, she would be heading down until she dropped to the point where the water tore her apart.

"Decoys have filtered off one of the Mark 37s. The other one is still coming for us." The report was neutral, calm and collected.

"Shut all watertight doors, rig for collision." Wicklow paused for a second. *To head for the surface or not?* "Take her up."

Collingwood started to rise but it was too late. The Mark 37 had been about to run out of fuel when it struck the nuclear-powered submarine's screw and exploded. The shaft whiplashed from the blast, then ran out of control as the mutilated propeller started to shake itself apart. The shaft seals and bearings ruptured, causing flooding throughout the whole machinery space. *Collingwood* never got to make it to the surface. Her stern flooding and her machinery gone, she was already sinking fast. The control room crew had time to scram the reactor before the hull collapsed under the pressure. In the space of less than half an hour, three more ships had joined the long list of wrecks at the bottom of the Drake Passage.

Seer's Home Philotas, *Saranac River Valley, Adirondacks.*

"You do realize that Sir Robert has a long history of chasing every female in sight don't you?" The Seer sipped his whisky and sighed gently. He was reasonably certain this was not the sort of conversation a man was supposed to be having with his daughter.

"Of course. I just have to run not quite fast enough. Although I've as good as told him he's going to catch me." Igrat was sitting on the couch, freshly showered and wrapped in a thick cotton robe, her legs drawn up beside her. She'd caught a rotodyne out of Washington International and it had dropped her off at the airstrip attached to the house. What had once been a long drive up here was now a convenient ride on a puddle-hopper. She didn't mind paying the extra fee for the additional stop. The views alone made it worthwhile and she needed the rest. The constant flights across the Atlantic were more wearing than most people realized.

The door to the living room entered and Raven entered, pushing a trolley loaded with plates. Igrat whinnied slightly with delight at the smell of rich stew. "Wild turkey, Raven?"

"Wild turkey." Raven confirmed that and took quiet pride in Igrat's open enjoyment. It had taken her some time to get used to Igrat's ways, especially her whole-hearted pursuit of life's pleasures. Privately she had thought that those pursuits would have dropped her into a mass of trouble if she'd lived on a reservation. Angry wives would have been coming for her in the night, Raven was quite convinced of that. "Achillea shot it and it's been hanging for just the right time. And, it really has been cooked according to an old Indian recipe."

Igrat and her father both burst out laughing at the comment. Raven was pure-blooded Shoshone and a superb cook. She'd even published a book of Shoshone recipes, under an assumed name of course. It had sold well. One of many ways customs and culture from the Nations had become popularized after being neglected for far too long. She started spooning the stew out of its casserole into serving dishes, making sure that the Seer had his favorite pieces, before adding slabs of corn bread. Igrat took hers and quietly took a few mouthfuls. In Naamah's absence, the job of food tasting fell to her. Nobody took it that seriously these days, but it was better to be safe than sorry. "Gods, Raven this is good. How do you get the turkey so soft? I keep expecting it to be like rubber."

"Cook cool and slow." Raven was smiling with happiness at the obviously sincere praise. "I put the chopped turkey into a dutch oven a whole day ago. So, how did you get along with Sir Robert Byrnes?"

"He dined me, wined me and made it very clear there were quite a few other things he wished to do to me. Some very naughty." Igrat closed her eyes with sheer pleasure at the thick gravy mopped up with freshly-baked cornbread. "But he said nothing that even hinted at the Auxiliary Units. The official line is they don't exist, never have existed and are just media speculation. Even mention them directly and I get the 'pat on the head, silly little girl' treatment. I thought Robbie might tell me something from the funding end, but not a word."

196

"What do you think Iggie?" The Seer absorbed the information and mulled its implications.

"The Auxiliary Units? Oh they exist all right. They've overdone the 'we don't exist' bit just a little too much. If they really didn't exist, there would be a few loose ends knocking round. You know the sort of things, little mysteries that nobody can quite solve and which curious-minded people could construct into an obviously-absurd legend. But there aren't. Somebody has gone around and carefully closed off all those loose ends, every conceivable one of them, and the only reason to do that is to hide something. The fact that there is so obviously no evidence at all is, in an odd way, the strongest evidence of all. Could I have some more stew please, Raven? I'm hungry."

"Plate." Raven served out some more stew and watched Igrat start to wolf it down. "How do you stay thin?"

"Lots of exercise." Igrat looked innocently around, an appearance that deceived nobody. "After all, I'm a Royal Courier now. I've got to run around like a greyhound. Father, do you want me to keep sniffing around for hints about the Auxiliary Units?"

"Amongst our friends over there, sure. No need to take chances though. At the moment it's just curiosity. But if the Auxiliary Units do exist, it would be nice to know about them."

SBS Unit, Penguin River, South Georgia

To his dismay, he was now certain that the Argentine force was larger than the original sighting had suggested. More of the swimmer-commandos had appeared, working their way through the field of ice-covered rocks that led up to the Penguin River. There were at least 18 by now, and Marine "Tiny" Stroud was sure there were six more somewhere. Assuming there were 50 swimmer-commandos in the team that had occupied Grytviken, that meant at least half their force were up here. It was certainly more than the five SBS men were capable of handling.

Stroud had already picked his target. One of the swimmer commandos had moved into an overwatch position and was scanning the rocks with the telescopic sight mounted on his FAS rifle. Stroud assumed it was the FAS. The Argentine swimmer-commandos and Marines both used the Belgian-designed rifle while the Argentine Army used the much cheaper Russian-designed SVK. He was in no doubt about the scope though. He had seen light flash from the rising sun flash off its lens. Stroud was quietly confident he hadn't been seen yet. Partly, that was because nobody was shooting at him but there were other reasons as well.

One of them was the rifle he was carrying. The original L1 had been equipped with the traditional wooden furniture. That had been replaced in the L1A2 version with the lighter and stronger plastic stock and grips. At first, those had been made in black. At some point a great light of inspiration had engulfed somebody and it had been realized that the plastic furniture could easily be made in any color. So now, the L1A2 had a range of camouflaged components that could be switched over to make the weapon unobtrusive in any environment. The rifle itself was a bullpup design with the magazine behind the pistol grip and trigger. That had been a controversial decision and other rifle designers had ridiculed the resulting design. They had suggested it was best suited to inserting hot

197

cartridge cases up the nose of anybody using it. Certainly it gave left-handers problems, but the layout had provided a compact weapon with an unusually long barrel for its overall size. The resulting accuracy was exploited by the provision of an optical sight, making the British Army the first to issue such sights as standard equipment.

Stroud was using that sight, confident that with the sun behind him he would not be betrayed by a reflection. He had placed the red dot just below the chin of the man he had chosen. A gentle squeeze of the trigger and a five round burst struck his target. That was another advantage of the bullpup configuration; the rifle recoiled straight backwards and it was very easy to prevent muzzle climb. A short burst put all the bullets where the shooter intended, not sent them skywards. His target slumped downwards. The red stains from the bullet wounds spread across the rocks and glistened in the sun. Stroud didn't stay around to watch. By the time the 7mm bullets had struck, he was already beginning to move out of his firing position and shift to an alternative.

The speed of that move saved him. Despite the flash suppressor built into his rifle, there had been enough of a firing signature to tell the Argentine commandos where the shots had come from. Their return fire sent bullets all around his just-vacated position. The heavy 7.65mm bullets whined off the frozen ground or splattered against the rocks. The full-power 7.65x54mm had a lot more striking energy than the intermediate power 7x43mm used by the British rifle. It was enough to send rock fragments skittering around the impact area. One of those fragments sliced across Stroud's cheek, leaving a long but shallow cut. He ignored it, knowing that soon he would have much more serious things to worry about.

Swimmer-Commando Team, Penguin River, South Georgia

The short burst had felled the overwatch sniper without warning. Lieutenant Marcos Rafa cursed as he saw the man's body tumble from the rocks and sprawl on the frozen ground below. He had been relying on the sniper to pick off any British troops the Swimmer-Commando unit would run into while they closed on the observation point the British had positioned somewhere up here. Instead, the enemy had scored first blood and taken the man out. Rafa decided that he would make sure any prisoners his unit took paid for that. The thought was drowned out by the hammering of rifle and machine gun fire. It was one thing the Swimmer-Commando units had learned during their long fight against the guerillas who plagued the Argentine countryside. Ambushes had to be dominated by an immediate mass return of fire. It would pin the ambushers down and allow them to be isolated and picked off.

One regret Rafa did have was that his unit didn't have any heavy weapons with it. A small detachment, they had left their 60mm mortars back with the main body of the unit in Grytviken. Those mortars would have been invaluable against the opposition they now faced. Still, even if they had wanted to bring them, the rough ground between their base and this position had precluded the option. This would have to be done the old way.

"How many are there, Sergeant?"

"Ten, perhaps fifteen?" Mateo Marcelo sounded confident, but he really had no idea of what the unit was up against. He wasn't that interested in finding out either. He was much more in favor of gathering intelligence when he and his men were the only armed people around and he'd seen how surgically accurate the gunfire that had taken down one of his men had been. He didn't really want to chance that.

Rafa had a shrewd idea that his Sergeant was more interested in saving his skin than carrying out the mission assigned to this patrol. That was an issue he would address later. At the moment, he had a more pressing concern. That was driving in the defenses of this observation post. First job would be to expand the front sideways and try to envelop the defenses ahead of them. "Marcelo, take three men and move off to the left. Find the edge of the British position and move around it." *And try, for once at least, to act like a soldier.* "Everybody else, lay down grazing fire against the rocks up ahead. Pin the British down."

SBS Unit, Penguin River, South Georgia

Sergeant "Dusty" Miller had an interesting problem on his mind. *Would the Argies move left or right?* After Stroud had taken down one of their men, they'd try and pull a flanker. He was sure of that. The question was, which flank? Right would take them to the camp more quickly; left would take them through easier terrain. Only, they weren't sure that the camp was there, or if it was, exactly where it was located. Also, these were swimmer-commandos, not infantrymen. They weren't used to fighting a killing match in bad ground. *They are more used to raids on hide-outs and that,* Miller guessed, *is what they think they are doing here.* He paused for a second, weighed up the balance and made his decision. *Left. They'll extend to their left. Straight into my loving arms.*

His thought train was interrupted by a blast of gunfire from the Argentine positions. The sounds told him a lot. He could count two light machine guns and at least six rifles. That meant, what, ten men holding the baseline to the front. Plus their officer and the man Stroud had killed. So, four men or six pulling the flanker. Either way, it wasn't good. Miller was the only man positioned to block them. That underlined a simple fact. There just weren't enough SBS men to defend this position properly.

Movement in the rocks caught his eye and he looked carefully through the optical sight on his rifle. Four men. The magnification of the eyepiece showed him one of them shouting at the others. Fair enough. He took a deep breath, steadied himself and fired a short burst at the shouting man. Miller saw him start to go down but he was already rolling away from his firing position and moving to an alternate. Ironically, that one would put him in a slightly better position. He heard bullets hit the rocks around his old post, then he was nicely set up in the new niche. In front of him, the man who had been shouting was down right enough, but he was trying to drag to the cover of some rocks. Miller guessed the burst had hit him in the legs. Shooting slightly downhill was always complicated and he'd probably over-compensated. The three other men were hidden in the rocks, firing wildly at the area he'd been in a few moments before. One of them was only partly in cover; his head and chest were shielded by the rocks. What he didn't realize was that Miller's change in position had left his lower back exposed.

Miller took careful aim and fired another short burst. He wouldn't be able to kill his target from this angle, but the shots would shatter the man's spine and leave him pinned down. Better still, with two wounded men on their hands, the ability of the Argies to move and fire against him would be seriously reduced. So far, so good. Curled up in the rock field, he patted his rifle and started to shift to a third position. There was one thing troubling him. Every time he and his men moved, they were falling back on the base camp and that was not the way the battle had to develop.

199

Across the Rockfield that led to the sea beyond the Penguin River, Private Keith "Jocko" Gillespie had worked his way into a comfortable firing position. From his vantage point he could take the likely lines of approach under what the manuals called 'a brisk enfilading fire.' To do so, he had the light machine gun version of the L1A2 rifle. The L3A2 had a longer, heavier barrel, a bipod and a much more powerful optical sight than the L1. It still had the 20-round magazine though. Many older soldiers still preferred the Bren Gun with its larger, top-mounted magazine. Some Army units actually had them but the SBS hadn't had time to 'acquire' any. In any case, Gillespie wasn't one of those who hankered after the weapons of the past. He liked his L3 and appreciated its virtues.

In front of him, he could see that the Argentine advance was stalling. It hadn't taken much. They'd lost one man certainly dead and two wounded, but few of the swimmer-commandos seemed keen to mix it with professional Marines. They'd laid down a lot of fire on the center of the presumed British line. That had probably forced the other two members of the unit, Harding and Meriwether, back. Stroud and Miller had also dropped back after they'd drawn blood. That left Gillespie as the only one in their original positions. It also meant that it would be his turn. With that thought, another movement in the icy rocks caught his eye. It was the shape of a man moving forward, probably trying to probe the British positions. Gillespie took careful aim and squeezed out a ten-round burst. The figure lurched and was still.

It was the extra size of his weapon and the length of the burst that killed Gillespie. They delayed his move from his firing position by a fraction of a second. That brief pause was enough to expose him to the counter-fire from the Argentine unit. The 7.65mm bullets raked his position, ricocheting of the rocks around him and sending splinters of rock and ice through the air. One of the ricochets hit Gillespie just above his right temple and exited through the nape of his neck. The tumbling and distorted bullet killed him instantly.

Field Exploration Camp, Penguin River, South Georgia

Georgina Harcourt gasped at the explosion of gunfire. It was one thing to go through the motions of handling a rifle and learning how to use it, quite another to hear the crackle of gunfire and know that the shots she was hearing were intended to kill. She was also a quick learner and could tell the difference between the ripple of light cracks from the British rifles and the heavier, rhythmic thudding of the Argentine weapons. There was a disturbing preponderance of the latter.

"Cynthia, it's started."

Across the hut, her companion nodded. The hut seemed strangely empty after accommodating seven people for so long. She started to say something but was interrupted by another barrage of rifle fire. This exchange was noticeably closer than the earlier one. It ended with something new; the blast of a grenade exploding. Both women looked down at the hand grenades they had been given, suddenly understanding the lethality of the heavy metal eggs. "We'd better get out of here."

Georgina nodded and led the way out of the hut into the rocks that lay between it and the shore. Once outside and moving north, the noise of the fighting behind them was drowned out by the clamor of the hysterical penguins.

SBS Unit, Penguin River, South Georgia

Miller cautiously looked over the edge of his new position and tried to spot where the Argies were pushing forward. *Everywhere* was the answer that forced itself on him. He and his men had killed at least three and left two more badly wounded but they had lost two of their own in the process. Gillespie caught by gunfire and "Happy" Meriwether killed by a grenade. Odds that had started at eighteen to five were now thirteen to three. The problem was that the situation they faced was a nightmare for units like the SBS. Normally, faced with these kind of odds, they would disengage and slip away. Here, there was nowhere to slip away to and they were anchored in place by the two women. That left them very few tactical options.

Another blast of fire saturated a pile of rocks off to his left. The Argies were predictable all right. They would lay down a heavy blast of covering fire, then a few of their men would try and rush forward to seize a new position. Sound basic tactics but against the tiny handful of SBS men scattered in the rocks, the covering fire served only to give notice of the impending move. Sure enough, a group of six swimmer-commandos broke cover and tried to move up to another line of rocks. Five of them actually made it but the advance cost them the sixth. He was left sprawled over the rocks, the shining white of the rock disfigured by the flow of red down its sides. The odds were now twelve to three but the Argies had seized another few yards of ground.

Swimmer-Commando Team, Penguin River, South Georgia

Almost a third of his unit was dead or wounded. That alone made Rafa believe that he was up against a much more powerful force than he had originally thought. He now seriously questioned whether it would be possible for him to clean out this observation post the way he had been ordered to. *There had to be at least a dozen or so British troops in front of him, probably the survivors of the garrison at Grytviken.* Thinking about the damage those troops had inflicted on the *Punta Alta*, a dozen was the smallest number he could expect. Rafa did the calculations quickly. *Assuming twenty or so troops had been in the small port, six had been killed there and probably two more here. That made a dozen sound right.* It also meant that he was, at best, now equal to the defenders in numbers and might well be outnumbered by them.

It was time for another push forward. His remaining sergeant had picked out the most likely point for the British defenders to occupy. The blast of fire from the two machine guns sent tracers scouring into the rocks. A group of his men sprinted forward under its cover. As soon as they were in the open, the volume of fire from the guns suddenly slackened. That appeared to encourage the British. The rifle fire that greeted the assault team was much more intense than the isolated bursts that had been experienced to date. Rafa instinctively made the estimate.There were at least three machine guns firing this time and their effect was obvious. Four of the six men went down. Two obviously dead; two more still moving. The other pair scuttled back to cover.

Furious, Rafa wormed his way through the rocks to the position held by his men. *That latest push might have been decisive if one of the machine guns hadn't ceased fire* he told himself. In the forward position held by his men, Rafa was met by his surviving sergeant. "Sir, you had better look at this."

'This' was one of his machine gun crews. Both men were dead, neatly shot through the head by bullets that had penetrated their helmets. Rafa had seen damage and injuries like that many times before. They were the result of armor-piercing 7.65mm rounds. The steel-cored bullets had sliced through the protection afforded by the men's helmets but it was the sheer precision of the shots that was impressive. Rafa looked at the bodies, imagining how they had been positioned while they had been firing on the British in front. That made it very obvious. The bullets had come from behind the Argentine positions.

The sergeant had come to the same conclusion. "Sir, they were killed by our own people. We have traitors amongst us."

Rafa nodded. It was possible some of the Argentine Marines had followed the Swimmer-Commando unit and decided to take the opportunity of eliminating some of the hated commandos. That was more palateable for him than the possibility some of the men in this unit had turned their coats. He wasn't able to take that line of thought much further since the air was filled with a curious whistling roar. He looked up as the two Rotodynes started a strafing pass. Observation point or not, it was time to leave.

SBS Unit, Penguin River, South Georgia

Miller looked up. Two Junglie rotodynes swept overhead. Their under-nose gun turrets sprayed fire into the rocks in front of them. *Talk about the cavalry arriving at the last possible minute* he thought. The last Argentine assault had been pushed back, but Harding had been badly hit by the rifle fire. There was a good chance he wouldn't make it out. The Junglies had arrived in just the nick of time. They passed swiftly over the area and were now circling around, clear of the battle area. A rotodyne was about as fast as a Second World War fighter when the pilot was suitably nervous. They didn't hang around over hostile ground. One of the rotodynes swept in again, firing its underwing rockets. The other one headed for the location of the camp hut.

Wearily, Miller squirmed backwards through the rocks, meeting Stroud on the way. "Harding?"

The question was terse. Stroud's response equally so. "Gone."

The two surviving SBS men made their way back to the camp and the Rotodyne that had landed near it. A group of Royal Marines were already spreading out to secure the perimeter. Conscious that he and Stroud were being covered by half a dozen rifles, Miller sought out their commander, carefully avoiding any suggestion the person he was speaking to was an officer. "You made it just in time. Things were getting pretty sticky out there."

"We were heading inland but got a radio message to divert here." The Marine officer looked at the two SBS men with a tinge of awe. They may have been dirty and distinctly malodorous, but they'd secured British sovereignty here on South Georgia for weeks.

"A radio message. Must have been the girls." Stroud looked around for the two women. To his relief he saw them coming in, escorted by a pair of Marines.

202

"What happened to the others?" Cynthia asked the question, although she and Georgina must have known the answer. At any rate, they didn't wait for the answer before starting to cry.

Miller shook his head sadly. "They're out in the rocks. We'd all be there if you hadn't got that radio message out."

Georgina snuffled, then frowned. "Radio? We didn't get a message out. We just hid in the rocks like you told us to."

"Women doing as they are told? You got these two well-trained." The Marine officer faked incredulity then yelped as Cynthia kicked his ankle. Miller shook his head then looked around at the hills. Somehow, they seemed oddly friendly.

HMS Lion, *Flagship, Cruiser Squadron, Off South Georgia*

It was a sight that had not been seen on the world's oceans for more than sixty years. A formation of ships had formed line of battle and were about to open fire on the enemy. There had been naval battles since the First World War of course, but they had been wild scrambles between diffuse formations of ships. They had lacked the stately majesty of the sight Admiral Timothy Tyrrell Chupe saw. The three cruisers lined up astern of his flagship was a sight to be viewed with something like quiet satisfaction. The cruiser squadron had only formed up a few days before. Now it was tasked with supporting the South Georgia landings. HMS *Panther* had come in from China Station, although the long high-speed run from Singapore had strained her old engines. *Tiger* had been hustled out of a remarkably accelerated refit while *Leopard* had come in from Mediterranean Station. At first, they had been assigned to screen the two carriers but they had been relieved of nursemaid detail so they could take part in Operation Parakeet.

"Any word from the booties?" Chupe's question seemed aimed at vacant space but nobody was under any illusions who would have to answer. Chupe ran a taut ship and his officers knew their trade. They also knew how he liked his bridge to run. The key word there was 'smoothly'.

"The Rotodynes relieved the observation point on the Penguin River Sir." The communications officer didn't need to consult his notes. "They rescued the survivors of the SBS team and the two civilians. The SBS were under attack at the time. The Rotodynes gave them fire support but they lost three men out of five. The Marines have the observation point now and are on the radio, prepared to direct fire. One of the Rotodynes is heading over to *Argus* to deliver the survivors, the other inland to pick up the other SBS group and the Antarctic Survey Group survivors."

It was a neat, concise report that earned the communications officer an approving nod. Chupe turned around and looked at the three cruisers following him again. "Order all ships to commence firing on my signal. One salvo, then wait for range and bearing corrections." His attention was still riveted on his four cruisers. He had no intention of missing the historic sight. Chupe paused and took a deep breath. "Signal, open fire."

The sixteen six-inch guns on the four cruisers fired simultaneously, crashing out a single, deafening statement of intent. It was as impressive a sight as Chupe had ever seen.

203

For a moment, he felt a twinge of nostalgia that the days of line of battle and broadsides had gone.

"We have a fire correction, Sir." The communications officer spoke quickly. "Drop range two hundred yards, bearing change plus one degree."

The firing corrections were transmitted to the fire control stations on the four cruisers. The twin turrets on the cruisers shifted slightly. Then the guns crashed again.

"On target, Sir. That lot landed dead center of Grytviken. Spotter says fire for effect."

"Does he indeed? Order all ships; set rate of fire for 20 rounds per minute. One minute barrage."

The orders went out. Chupe waited for a moment then gave the signal for the bombardment to start. Eighty six inch shells arriving in a minute would, he hoped, have the desired effect on the Argentine garrison unfortunate enough to be in Grytviken.

HMS Argus, *Helicopter Support Ship, Off South Georgia*

The whistle of the Rotodyne powering down made the rumble of thunder all the more obvious. Georgina Harcourt shivered as she stepped out of the back of the aircraft. "At least that was one thing we were spared. I hate thunderstorms."

"That's not thunder Ma'am. That's the cruisers bombarding the Argie garrison at Grytviken." Stroud listened to the gunfire with satisfaction. "They're really working the place over."

"But there were people in there! I mean our people."

"Miss Harcourt?" An officer had come out to meet the party. As he got close, Georgina saw his nose wrinkle. She decided to get a shower as soon as humanly possible. "Do you have relatives in the Antarctic Survey Group or the civilians in Grytviken?"

"No, but Cynthia and I met them when we arrived."

"Well, most of them were evacuated inland just before the invasion. They're being picked up now. Three were left in Grytviken: the Postmaster, one other fit person and another who had a leg injury making him unfit to travel. All three are reported to have been killed." The Officer paused, uncertain about how much the two women needed to know. "We have every reason to believe that you two were intended to join them. Anyway, you're safe now. May I offer you the hospitality of HMS *Argus*?"

That was, Georgina decided, a pointed suggestion that she ought to get her shower and some fresh clothing. "Why, thank you Lieutenant . . . . ."

"Dunwoody Ma'am. Harold Dunwoody. Seamen Styles here will show you to your quarters. Sergeant Miller, Marine Stroud, the First Officer wishes to debrief you two immediately. If you would follow me, please."

Thirty minutes later, Dunwoody was back on the bridge. "How are our guests?"

"Very good, Sir. The two women are having a long and much needed shower now. We've issued them with new clothing from the stores. Our two SBS friends are telling the men from Northumberland Avenue everything they know. Any developments in the situation, Sir?" Dunwoody was the ship's Operations Officer, responsible for keeping the tactical plot up to date.

"Go look at the plot." Captain Anthony Ralph grinned. "It is up to date. You've trained your team well. To save you a trip, there are two Bananas doing a swing south and east, another pair are scouting south and west. That's all. The Rotodyne on the deck is taking off soon, going over to Grytviken to see if the Argies want to chuck in the towel. I almost hope they don't. The things I've been hearing about those swimmer commando people turn my stomach.

Dunwoody nodded; both agreeing with the sentiment and appreciative of being saved the trip to the Ops Room. *Argus* was a conversion from a civilian ship and a lot of equipment had been fitted in wherever there was room for it. That meant the Operations Room and its plot were three decks down from the bridge. It was fortunate that telephones had been invented to keep the two in communication, a point that was demonstrated by said telephone ringing.

"Ops Room here. We've just had a message from Spyder-One. They report seeing a small freighter, no more than a trawler really, a bit to the south of where our operations are taking place. Freighter has identified itself as the motor vessel *Nikogaš Nevidel*." The speaker's voice stumbled badly over the name and paused before recovering. "She's on the Macedonian registry, Sir."

"Macedonian? What the devil is she doing down here? Check the confidential books, Harry; see if she's mentioned. Ops, tell the Bananas to keep an eye on her."

Dunwoody vanished for a few minutes and then returned with a grin on his face. "No mention in the CBs, Sir, nor in the naval reference book. But, I checked through the Admiralty Bulletin and she is mentioned in there. Small freighter, Macedonian Registry, was carrying supplies to South Georgia but was unable to complete her voyage due to the Argentine Occupation. Her skipper negotiated an agreement with the Admiralty to stay in these waters in case she was needed to pick up splashed aircrew."

"A service for which their Lordships are paying handsomely I would guess." Ralph snorted in indignation. "I suppose it's one less thing our ships have to do. Pass the word through to the Bananas. Tell them to buzz her and then proceed with their patrol."

Grytviken, South Georgia.

"There can be no doubt that Grytviken is indefensible. With the ships sunk, there is no need to stay here. We will retreat to our original position at Leigh Harbor." Astrid gave out the orders without any sign of emotion. Around him, the Argentine naval facility at Grytviken was a blazing shambles. The barrage of heavy gunfire had been short, sharp, and incredibly destructive. There was little left of the supplies and equipment that had been assembled for the occupation of the other islands in the chain.

205

"And Leith Harbor is any better protected from bombardment and air attack?" Marine Captain Teobaldo Castro spoke with heavy irony larded thick in his voice.

"No, but we have supplies there we can use."

"And how are we supposed to get there? Have any of the Snowcats survived to carry us?"

"Of course." Astrid sounded impatient with the argument. "Some were lost but there are enough to carry my men to Leith Harbor."

"Your men." Castro's voice was flat. "And us?"

"You will act as the rearguard. Fight the enemy here and delay them. Deny this harbor to them as long as possible."

I had thought as much. Internally, Castro seethed with anger at the obvious plan that lay underneath Astrid's words. *To throw the Marines to the wolves while the Swimmer-Commando group made its escape. Doubtless, they plan to be picked up on the coast somewhere. Probably by submarine. Time to throw some obstacles into this set-up.*

"A very courageous decision, Captain Astrid. Certainly, to try and hold Grytviken now, even as a rearguard will be a desperate task. To undertake the journey to Leith Harbour by Snowcat under constant air attack in the hope of one last glorious stand, that is truly heroic."

Astrid paled slightly but looked suspiciously at the Marine Captain. *I know what he's thinking.* Castro looked at Astrid steadily. *He thinks I'll hand this place over to the British as soon as he's gone and tell them where he is heading for. Nobody said he was stupid, that's exactly what I'll do if he goes through with pulling out.*

"Perhaps to split our forces in the face of the enemy is not the best of plans." Astrid sounded pompous. He paused and went over to speak with some of his men. Castro couldn't hear what they were saying, but they quickly left the room. "We will concentrate our forces here, in Grytviken. And fight to the last man."

You mean fight to the last of my men. What the hell have you got planned? Castro stared at Astrid again and tried to work out what was running through his mind. Whatever it was, it wouldn't end well for the marine detachment, Castro was very sure of that.

The long, silent wait was interrupted by the radio crackling. "Commander, Argentine Garrison in Grytviken. This is Royal Navy Rotodyne Dog-One. We have you under our guns and you are defenseless against naval bombardment and air attack. In order to prevent unnecessary loss of life, we offer you the opportunity of surrendering immediately. If you fail to do so, the bombardment will resume. The burst of fire earlier was just a small example of the firepower at our disposal."

Astrid looked around at the other occupants of the room before picking up the radio microphone. "Dog One, this is the Argentine expeditionary force commander. In view of the hopelessness of our position, we are prepared to negotiate surrender terms. Please land your Rotodyne on the helicopter pad just south of the Grytviken area."

As Astrid finished, Castro saw an evil grin spreading over the Swimmer-Commando officer's face, His mind flashed back to the surreptitious orders a few minutes earlier and his stomach sank. *What has this idiot done?* He lunged forward and grabbed the microphone from Astrid's hands before he react. "Royal Navy rotodyne, do not, repeat do not land on that helicopter pad."

Royal Navy Rotodyne Dog-One, Over Grytviken, South Georgia

"What the hell is going on down there?" The scream of warning and the sounds of fighting came clearly over the radio. In the back of the Rotodyne, Admiral Chupe and the party of Royal Marines were on edge.

"Don't know Sir. We got warned off, then they're fighting amongst themselves. Fists and feet by the sound of it. We're having a look at that helicopter pad right now."

The rotodyne copilot was scanning the area through the thermal imager built into the Fairey Defender's under-nose gun turret. He sucked his teeth very audibly. "Interesting sight down there, Jim. Most of the ground is cold but the helicopter pad has a number of warm spots on it. About a dozen of them. The sort of spots one gets when digging a shallow hole and burying something."

"Something like a landmine?"

"Something exactly like a landmine. The bastards."

"Not all of them. We got warned off, remember? Admiral, Sir, the proposed landing point was a minefield. We're circling around again."

The ground link crackled back into life. "Royal Navy Rotodyne, this is Captain Castro, Argentine Marines. We wish to negotiate a surrender, but as you value your life, don't go near that landing pad."

"We won't, Captain. It's mined. Who was the first person who spoke?"

"That was Captain Astrid."

In the back of the Rotodyne, Chupe's head snapped up. That name featured heavily in his secret orders. "Who commands there now?"

The Rotodyne pilot relayed the message. The answer was immediate. "I do. Captain Astrid has been . . . detained." There was an almost humorous undertone to the message. Chupe formed a picture in his mind of Astrid prone on the floor with half a dozen marines sitting on him.

"Tell Captain Astrid that we will land on that pad provided he leads a line of his men in marching backwards and forwards over it."

There was a pause.When Castro spoke again, the amusement was more obvious. "Captain Astrid respectfully declines the invitation. We are in the Kino Building, this is our headquarters. You know where it is?"

Chupe nodded. There was more to that message than it sounded. By revealing the location of their headquarters, the Argentine Marine Captain had given a clear indication that his intentions were genuine.

A few minutes later, the Rotodyne had landed beside the Kino Building. Two dozen Argentine Marines were gathered around the building, surrounding another dozen or so men who were sitting on the ground with their hands on their heads.

"Captain Castro?" Admiral Chupe picked out the Marine Captain and acknowledged the salute. "I must thank you for your warning. Had we landed on those mines, there would have been a bloodbath here."

"I think that was the intention Admiral. To make any kind of surrender impossible while the perpetrators of that crime slipped away in the chaos of the fighting."

"I agree. Is Captain Astrid here?" The question was rhetorical. It was answered by a dishevelled figure being pushed forward. "Ah, Captain Astrid. I must advise you that you are under arrest as a suspect in the murder of Postmaster Walsingham."

"You cannot . . . "

Astrid's words were interrupted by one of the Argentine marine sergeants. He spoke after glancing at Castro and getting a nod of approval. "Admiral, Sir, I and my men, we all saw that happen. A brutal, cowardly murder of a brave old man." There was a stir of approval and agreement amongst the Argentine Marine unit.

Mixed up with the British Marine contingent, Sergeant Miller heard the description. He whispered to Stroud, "Actually, he was a cantankerous old fart but he'll never go down in history that way now."

CHAPTER TWO
SHAPING A BATTLEFIELD

Royal Australian Navy Submarine Rotorua, *East of the Beagle Channel, South Atlantic*

"The underwater navigation equipment is remarkable." Lieutenant Marco Elorreaga was genuinely impressed. *Rotorua* had spent her time at sea in a cruise down to Chilean waters on the Pacific side of Tierra del Fuego then nosing around the maze of inlets and channels that characterized the coast. As she had done so, Elorreaga had become steadily more impressed with the submarine's handling characteristics. Those were waters he had been familiar with. Indeed after two years on the Chilean Navy submarine *Simpson*, he considered himself intimate with them. For all that, the *Simpson* had never gone through the Beagle Channel submerged. On the rare occasions a Chilean submarine had gone through the Channel, she had made the run surfaced.

Not *Rotorua*. She had made the run submerged, all the way. The transit had been made possible by the submarine's bottom-mapping sonar. It allowed her to thread her way through the maze of channels and reefs that had obstructed the passage. There had been a few anxious moments as the seabed had reared up and appeared to block the way but *Rotorua* had managed to find her course through despite her bulk. All in all, it had been a stunning demonstration of navigational expertise. Elorreaga had been mesmerized by the continuous picture the bottom-mapping sonar had revealed. The bottom of the Beagle Channel had never been mapped properly before. The structures that the sonar revealed were as unfamiliar as the far side of the moon.

Despite the equipment and the skill with which it had been used, Captain Beecham and the rest of the crew were heartily pleased to get out of the narrow waters that had confined them. The narrow channel was no place for a submarine; there was a danger *Rotorua* would have been run down by a merchant ship in the shallower sections. Even in deeper areas, their room to maneuver was severely limited. There had been a collective sigh of relief around the submarine when she had finally debouched from the Beagle Channel into the comparatively unrestricted waters around Picton Island.

"These submarines have gathering electronic intelligence as one of their primary purposes." Beecham was uneasily aware he was dropping into sales pitch mode again. "That means we have to get into and out of some pretty tight places sometimes. The bottom mapping sonar was developed just after World War Two as part of the effort to find out

209

how bad the radioactive contamination of the North Sea was going to be. Nobody liked the answers we got, of course, but we learned much about seabeds and their history in the process. The current Australian FOSM, Admiral Fox, made some of those early voyages in the submarine *Xena*."

Elorreaga nodded. The disaster that had struck the North Sea after the 1947 bombing of Germany was still forcing the world to deal with its consequences. An entire sea had been left an unusable wasteland, its fish and resources unobtainable. Only in the last few years had the slow decline of the contamination begun to open it up again. He decided it was time to try one of the more provocative questions he had been instructed to ask when the time was right. The answer was anticipated; the important thing was how that answer was given. "Electronic intelligence gathering. From the Chipanese I suppose?"

Beecham smiled, very well aware of how the game was played. "You might think so, I couldn't possibly comment. We are very well equipped for the work though. We have both communications and radar intercept antennas, installed on separate masts. The processing and analysis units are in the communications room just aft of this compartment. We like to think we can give a Septic nuke boat a run for its money in that area. Both scopes have radar warning systems as well, of course. As does the snort. We don't want to be caught by a patrol aircraft using any of our masts."

"What about our own navigational radar? Isn't using that a risk?"

Beecham paused, thinking carefully. "We have a frequency-modulated continuous wave navigation radar. Its maximum power output is low so detecting it should be difficult. Having said that, personally, I prefer not to use it. I don't think a submarine should emit anything unless it has to. We came through Beagle relying on our mapping sonar and that's the way I like it. The mapping sonar itself is detectable of course but it's a lesser risk than the radar set."

"I wonder what's going on up there." It was phrased as an abstract question about radar and communications emissions but Beecham knew Elorreaga really meant news about the war.

"Let's find out." Beecham turned away to give the orders. "Sonar room, any signatures out there?"

"No, Sir."

"Good. Bring her up to periscope depth. Comms, be ready to raise COMINT and ELINT masts and gather all electronic data."

Rotorua creaked slightly as she changed depths. When she leveled out, the creaks were replaced by a subdued whine as her periscope extended. Beecham's standing orders were that whenever his submarine came to periscope depth, the surveillance scope should be raised unless he had specifically ordered to the contrary. As the eyepiece rose, he grabbed hold of it and did a rapid 360 degree scan. As soon as he'd finished, he made a sharp gesture with one hand and the periscope slid down.

"Up surveillance masts."

"You are very concerned about what is happening on the surface." Elorreaga wasn't critical, if anything his voice carried approval.

"This is a war zone and we don't want to get sunk. Really, we shouldn't be here. However, my main concern is getting hit by a merchie. We think we probably lost *Penelope* that way."

The reference caused a momentary sadness around the control room. The Australian submarine service was a small and close-knit family. The disappearance of the submarine *Penelope* a year earlier had been a blow, one made worse by nobody knowing what had happened to her. She had simply left on patrol and never returned. The consensus of opinion was that she had been run down by a merchant ship, but there were other, dark rumors of a Chipanese boat ambushing her. Nobody knew. Unless her wreck was found, nobody ever would.

"Comms here, Sir. You'd better come and see this. We've got contacts all over the sea."

"Follow me, Marco." Beecham led the way into the Comms Room. Standing at the hatchway, he could see what the problem was. The big multi-colored display showed a mass of contacts to the north, and east of them.

"We're picking up radar, comms and datalinks. Recording everything, of course. Most of this is Argentine." The ELINT operator on duty thought quickly. "I'd say this is an ASW operation, Sir. We've got radars from ships and aircraft plus datalinks between them. If this was normal times, I'd say we were watching an exercise. Under the circumstances, I'd say this is the real thing."

"And something we'd better keep well clear of." Beecham looked around quickly. "Record everything you can and store it. What we can't decrypt or analyze, the boys back home will. If any of that lot starts to move our way, alert me immediately.

Beecham returned to the control room. "We have an ASW operation going on north and east of us. We'll stream our tail and hang out our ears for whatever we can pick up. Otherwise, we can head south and get away from this."

Rotorua swung south, shuddering slightly as her towed array was deployed from its nest between her twin screws. Soon, it too was adding its input to the information on the Argentine ASW operation behind her.

Ministry of Defence, Whitehall, London

"Good afternoon, General." Igrat smiled at General Howard and sipped delicately at the tea she had been offered. "I have the latest reconnaissance pictures and other data your command staff will need. Also, I have words for you."

Howard smiled politely, and listened to her voice adopt the flat, disinterested tones of The Seer. As usual, the 'words' were mostly opinions and analysis rather than facts although a few of the latter were included. As always, they were ones that were too sensitive to be put in writing. Idly, Sir John Howard wondered just how many profound secrets Igrat carried in her head. To his surprise and discomfort, Igrat appeared to have guessed what he was thinking.

"I forget them. Not deliberately, but I do. In a week's time, I will never be able to remember anything I have just told you." Igrat had finished the 'words' and was speaking in her own voice. "Experts who have studied memories tell me people can either remember things like messages for a long time or they can remember them very accurately but not both. I do the latter. I remember the words until I deliver them, then they fade away quickly." She grinned at him, knowing her ability to guess what people around her were thinking had caught him unawares.

"Igrat, I have news for you although I'd guess the Seer already knows most of it. The Argentine forces on South Georgia have surrendered. They're being taken to HMS *Argus* now for delivery to Uruguay."

"Alberto Astrid?" Igrat's heavy-lidded eyes had opened slightly at the news. She wasn't absolutely certain why The Seer was so interested in that one man but he was and so she took it on herself to gather as much data as she could for him. "Do you have him?"

"We've got him. We're charging him with the murder of Postmaster James Walsingham. There's a lot of complications of course, we're already getting representations from four governments . . . ." Howard saw Igrat's interest and enlarged on the subject, "Italy, Sweden, France and Spain. They all have citizens who have disappeared in Argentina over the last few years and they seek an accounting. At the very least, they want to talk to him. The problem is that we have already heard from the Argentine government as well. They have waxed furious over the charges we are bringing against Astrid and are threatening reprisals against prisoners of war they hold if we continue with them."

Although Igrat gave no outward signs of it, internally she winced. That sort of action would not go down well in the United States. This was probably the hardest part of her job, one that she had learned over thousands of delivery trips around the world. She had sat in on meetings where the information she had brought was needed and had to bite her tongue to stop herself speaking. Her position meant that any words she uttered would be taken as official U.S. policy. The consequences of voicing her own personal opinions could be disastrous. At the very least, it would mean a complete loss of trust in her. That was something she was not prepared to countenance.

"Do you have words for me to take back to Washington?" Igrat's husky voice was dead level and showed no sign of her own internal conflict. The question was her way of getting back her mental equilibrium.

Howard smiled at her. He had dealt with high-grade couriers many times and he had a shrewd idea of what had just passed through Igrat's mind. "Yes, indeed. Please pass on the message that we have Astrid and we have received messages demanding he be transferred to the custody of other countries for trial and from Argentina demanding he be treated like any other prisoner of war. Please also add that observation of our other Argentine prisoners of war indicate that he is much feared by them and equally hated. At the moment, there are no British PoWs in Argentine hands, so their threats are mere posturing. That's the end of my words on this issue. May I offer you another cup of tea?"

He pressed a button on his desk and the door opened with the tea-trolley. "General, the Prime Minister is about to make a public announcement." The tea lady was arranging a fresh pot of tea and a plate of Jaffa Cakes on Howard's desk. She smiled at the General, looked coldly at Igrat and then left.

"Let's see what he has to say." Howard turned on the television. It was already tuned to the BBC and the picture formed quickly.

Prime Minister Newton was speaking. "Ladies and gentlemen. The Secretary of State for Defence has just come over to give me some very good news and I think you'd like to have it at once. We have received the surrender of all Argentine forces on South Georgia. The news has been confirmed by the following message from Admiral Chupe, commander of the British forces in the South Georgia region. 'Be pleased to inform Her Majesty that the White Ensign flies alongside the Union Jack in South Georgia. God save the Queen.' Now is the time to rejoice at this news and congratulate our forces and the marines while not forgetting the stern tasks that are still ahead of us. Rejoice." Newton turned away to the door of Number Ten and vanished inside.

Naval Headquarters, Buenos Aires, Argentina

"We can't hold Las Malvinas without controlling the seas around the islands. We can't do that while the British Navy is operating there unchallenged. So, we have to challenge them. Get the fleet to sea and do just that." Admiral Jorge Anaya had just come from another bristling meeting with President Galtieri; one that had centered around the fall of South Georgia. Anaya had his own worries about that; not least was the fact the British had captured Captain Astrid alive. So, in the great manner of things, he was about to relieve his problems by giving Vice-Admiral Juan Lombardo a hard time. Lombardo would doubtless pass that down to his flag captain who would transmit the nausea with interest to his lieutenant. The lieutenant would go home and beat his wife who would then kick her dog. The dog would then go out and harass a cat that would respond by killing the nearest rodent it could find. Such was the way of the world

"We only have the one carrier available." Lombardo was thoughtful. "Of course, we carry more aircraft than the British carriers and we have a better screen. Yes, Admiral, I think we can do this."

Anaya stopped in his tracks. He had been expecting protests and explanations as to why it couldn't be done. Lombardo's thoughtful and considered approval took the wind out of his sails. That left him only one line of attack. "Then why aren't the ships at sea?" The question came out with menacing undertones.

"The British carriers have only just come within our range." Lombardo still sounded thoughtful, apparently unaware of his superior's urgent need to scream in rage. "There was little point in wasting fuel cruising around waiting for them. But now is the perfect time to stage our attack. The two carriers must be split, one coming up from South Georgia, the other already in our area. If we move quickly, we can catch them apart and destroy them piecemeal. Admiral, I suggest the ships put to sea without a moment of delay."

Anaya was almost crying. *Why was it, the one time I really needed to throw a furious tirade at somebody, they all kept anticipating what I want and agreeing with me?* "See that it is done. And we need to reinforce the garrison on the Malvinas immediately."

Lombardo looked at the situation display. "We lost a freighter west of the islands. We have also lost contact with a submarine that was in the same area. We believe that both were the victim of a British submarine that was in the area. Almost certainly one of their nuclear-powered boats. We are conducting a hunt in the area now but so far we have made no contact." That had hardly surprised Lombardo. Trying to find a nuclear attack submarine with the resources the Argentine Navy had available was a triumph of optimism over reality. The British submarine that had killed the merchant ship and the submarine, he had no doubt that both were lost, was certainly long gone from the scene by now. "It would be unwise for us to send another slow merchantman into that area now. Instead, I suggest that we use the two assault cruisers. They can make the voyage at full speed and deliver additional anti-aircraft equipment to the islands. We have the destroyers *Catamarca* and *Entre Rios* to act as escort for them. We'll need the other three missile destroyers to screen the carrier of course."

Lombardo paused at that point. He was actually unhappy about detaching the *Entre Rios* to screen the assault cruisers. Another missile destroyer, *Mendoza*, should have been available but she had stripped a main reduction gear a few weeks earlier and was in dockyard hands. That left just three such strips to screen the carrier. Quietly, he cursed the state-owned Argentine naval shipyard. They had two more missile destroyers under construction but they were running years late. They should have been in the fleet already, but it would be a long time before they arrived. That left the navy short of anti-aircraft firepower.

"You would trust such important ships to a mere two destroyers as escort?" At last Anaya had found something he could rant about.The relief was cathartic to his troubled soul. He let loose with a flurry of choice epithets and stomped over to view the ready board. "You will add *Santissima Trinidad* and *Almirante Garcia* to the squadron immediately. And see that those ships are at sea without any further delay. Then he stormed out of the room.

Lombardo made the necessary additions to the plans. He admitted to himself that adding the two old American destroyers to the screen made a certain amount of sense. They were Gearing class DDEs, fleet destroyers modified to act as fast escorts for aircraft carrier groups. Their twelve three-inch guns gave them good anti-aircraft firepower by gunnery standards. They had Otomat anti-ship missiles in case enemy warships intercepted them. It was their capability against modern submarines that was sorely lacking. Still, there was nothing in the Argentine fleet that was much better in that respect.

He looked at the resulting naval operations plan and shrugged. A carrier group to hammer on the British and the assault cruiser group to run additional equipment to the garrison on the Malvinas. It was about as workmanlike a plan as he could come up with.

Military Transport Drakensburg *South Atlantic.*

"I think we have found the rest of the amphibious squadron." Lieutenant Colonel Rigsby looked around the bridge of the *Drakensburg* with a measure of satisfaction. He was painfully aware that the British troops on the ship were inexperienced by comparison

214

with the hardened South Africans but the sight of the ships arrayed around them was compensation. There was no way South Africa could match the sea power that was on show here. And that didn't allow for the cruiser squadron and the aircraft carriers that were already closing on the Falkland Islands.

"I thought the carriers were running ahead of us." Shumba Geldenhuys looked at the two massive ships off to port with curiosity. "Are we to go in as a single group then?"

"Those aren't carriers Shumba. They're the assault ships *Albion* and *Bulwark*. They're putting the AirMech brigade ashore. They've got the Rotodynes for the job. See over there? The two LPDs? They're *Fearless* and *Intrepid*. They have the bulk of the armor on board for the landing at San Carlos. The infantry is aboard the two liners." Rigsby waved at the two liners slipping through the waves behind the warships. Their elegance tended to emphasize the chunky functionalty of the warships. The two liners were exuding a faint air of embarrassment, rather akin to two society ladies who had accidentally found themselves in a bordello.

"God have mercy on them if they are hit." Geldenhuys spoke with deep sincerity. He suspected the ships had limited internal subdivision and were stuffed with inflammable materials.

"It's not quite as bad as that. They were designed with experience from the *Titanic* and *Britannic* in mind, so the subdivision is a lot better than you might think. Also, they've been thoroughly stripped inside. Lord knows what Cunard will think when they get them back. It's the size of the target they offer that worries me. An Argie pilot will be hard put to miss them. We'll just have to hope they won't get that close."

Geldenhuys looked around at the six destroyers escorting the amphibious formation. "The big ones over there, the cruisers? Can we persuade them to stay close to us?"

Rigsby laughed. "Well, if your farms can get fresh steaks out to us, they'll stay close all right. Best beef in the world so I'm told." He'd done his research on the South Africans. One of the things he'd learned was that to the Boers, their farms held a special place in the national consciousness. Praising their produce was a sure way to make friends and influence people. "The two big ones are H-class destroyers. *Hero* and *Hotspur*. *Hero*'s in good shape but *Hotspur* is fresh out of the builder's yard. Still got dockies on board finishing her off."

Rigsby paused for a moment. Ugly memories tugged at his mind. "Last time we sent a ship to sea like that was during the Great Escape. The battleship *Howe*. She was only partially complete and the only operational guns on board were a few machine guns. The other battleships in the group were fully armed and could put up a pretty lethal barrage so the Germans picked on her. She caught hell from German Condors and only just made it out. The crew just had to sit there and take it. For hour after hour without any help. If the Condors had torpedoes, it would have been all over for them because the rest of the fleet couldn't stop to pick up survivors and the Germans had no intention of doing that. But the Condors didn't and so they made it to Canada."

Geldenhuys spoke gently, understanding the depth of the memories being evoked and noted Rigsby's age. He'd already noticed that the British Army was a young force. Its officers were, on average, five or six years younger than their equivalents in other armies. He still hadn't decided if that was a good or a bad thing. "You sound like you knew this personally. Your father was on board?"

"My father. After they got to Canada, *Howe* was completed in an American yard and spent the first part of the war escorting convoys in the North Atlantic. Then she and the other members of the class went out to Singapore as the British Pacific Fleet and sort of deterred the Japanese. After the war, he came back to the U.K. He had the chance to go to Australia but he wanted to come home and help the old country recover. I remember waking up at nights, hearing him have nightmares about the Great Escape. Not about the Arctic Convoys; although Lord knows, they were bad enough. It was the Great Escape that haunted him. He didn't talk about it until I joined up and then he spent a whole evening telling me the story. That's one reason why I went into the Army, not the Navy."

"I had no choice there. Our navy is too small to offer a worthwhile career. It was the Army. The only choice was whether to do three years as a conscript or volunteer and become a professional. Not much for me back home, so a volunteer I became. Good choice for a Griqua. Fighting is what we do best."

"And very lucky for us." Rigsby was fervent on that point. "You've brought good men with you and we need the expertise. Lord knows we've trained enough but we're as green as grass compared with your boys."

"You should believe me on this; the fighting on our northern border is no work for a real soldier. Fighting those gangs of murdering thugs is nothing like a real war. Take Lieutenant van Huis. Fighting the 'Stams is the only thing Bastiaan has ever done. He knows as little of fighting a real army as your young Lieutenant Cross does. We're all learning this together. Let us just pray there'll be enough of us left to pass on what we have learned."

"Amen to that. Cross comes from good stock though. His father was a German panzergrenadier." Rigsby hesitated slightly. "There's something a little odd there. His old man is a housepainter; nothing special, but some of the records are sealed. Something happened with that family back in the '50s that isn't for publication."

Geldenhuys shrugged. "Who knows? Bastiaan comes from the second richest family in the Republic and his wife comes from the richest. That's why the men call him Lieutenant Geldsakke. Lieutenant Moneybags. He could have bought his way into a comfortable desk job in Pretoria, but he's out here with us instead. Just like your Lieutenant Cross. We're all here now. That's all that matters. True my friend?"

"True." Rigsby looked out at the amphibious squadron that was shifting positions to absorb the new arrivals from Simonstad. "And there's no way we can get out and walk home if we change our mind."

Sea Mirage F.2 XS-576. Over the South Atlantic

There were times when a fighter needed two crew members. One to fly the aircraft and another to watch the radar set. This was not one of those times. That was fortunate because the Sea Mirage was a single-seater. Lieutenant Commander Dudley Pope was flying his Sea Mirage with its radar emphatically turned off. He was relying on radar

216

input from the ships to steer him in on his target, an Argentine Navy Superstream I executive jet that had been bought on the civilian market and converted for maritime reconnaissance. The equipment fitted to it had included an elaborate ELINT system, probably housed in the great pod that hung under its belly. That system was undoubtedly picking up radar emissions from the British warships. In fact, the crew were probably depending on those emissions to find the ships. If they detected airborne radar emissions coming for them, they would run.

The Superstream I was a derivative of the old RB-58C with its fuselage reprofiled to include a cramped cabin for eight passengers. It was still powered by the J-79 engines that could drive it up to Mach 2.4 at high altitudes but it would have to go to full reheat to do so. That meant that would burn its fuel fast. The catch was that if the Superstream I went to full speed, Pope would have to do the same. His Sea Mirage was barely 30 mph faster than the executive jet. In a tail chase, he would run out of fuel long before he got within missile range. So this intercept was an ambush. The plan was that by the time the Superstream detected his presence, it would be too late to run. Idly, Pope gave thanks that the target was a Superstream and not a SAC RB-58G. Trying this on the latter would get a fighter pilot a nuclear-tipped air-to-air missile fired into his face. Ever since *Marisol* had gone down almost twenty years ago, the Septics had been very unforgiving about people trying to intercept their bombers.

"Target is 20 miles in front of you. Continue steering two-eight-zero. Target altitude is angels 35." The voice from ground control was dispassionate.

"Acknowledged. Still in cloud layer." Pope's response was equally calm. The weather was bad, all right. The cloud levels were thick and stretched all the way up to 30,000 feet. The next part of the plan was to accelerate within the cloud layer and then zoom up to stage the intercept.

"Target is turning now." The Superstream was on a racetrack; an oval holding pattern that allowed its sensors to scan a wide area of ocean. It was reaching the end of one of the long sides of that oval and would be turning towards him. Pope had the relative positions in his mind. This would be a collision course intercept. For that he would need the R-530 missiles hanging under his wings. He switched over to them so the electronics would start to warm up.

"Acknowledged. Starting bounce now." Pope firewalled his throttles, feeling the two Atar 9 engines in his fighter surging to full power. The Sea Mirage surged forward, sliding through the sound barrier easily. It took only a gentle pull on the control column to cause the aircraft to leap upwards, breaking through the top of the cloud layer. Pope flipped on the radar set and saw the blip from the Superstream blossom on the scanner. The data from the contact was already being relayed down to his missiles and readying them for firing.

Something was wrong. The Superstream was there, all right, but it was a lot further away and a little higher than the ground controlled interception reports had suggested. Pope guessed what had happened. *The Superstream has a deception jammer on board to hide its true position in case somebody tried this.* The executive jet was already turning fast and diving away. Pope could see the misty concussion wave forming around its fuselage as it accelerated and the brilliant red flare of its afterburners shone against the sky. He quickly glanced down. The aircraft's true position was painted on his radar screen and he was closing fast. The problem was the rate of closure was dropping quickly as the Superstream accelerated away from him.

He did the mathematics in his head. By the time the Superstream was up to full speed, he would be within eight miles of it. That was within the range of his R-530 missiles, but they would be in a tail chase and the margin of speed wasn't that high. His two R-510 infra-red homing missiles were the better weapon for a tail chase. They were faster but shorter-ranged. On the other hand, the brilliant glow of the Superstream's afterburners would be an easy target for them. He took a split second to decide and then flipped over to the infra-red missiles. In his earphones, the broken notes of the annunciator system wavered for a second and then settled down to a constant, steady tone. The missiles were locked on. Down on his radar screen, the dot representing the Superstream now had a diamond carat around it.

Pope exhaled, held his breath slightly and squeezed the trigger that sent the two R-510 missiles streaking off towards the fleeing reconnaissance aircraft. They wavered slightly, then settled down to track the Superstream in front of them. For a moment, Pope thought he had his kill but the Superstream crew had a few tricks left. One was a brilliant ruby-colored light that started flickering under the tail. Another was the mass of white trails that erupted from both sides of the aircraft, trails that terminated in glaring red flares. Pope knew what both were. The light was an infra-red jammer; it was carefully calibrated to burn out the guidance head on his missiles. The flares were decoys designed to lure the missiles away from their target. He didn't know which system had worked, but his missiles went straight on when the Superstream made an evasive turn. Two clean misses. In the far distance, well away from his target, he saw the patches of cloud as they exploded at the end of their run.

To his frustration, Pope saw the Superstream pulling away from him. It was much heavier than his fighter and that gave it the edge in a dive. Given long enough he would catch it up but his engines were burning fuel at a prodigious rate. It wouldn't be long before he had to pull away and return to the carrier. The Superstream was gulping fuel as well, but it had much more of it and its B-58 forebear had been designed to hold speed for prolonged periods under just these circumstances. Pope did the calculations in his head again. His R-530s were really marginal and he would be out of fuel by the time they got to be anything more than that.

One other factor ran through his head. The British carrier groups were fighting with what they had. There wasn't any more. He'd already wasted two missiles. Throwing away two more would be inexcusable. As if to reinforce that thought, the red fuel warning light on his instrument panel clicked on. It was time to go home.

"Bandit got away. Used deception jamming to hide position. Flares and an IR jammer to evade two missiles. On bingo fuel and retuning home."

"Acknowledged. At least you scared him off."

Argentine Aircraft Carrier Veinticinco de Mayo

"The reconnaissance aircraft has called in, Sir." The communications officer had made it to the Admiral's bridge in record time. They were chased off by a fighter but before that they got contact on the British carrier group. It's almost exactly due west of us, 407 nautical miles out. A long way for our Skyhawks."

Vice-Admiral Juan Lombardo gazed at the attack plot. "The Superstream spotted both carriers?"

"No, Sir. Just the one. Steering slightly north of west."

"Then the one from South Georgia hasn't had time to join up yet. Interesting. We still have a chance to catch them apart."

The mathematics were easy and, as it happened, very convenient. The Skyhawk had a tactical radius of 340 nautical miles with four thousand pounds of bombs on board. That mean the British carrier would be on the edge of that radius in two hours. It would take two hours to get a strike ready. That meant that there was a good chance the *Veinticinco de Mayo* could get her strike in first. In carrier warfare, getting a strike in first was all that mattered. She had 54 aircraft on board, 24 Skyhawks and 30 F9U Crusaders. Six more Crusaders were overhead flying combat air patrol. Lombardo had read of how the American carrier *Shiloh* had been caught without her combat air patrol and had no intention of following the same example.

"Prepare a strike. Eighteen Skyhawks and twelve Crusaders. After they're gone, we'll get another twelve Crusaders on deck alert in case the British get their strike in. The remaining aircraft, get them ready for a second anti-shipping strike in case the second carrier turns up."

His Air Group commander started rattling out orders. Then, he paused for a second, "Admiral, thousand pounders and Bullpups on the Skyhawks?"

Lombardo nodded. "Make it so."

CAG finished his orders off. By the time the last words were out, the results had already started to become apparent. Skyhawks and Crusaders were being rolled out of their positions in the deck park and towards the lifts. They were being struck down below, ready to be fuelled and armed up. Below decks, men would be pulling the thousand pounders from the magazines and installing the impact fuses on them. Other crews would be in the missile magazines getting the Bullpups out of their racks and readying them for installation on the Skyhawks. Beside them, other men would be getting the Sparrow and Sidewinder missiles out of storage and readying them for the Crusaders.

"Sir, the Crusaders can get to the carrier position now. Should we launch a fighter sweep first?" CAG was as undecided as he sounded.

Lombardo thought it out. *The F9U had a tactical radius of 435 nautical miles. They could get to the enemy position very quickly; in less than 15 minutes if they went out on full power all the way. Of course, if they did that, they would be running desperately low on fuel. And if they did show up, they would be telling the British that the strike planes were following. Doing a fighter sweep first was American doctrine that was certain, What worked for Americans with their huge resources was not so good for others.* Another thing weighed with Lombardo. He was reading a history of the Battle of the Orkneys, *'Shattered Club'* it was called. It made great play of how the German carrier admiral had been so

219

desperate to get off his strike, he hadn't got his full fighter force up when the American strike groups hit. Lombardo had shaken his head at that. Now he realized just how easy it was to be seduced into thinking the strike was the only thing that mattered.

"No. Our first blow will be the heavy one. We must try and catch the British before they launch. And make sure the crews down below get the rest of our fighters ready as soon as the strike is spotted on deck."

Lombardo turned away and looked out of his bridge windows on to the turmoil below. It was hard to see order in the maneuvers going on down there but getting aircraft struck down to the hangar deck and then moving them back up to the spots on the flight deck was well-rehearsed. As he watched, the elevator forward between the two catapults started to drop. Almost unconsciously, he started counting seconds. He reached 45 when the empty elevator re-appeared and another F9U was pushed on to it. For a round trip that involved getting the aircraft off the lift as well, 45 seconds was very good. The flight deck crews might be in turmoil but it was a well-ordered turmoil. The crews knew what they were doing.

Going into the first carrier battle in the history of the Argentine Navy, Lombardo just prayed that he knew what he was doing.

Control Room, HM Submarine Saint Vincent

"Lot of surface ship propeller noise, Captain. Many screws in the water, I think we're hearing multiple twin-screwed ships and at least one four-screwed. Bearing is of-four-seven, course due west."

"The Argentine carrier group?" *Saint Vincent* was one of four nuclear-powered attack submarines strung out as a picket line between the Falklands and the Argentine naval bases. There should have been five but *Collingwood* was off the air and showed no signs of reappearing. That was causing an increasing level of concern. Her absence had been made up by *Vanguard* arriving from the Pacific.

"Could be, Captain. The sound signatures are distorted but I think one of the ships is an Essex class. Unless either the Brazilians have joined in or the Argies got the *Neuve de Julio* working, it's the *Veinticinco de Mayo*. And that means the main Argie fleet is out."

Captain Wiseart tapped the screen showing the plot. It was a long-range passive sonar contact. That meant the range data was very approximate. "What was the weather report? Wind direction?"

"Wind's from the Southwest Captain. It's a prevailing pattern, unlikely to change much."

Wiseart nodded thoughtfully. "If they're getting a strike off, their A-4Ds will be loaded to the max and the F-9Us are marginal for an Essex anyway. Even a rebuilt one. They'll swing into the wind. That means they'll be coming this way. We'll establish a baseline. Reel our tail in, then make thirty two knots course one-eight-zero for thirty minutes. At the end of that time, stream our tail and get another bearing and course."

It was a standard maneuver, one the *Saint Vincent* had practiced many times before. This time there was a tension during the 30 minute run due south that betrayed the fact this time the circumstances were different. After what seemed an age, the submarine slowed down and streamed her towed array. It took another few minutes for the data to be analyzed and plotted. When it appeared on the screens, it caused Wiseart to stare intently at the plot.

"She's there, but heading south west?" The question was rhetorical only. "To do that she must have turned almost as soon as we stopped our run."

There was a nod of agreement around the control room. The weapons officer voiced the thought everybody else had in mind. "Getting ready to launch now."

"And the airdales need to know that." Wiseart snapped out the orders that followed his conclusion. "Periscope depth, establish satellite link and get the warning out to *Furious* and *Glorious*. Comms, tell them they've got visitors coming. Then set up an intercept course for that carrier group."

Flag Bridge, HMS Glorious, *North East of the Falkland Islands*

"That recon bird *Furious* saw off must have reported back." Admiral Charles Lanning was stumping backwards and forwards, running the permutations through his mind. "But there's not much land-based aircraft can do to us out here."

"The marines left on the Falklands say that there's at least a squadron of Macchi Ciclones at Stanley Airfield." Lieutenant Dunbar was leafing through the intelligence reports. "And we have satellite data that the Argentine carrier may be out."

"Is out, Admiral. Permission to enter?" Captain Wales was standing at the hatch leading to the Admiral's Bridge. By convention, even a ship's captain had to ask permission before entering the Flag Bridge.

"Step right in, Charles. You've got word for us?"

"Hot line from Northwood. *Saint Vincent* has radioed in. She's picked up what she thinks is the enemy carrier group almost due west of us. About 400 miles west of us. She says the group turned south west just as they made a position fix. *Saint Vincent* is steering to intercept and attack. Their message was dated just under twenty minutes ago."

Lanning reminded himself that he was not supposed to salute Captain Wales. Not here, anyway. "They're launching aircraft. Must be. They'll fly due east and if we turn into the wind to launch . . ."

All eyes turned to the tactical display. Dunbar typed the position of the report in and then added the course of the two British carrier groups if they also turned to launch. The conclusion was obvious. If the Argentine strike flew due east based on the Superstream's report, they would miss the *Furious* group but pile straight into *Glorious*. Lanning wasted no time in his decision. "Get the fighters up now please, Captain Wales; no delay. That strike could be on us in 30 minutes."

Captain Charles Wales spoke quickly into the intercom. "We can get twelve more Sea Mirages up, full point defense load, two 530s and four 550s each. We've got four Sea Mirages up now. They've got 450 gallon drop tanks and they've been tooling around saving fuel. Bad news is they're short on missiles; one 530 and a pair of 550s each."

He was interrupted by the sound of the bow lift bringing the first of the Sea Mirages up from the hangar. Almost simultaneously, the aft lift was striking down one of the deck park of Buccaneers. Wales looked at the Sea Mirage moving forward on to the catapults. Behind it, the lift was already descending. "We'll have these off in just under ten minutes, Sir. Then we can spot and launch a deck strike of Buccaneers. CAG says we can have sixteen off but they'll only have four Sea Mirages to escort them."

The pensive silence was interrupted by the blast of the first Sea Mirage taking off. "You've done well Charles. How did you have the birds ready?" Lanning was buying time to make a very unpleasant decision and everybody knew it.

"We were readying the group to hit Stanley Airfield. The load on the Bananas is a long way from optimal for a shipping strike. They've got four one thousand pounder retarded bombs and a pair of Bullpups or Martels each. But, better they're in the air with anything than . . . ."

" . . . . than on the deck here when that Argie strike gets in. I know. It's still going to be rough on them going in that way. Launch the strike as soon as the CAP is up. What about the four remaining Bananas? "

"Hangar deck will inert them. We can't get them fuelled, bombed up and off in time."

"Sir." Dunbar spoke quietly. "*Furious* is south of us. Can we assume they got the message?"

"We'll have to. If we start transmitting, it's a come-and-get-us invitation. That Argie strike is going to be bloody enough as it is. No need to give them an engraved invitation."

"Oh, I wouldn't say that." Wales sounded vaguely amused. "My mother always says that nothing scares people quite like one of her engraved invitations."

Flag Bridge, HMS Furious, *North East of the Falkland Islands*

"*Glorious* is going to catch it." The word around the bridge was unanimous. Both *Furious* and *Glorious* would turn into the wind. That would take *Glorious* right into the path of the inbound strike from the Argentine carrier. The same maneuver would take *Furious* well clear. She had been south east of the *Glorious* to start with. That position plus her maneuvers to launch had left her even further south east. The Argentine pilots would find *Glorious* first. That was very hard luck for her, but it gave the strike aircraft on *Furious* a real break.

"And Charlie knows it well." Admiral Kinnear sighed slightly. "He's getting his CAP up now and throwing whatever strike aircraft he can get ready out. And praying he

222

gets his decks clear and hangar inerted before the Argie strike arrives. We've got a chance to do a bit better."

"Anti-shipping strike, Sir?"

"With everything we've got. We'll swing a little south and then come at the Argies from the south. All twenty Bananas. The Highball-fitted aircraft carry those; the rest Martel anti-radar missiles and retarded thousand pounders. We'll give them eight Sea Mirages as escort and keep a dozen more back here as CAP."

There was a moment's hesitation on the bridge. Kinnear sensed it and looked around. "Our strike will be going in an hour later than Charlie's. The Argie skipper will have most of his CAP down for refueling and rearming. Plus he'll have his deck full recovering what's left of his strike. He won't have much up in the way of fighters. What he does have will be out to the west, either intercepting Charlie's birds or chasing them back to their carrier. But, he might have a reserve strike held back in case we turn up. So we need our CAP." There was a slight pause. "And we know the F9U has a hell of an edge over our Sea Mirages. It's four hundred miles per hour faster, it can out-climb and out-turn them and it's got better missiles than we do. If they're escorting a strike in we're going to need that CAP."

He relaxed and watched his command group go to work. All he had to worry about now was whether the Argies really would lob their strike at *Glorious*.

Savoy Hotel, London

Igrat liked the Savoy. There was something about the place that appealed to her more old-fashioned instincts. The renovation that had been finished a few years before had only added to the charms it held for her. It had needed the work badly. Bomb damage from the war and almost twenty years of near-total neglect had come close to leaving the hotel derelict beyond restoration. But, it had been saved. The new owner had invested almost another decade and millions of sovereigns in rebuilding its glories. Now, it was something quite unique. It was a hotel that appeared to belong in the 1920s. It was full of the promise of a golden age before the horrors of the depression and World War Two had given the world a darker and less optimistic shadow. Yet within the shell of the past was a modern and very well equipped hotel. Igrat approved of the blend.

What she didn't approve of was the way her instincts were working overtime to tell her something was wrong. It was a lesson she had both known for herself and one that she had been patiently taught. The one had reinforced the other. *Instincts are your senses picking up information below the level at which you are consciously aware of them. But, your brain knows they are there and is frantically screaming warnings*. Then one thing did catch her eye. She had left a horse hair trapped in the doorframe when she had left. That hair was now on the carpet.

Casually, seemingly by accident, Igrat lightly kicked the door of the room next to hers twice. The kicks were too rapid to be a real accident. A slight pause and then a third kick. Then she went into her own room. Her senses kicked into overdrive. Heather Watson was already there.

"You're a whore." Her voice was a near scream, loaded with viciousness and spite. There was even a trickle of saliva from one corner of her mouth. Heather's sheer rage seemed to charge the air in the room with electriity

"I know," Igrat smiled politely. "I'm one of the best whores around. Everybody knows that. It's just that I stopped charging for it a long time ago; well, mostly anyway. Now, I just accept the presents they give me. Just out of interest, how did you get in?"

"I've got a greyhound badge too. I told the floor manager I had messages for you."

Igrat shook her head, tut-tutting theatrically. "You're only supposed to use it on official business. You're a naughty girl, Heather."

To Igrat's secret glee Heather actually flushed with guilt before her anger reasserted itself. "You, you call me names? You're a . . ."

Igrat listened to the outburst, ostentatiously counting on her fingers. When Heather paused for breath, she cut in on the tirade. "You missed out tramp and slut. But they're Americanisms so I'll forgive you for those. You ought to try for a comprehensive description though. A description is useless if it isn't complete." Behind her air of amusement, Igrat was watching Heather carefully, intentionally goading her into losing her judgment. Another thing Igrat had learned a long way back. When she kept herself cool and the person threatening her didn't, the odds swung dramatically in her favor.

It was working. Igrat saw the skin around Heather's eyes flush red and the corners of her eyes and mouth tighten. Heather had one hand in her bag when she screamed in rage. "Keep your hands off him, you bitch!"

She dropped the handbag, clumsily drawing a knife in the process. Her hand lashed out, holding a kitchen carving knife with a six-inch blade. She slashed at Igrat who delicately side-stepped and grabbed Heather's right wrist. Igrat then took a pace forward and made a half turn before she hooked her foot behind Heather's left leg and jerked it out from under her. Heather Watson swayed for a split second before she crashed to the floor with Igrat on top of her. At some point in her fall, the hand holding the knife had been twisted up Heather's back, keeping the blade well away from Igrat's body. Once she was convinced Heather was pinned down, Igrat used her free hand to press a nerve center in the wrist. Heather's hand went slack and the knife slipped from between her fingers.

An ironic burst of applause echoed in the room. Igrat picked up Heather's knife, then half-turned to look at Achillea who was standing in the communicating door between the two rooms. Henry McCarty was behind her, one of his Colt revolvers drawn. "Well, do you approve? You can have the knife for your collection if you want."

Achillea shook her head. "You were a little slow in taking her down. As to the knife, why would I want a cheap thing like that? Not worth the shelf space. Heather, when you're buying a knife you get what you pay for and paying top dollar is worth every cent. Take a look at this." She walked over to the desk, trapped the knife blade between the frame and a drawer, then jerked sharply downwards. The blade snapped with a dull click. "Hear that? Third or fourth-rate steel, no better than a table knife. It'll break just when you need it most."

224

"And it's too big." Igrat chimed in. "Distance from the skin to vital organs is three inches, four at the outside. Anything more than that just makes the knife clumsier to use. Incidentally, do you plan to lie on the floor all evening?"

Heather got up, crying from a mixture of shock and humiliation. Even so she was shocked to see that she was at least four inches taller than Igrat. Somehow, in the brief seconds of the fight, Igrat had kicked her stiletto heels off. Her sobbing redoubled.

"You have every man you want. Why did you take mine away?"

Igrat shook her head. "I haven't taken him away. I just borrowed him, tried him out and returned him. Look Heather, you know Robbie always was a womanizer. I'm what you called me, a whore. Leopards never change their spots. Not me, not Robbie. You either have to accept it or leave him. Your decision. If it's any consolation my partners have faced the same choice. They mostly leave."

Igrat patted Heather on the back sympathetically, hoping that Heather wouldn't ask any more questions. The one thing Igrat didn't want was to explain the real reason why Sir Robert Byrnes had ended up in her bed. *Well, actually one of the Caledonian Club's beds* she reminded herself. The fewer people who knew she was interested in the Auxiliary Units the better. Sir Robert Byrnes had been a possible lead in to them from the financial side. They had to get funded somehow. Yet, if even half the stories were true, finding anything out about them was terminally dangerous. That train of thought caused her look at Heather sharply. The fight between them had really been very easy.

"Anyway, Heather, if you decide to stay with him, look after him. Did you know he's pining to have a kipper for his breakfast? Get him one now and then, even if you have to work hard to get it for him. A little bit of tender care like that and you'll avoid most situations like this. Learn to live with who he is or accept being very lonely for a very long time. Now get out and never, ever, pull a knife on me again. This time I disarmed you. Next time. . . ." Igrat waved at Henry and Achillea. "They'll do what they have to. Which is whatever it takes to protect me. Capische?"

Heather left, slamming the door behind her. McCarty relaxed and returned his Colt to its holster. "Well, Iggie, do you think . . ."

Igrat shook her head and rubbed her ear frantically. She had been putting facts together and the whole incident had been just too pat. It was a set up of some sort. The only question was why? The logical assumption was that this room was bugged. *In fact,* Igrat thought, *that had to be why Heather had been here. She's been bugging the room and I walked in on her. Everything else was a bit of inspired acting.*

McCarty nodded slightly. He'd followed the logic and come to the same conclusions. He picked up where he had left off smoothly. " . . . this will be a lesson for you? The only thing that puzzles me is why you don't have angry wives coming after you more often. Or angry husbands for that matter."

"Raven says that if I'd grown up in her village, I would have had my nose cut off. Just the way I'm made, I guess. Heather just wanted to scare me off, that's all. It's all over now and she won't be back. I guess poor Robbie won't be getting anything from her for weeks and weeks. I'll have to try and make it up to him."

225

Achillea made a snorting noise; McCarty just laughed. Igrat bobbed her head slightly to acknowledge the response. "Thanks for the help guys."

The connecting door closed, leaving Igrat alone in her room. Before she showered and went to bed, Igrat looked around the room speculatively. *I wonder here she put them?*

CHAPTER THREE
SLUGGING MATCH

Sea Mirage F.2 XD-321. Over the South Atlantic

"Here they come." Lieutenant Commander Toby Matthews heard the frantic bleeping of his radar warning system and passed the alert out to the other three Sea Mirages in his formation. Their radar warning equipment should sound the alarm as well, but there was no extra hazard in giving the verbal warning. There was always the possibility that somebody's radar warner was on the fritz. He had already blown his drop tanks, taking a grim satisfaction in the act. The big tanks were in short supply and orders were to bring them back if possible. Nobody would argue that facing over a dozen Super-Crusaders made bringing them home impossible.

Long white fingers of smoke were already reaching out towards him. He pulled his Mirage up into a loose barrel roll while he fired off the chaff dispensers built into his missile launch rails. Faced with over a dozen Sparrow missiles heading at his section of four fighters, he hoped that the chaff and the output from his jammer would be enough. The Argentine fighter pilots had probably fired off a single missile each, holding back their other pair for when the situation had matured. Matthews's section was taking the Argentines head-on, hoping to fix their attention forward. That would exploit one of the F9Us weaknesses, the narrow scan of its radar. The large nose of the twin-engined Super-Mirage gave the radar mounted there a wider field of view. The hope was the dozen additional fighters coming up from *Glorious* would be able to stage an ambush.

That put the four original CAP fighters into the unpleasant position of being bait. They were scattering in the face of the barrage of inbound missiles, each maneuvering to get away from the fingers that were reaching out to touch them. Half way between the groups of aircraft, Matthews saw a black ball of smoke, quickly followed by a second. It looked as if the AIM-7 Sparrow was following its known habit of exploding prematurely. The next explosion wasn't so harmless. It enveloped one of the four Sea Mirages in a ball of fire. That left just three of them. Their trio of R-530 missiles seemed as puny a counterblow as it really was. The AIM-7 was a flawed and faulty missile that had never fulfilled its designers expectations; everybody who had studied weapons knew that. They also knew that the R-530 was even worse. All three missiles missed hopelessly.

Matthews watched glumly as the radar contacts that represented the Argentine formation accelerated. The F9U could reach 1,900 miles per hour; its single J-93 engine gave as much thrust as the two Atar 9s on his Sea Mirage. It could outclimb and out-dive him as well, by a wide margin. The only edge he had was that his larger wings meant he could out-turn the dark blue Crusaders. Sure enough, the Argentine formation started to swing upwards in an obvious preliminary to a dive through the Royal Navy aircraft before zooming up to high altitude again.

That was when the trap was sprung. With their nose pointing upwards and their limited search scan, the Argentine formation had no warning of the salvo of R-530 missiles that engulfed them. The ambushing Sea Mirages had fired both their R-530s in the hope that if some didn't bite, others would. The sky around the Argentine formation blackened with explosions and Matthews saw at least three of the Super-Crusaders dissolve in the black and red balls of flame. The Argentine formation had completely shattered with the assault. Their aircraft were all over the sky, their pilots trying to get them back under control. *That was the trouble with the Mach 3 hot-rods* Matthews thought. *Once the pilot lets the bird get ahead of him, there's no recovering.* That wasn't strictly true, but the fighter escort for the Argentine attack formation was all over the sky. The way was open for his group of three aircraft at least to engage the Skyhawks skimming the sea below.

Those attack planes presented him with a target-rich environment, of that there was no doubt. The Skyhawks were spread out across a wide area. Nobody bunched aircraft together in tight formations any more. The use of nuclear-tipped air-to-air missiles had ended that. Here, the spread-out group of aircraft meant that engaging them would be hard and time consuming. Matthews put his Sea Mirage in a long curving dive that would bring him out behind the nearest Argentine aircraft. His annunciator was already growling when he saw four of the Skyhawks jettison their bombs and missiles. Those four were turning to meet his fighters. He could see the Sidewinder missiles on their outer wing hardpoints. He switched targets quickly; those four aircraft were no longer a threat to the surface ships.

His wingtip R-550 missiles streaked out towards one of the bomb-carrying aircraft. One of the heat-seeking missiles flew straight into the sea; foxed by the flares the attack aircraft were dropping or perhaps seduced by heat reflecting off the surface of the sea. The other missile exploded right behind the Skyhawk. It cartwheeled into the sea. Matthews pulled out of his dive and tried to climb clear. The four Skyhawks that had assumed the role of escort were closing in fast. He rolled, racking his Sea Mirage around in a turn that sent his vision graying out. It was too close for missiles even if he'd had one left but his two 30mm cannon still had the punch needed. Their shells slammed into one of the attacking Skyhawks. He saw its pilot eject a split second before his aircraft exploded.

Matthews climbed clear for a second, while he watched another one of the Skyhawk bombers crash into the sea and a third start to trail smoke. For a moment he wished he'd been armed with the R-510, the missile intended to shoot down America's B-52s. It was slower and less agile than the R-550, but it had a much larger warhead. Then he saw that two of the Argentine Skyhawks that had come after his fighters had survived. More than that; they had finished off another one of his Sea Mirages. Everybody was down to cannon now. That meant those two Skyhawks had to go before he could get back to attacking the bombers that were now perilously close to *Glorious* and her escorts. He curved after them and watched them respond in kind. They might be slow and poorly armed, but the little Skyhawks could turn tighter than any of the supersonic jets could manage.

They proved that by turning into the two attacking Mirages. Matthews could see the flashing from the wing root-mounted 20mm guns. Balls of fire streaked past his cockpit. He squeezed the trigger on his own guns, sending the 30mm shells out in return. Some of them bit home. One Skyhawk lurched and headed downwards. Matthews racked his Sea Mirage around to administer the coup de grace but it wasn't necessary. The Skyhawk had made an emergency landing on the sea and was already sinking, its tail pointing upwards as it slipped under. Beside the fuselage, the Argentine pilot was scrambling into a rubber raft. *What had happened to the other Skyhawk and the one remaining Mirage of his section?* Both had gone and Matthews guessed what had happened. The two pilots had been so fixated on firing at each other they had left pulling out too late and the two aircraft had collided head-on.

Feeling very lonely and wondering what had happened to the other CAP Sea Mirages, Matthews set off after the distant Skyhawks. They were already closing on *Glorious* and her escorts. He guessed he wouldn't get there in time to do any good. In the event, it wouldn't matter. He felt a violent explosion aft and saw the engine dials on his instrument panel had either gone dead or flipped into the red zone. Behind him, a pair of F9Us were already arching skywards. The AIM-7 might be a tricky and unreliable beast, but the AIM-9 was simple and trustworthy. One of them had taken both his engines out. Matthews had just enough control left to ditch his fighter. Then, he too was struggling to get into his raft before the plane sank under him.

Operations Room, HMS Glowworm

"Air Warfare Team ready, Sir." Lieutenant Commander Simon Baxter was standing in the Air Warfare Alley, beside the main plot. The screens were a confused mass that showed the dogfight going on out along the threat axis and the raid that had broken through the combat air patrol. Admiral Lanning had his three Sea Dart armed G-class destroyers out along the threat axis. The Sea Slug-equipped *Electra* and *Eclipse* were guarding the back door. That put *Glowworm, Grafton* and *Greyhound* right in the front line. *Our job, if necessary, is to die gloriously in defense of the carrier.* Baxter winced to himself at the involuntary pun. There was a strange quiet in the Ops Room; the kind of quiet one felt rather than heard. It reminded Baxter of a public library full of well-behaved citizens

"Fighters are breaking off, Sir." Air Warfare gave the status report unemotionally Baxter looked at the plot. It showed twelve tracks coming over the radar horizon in a great arc. The Argentine pilots knew their business. They'd spread out to prevent the radars on the defending destroyers from engaging multiple targets. *This is going to be hairy.*

"Engage designated targets."

He felt *Glowworm* lurch under his feet as the first of the missiles in her vertical launch silo amidships left its tube. Ten second later it was followed by a second and then a third. On the target display, the missiles reached out to touch the inbound Skyhawks. Other tracks came from the *Glowworm's* sister ships. The position of the Skyhawks blurred as their jammers tried to deceive the missiles. Then their tracks vanished completely as the chaff clouds masked their position. The interference cleared quickly as the radars switched to different frequencies.

At least five of the twenty seven Sea Dart missiles launched by the three destroyers scored. More may have hit. If they did, then they were multiple strikes on the same aircraft. The stricken Skyhawks vanished in electronic flares. Their echoes faded out as the sweeping radar scans showed no tracks to be refreshed. Baxter felt *Glowworm* shaking under his feet, a shuddering blow that told him the ship had been hit and hit hard. The lights blinked out, then picked up again as the emergency generators cut in. Any other sounds were temporarily blanked out by the wailing of the emergency sirens. The repeated insistent "fire and rescue parties amidships" calls told of the effects of the hit.

"Number One, report to the forward bridge immediately." The message was urgent and allowed for no delay.

"Air Warfare, take over the Operations Room."

Baxter paused while the Air Warfare Officer slid into his seat, then took off, heading upwards and forwards to *Glowworm's* bridge. When he got there, one thing was obvious. The forward bridge with its low position had paid off. Whatever else had happened, the bridge and its crew were intact.

"What happened, Sir?"

"Skyhawk hit us with two Bullpups. One's hit the foremast and knocked out our primary radar. The other's hit the 35mm mounts aft. We're burning back there. I want you to go aft and take over the damage control effort. You'll have to go back below decks. We've got wreckage and fires amidships and the way above decks is blocked." Captain Foster looked grim. "The Skyhawks hit *Electra* as well. Bullpups and at least two bombs. She blew up; she just blew up. Still, we're not down yet, Simon. Now get some foam on that fire aft."

"On my way, Sir." Baxter started his way aft, going down a level and then along through the forward mess deck. The heat was making him stream sweat. He could hear the noise of the damage control efforts over his head. The blast from the Bullpup hadn't penetrated down here. All that he could see and hear were the secondary effects of the blast. At one point, there was a loud crash that made him think an overhead had collapsed. Whatever it was, it had taken place in the forward superstructure. Further aft, he had to head towards the ship's centerline since the boxes of the vertical launch system were blocking the way along the ship's sides. Ordnance crews were already checking the missiles that were left, making sure they were ready to be fired when the next wave or Argentine aircraft struck. There would be another wave; Baxter was sure of that.

He could feel the heat rising further. He climbed upwards, emerging on to the open deck by the wreckage of the 35mm mounts. Both were gone, shattered. It looked as if the fiberglass weather shields had just disintegrated when the blast from the missile had hit them. Around them, the damage control teams were spraying foam on a fire around the aft superstructure. It looked as if the Bullpup had hit the bottom section of the aft tower mast. The mast structure was twisted and hanging drunkenly to one side, its radar inert. Instinctively, Baxter looked around for a Chief Petty Officer to get an accurate picture of what was going on.

230

The nearest CPO had seen the officer arrive and knew what he would need. By the time Baxter had made his brief inspection of the area, the CPO had a concise report ready for him.

"No sweat, Sir. We've got this one under control Could have been a lot worse. A few feet forward and we would have taken the hit in the missile silos. Then we'd have gone up just like *Electra* did."

"Just like *Electra*." Baxter looked at the work in progress. One of the fires was out. The hose teams had switched to water to cool the area down and prevent reignition. Across the hull, around the starboard 35mm mount, the other team was putting the final coat of foam down. That fire too was dying. Then he looked forward. The damage to the foremast was less spectacular, but it was obvious their primary radar was out.

The CPO saw where Baxter was looking. "Funny they got both our radars, wasn't it, Sir. Reckon those Bullpups were radar-homing?"

Baxter glanced around. In his experience, when a CPO engaged in speculative conversation with an officer, it was because there was something going on he wasn't supposed to see. That called for a quick value judgment. *Was it better to go on not seeing it or should he find out what was going on. I can't see anything wrong or irregular, better to let sleeping dogs snore undisturbed.* "Could be, Chief. There are radar-homing variants of Bullpup but it might be that the missiles just homed in on the most prominent parts of the ship. Whatever it was, they've taken us right out of the battle. We've lost both 35mm mounts, both sets of radars and the Seawolf launchers forward aren't looking too healthy. We're down to our four-inch gun and the Rotodyne. Still, we can hunt subs with that I suppose. And we're still secure below the waterline."

"There's that, Sir." The CPO didn't seem that convinced. Looking around him at the mess the two Bullpups had created, Baxter could understand why.

One of the ratings from the damage control group ran up and started to report. He began to address the CPO, but a discrete wave redirected him to Baxter. "Remaining fire is out Sir. We're putting more foam down and cooling off with seawater, but it's out. Just making sure it won't reignite."

"We're pretty much done here, Sir. It's all tying up the loose ends now. I hope they're on top of things over there." The CPO waved off to port. Baxter turned and saw that *Glorious* had been hit as well. She was listing and there was an ominous pyre of black smoke rising from her hull. "Damn, they got her as well. I thought we had them licked."

Flag Bridge, HMS Glorious, *North East of the Falkland Islands*

"Damage report?" Lanning snapped the question out. The Argentine Skyhawks, what was left of them, had vanished leaving chaos behind them. *Electra* was gone. *Glowworm* was hit and burning. That much he could see. What Lanning needed to know was how badly *Glorious* had been hurt.

"We're on top of it, Admiral." Captain Wales was smoke and dirt-stained but he had the situation on his ship under control. "Our first priority is to get the wrecked Skyhawk off our flight deck. As soon as we do that, we can bring the fighters in. I've got the handling crane pushing most of the wreckage over the side. The deck crew are picking up the smaller pieces and throwing them over."

Lanning grunted. That had been one of the more nerve-racking parts of the attack. A Skyhawk had been hit by a MOG missile from *Eclipse* and sent skittering through the sky. The heavy warheads the Ozwalds liked to build into their weapons should have taken the little Skyhawk right out of the sky. Somehow the pilot had kept going long enough to unload his bombs. One of the thousand pounders had landed in the sea alongside *Glorious's* aft quarter. Another had hit the flight deck aft and slid off without exploding. The Argentine pilot had deserved better luck, especially since his aircraft, even without the weight of its bombs, had simply run out of altitude and airspace. It had slammed onto the flight deck aft, slid across it and then hung up on the port aft four inch battery.

The pilot had ejected and come down on the flight deck a bit further forward. He's been detained by the crew who had got him down to the sick bay, suffering from broken legs as a result of his hard landing on the steel deck. His rescue might have counted as being fortunate for him had it not been for one of his wing-mates who had put two one-thousand pound bombs into *Glorious's* midships section. One bomb had set the starboard boat storage area on fire. The other had pierced the side plating and exploded in the sick bay. The Argentine pilot was presumably one of the dead in there. The compartment devastation was such that nobody who'd been in it was ever likely to be identified.

Glorious had taken two more very near misses just forward of the island. They were the ones that were causing all the real problems. They had exploded underwater; the mining effect had opened up seams in the ship's side and caused enough flooding to give the ship a marked list. The damage control teams were trying to establish a flooding boundary. Once they'd done that, work could start on bringing the ship back to an even keel. That brought a question to Lanning's mind.

"Can we bring them in with this list? And how many are there?"

"It will be a difficult landing, but yes. We're within limits for bringing aircraft in. We've got seven Sea Mirages waiting to land. The pilots are singing 'why are we waiting' over the radio."

"Seven out of sixteen?" Lanning knew that the Sea Mirages had had a hard fight but the final figure was still shocking.

"Preliminary count is that the fighters got six Crusaders and six Skyhawks. The missile ships got six more and we got one with our four inchers. Five got away, three trailing smoke. We didn't do badly, Admiral."

A destroyer exploded, another one crippled and the carrier hit. Nine fighters down, more casualties still to come in when our own strike gets there. If this isn't doing badly, what is the final butcher's bill going to look like?

"Thank you. Carry on, Charles." Lanning turned away and stared out of his bridge windows at the work on the flight deck aft. He saw the deck crews clearing away and the first of the surviving Sea Mirages coming into land. *Glorious* was still in business. For how much longer was a good question.

232

"Here they come." There were three enemy formations approaching, one group accelerating ahead of the rest. *That would be the fighters coming in as a preliminary sweep.* Lieutenant Anton Marko thought. The other two groups would be the bombers running in behind them. They could wait for a minute or two, the first priority would be to bring down the enemy fighters. Then shooting down the unarmed Buccaneers would be a formality. He glanced down at his radar display, the fighters were already spreading out but there were only four of them. This strike was virtually unescorted. His radar warning receiver went frantic as his fighter was designated and the sky filled with radar homing missiles. A dozen or so AIM-7Es heading out; about the same number of R-530s coming in.

Marko firewalled the throttles, feeling the thrust of the J-93 engine behind him send his speed soaring. The problem was that the narrow scan on his radar meant he couldn't turn much or he would lose the paint on his selected target and his missile would miss. The Sea Mirages he was targeting had a much greater degree of freedom in that respect and they were already turning to take advantage of it. Marko had to rely on his jammer and the chaff his aircraft was already strewing in its wake to protect him against the British missiles. To his relief, the missile threatening him either malfunctioned or was seduced by the countermeasures. It missed by a wide margin. Three of his squadron mates weren't so lucky. Their dark blue F9Us vanished in fireballs almost in the same instant as two of the British fighters blew up. Twelve aircraft against four had just become nine against two.

Freed of the need to guide his missile to its target, Marko pulled the control column back into his stomach and let his fighter climb. This was something the British fighters couldn't even begin to match. His mind held a picture of them turning below him. He rolled his Super-Crusader on to its back and then dropped, seeing the two slate gray Mirages far below him. He felt his vision starting to blur as he dived on them, watching with frustration as three fighters closer than his closed in first. They swept in behind the two Sea Mirages but the two British fighters suddenly turned towards each other. They racked themselves around in tight banks. Two of the Super-Crusaders broke away but the third tried to press home his attack. He picked one of the fighters but in doing so he opened himself to the other. A radar homing missile took the aft section of his fighter apart. The pilot punched out as his aircraft disintegrated around him.

The tight turn had left the pair of British fighters wallowing. Marko realized that his late dive had been a blessing in disguise. His AIM-9s were already locked on and he fired a pair of them. Both guided perfectly to their target. The stricken Sea Mirage turned end-over-end, streaming white vapor as it broke up and burned. The nine Argentine fighters converged on the single remaining Sea Mirage.

"Forget him; get the bombers." The fighter controller shouted the orders into the earphones of the pilots. They peeled away and started to turn towards the nearest of the Buccaneer groups. Only, they'd vanished from the radar picture. Marko picked them up visually; not by direct sight of the aircraft but by the white streaks they were leaving on the water behind them. The British bombers had dropped down so they were skimming only a few feet above the waves. They hadn't dropped any speed in doing so and they had already pulled far ahead of the pursuing fighters.

233

That didn't disturb the Argentine pilots. They had a 1,200 mph speed advantage over the Buccaneers. They closed the difference quickly, leaving a single Sea Mirage behind them to escape back to *Glorious*. Marko locked one of his AIM-7 Sparrow missiles on to a Buccaneer, then fired it as he dived down to intercept the bombers. It missed, hopelessly, exploding in the sea far behind the racing Buccaneer. Marko cursed and fired again. He watched helplessly as his second Sparrow follow the first. That was when he realized what was wrong. His radar was locking on to the cloud of spray behind the bombers. By now, he was closing on them fast. He flipped over to his remaining pair of AIM-9 Sidewinders.

As if they had sensed his intentions, the Buccaneers dropped even lower, nestling into the waves that were now barely a few feet underneath them. To his frustration, Marko realized he wasn't getting an annunciator tone from his missiles. The same spray cloud that had foxed his Sparrows was shielding the engine exhausts from the infra-red homing systems on the AIM-9s. Worse, his Crusader was being bounced all over the sky by the turbulence this close to the sea. The F9U was like all American aircraft; optimized to fly high and very fast. Down here, a few feet above the waves, the shocks reflected from the sea surface were literally shaking his aircraft to pieces. Marko started to fire short bursts from his four 20mm cannon as he closed on his chosen target. He could see the tracers going wild as his aircraft bounced at critical moments in the attack run. He felt like screaming in frustration. This was a totally different kind of environment from the stately, choreographed battles he and his fellow pilots had trained for.

Finally, his gunsight settled on the Buccaneer for a few seconds. He got in a quick burst that finally, eventually, struck home. He saw the Buccaneer lurch, fragments flying from its fuselage, but to his utter disbelief the damaged aircraft kept flying. He was within the danger zone now, the area where missiles from the destroyers would be targeting him as well as the hostile bombers. He had to make one last effort to put the infuriating British bomber down. He was lined up for another burst and finally managed to get it off. This time, the bomber didn't survive. It hit the sea below, bounced high into the air and broke up. Marko saw the two ejector seats going skywards and the white blossom of parachutes forming. By then he was climbing away from the pounding nightmare a few feet above the sea, and getting back to where his fighter was happy.

Argentine Aircraft Carrier Veinticinco de Mayo

Vice-Admiral Juan Lombardo swore to himself. The fighters had taken their own sweet time about it but they had knocked down three of the eight inbound Buccaneers. The other five were angled away from his aircraft carrier; apparently heading for two members of his screen. A quick glance at the plot confirmed that. They would pass ahead of him and hit the destroyers *Cordoba* and *Rivadavia*. The *Rivadavia* was already spitting missiles at the five inbound bombers. She'd put a dozen Folgore missiles into the air. Lombardo felt like cheering when two of them sent Buccaneers spinning into the sea. His delight was short-lived because one of the three surviving bombers let fly with a salvo of four missiles. The other two were also firing missiles but singly. That told him they were Bullpups. The four missiles were an entirely different matter. Lombardo realized they had to be anti-radar weapons. *Rivadavia's* Captain must have made the same conclusion but the missiles were too fast and the range too short. The missile destroyer's superstructure vanished beneath the four explosions and her missile fire ceased instantly. Lombardo knew she was out of the game for a long time to come.

The *Cordoba* was thumping away with her old, slow-firing 5.3-inch guns but they were anti-ship weapons and their use against the low-flying bombers was hopeful in the extreme. The other gun destroyer out there was the *Hippolyte Bouchard*. She was an old American DDK Gearing, accompanying the fleet to provide anti-submarine cover. She had four five inch guns and six three inch, for all the good they would do her. One of the Buccaneers was heading for her. Lombardo winced as a Bullpup plowed into her bridge. Another Bullpup was heading for *Cordoba,* but the old ship brought it down with her 47mm guns. Her luck held. The Buccaneer heading for her actually flew between her funnels but the salvo of retarded bombs was badly late and exploded well beyond her. *Must have been a release failure, the bombs hung on their ranks for some reason.*

Rivadavia wasn't so lucky. Already hurt by the Martel missiles that had gutted her fire control systems, the four one-thousand pounders bracketed her beautifully. One went into the water just short, two slammed into her midships section and the third was just over. By the time the water subsided, Lombardo could see the ominous sight of her wallowing. Her bows and stern moved differently. Any seaman's eye would realize that her back had been broken by the blasts. *Hippolyte Bouchard* was better off, but only just. An older ship, built in an American yard, she was tougher than the more modern Italian-built ships. The bomb hits hadn't been quite so devastating. They'd gone aft; that had helped as well. The destroyer's stern guns were a shambled mess and the structure there was burning, but Lombardo could already see that the damage wasn't fatal.

"Admiral, look!" The cry from the bridge wings caused Lombardo's head to snap around. Another formation of eight Buccaneers was heading in. This one had got past the fighter screen untouched. They appeared to be heading for a group of four destroyers; the missile destroyers *Cervantes* and *Juan de Garay* and another pair of Gearing DDKs. For a moment, Lombardo felt a sense of relief that inbound bombers would have to get past the four ships first. Something about the flight paths disturbed him. It took him a split second to realize what it was. When the realization struck home, he knew he had missed something very important. *The Buccaneers aren't trying to get past the screening destroyers to their primary target. The screening ships are their primary target.* He watched while *Cervantes* and *Juan de Garay* started pumping out missiles, sending more than two dozen at the inbound formation. Three Buccaneers went down, but the inevitable was already under way. The anti-radar missiles were already launched and they were fire-and-forget weapons. It didn't matter to them that their launching aircraft was already fragments sinking in the chilled waters of the South Atlantic. They were locked in on the fire control radars of the two missile ships.

They didn't do as well as the four fired at *Rivadavia*. The skippers of the *Cervantes* and *Juan de Garay* had realized what was coming. Their fingers must have been poised over the emergency shut-down switches. The destroyers' radars went silent. The two ships accelerated, turning tightly to present the smallest possible targets to the Martels. It didn't save them, quite. Both were hit but the missiles took out the ships' after superstructures. The forward area with its vital command and control spaces escaped.

Lombardo held his breath as the five surviving Buccaneers made their runs. It was almost a repeat of the first groups attack only the *Cervantes* and *Juan de Garay* were already presenting their sterns to the bombers. That was good against missiles; not so good against bombs. *Juan de Garay* got away with it. The bomber targeting her made an error in deflection and that, combined with her turn, meant the bombs went clear. *Cervantes* suffered for her sister; the aircraft attacking her made a perfect run. Four bombs were neatly spaced along her deck. Lombardo saw the rippling explosions and the gouts of black-orange fire that erupted from the stricken destroyer.

That was when the Admiral realized how much his chest hurt. He had been holding his breath during the bombing runs and he was slowly turning blue. He forced himself to breathe, then looked out again where the surviving Buccaneers were heading for the horizon. *We got eight*, he thought, *eight out of sixteen*. Then he shook his head. He had the maths wrong. *The British had concentrated on my screening ships and done a good job of wrecking them. Two of my three missile ships are sinking and the third is badly hurt. One,* Lombardo looked out of the bridge and corrected himself *two of my ASW destroyers are hurt as well. The second British carrier has to be out there. If the British weren't certain another strike was on its way, they'd have thrown everything at our carrier.*

"Air group situation?" The question was blunt and terse.

The answer he got was equally so. "We've got eight CAP and seven escort fighters coming back. All low on fuel and ammunition. We have five Skyhawks from our strike on their way back. All damaged. We have a reserve of six bombers and six fighters ready to go."

Lombardo nodded. "Reports?"

"Fighters are claiming more than forty enemy fighters shot down. Bombers claim they have sunk two cruisers, two destroyers and left the British carrier burning."

"Get our second strike off. There's another British carrier out there. Send the planes south west of the original mission plan. The returning aircraft will have to wait until the strike is on its way. Then get them down, reload the fighters on the deck and get them off again. There's another British strike coming."

"Sir, we've got six more Crusaders armed and fuelled, they're part of the CAP that we couldn't get up before the British hit us. What should we do with them?"

"Get them up as CAP of course." Lombardo was furious that precious seconds were being wasted with stupid questions. "With the CAP aircraft out of fuel and the missile ships hit, we're defenseless."

Naval Attache's Office, Australian Embassy, Santiago, Chile.

There were a number of reasons why Lieutenant Graeme Gavin considered himself a fortunate man. It wasn't just that he had a beautiful and wealthy wife although that was a great deal of it. It was also that every morning he had a packed lunch waiting for him to bring to the office. Not just a cut lunch either; a proper meal, with a half-bottle of local wine to wash it down. One or two days a week, Emilia would come in herself and they'd eat together in his office. He wasn't just a fortunate man; he was also a very happy one.

"Have you heard the news, Garry?" Captain Lachlan Shearston, the Australian Naval Attache to Chile stepped into the office. He looked at the lunch Gavin had just taken out and sighed. "You know, I told Narelle about your lunches and suggested she might do one for me. Her reply was indescribable. Basically, it boiled down to asserting that the cut lunches her mum made had kept her old man working for years and now one would do me."

"Grab a fork and tuck in." Gavin was beginning to get the hang of the diplomacy thing. "Emilia always makes sure there's plenty of food. Why don't you and Narelle come up one weekend? We have great barbeques. What's happening in the outside world?"

"For us? Chilean Navy is biting on the R-class submarines. The Lieutenant they've got out of *Rotorua* is most impressed and the commercial boys have been negotiating like mad. The Italians and French are most displeased with them. Anyway, the Chilean Navy is going to order four Batch IIs. Looks like you'll be staying here a bit longer than expected to help get them into the fleet. The real news is the poms out in the Falklands. Word from the Septics is there's a hell of a carrier battle going on. One of their manned orbiting stations radioed the news down. In clear, by the way, so the whole world is getting the message. Burning ships on both sides, so they say. My God, this is good. What is it?"

"Pastel De Choclo. It's a sort of chicken and sweetcorn stew with raisins and hardboiled eggs. Have some wine. Emilia put in a half of the family white to go with it. Any word on how many ships lost?"

Shearston looked sadly at the rapidly disappearing meal. "I suppose I should offer you my sammies in return, but cheese and bread would be a come-down after this feast. Don't know yet; all we have is ships on both sides burning. Now we'll find out whether the British are really back or not." He hesitated for a moment. "I don't suppose Emmy gave you any afters, did she?"

Sitting Room, Private Apartment, 10 Downing Street, London.

"The latest expression of developments within current military affairs has just arrived Prime Minister." Sir Humphrey Appleday had brought the messages up himself. "There appears to be a major exchange of hostilities between between the Task Force and the Argentine fleet. Message from Admiral Lanning says the destroyer *Electra* has been sunk, *Glowworm* badly damaged. *Glorious* has been hit but she's still operational. Our own strike is claiming five Argentine destroyers sunk. I think it would be fair to suggest that a major naval battle is in progress."

Prime Minister Newton wiped his mouth and put down the egg sandwich he was eating. "Aircraft losses?"

"The reports from the personnel involved in executing hostilities suggest that claims at least fifty Argentine aircraft shot down in exchange for twenty of ours would not be amiss. If the claims of the forces there have anything like a reasonable level of veracity, I would say that we have made a substantial start of eliminating Argentine naval aviation capability vis a vis their aircraft carrier force."

"It isn't true, Humpty. You know that. Divide by three; that's the rule. I'd say we're probably running loss for loss at the moment. How are the forces taking it?"

"Here, Prime Minister? The greatest concern of the forces remaining in the national homeland is that the war will be over by the time they are able to complete their transit to the theater of operations. The second wave of expeditionary forces will be ready to implement its departure shortly. *Courageous* is completing her refit and will be extracting herself from drydock next week. The Navy has been working on assembling a new air group for her exploiting the assets still remaining in this country, accepting that some of them may not represent the peak of our military capability."

"In other words, the Navy is scrabbling around trying to find enough aircraft to put on her." Newton sighed. "I thought two airgroups for three carriers was a bad idea. We'll have to fix that in the future. How goes the other matter?"

"The question of the culpability assignable to Astiz and our ability to implement the required legal action necessary to bring him to the justice many, indeed I would say a majority, of the non-Argentine population of the world in which we have the good fortune to reside believe he so richly deserves?"

"That's right. When can we sell him to the highest bidder?"

Sir Humphrey Appleday looked appalled. "Prime Minister, I must object. Our decision on to whom we should render Astrid for trial should be taken in full accordance with international law and with due consideration for the strength of the case that can be brought against him and whether the appropriate legal penalties can be imposed under the system of national law prevailing."

"Humph. Not soon then. Thank you Sir Humphrey. Please make sure I get the news as it comes in."

"Yes, Prime Minister."

Flag Bridge, HMS Glorious, *North East of the Falkland Islands*

"We've got eight Mirages and a round dozen Buccaneers left." Captain Wales sounded tired. So far he'd lost half his air group and the enemy carrier was still out there, unhurt. "A lot of the birds are damaged; how some of the Bananas got back is beyond me. The good news is our fires are out and we've got the flooding perimeter established. We're counter-flooding to eliminate the list now. We'll be able to get twenty-four, possibly twenty-six knots as soon as we've sealed up. Flight deck is operational although we've got precious little to fly off it right now. We're down to our missile ships for cover against the next air attack."

"You can expect it soon enough, Charles. Can you get at least something up as CAP? And throw out another strike? The Argies will be hurting as badly as we are."

"Worse. The Bananas really did a number on the screen. We've got two Seadart and a Seaslug ship left. We don't think the Argies have anything. They're wide open."

"Remember we're not in this alone. *Furious* is south of us somewhere. She'll be throwing a full strength strike at the Argies any time now. All twenty Bananas; some of them Highball birds. Charles, don't worry about getting out another strike. Get everything up on CAP that you can. If we can ride the next strike out, we'll be through it. Get the Bananas sealed down and inert the fuel system as soon as CAP is up."

238

"Sir, report from *Glowworm*. Fires are out and machinery is undamaged but she's down to her four-inch gun and that's it. She's moving on to the threat axis as a bomb sponge."

"That is exceedingly nice of her." Lanning looked around his bridge. "Well, it is. Charles, I suggest you invite Captain Foster to your mother's next garden party."

"If you insist Sir, but I'd rather do something nice for him." A chuckle of relieved tension ran around the bridge. It was interrupted by a whine forward as the bow elevator brought a Sea Mirage up to the flight deck. The ballet on the deck started as the aircraft was moved forward to one of the catapults. By the time it was in place, a second Sea Mirage had been brought up. "We've loaded them to the max, Sir. Four R-530s and four R-550s. Cut the fuel load back to compensate. Launching now."

There was a bang and roar as the two Mirages were catapulted off. They dipped slightly on leaving the carrier but recovered and swept upwards. Lanning had his combat air patrol up and felt absurdly pleased at the effort. It was absurd; he knew it. Two aircraft was hardly an adequate air defense against the strikes that were being thrown, but it was all he had and it was much better than nothing. He felt a bit better about it a few seconds later when another pair of Sea Mirages were brought up from below. With four aircraft up, *Glorious* had a fighting chance.

Blackburn Buccaneer S4H XT-279, HMS Furious, *North East of the Falkland Islands*

Catapult launching was always an interesting experience, especially when it took place in a heavily-loaded Buccaneer. Lieutenant Commander Ernest Mullback positioned himself carefully; his head resting firmly on the padded seatback. His harness straps were as tight as he could pull them, his arms and legs positioned just so. The last thing he wanted now was to screw up his launch and miss what he knew would be the culmination of his career. Training missions were a bore. Hitting ships in harbor was close to shooting fish in a barrel. But a strike against an enemy carrier at sea was what he had trained for. His faithful Banana had her two Highballs in her belly. That was all she could carry; her wing racks were empty. The same wasn't true of the aircraft waiting behind her. The Highball aircraft were being followed by eight conventional strike birds with eight one-thousand pound bombs each and four missile-armed anti-radar aircraft. They, along with the eight escort Sea Mirages, were still in the hangar. The aft elevator would be bringing them up as the on-deck aircraft were launched. It would take a little time for the strike to form up, but it was worth taking in order to deliver a coordinated punch at the enemy.

The launch control officer dropped his flag. Mullback felt the slam as the steam catapult hurled XT-279 forwards. He heard the odd thwang noise as the bridle catcher retrieved the cables that had secured his aircraft to the catapult. Then, he saw the sea appear in front of him as the Buccaneer nosed down. Then, the Spey engines pushed him upwards and away from the sea. Mullback relaxed; the dangerous part was over now until he and the other Buccaneers would have to punch though the enemy defenses. Then, all that was left was to find his carrier and land on it. Put like that, he wondered why he didn't find himself another profession.

It took two orbits for the strike to be launched and then to form up properly. The problem they had now was that the position for the Argentine carrier group was already almost an hour old. It would take another 30 minutes to reach them, so they could be anywhere within a 45 mile circle of their reported position. That wouldn't sound much to a landsman but Mullback was part of a Navy and knew better. A circle with a radius of 45 nautical miles covered a lot of sea and a ship was a small target. In the old days, finding a ship group would have been a matter of chance, but radar changed that. The Sea Mirages were already moving to the front of the formation, their Cyrano V radars searching for the enemy ships. That was the other reason why the fighters ran ahead of the bombers. It wasn't just to protect them; they had to find the targets as well.

"Targets located." The message over the radio was terse and to the point. "Bearing three-four-eight. Range eight-five miles; course south-west." Mullback watched the exhausts on the twin engined Mirages light up as they swept ahead in an effort to get the Argentine fighters before the Argies got through to the bombers.

Argentine Aircraft Carrier Veinticinco de Mayo

"Strike is off, Sir. We got six Crusaders and nine Skyhawks out." The Air Group Commander sounded justifiably proud of the effort. He'd not only got the reserve strike out, but his deck crews had managed to refuel and rearm three Skyhawks in time to rejoin them. The same crews had managed to get eight more Crusaders armed and fuelled and they were launching as well. That left four Crusaders and two Skyhawks on the decks. There was no hope of getting them ready. There wasn't time and, anyway, they were too badly damaged. Lombardo briefly considered pushing them over the side but rejected the thought. *Who knew, the way this aerial slugging match was working out, there might come a time when four damaged fighters and two shot-up bombers were the margin that brought victory.*

"Well done. The remaining aircraft, are they safed?" Lombardo meant 'were the aircraft defueled and their armaments stored?'

"They are, Sir. And we're inerting the carrier fuel system now."

"Bandits, Sir." Air Warfare had sent the message up from the CIC below decks. "At least 30 aircraft coming in from due south. Two formations; a small one leading, much larger formation behind them."

There was a brief but agonizing pause before the CIC updated the report. "The larger formation is dropping of the radar now. Our fighters are moving in to attack."

Super-Crusader 3-A-204. Over the South Atlantic

Overhead, the six fighters that had taken off earlier were engaging the British Sea Mirages. Anton Marko twisted around in his seat to see if he could work out what was going on up there but it was a brief effort. His job was to go after the Buccaneers that were already streaming towards his carrier. The long rooster-tail of white spray both revealed their position and masked them. These pilots were more skilled than the ones from the other British carrier, Marko could see that easily. They were flying lower, if that were possible. Their pilots were holding them steadier in what had to be a barrage of turbulence from the sea surface a scant few meters underneath.

Behind him, the remaining Super-Crusaders were burning fuel in an effort to get out as far as possible. That would give the maximum possible time for intercepts. The

240

Argentine pilots already knew that the Buccaneer was hard to hit that close to the sea and the aircraft could take a phenomenal amount of punishment before going down. Every second spent in engagement was essential. *Especially with the missile ships crippled*, Marko thought grimly. *Rivadavia* had already sunk. *Cervantes* was a blazing wreck; not much longer for this world. If the fighters failed, their carrier was wide open.

He picked a Buccaneer and fired off two of his AIM-7 missiles at it. Neither hit since both homed in the spray thrown up by the bomber. The fragmentation from their warheads did nothing more than stipple the surface of the sea. He racked his Crusader around, hearing the structure of the fighter groaning with stresses than pushed it far beyond the limits laid down by the manufacturer. His annunciator was warbling but the tone was intermittent, not steady. That told him the missiles had a partial lock at best. Still, he fired one pair. Sure enough, one missed but the other exploded close behind the Buccaneer. It lurched in mid air, while black smoke erupted from both engines. Incredibly, it kept going. *What did Blackburn build in their English factory* Marko asked himself, *aircraft or tanks?*

The British formation was splitting up. One group of four were clearly the anti-radar missile carriers; they were going ahead of the rest, obviously readying to fire their missiles at the anti-aircraft ships. *Well, they'll find few pickings this time. The previous wave did their job all too well.* Another group of eight had clean wings and were accelerating ahead of the rest. Lacking the drag of underwing bombs and missiles, they were probably just a critical few knots faster than the others. The other twelve had the expected underwing bomb load. Marko marked them out as the dangerous ones; the heavily-loaded ship-killers. One of them had been the aircraft he had just damaged.

Marko closed in on his prey. The damaged Buccaneer was wallowing, obviously losing engine power and the pilot was having trouble staying airborne. That made him an easier target. Marko came in from high above and raked the aircraft with 20mm fire before buffeting could throw off his aim. A stable gun platform compensated for long range. The Buccaneer went into the sea.

There was still work to be done though and Marko had traded off his height advantage. Now he was following the Buccaneers at more or less sea level. This close to the water, it was the British bombers that had the speed advantage. Marko climbed a little and then pushed down his nose to try and catch up. His first burst of 20mm went wild when buffeting threw off his aim. Before he could fie again, something weird seemed to happen. One of the bombs under the Buccaneer's wings detached and fell away. A split second later it hit the sea and exploded. Marko realized too late what had happened. The bombardier on the British aircraft had timed the drop beautifully. When the thousand pound retarded bomb exploded, it did so directly in front of Marko's aircraft. His J-93 gulped at the towering column of water a split second before the sheer impact of the waterspout ripped the wings from his Crusader. The whole aircraft came apart around him. He never even got a chance to resent the idea than an unarmed aircraft had shot him down.

Blackburn Buccaneer S4H XT-279, North East of the Falkland Islands

In theory at least, the Buccaneer could fly underwater. Not literally, of course; but in theory, the compression wave generated by the aircraft would push the sea underneath into a dish-shaped depression. A really ballsy pilot could, in theory, drop his Banana down so that it was actually flying in that depression and thus be technically underwater. The critical words there were 'in theory.' Mullback wasn't prepared to go quite that far but he was nestled down so far that the sea level appeared to flow around his aircraft. The pounding turbulence from the sea surface was murderous but the Banana was designed to fly in this environment. It was just that tiny touch more stable this low down that anything else. That gave them their chance of survival against modern naval air defenses. How low they would go depended on the pilots but the suggestion that people standing in front of a low-flying Buccaneer would be well-advised to duck when it passed over was not a joke. Flying between buildings and under bridges were regarded as elementary tricks for beginners.

The radio chatter was increasing as wireless discipline broke down. The Sea Mirages were taking a bad beating. They seemed to have knocked down at least three F9Us with their missiles but they'd taken two losses themselves. Even outnumbering the Argentine fighters two-to-one, they were still getting the worst of the dogfight. The Crusaders were just too fast and they slashed at their enemy in dive-and-zoom attacks that gave the Sea Mirage little chance other than to evade and hope. Up ahead, Mullback saw the missile-armed defense suppression aircraft firing off their Martel anti-radar missiles. His own radar warning display was showing very few threat signals from the ships ahead. He devoutly hoped that the sacrifice made by *Glorious's* air group hadn't been in vain. If it had, there were enough anti-radar missiles heading in to suppress the defenses. He hoped.

It was time. He lifted his nose slightly and climbed to the recommended Highball drop altitude of sixty feet. The familiar green lines on his head-up display were already beginning to converge as the Blue Parrot radar sent its pulses out to measure the range to the aircraft carrier in front. It was firing its own guns at the Buccaneers. Mullback knew she was supposed to have been refitted with the fast-firing OTO-Melara 76mm guns. The streams of tracer fire confirmed that. Beside him, a Buccaneer with a SAC-like band of green and dark blue-gray tartan painted under its cockpit took a direct hit from a three-inch round. That was more than even the legendary Buccaneer could take. The aircraft disintegrated. *Good bye, Jock. See you in Fiddler's Green.*

The green lines touched the bow and stern of the carrier but Mullback was looking for more than that. He had to drop his Highballs so they would skim the tops of the waves, not get trapped in the troughs between them and sink. He paused slightly to get the pattern of waves right and then dropped the two spherical bombs. Despite his care, one hit the side of the waves and sank almost immediately. The other hit, skipped and was on its way. Accelerating ahead of the bombs, Mullback dropped down to seaskimming altitude again, as he saw the flash of tracers go over his head. The guns on the carrier simply couldn't depress enough to bear on him. Then he had to lift his nose again as the carrier swelled in front of him.

He passed between the radio antennas lining the flight deck and left the flight deck crews sprawling on the surface. Over the carrier he dropped his aircraft down once more and started his run out.

"Six of us made it, Jerry. Four of us dropped on the carrier and two on a big destroyer. Alasdair bought a farm from flak and that new kid, Freddie Kingsman, went in as well. Fighter got him, I think." Alex Peters sounded flat and depressed. Then he looked backwards. The aircraft carrier behind them was a twisted, broken wreck. Her bows had been torn clean off and her whole structure sagged. Off to one side, the biggest of the Argentine destroyers had broken in two. Her severed stern was already on its beam ends, going down. "They've taken a fine honor guard down with them though."

242

Argentine Aircraft Carrier Veinticinco de Mayo

The British pilots had to be mad. The bombers were skimming so low over the sea that it appeared their bellies were actually cleaving the surface. That was an illusion of course but nobody sane flew that low over the waters of the South Atlantic. One larger-than-normal wave and the aircraft would be engulfed. Lombardo had watched the six fighters of his CAP take on the eight British fighters, knock down five of them for two losses and send the rest scuttling away. The deck-launched intercept had engaged one group of twelve Buccaneers, downing five of them before they'd had to pull away. That left a group of eight heading straight for the *Veinticinco de Mayo.*

What Lombardo saw next bewildered him. The British bombers appeared to be dropping their bombs several hundred meters short of his ship. At first, he thought they were torpedoes but they dropped like bombs. There was no doubt of that. Then he was distracted by the bombers passing over his carrier. The anti-aircraft guns had got one of them and possibly damaged another. The rest had hurdled his carrier as if they were daring athletes. He looked down on one of the bombers as it passed in front of the island, below the windows on his flag deck. Another went between the aft end of the island and the radar mast, banking by at least 45 degrees. Two others went further aft, also skimming a few centimeters over the flight deck. To his dying day, Lombardo would swear that he could see streaks of white belly paint left on the deck, scraped off by the Buccaneers as they overflew the carrier and escaped.

He was still in a state of near-shock when he remembered the bombs dropped by the British bombers. He'd expected to see towering columns of water where they had exploded at the drop site. Instead he caught sight of the first one as it bounced off the surface of the sea and struck the hull plating just below the hangar deck. It disappeared from view. For a split second, Lombardo thought it had suffered a fuse failure.

What happened next was beyond any experience he had ever had. The explosion from that first bomb was devastating enough; it lifted the whole forward section of the ship. The shock wave from the blast hurled him off his feet and into the bulkhead behind. Stunned by the shock, he felt rather than saw the bow of the ship being sucked downwards. Then, a mighty column of water erupted through the forward part of the flight deck, spraying wreckage in a wide arc. Lombardo dragged himself to his feet in time to see the forward section of his ship detaching completely and twist through ninety degrees. The bulkheads formed great cliffs in the water that diminished as the bows began to settle.

That one hit alone would have been enough but there were four more; all aft of the center of the ship. Each blast was terrible. Each did more damage to a ship that was already destroyed beyond any hope of recovery. Lombardo gave his last order as Admiral of this fleet. It was a very simple one. "Abandon Ship!"

Veinticinco de Mayo was sinking very fast. Lombardo grabbed one of the seamen on the bridge and started to pull him towards the edge. The man had been unlucky. Perhaps he had been standing on a resonance point of the shock waves; perhaps he had been thrown into something. Whatever it was, the angle of his feet and the shape of his legs showed that his ankles and calves had been badly broken. Other men had been thrown into the overhead and were laying dead or unconscious on the deck. Panic stricken messages were coming on over the few internal communications lines that remained working. Internal hatches had been jammed throughout the ship by the shockwaves from the underwater explosions that had torn her apart. Lombardo knew that most of the crew would be trapped below decks and could not be rescued in the very few minutes that were left while the carrier stayed afloat.

He helped where he could, dragging men to the rafts and pushing them away from the sinking wreck. In doing so, he saw *Cordoba* blown in half by the strange bouncing bombs that had done for his carrier. He knew the same scenes and the same deadly pattern was being repeated over there. *Cervantes* had been hit by more bombs and had already gone down. *Juan de Garay* had been raked by conventional thousand pound bombs and was on her beam ends. Oddly, the British had left the four Gearing DDKs alone. Perhaps they had recognized that they were the only chance of survival the crews from the stricken warships had of surviving the cold of the South Atlantic. As he took the last place in the last raft off the *Veinticinco de Mayo,* Lombardo knew he was a part of the worst naval disaster since the Battle of the Orkneys.

Super-Crusader 3-A-211. Over the South Atlantic

Air combat is a brutally Darwinian process. The first combat mission flown by a pilot is by far the most dangerous; novices often do not survive it. The increase in combat skills for the survivors is exponential; veterans of even a two or three missions take the first-mission novices out with comparative ease. Three of the pilots flying Argentine Skyhawks were now two-mission veterans. So were the pilots of two F9U Super-Crusaders who had replaced novices in order to give the small formation at least a fighting chance. The problem was that the four Sea Mirage pilots that faced them were now also two-mission veterans. They had split into two pairs and were coming at the Super-Crusaders from two directions. Their missiles formed a web around the intended targets.

The Argentine fighter pilots had learned much. They were coming in higher and much faster than before, flying their F9Us at the limits of their performance. They didn't even bother to launch any of the three AIM-7 missiles carried by their aircraft since that would trap them into the narrow cone defined by the scanning arc of their radar. Instead, then dived on the British formations and maneuvered to avoid the incoming missiles. Five of the six made it. The sixth continued to dive, losing parts of its airframe all the way down, until it hit the sea and exploded.

The Sea Mirages were skidding all over the sky in their efforts to out-turn the Crusaders. The Argentine fighters were relying on their simple and reliable AIM-9s to bring down their opponents. It paid off. One pair of Sea Mirages was targeted by three Crusaders, two of which were flown by veterans of the earlier strike. Both British aircraft went down as the Argentine AIM-9s homed in on their engines and shredded their tail surfaces. Their pilots punched out and floated down to the sea that was slowly being covered with shot-down pilots.

The other pair of Sea Mirages did better. They were faced by novices and they managed to avoid the sub-optimal shots fired by their opponents. As one of the Crusaders started his zoom skywards, the heat flare from his engine drifted into the acquisition arc of a British fighter. Two R550 missiles took the whole rear of his aircraft apart.

By then, the Skyhawks were clear of the CAP fighters. The four surviving F9Us climbed away, setting course for Stanley base in the Malvinas. Their pilots knew all too well that their carrier was finished and the airfield at Stanley was their only hope. Even getting there would need very careful fuel management, but the only other choice was crashing in the sea.

Forward Bridge HMS Glowworm

"They're not falling for it." Baxter watched the inbound Skyhawks fanning out to break through the air defense screen. They had already started to fire their Bullpups while *Grafton* and *Greyhound* had opened fire with their Seadarts. In doing so, they had revealed that *Glowworm* had been left toothless. The pattern of inbound missiles showed that the Argentine attack pilots had realized the implications of her silence and were simply ignoring her.

Of the nine Shyhawks, three had peeled off to attack *Greyhound* and another three to deal with *Grafton*. The other three were heading straight for *Glorious* and they had little opposition in their way. *Eclipse* was firing her Seaslug and MOG missiles but neither were having much effect. *Greyhound* was on her game though. Baxter watched the plot as she neatly knocked down all three Skyhawks heading for her. She then switched fire and sent missiles off in tail-chases after the Skyhawks that had attacked *Glorious*. It was a hopeless gesture, even if the missiles hadn't gone ballistic shortly after launch.

Grafton had done less well. She knocked down two Skyhawks but the track of the third overflew her position. She joined the three Skyhawks that had attacked *Glorious* and headed out to sea. From their course, it was obvious they were heading for the Falklands. "Damage reports?"

The reluctance with which the reply came back was proof of Baxter's worst fears. "*Grafton* took three near misses that opened up her side. She's rolling over. Abandon ship order has been given. *Greyhound* took a Bullpup in the bridge. She's reporting she's lost forward missile control but otherwise she's all right."

"What about *Glorious*?"

The message came back with even more gloom and reluctance. "Five direct hits; three near misses. Two Bullpup hits as well. One of the hits failed to explode but another took out the bridge. Admiral Lanning is dead. Captain Wales is missing. *Glorious* is being conned from her emergency station." The speaker hesitated, then plunged on. "She's got fires on the hangar deck, her machinery is damaged and she's not under control. *Eclipse* had to get out of the way pretty sharpish."

"Captain Wales is missing?" Baxter felt the stab deep inside him. It had been a long, long time since an heir to the British throne had died on a battlefield. The butcher's bill for this operation was mounting with terrifying speed and the actual invasion of the islands was still to come. Baxter only hoped that by the time this battle was over, there would be enough ships left afloat to stage it.

Savoy Hotel, London

"That's a bit much," Achillea was looking at the pile of transmitters and wires on the table. She and Henry McCarty had carefully searched Igrat's room and come up with five bugs that had been planted there. "We're here to help them after all."

245

"Our room was clean," McCarty looked around to make sure that this conversation at least was in private. He privately gave thanks that years of practice had made sure that they were all very careful what they said, even in presumed privacy. "So the target of this bugging was Igrat."

Igrat's mind was suddenly filled with a picture of a mysterious darkened room with her tied to a chair in the middle of it. A fist coming out of the darkness and the crunch as her nose had been broken. There had been the sickening fear that she would be disfigured and then the time it had taken for her to recover from the beating she had received. Although she wasn't aware of it, she went white and started to shake. She did know her heart was pounding and she started to breathe deeply to slow it down. Slowly, the panic attack passed. "I could take that personally, you know."

"We are assuming that this is political." McCarty had noted Igrat's reaction and moved the conversation to ground where she would be more comfortable. It had taken a long time for her to get her self-confidence back after Geneva. Even now, he knew that flashbacks still hit her hard. "Might be that somebody took a liking to you in the bar and wanted to know a bit more about you."

"One of the penalties of being the most glamorous woman around." Achillea chimed in, realizing what McCarty was trying to do.

"Any girl can be glamorous," Igrat said. "All she has to do is stand still and look stupid."

McCarty snorted with laughter. Igrat was far from stupid and people who assumed she was tended to end up deeply embarrassed and without their wallets. "And nobody does that better than our Iggie."

"Thanks, Henry. I think. Anyway, your efforts to cheer me up are appreciated but we all know this is political. So I think we had better have a nice long chat with Sir Humphrey.

Royal Australian Navy Submarine Rotorua, *North of the Falkland Islands*

"Now there's a sight you don't see very often." Captain Steven Beecham was fascinated by the sight in his periscope. An Argentine was making a dead-stick ditching in the sea. It was obviously out of fuel. Its three flight mates were circling around; one obviously making preparations to ditch as well. He swung the periscope to watch the first plane to crash. It was sinking fast, but the pilot was out and already in his rubber raft.

"What's happening up there?" Cardew was fascinated. His Captain had never spent this long on the periscope before.

"Four Argentine Skyhawks ditching. One, no, make that two, are already in the water, the others getting ready. First bird dead-sticked, the second came in under power. Looks to me like they were heading for Stanley but ran out of fuel. I'd guess they decided to stick together once the first bloke ran dry. There goes number three."

Cardew thought for a second. "Number One, prepare to surface. Rig for picking up survivors. What's the largest Australian Ensign we have on board?"

246

"We have a 12 by 18 foot Ensign, Sir."

"Then hoist it. As prominently as you can as soon as we surface. Come to think of it, if we have any other Australian ensigns, hoist them. Then have every lookout available up top and watching. If the radio traffic we have picked up is anything to go by, there'll be shot-down pilots all over the place. As soon as we're topside, elevate the ESM mast and listen out for distress beacons."

Beecham felt the submarine angle upwards as the control room crew brought her to the surface. As soon as she was soundly 'upstairs,' he transferred up to the surface conning station built into the front of the sail. By the time he got there, a detail from the crew was already on the deck forward and getting ready to pull the four life rafts in. Three of the Skyhawks had already sunk and the fourth was about to go under. Beecham watched it go. Then he realized that by doing so, he had missed the rescue of the first Argentine pilot. He was already wrapped in a blanket and being hustled down the forward hatch. The Argentine pilots realized what was going on and were paddling over to the waiting submarine.

"Sir. First pilot is in the wardroom with a tot of rum inside him. It's as we guessed. They're refugees from the Argentine fleet. The British got their carrier and they were trying to make it to Stanley. One ran out of fuel so they decided to go in together. He says there are dozens of aircraft down, all over the area."

"Well, we'll have to start picking them up then. We're probably better off on the surface anyway. Make sure the pilots get as much rum as they need."

Cardew grinned. Shock at ditching, a quick rescue and a few shots of hundred percent proof naval rum worked wonders when it came to getting people to lose control of their tongues.

Stanley Airfield, Falkland Islands

The wailing air raid sirens blasted out. Men spilled out of their tents and ran across the airfield. Major Grigorio Mazza was already at his action station, inside the control cabin for his Scudo air defense system. Six twin 47mm anti-aircraft guns with one fire control radar for each pair of mountings. Three triple mounts for the land-based version of the Folgore anti-aircraft missile. The radar plot showed a small formation of aircraft coming in from the sea. Mazza checked the inbound flight schedule. It showed a Pelican transport aircraft from the mainland would be arriving that night but no other air activity.

"All guns and missiles prepare to engage inbound aircraft." Mazza checked the display. The bearing was constant, but the height finder radar showed the inbound aircraft were steadily losing altitude. It was a slightly strange attack pattern for aircraft that were about to engage a heavily-defended base. Despite the incongruity, the 47mm guns were already lining up on the target. The approach altitude was already too low for the Folgore missiles. Mazza shook his head and scanned the area with his binoculars. Wherever the aircraft were, whatever they were, they were invisible in the gray mist.

Mazza sighted the lead aircraft a split second before his guns opened fire. He recognized the long fuselage, the dark blue paint job with the light blue and white-striped rudder,. They were Navy F9U-5 Crusaders, undoubtedly from the *Veinticinco de Mayo*. Whatever he may have thought next was interrupted by the crackle as his guns opened fire.

"Cease fire, cease fire immediately. Aircraft are friendly! Say again those are our aircraft!"

The Argentine gun crews were well-trained. The fire stopped instantly but the damage was done. The lead F9U was bracketed by the shell bursts and crashed just short of the runway. About the only redeeming feature was that the pilot managed to eject and floated down well clear of the wreckage of his aircraft. The other three Crusaders managed to come in to land without problems. *On the whole*, Mazza thought, *it would probably be better if I didn't go over and introduce myself to the Navy pilots.* Then, as he always did at times of stress, he reached out and touched the picture of his wife and child pinned over the main fire control display.

Flag Bridge, HMS Furious, *North East of the Falkland Islands*

"More orphans coming in, Sir." Admiral Kinnear watched the deck crew at work. What was happening down there looked like a well-rehearsed ballet dance but it was deadly serious. Thirteen of the twenty Buccaneers had made it back along with three of their escorts. With his own twelve planes up as CAP, that meant *Furious* had seventeen fighters and thirteen bombers left. She'd lost a quarter of her air group; but in doing so she had gutted the Argentine Navy. The camera film was conclusive. The *Veinticinco de Mayo* was a goner, along with her escorts.

Things had improved a little since then. For *Furious* anyway, although Kinnear was worried about the larger picture. Two Sea Mirages had landed from *Glorious's* CAP. They had told a story of a bombed and burning carrier, dead in the water and with a wrecked flight deck. Now four Buccaneers were coming in and they had to have the oddest configuration he had ever seen. They'd been inerted on *Glorious's* hangar deck but in the few minutes the hangar deck crews had available, they'd got them off. They hadn't had time to purge the internal fuel tanks, so they'd hung drop tanks on the inner wing pylons and the aircraft had flown down on those. Kinnear hoped that the pilots wouldn't absent-mindedly jettison the tanks before landing.

Assuming they got in all right, he would be nearly back to his pre-war air strength. Thirty two aircraft; half bombers, half fighters. *Furious* was still in business.

"CAG, get the Bananas bombed up for an anti-shipping strike."

"Target, the carrier group, Sir?" CAG was surprised. *The four old Gearings left afloat weren't worth another strike surely?*

"No. Just have them ready to go. We can't guarantee that there isn't another carrier out there. Until we can, we keep our guard up. The Argie Admiral forgot about us and I don't want to emulate his mistake. We'll keep a CAP and strike group ready until we're more than sure there's no more threats from the Argie Navy. If we get smacked as well, the task force is screwed beyond redemption. Signals? There you are. Get a message out to somebody in *Glorious's* group. I want to know what is happening up there. Find out if we're alone or not."

Savoy Hotel, London

"Guys, come and watch this. Looks like our discussion with Sir Humphrey will have to wait." The television in Igrat's room showed a picture of the MoD press briefing room. Ian Macdonald was just entering, "Hurry up! It's got to be real news. The speak-your-weight machine is on."

"Ladies and gentlemen. Over the last twenty four hours, a major naval action has been fought between the Argentine Navy and the Royal Navy task force operating in the South Atlantic. During the course of this action, the Argentine aircraft carrier, the *Veinticinco de Mayo*, a light cruiser and three destroyers have been sunk. Two other Argentine destroyers are reported to have been damaged and at least sixty Argentine aircraft have been shot down. While carrying out their duties as part of the Task Force, the Royal Navy destroyers *Electra* and *Grafton* have been sunk. The aircraft carrier *Glorious* and the destroyer *Glowworm* have been damaged. British aircraft losses are reported to be approximately forty aircraft."

"Have we any idea of casualties?" A woman from the Telegraph was first to jump in.

"We believe that at least four hundred of our sailors and airmen have lost their lives. We have no idea what Argentine losses are like, but we must presume they are proportionately as heavy as our own."

"The Prince of Wales is Captain of *Glorious*. Is he safe?" This time it was a gentleman from the Times.

"I'm sorry, I have no information on that topic."

"Why has it taken so long to get this information to us?" The speaker was Bernie Tatlock, a well-known nemesis of the Government in general and the Ministry of Defence in particular.

"Mister Tatlock, I seem to recall that it took six weeks for news of Trafalgar to reach England," MacDonald said with a degree of languid exasperation. "I don't think anyone much complained then. I regret that I cannot answer any questions or provide any further information at this time. Thank you."

MacDonald picked up his papers and left the room amid a buzz of confusion. The camera panned over the journalists struggling to be first out with their stories. Somewhere in the confusion, Tatlock yelped as a stiletto heel jabbed into his foot. His professional colleagues did not appreciate the shut-down in question time that had followed his aggressive intervention.

Igrat switched the television off. As if the two instruments were linked, the telephone rang as soon as the picture faded. She reached over and picked the phone up.

"This is she. . . . . Why, General Howard, Sir, I didn't know you cared. . . ." Igrat dropped the attitude a split second later. "I see Sir. That will be no problem. I'll be right over. I'll have two bodyguards with me. There's a Sonic Clipper leaving London in two hours. I can be on that. . . . Yes, Sir, that will be very helpful. . . . . I'll call ahead and make sure The Seer is in his office ready to receive them. . . . . Yes, Sir, I do have that degree of discretion in such matters."

Igrat paused and looked around. "Move, everybody. We've got to go to the MoD to get the preliminary action reports that have just come in. General Howard wants the Boss to have them ASAP. He says there is a lot in there our Navy needs to know."

CHAPTER FOUR
INVASION

Operations Room, HMS Bulwark, *East of the Falkland Islands*

"Colonel Jones, you will take Second Battalion, The Parachute Regiment and carry out an air-mech assault on the Argentine fortress at Goose Green. Herbert, you will seize that base and its associated airfield, securing the same for our use. You may expect an Argentine counter-attack and will prepare your defenses to defeat the same. Are these orders clear to you?"

"Yes, Sir." The enthusiasm in the response was immediate and obvious.

"Good man. Colonel Hill, you will take First Battalion, The Parachute Regiment and carry out an air-mech assault on Mount Tumbledown and Wireless Ridge. John, you will seize and occupy that position and prepare it for the field guns that will be lifted in to join you. You may expect an Argentine counter-attack and will prepare your defenses to protect the guns and defeat that attack. Are these orders clear to you?"

"Yes Sir." No less enthusiasm and possibly some exultation. It would be One Para that closed the noose on Stanley. A sharp twist of the tail to their old rivals in Two Para.

"Excellent. Colonel Hartmann, you will take First Battalion, the Royal Regiment of Marines and carry out an air-mech assault on Mount Kent. You will seize and hold that position until relieved by the troops advancing from San Carlos. Karl, you have the hardest job here. You will have to wait here in the assault ships until the Junglies that landed One and Two Para have returned and rearmed. That means you will be going in some three hours later than they will. One and Two Para will have the advantage of surprise. You will not. Your Marines can expect a heavy counter-attack developing early. You will stop that attack in its tracks. Are these orders clear to you?"

"Jawohl! I mean, Yes, Sir."

A ripple of laughter at the deliberate 'mistake' ran around the briefing room. "Gentlemen, the Marines have a deadly task here. We don't have the capacity of going in as one wave; the cancellation of *Centaur* saw to that. We had to seize two out of three objectives and leave the third for a second wave. We can thank the dockies who worked triple shifts to get both our amphibious transports ready that we are able to hit two. Before *Bulwark* came out of dock three months early, we were going to have to assault each target in turn. But, two out of three it is. On the way down, the operations staff went over all the possible permutations of landing. We evaluated taking Goose Green and Mount Kent, Mount Kent and Mount Tumbledown and Goose Green and Mount Tumbledown. Each permutation had its advantages and disadvantages. We decided that the element of surprise would be critical in taking Goose Green and Mount Tumbledown but less so on Mount Kent. Yet without Mount Kent we would have two isolated positions at almost opposite ends of the island. With Mount Kent we can give the troops advancing from San Carlos a smooth highway garrisoned by our brigade all the way to Stanley."

"A smooth highway, Sir? Here?" Again a ripple of laughter at the disbelief in Jones's voice spread around the briefing room.

"All right, a smooth dirt track with occasional swamps, streams and rocky outcrops. But it will be garrisoned by us and that makes it as good as a smooth highway. By the way, reinforce the warning to all your men. Nobody drink the water here, it's got liver flukes in it."

There was a murmur of agreement. Strachan waited for a moment and then continued, "Karl, with your permission, I would like the honor of accompanying your Marines on their assault."

"The honor would be ours, Sir."

"Thank you. Any other questions?"

There was a long pause as the officers studied the maps showing the battle plan. They'd all had their own parts of it for some days but this was the first time everything had been put together for them. "I'll say one thing. The Septics couldn't even begin to pull this off." Hill's voice was loaded with satisfaction.

"They wouldn't even try. They'd just drop a damned great nuke on the place and call it quits." Jones sounded slightly derisive. "The last time they tried an opposed landing, the Caffs wiped the floor with them."

"It was not quite that bad." Hartmann felt compelled to defend his brother Marines even if they were Septics. They held the beach and blocked the way to where the rescue was carried out. Those were their orders, yes?"

"One other thing." Brigadier Strachan rapped sharply on his podium. "I have just received word from HMS *Glorious*. Her fires are out and the flooding has been contained. She is now retiring to South Georgia, escorted by *Glowworm* and *Greyhound*, where she will make further repairs before heading home. Her surviving aircraft have been transferred to HMS *Furious*." He paused, bringing his voice under control before the next part. "I regret to have to inform you that the body of Captain Wales has been located and recovered from the wreckage of the island. It appears that the Prince of Wales died in the finest traditions of the Navy, remaining at his station and doing his duty. He will, of course, be buried at sea along with the other casualties from *Glorious*. Gentlemen, his

252

funeral will be taking place while you are carrying out your assaults. Let us make very sure that our conduct honors the sacrifice he has made."

Darwin Road, Port Stanley, Falkland Islands

Major Patricio Dowling was a very angry man that morning. For night after night, he had been woken up by a series of telephone calls at unspeakably early hours of the morning. Each call had been routine reports that were nothing to do with him. He had asked one caller why would anybody think he was interested in the number of sacks of garbage removed from the cookhouse? The caller had simply hung up. After the fifth call in a two and a half hour period, he had realized the calls were not intended for him at all. They were routine calls that had somehow become misdirected in the telephone exchange. By the time he had finally got back to sleep, the sun had been rising and it was too late for any rest that night. He had spent the first few hours of the new day having the telephone switchboard checked thoroughly. The problem hadn't been there. The telephone engineers had suggested that water seeping into the lines from the bogs had caused short-circuits.

It was not as if the work here was going the way he had planned. He had expected this to be a relatively simple job. The garrison would be eliminated, the islanders rounded up and either deported or otherwise disposed of. He'd had files on all the local leaders. They would have been the first to disappear. Nothing had gone the way he has expected. The British garrison had been brutally mauled, but the Argentine Marines had made sure their prisoners had been safely delivered to Uruguay and the care of neutral powers. The surviving Royal Marines had been waging a steady war of attrition; nothing elaborate but a man shot by a sniper here, a mine placed in a roadway there. And always, the litany of stupid accidents that seemed to accompany the Argentine Army wherever it went. Fuelling accidents, trucks running off the road and into the swamp or over sharp drops. The list seemed endless. Minor, avoidable accidents all of them but each bringing its toll of dead and wounded.

Dowling had begin to think the Argentine Army on the Malvinas was cursed. There had been so many accidents. The number was so far above the norm for any reasonable kind of operation. As any good intelligence officer would do, Dowling had started to look at those accidents with growing suspicion. When losses from sheer stupidity reached those levels, they stopped being accidents and started to become sabotage. Dowling was becoming increasingly convinced that the Army was infiltrated by traitors. If he couldn't bring them in for judgment, he was uneasily aware that he might be considered in league with them.

That thought made Dowling hit the accelerator hard as he came over the hill top and start the long descent down. He was on his way to the airbase at Stanley. There had been another accident. One of four Argentine Navy Crusaders making an emergency landing had been shot down by the air defenses. That was another uneasy thought. Dowling had heard there was a great naval battle going on offshore, but he had no idea how the battle was going. The Argentine communications network was being remarkably quiet about it, but the fact that four orphaned Navy aircraft had tried to make it back to Stanley did not bode well for the battle.

Half way down the slope, Dowling realized he was going too fast to make the turn at the bottom safely. One more annoyance to add to a day that was already one he would rather forget. He stabbed at the brake pedal with his foot but the mushy response

253

told him there was something seriously wrong. The Landrover showed no sign of slowing down. Thoroughly frightened, Dowling yanked on the handbrake but that simply caused the vehicle to swing out of control. Dowling twisted the steering wheel with one hand, trying to stay on the road, while with the other he knocked the gear lever into neutral. By then it was too late, and he saw the white concrete cylinders that marked the end of the bridge railings looming in front of him.

A few minutes later, Dowling found himself returning to semi-consciousness. That was when he felt one hand take a firm grip on his neck while another grabbed his chin. He knew what was coming next. It was no surprise when he felt the rapid jerk and his body went numb as the bones in his neck separated. He remained alive just long enough to feel himself being dragged somewhere.

Blackburn Buccaneer S4H XT-279, Approaching Argentine Airbase, North East of Stanley

XT-279 was coming in light. The Highball equipment in her belly prevented her from carrying normal bombs in there so she was restricted to the four Martel anti-radar missiles carried under her wings. The six surviving Highball aircraft had been joined by the three remaining dedicated anti-radar aircraft. Together their barrage of missile devastated the anti-aircraft fire control radars and the airfield search systems. The nine aircraft turned away long before the guns ringing the airfield could engage them.

Mullback knew this mission was a milk-run. The Highball aircraft and the anti-radar birds were now too precious to waste on pounding airfields. That had been left to the eight bomb-carriers. They made their low-level runs over the airstrip. Each deposited eight thousand pound retarded bombs over the parking area and taxiways. Mullback saw the sky stained by the flak bursts from the 47mm guns and the eruption of primary and secondary explosions from the airfield area. There were also two columns of smoke rising away from the airfield, columns that Mullback recognized as graves of crashed Buccaneers. By the time the bombers had formed up again for the flight back to *Furious*, Mullback had done the maths. He came to the grim conclusion it was only a matter of time before the British fleet ran out of aircraft.

Control Room, HM Submarine "Saint Vincent"

"We've got another contact, Captain. Multiple screws, moving fast. Estimated speed 27 knots."

"Up scope." Captain Wiseart waited until the periscope tube was passing him on its way up, then grabbed the controls on either side and did a quick scan. "Down scope."

The exposure had been less than 15 seconds, a tribute to much training and long practice. Wiseart was grinning broadly when he turned to his control room crew. "Welcome to my parlor said the spider to the fly. Five ships out there; a cruiser and at least four destroyers. The cruiser is one of those weird Argentine assault cruisers; the ones with eight inch guns forward and quarters for a marine landing force aft. She's coming straight for us. Sonar, target data?"

"Course is one-oh-three, Sir; estimated speed still 27 knots. Range is 12,000 yards and closing quickly."

"Prepare tubes one to four with Mark 2s. We'll take the cruiser with tubes one to three, the nearest destroyer with tube four. Then we'll make a quiet and dignified departure. Or, alternatively, run like hell depending on which seems most appropriate."

"Course and speed constant, Sir."

"Fire control solution?"

"Set and ready to go."

"Fire all tubes. Then turn onto a reciprocal bearing and get us out of here."

Saint Vincent lurched as the heavy torpedoes fired in sequence from her bow tubes. The ticking of the clock seemed to slow down as the entire control room crew waited for the dull thunder of torpedoes striking home. Eventually, Wiseart had to admit at least one failure. "First torpedo missed."

Anything else he might have said was interrupted by a long low rumble followed quickly by a second. Then, there was a long pause before a third explosion. The control room crew erupted into cheers.

"Up scope." Wiseart repeated his scan. "We got her. Her bows are half-hanging off and her back is broken amidships. She's burning like a torch. No way she is anything but a goner. We clobbered one of their old Gearings as well. She's broken in two and is going down fast."

"Go back for the other destroyers, Sir?"

Wiseart shook his head. "They're closing in on the targets. Picking up survivors I think. We've neutered that group. Leave the rest to go home."

Destroyer Catamarca, *Standing by Argentine Assault Cruiser* La Argentina, *Falkland Islands*

The blow had been swift, deadly and utterly destructive. *La Argentina* had been hit twice; once under the forward turrets, once just aft of her machinery spaces. The hit forward had blown her bows off. The whole bow assembly was twisted to one side and sinking fast. What had happened aft was far worse. *La Argentina* had been loaded with anti-aircraft missiles and guns in her hangar and on her flight deck, but she had been carrying drummed fuel in the living quarters for her Marines. The under-the-keel explosion of the Mark 2 torpedo vaporized that fuel and spread the explosive mixture through her hull. Then, that mixture had ignited and turned into a fuel-air explosion. The fireball raced through the ship, killing and burning everything in its path. The assault cruiser was an inferno. The survivors on board frantically jumped over the side to escape the ghastly alternatives of being burned alive by the fires or sucked down when the cruiser sank.

Captain Isaac Leonardi had already started to bring *Catamarca* in to assist the stricken ship when one of the other destroyers, the *Santissima Trinidad* was hit. The blast was dead amidships and the old destroyer was overwhelmed. She broke in half and was sinking so fast that few of her crew would escape. Leonardi had already seen the casualty figures from the carrier battle further north. More than fifteen hundred men had died on the

Veinticinco de Mayo. The dead on board the three destroyers that had gone down added at least another five hundred to that total. Now, with *La Argentina* crammed with her own crew and the complements of the anti-aircraft systems she had on board, Leonardi guessed that more than a thousand more were in extreme danger.

And so, for the third time in barely more than a few weeks, *Catamarca* closed on a wrecked and burning ship and did what she could to succor the survivors. All the time, Leonardi was waiting for the slam under his feet that would tell him that another British torpedo had stuck home and that his own ship and crew were to be added to the horrifying butcher's bill. But, the slam never came and he slowly relaxed. He guessed that the British captain was first of all a Seaman also and he would not fire on ships that were saving the lives of stricken mariners.

He looked down at his ship and saw the sights that had become all too familiar to him. Nets over the side of his ship; survivors being brought on board to be wrapped in blankets and rushed below. Even a few minutes exposure to the waters of the South Atlantic would be fatal. The Arctic Convoys had taught navies much about helping their crew survive in frigid waters but there was only so much they could do. A swift rescue was still the best way of saving survivors. He watched as men from his ship jumped into the water to pull the survivors too badly wounded or exhausted into safety. And so it was that *Catamarca* slowly filled with the survivors from the sinking cruiser.

By the time the wreckage of *La Argentina* had sunk, every spare space on *Catamarca* was filled. The missile destroyer *Entre Rios* had joined the rescue effort while the remaining Gearing class was picking up survivors from her sister.

"Our contribution to this war seems to be restricted to picking up survivors." Lieutenant Brian Martin was also watching the rescue effort. He had to, his cabin was one of those that had been taken and filled with badly wounded men from the *La Argentina*

"We started this remember, by sinking *Mermaid*." Leonardi's sadness was evidence in his voice. "Perhaps this is our penance for that act. We are to survive while the ships around us are sunk and be tasked with picking up those men from them whom God has in his mercy spared."

He was interrupted by an officer from *La Argentina*, a young ensign whose hands had been burned and were bandaged as well as the desperately-overloaded medical team on *Catamarca* could manage. "Captain Leonardi, I wanted to thank you and your crew, on behalf of my men, for what you have done to rescue us. Truly *Catamarca* is a ship crewed by the angels of deliverance."

Darwin Road, Port Stanley, Falkland Islands

The convoy of trucks came to a halt; one more annoying incident in a day filled with them. All the trucks were overloaded since the plan had been to make up the unit's requirement by confiscating vehicles from the civilian population. The planners had overlooked something, most of the confiscated light trucks were gasoline powered while the Argentine Army's own vehicles were diesel-engined. Last night, the inevitable had happened. During the preparations for this move, somebody had filled the tanks of the gasoline-engined vehicles with diesel fuel.

256

Colonel Alfonso Fernandez got out of the lead truck and walked down to the bridge. It was easy to see what had happened. The Landrover had smacked into the bridge abutment, ricocheted off and overturned. The driver was on the ground beside the overturned vehicle. From the way his head was twisted, he had obviously been killed on impact and thrown out. He walked over to these scene of the accident and looked at the victim.

"That's Major Dowling. At least nobody human has been killed." Captain Vazquez made the observation with at least some satisfaction in his voice.

"Shut up you fool. Somebody will hear you." Fernandez looked at the bridge again and sighed. His battalion had been tasked to take possession of Mount Tumbledown and Wireless Ridge overlooking Stanley. Nobody had admitted it but it was widely known that the Argentine Navy had fought an engagement with the British. It had not ended well for them. Now, the British amphibious ships were closing in to land their troops. According to the last reports, they had been some 600 kilometers out, so the counter-invasion was expected in around 24 hours time. Fernandez was supposed to be holding the back door to Stanley in case the British did an end-run and tried to hit the position from the South. Only, everything had gone wrong as usual. *Now this idiot from military intelligence has gone and blocked the road.* "Organize a work team and get that wrecked Landrover out of the way. And put Dowling's body somewhere appropriate."

Fernandez tried not to hear the splash as the dead Major's body was thrown over the parapet into the swamp. The simplest way to get the Landrover off the bridge would be to push it off with a truck. To do that efficiently and without damage to a scarce truck, it would have to be righted and put on its wheels first. A group of men from Vazquez's company had just started that when Fernandez heard a strange whistling noise; one that seemed to be modulated by a low-pitched drone. He spun around just as the stream of British Rotodynes burst over the ridgetop and opened fire on his battalion, helplessly strung out along the road.

Fairey Defenders, that's what they're called, Fernandez thought, hardly able to credit himself with remembering that at such a moment. *Those are the assault versions, troop carriers armed with unguided rockets, guided anti-tank missiles and a 20mm gatling gun in a nose turret. And they are all trying to kill me.* It was that last thought that broke the strange freeze in his mind and he dived into the ditch for cover.

Armies had learned from the damage wrought by low-flying fighter-bombers in the Second World War. The Argentine Army was no different. One man in five carried a shoulder-fired anti-aircraft missile. But the Defenders were flying as low as helicopters and as fast as aircraft. They were skimming terrain features, using buildings and trees as cover, flying down roads and around hills rather than over them. More frighteningly than that, each Rotodyne carried six 38-round packs of 3 inch unguided rockets. They were firing a constant stream of them into the battalion strung out along the road in front of them. They also had Adder anti-tank missiles on their wing racks and had used those to pick off the four vehicles in the battalions anti-aircraft platoon. Lastly, each had a 20mm gatling gun that poured a hundred rounds a second at its target. For all those reasons, not one of the Argentine soldiers managed to fire his missile. Most died in their trucks as the rockets reduced the convoy to blazing chaos. The rest saved their lives by throwing away their equipment and running.

Fernandez was one of the survivors. Vazquez and his team were not. They died as they ran, caught on the bridge where there was no cover and no hope of finding any. The Colonel shook his head and watched the Rotodynes overfly the remnants of his battalion and land on the hills he had been supposed to garrison. Troops poured out of the bellies of their assault transport aircraft. Little armored vehicles left with them. Some had guns strapped to the sides of their hulls; others were obviously infantry carriers. The message was obvious. Mount Tumbledown and Wireless Ridge had been seized by coup de main and were held by at least a battalion with armored support.

Fernandez was a professional officer and he already knew the area assigned to him well. Now the British were established on the high ground, it would be the devil's own job to force them out. With his battalion gone and most of the rest of the Argentine Army the wrong side of the ridge, there was very little between the British and recapturing Port Stanley. Carefully, very carefully, he edged out of his ditch and worked his way between the wrecked vehicles that littered the road. Once on the other side of them, he set off for the Headquarters at Stanley.

Argentine Airbase and Garrison, Goose Green

The line of Junglies lifted over the ridge and poured rockets into the base that lay spread out before them. This was a classical air-mech assault. The Fairey Defender 'Junglies' had lifted the assault force into the dead ground on the other side of a ridge. Then, the armored vehicles, the troops they carried and the Junglies that had brought the assault force into position swept over the ridge in a single devastating wave. The Argentine troops had a few minutes warning of the assault but it had done them little good. If anything, it worked against them. When the assault hit, they were half way between being at minimum readiness and at full alert. All too many of them were in the open when the waves of rocket fire tore into the camp. They scattered and went to ground, pinned down by the barrage of rolling explosions and unable to resist the assault that was already breaking upon them.

The Junglies had used their speed and range to slip across the coastline in one of the many undefended areas. Then, they had swung inland, still using the terrain as cover, and approached the base from the Lafonia side. What defenses the Argentines had prepared faced north, in anticipation of an assault from the landing beaches on the northern half of the island. It was the right choice; the logical choice to make. There were no good landing beaches for armored vehicles in Lafonia. The ground was open enough to make an assault by unsupported infantry a potential bloodbath. Goose Green should have been a very tough nut to crack.

The assault that was taking place was something entirely new. The little armored vehicles brought by the Junglies streamed forward; their machine guns raking the ground in front of them. The Junglies followed behind, firing their barrage of rockets over the heads of their infantry. It was teamwork. The infantry kept the Argentine missileers from attacking the rotodynes, the Junglies saturated the ground with fire and kept the defenders from mounting a coordinated defense against the infantry. The whole mixture, armor, infantry, rotodynes, formed a whole that was much greater than the sum of its parts.

The defenders had armor of their own; a platoon of four M92 light tanks. Had the fortress been attacked by unsupported infantry, those tanks would have been decisive. They were well-positioned and their crews were good. One blew up as soon as it started to move, hit by a Cobra anti-tank missile from one of the Junglies. A second was hit by a 120mm squash-head round from one of the British Chevalier light tanks. They were tanks in name only. In reality they were a descendent of the pre-World War Two Bren gun carrier and had armor as thin as paper. Each Chevalier mounted two 120mm Wombat recoilless anti-tank guns, one on each side of its hull. The Argentine M92 took a direct hit from one of the guns, lurched to a stop and was hit again by a shot from the Chevalier's other gun. It started to burn; the crew bailed out into the torrent of rifle, machine gun and rocket fire that was already engulfing them

In the midst of the chaos, the Chevalier stopped and two of its crew jumped out from the back. Each was carrying a single 120mm round and they had the reloading drill down to a fine art. They had the guns reloaded just in time to see their vehicle hit by a 76mm high velocity round from the third M92. The armor on the Chevalier was barely capable of stopping a rifle round. It offered no resistance to the high-velocity 76mm shot. The Chevalier blew up, killing all four crew members. They would have been better off if they had gone to ground and reloaded under cover but their inexperience, shown as over-enthusiasm had got the better of them. Others would learn from the mistake they had never got the chance to correct.

The third Argentine tank got no chance to celebrate its kill. A Cobra missile exploded its fuel tanks and that set off the ammunition stowage. The explosion was spectacular; tanks brewing up always were. It highlighted the fourth and last tank as it tried to back away to a more defensible position. It died in the process, killed by the one-two tap from another Chevalier. By that time, the Argentine defense was collapsing. The British assault swept through the positions the infantry should have been holding but had never managed to reach. The battle was over before it had fairly begun.

Colonel Jones was already getting his own defenses set up when the Junglies took off for the long flight back to HMS *Bulwark*. Most of them anyway. One Junglie had crash-landed just outside the perimeter wire after an anti-aircraft missile had taken out one of its engines. It looked repairable, but that wasn't his call to make. The other aircraft had to go back and pick up the Marines and shift them to Mount Kent.

"Sir. Butcher's bill." Sergeant Ian Mackay had a single short piece of paper in his hand. "Eight dead. Four from one Chevalier that was knocked out and four infantry. Twelve wounded; mostly rifle fire. Argies have twenty dead, mostly from the four tanks, and about sixty wounded, almost all fragmentation injuries from the rockets. Our medics and theirs are working together to treat the wounded. We've got a joint field hospital set up."

"Twenty dead and wounded, and they took eighty. It could have been a lot worse Sergeant; this was a strong position. If we'd have had to take it unsupported, I doubt if either of us would have lived to tell the story."

"May be, Sir. But this air-mech stuff seems to be all that the top brass thought it would be. The Argies never got themselves together enough to put up a real fight."

"Sir." A Signals officer had a flimsy in his hand. "We have the word from Kingfisher-Two. Mount Tumbledown and Wireless Ridge are both secure. No casualties in the direct assault. Their Junglies caught the Argentine garrison moving up on the road and tore it up something horrible. One Junglie got nailed by a SAM when it took off again. Crew are MIA."

"Very good. Make back to Prime. 'Kingfisher-One objective secured. Most of Argentine garrison have been taken prisoner. Own casualties, eight dead. One Junglie damaged but secure."

Jones and Mackay looked around at the base, now securely in British hands. The Union Jack was fluttering proudly over it. When Jones spoke, his voice caught slightly, as if there was an obstruction in his throat. "Sergeant, I think we're back."

Operations Room, HMS Bulwark, *East of the Falkland Islands.*

Forty rotodynes had gone out, carrying the two paratroop battalions. Thirty eight had returned and were spread out between the two assault ships, being refuelled and rearmed. The Marines were waiting, ready to stream on board the aircraft that had landed on *Bulwark*. A couple of nautical miles away, the rotodynes were preparing to pick up the heavy equipment for the two existing airheads. Artillery mostly; the lightweight 25-pounders that would open the siege of Stanley.

Strachan watched a Marine driving his Chevalier light tank up the ramp and into the belly of the Rotodyne. Counter-intuitively, it had been loaded nose first and would back out of the aircraft when it made its touch-and-go landing. So much experimentation had gone into making tiny decisions like that. Backing the vehicle out meant that its guns would be facing the right way as soon as they cleared the Junglie's rear ramp. That, in turn, meant they would be available just a small fraction of a second earlier.

"Ready to launch in thirty minutes?" Strachan addressed the question to Hartmann who was watching replacement Adder missiles being loaded onto the wingtip racks of the Junglies.

Hartmann didn't answer immediately. Instead he spoke first into the intercom on the operational panel in front of him. "On schedule, Sir. A few of the Junglies have bullet holes in them but nothing to worry about. They're being checked out while my Marines load up."

"Then, we'd better get down to the flight deck and mount up ourselves, Karl. We don't want your booties thinking we're holding them up."

Position Kingfisher-Two, Mount Tumbledown, Overlooking Stanley

"Friend."

The voice from the rocks was exhausted, shaky and near-spent. But, it was in English and that made the paratroopers in the observation point take notice. "Firefly." That was the password and the reply was "Serenity."

"God knows what the watchword is. We've been stuck out here for weeks. We're just about done in."

"Identify yourselves." The paratrooper nearest the voice settled down a bit closer into the rocks. If this was a trick, things would get very bloody, very quickly.

"Sergeant Jordan, Royal Marines. Late of Naval Party 8901. We've been evading and resisting ever since the Argies landed. Bagged a few of them as well. Who are you?"

"Two Para."

"Oh God, a bunch of Toms. There goes the neighborhood."

"Yeah, we thought you booties were around somewhere; the sheep are terrified. Advance and be recognized."

A number of ragged figures rose from positions in the rocks. They were wearing a mixture of British military uniforms and civilian clothes. Only one was carrying a British L1A2 rifle, the others had a mix of FAS rifles taken from Argentine Marines and SVKs taken from Army troops. It was their faces that shook the paratroopers. They were gaunt, the eyes sunk so deep into their heads that they appeared to be black holes. The men had lost so much weight that their cheekbones stuck out over jaws that seemed to expose their teeth. The men looked almost like skeletons. The paratroopers grabbed them and hustled them into cover. There were eight of them in all.

"Get the medics up here, fast." A message runner took off, worming his way through the rocks towards the battalion headquarters area. Using radios was out. The Argentines could pick up the transmissions and use them to locate headquarters positions.

"Easy, we got you. You evaded after the Argie invasion?"

"There were a dozen of us to start with. Lieutenant Hallam bought it early on in a firefight with the Argies. Sergeant Fox a bit later. Then I took over. We ran out of 7mm, mostly, so we picked up Argie weapons. The SVK is a real piece of crap. Most of the ones we found had cracked receivers. We got a lot of help though."

"From the civvies?"

"Yeah them too. They gave us food, water and what warm clothing they could find. This here, where you are, is as far south as the Argies ever came. Beyond here, it's all still ours. But there's more to it than that. The Island is haunted. There are ghosts here. Argies just died for no reason." Sergeant Jordan shuddered slightly. "Couple of times we thought they'd found us, but they'd have these weird accidents and we'd manage to get clear."

The medics arrived and took over the Marine survivors. A Lieutenant drew Sergeant Tennent to one side. "They say anything of interest?"

"Yeah, the SVKs crack up. We knew that anyway. Their tactical intelligence is worthless. They think the Argies never came further south than this. They've no idea what's happening on the rest of the island. Oh, and the Island is haunted. They say ghosts were helping them out."

The Lieutenant shook his head. Stress from a weeks-long guerilla war against the Argentine forces had taken its toll. Those Marines would take a long, long time to recover. "They probably believe that too. They'll be saying there's an Auxiliary Unit on the Island next."

A gentle laugh ran around the observation point. "Right. Shape up and keep your eyes skinned. We just heard from the assault ships. The Junglies carrying the guns will be arriving here soon. When they do, the Argies will go spare. They'll have to take those guns out or Stanley becomes unusable."

The Lieutenant moved back to his platoon position, taking care not to stick his head up over the rockline. The surface landing force would be coming ashore at dawn. Once they were in and could advance along the carpet of Air-mech troops that had landed across the Island, the whole battle would be over. The end game was approaching fast and he didn't want to be picked off by a sniper before it happened.

Argentine Headquarters, Stanley.

"They're all over the Island. You say they took both Mount Tumbledown and Wireless Ridge?" General Mario Menendez asked Colonel Fernandez, even though he knew the answer.

"They took both. They caught us on the road. We didn't have a chance. My men, those who survived, are still trickling in."

And a damned good thing that they are or we would have almost no troops between the British and Stanley. Menendez shook his head, angrily aware that this was all not supposed to be happening. "And another British unit struck Goose Green. The last radio message we had from there was that the position was falling to armored units landed from Rotodynes. We have had reports from a Special Forces unit that a third British force has seized Mount Kent. Look, Fernandez, look what the British have done. They have seized positions right across the island and cut us in two. The best units we have are here, at Teal Inlet, ready to counter-attack the British when they landed on the beaches in the northern part of the Island. We're cut off from them."

Menendez studied the map again and shook his head angrily. "The runway at the airfield is out. That airstrike knocked out only three of our Ciclones but it reduced the runway to a shambles. Our men are still clearing delayed action bomblets off the runway and parking apron. The Air Force refuse to launch strikes from the mainland now. They say by the time they get here it will be night. They do promise us strikes in the morning though. By then it will be too late."

"What about the Navy?" Fernandez tried to think of other forces that could be brought in.

"What Navy?" Menendez was openly derisive. "They fought the British and got raped. We won't see their aircraft for a long time to come. If ever. There are three Crusaders parked at the airfield and that's all. The rest are at the bottom of the sea. If it is any consolation, there's an Australian submarine out there picking up the pilots. Don't ask me why she is so far from home. Probably left over from that naval garden party in Santiago a few weeks back."

"The British have made a mistake. Their landing forces are deployed over a wide area. If we can take the airborne forces deployed on Mount Kent out, then we will have split them into two non-supporting pockets that we can defeat in detail."

Menendez looked at the maps and nodded in agreement. "We can move the cavalry at Teal Inlet over to attack Mount Kent at first light. I'd like to move sooner but trying to redeploy a unit at night on this wretched island is a sure way to lose half of it and wear out the rest. By dawn we will have the airfield here back in action and we can use the remaining Ciclones to support the cavalry. Then, once Mount Kent has been retaken, the infantry at Teal Inlet can bottle up the force that took Goose Green while the cavalry relieve us here in Stanley. We can win this one yet, Fernandez, despite the mess the Navy made of their part of this operation. You have overnight to put your battalion back together, then deploy then in a defense line, here at Sapper Hill."

The orders Menendez was issuing were interrupted by lightning flashing along the horizon out to sea. It made Fernandez shake his head. "That's all we needed; a thunderstorm now to disrupt our counter-attacks."

Menendez was puzzled. "There were no thunderstorms in the weather forecasts." Any further comments he might have made were cut off by the howl of inbound artillery fire.

HMS Lion, *Flagship, Cruiser Squadron, Off Stanley Airfield, Falkland Islands*

Admiral Chupe watched as Stanley Airfield disappeared under a hail of six inch rounds. There was no messing round this time, no demonstration of firepower followed by an invitation to surrender. This was a bombardment intended to totally destroy the airfield beyond any hope of quick repair. The four cruisers had four semi-automatic six-inch guns each; the two H class destroyers each had another pair. That made 20 guns each firing 20 rounds per minute. A total of 400 shells had deluged the airport; shattering it and causing secondary explosions to erupt all over the area. As suddenly as it had begun, the gunfire ceased. The ships swung their weapons to engage other targets in the Argentine base area. The mass barrage that had opened the bombardment wouldn't be repeated. Not now the large target that had justified it was a sea of flame. The warships had secondary targets to pick off before they vacated the area and moved south to support the landings already under way at San Carlos.

"Air raid warning red, red, red!" The alarm was accompanied by a wailing of alert sirens. The radar repeater on the bridge showed six thin red streaks leaving positions on the island.

"Here they come." Chupe's comment had a note of the old Navy prayer 'for what we are about to receive, may we be truly thankful,' about it. "Let's hope the Heroes live up to their name."

HMS Hotspur, *Destroyer Screen, Cruiser Squadron, Off Stanley Airfield, Falkland Islands*

"Engaging with Seadart." Hargreaves gave the order as the anti-ship missile batteries around the Argentine base area unmasked and opened fire. There were six missiles in the first wave and four in the second. *Hotspur* was already shifting her six inch gunfire to the positions revealed by the missile launches. A few thousand yards away,

HMS *Hero* was doing the same. The positions were probably empty, the crews would have shot their missiles off and left as fast as possible but it wouldn't hurt to be sure.

"Engaging." *Hotspur* was a big destroyer; not substantially different in size from the cruisers she was escorting. The missiles leaving her vertical launch system hardly caused her any movement. The Air Warfare Officer had watched the ship's command system fire a stream of missiles at the first wave of anti-ship missiles. The radar screen dissolved in flare as the Seadarts tore into the Otomats and started to bring them down. Three inbound broke out of the kill-zone and closed on the line of British ships, skimming just a few feet above the surface of the sea. One was knocked down by a Seawolf from *Hotspur's* secondary battery. A second looped out of control as jamming disrupted its homing system. The last passed astern of *Hotspur* and slammed into the aft superstructure of HMS *Lion*.

The cruiser rocked with the blow and her aft turret ceased firing as black, oily smoke mixed with orange flames enveloped the ship's stern. Hargreaves looked at the picture on the electro-optical display and cursed. "I thought we had that lot taped."

"*Hero* got all hers; four for twelve missiles fired. We fired twelve Seadarts, two malfunctioned and went into the 'oggin. The other ten scored three hits. Also, fired three Seawolfs for one hit." Leading Seaman Goldsteam gave the report quickly. The reason as simple; the existing numbers didn't fit and that meant there were more anti-ship missiles out there. "We had six targets, Sir. *Hero* only had four."

"That won't help *Lion*." Hargreaves was still watching the screen with the night-vision picture of *Lion* on it. The ship was a shadowy green color, but the aft superstructure was brilliant white. It was mute testimony to the ferocity of the fire raging there.

"Three more missiles coming in, Sir. We're engaging." There was an agonizing pause as *Hotspur* opened fire again. "They're down. *Hero* is engaging the next set."

It was a weird feeling, sitting in the comfort of the Operations Room, with comfortable chairs, fresh tea and coffee available, breathing cool, clean air. Intellectually, Hargreaves knew that the battle against the anti-ship missiles was a desperate one. The stream of missiles from the shore batteries were a deadly threat to the cruisers that were the backbone of the bombardment force. The two H-class destroyers were all that stood between those cruisers and the missiles. Yet, Hargreaves had a strange sense of detachment, as if the punch and counterpunch of missile and anti-missile was a play he was watching on television. It all seemed very unreal somehow.

"Shifting targets again." That came from the Surface Warfare Officer. The six-inch guns were moving to their next target, independent of the air defense efforts of the destroyer. Despite the missiles coming in, the methodical destruction of the Argentine primary base continued.

Aft Superstructure, HMS Lion, *Off Stanley, Falkland Islands*

The fires burned red, deep red. The glare from them made the Fearnought fire-resistant suits of the damage control crews glow scarlet rather than their proper silver color. The men fighting the fires had lost their identities, hidden behind the heat-reflective surfaces and dark visors of their suits. All around them, the tangled wreckage of the aft superstructure twisted and crumpled in the flare of the fires. Mixed in with the roar of the flames and the thunder of high-pressure foam from the hoses were screams from the men who were trapped inside compartments and were now being roasted alive. For them, simply being burned to death would have been a mercy. Anybody who suddenly found themselves in the aft superstructure of HMS *Lion* that night would have been forgiven for thinking they'd suddenly been translated to Hell.

It hadn't been luck that had saved HMS *Lion*. It had been skilled ship handling. The ship's Number One had seen the missile break through the defenses and swung the ship around so that her stern quarter had presented to the inbound missile. That meant the missile that should have struck the machinery spaces had hit the superstructure forward of the aft six inch gun turret. The ship's watertight integrity had been preserved. She was hurt and burning, but she was not flooding. The first and probably the most critical battle had been won before the missile had even exploded.

Coming in from the stern had meant the missile hit at an oblique angle instead of perpendicular to the ship's side. The Otomat had a shaped charge warhead that blasted blazing fuel through the area it had ripped open. The damage looked much worse than it was. The missile had torn away a substantial proportion of the side plating on the aft superstructure decks but the damage was shallow, not deep. The Duty CPOs who were heading the fire teams had already realized that the damage was not fatal. Not now, not yet. They had confidence in the old cruiser's ability to survive the damage. That also was a battle won. Now, all they had to do was cement their victory by communicating that confidence to the young sea men who made up the rest of the damage control teams.

The flames flared up, increasing the glow as a section of steel, softened by the heat of the fires and deprived of support by the explosion, collapsed on to the deck below. One of the CPOs grabbed two members of the team he headed, men who were dangerously close to the collapsing structure, and pulled them clear. "Watch yourselves, you damned fools. You can't protect the ship if you don't protect yourselves first!" Then he smacked each of them hard on the back of their Fearnought helmets and pushed them back towards the inferno that was engulfing the decks.

The secondary fire was being beaten back as the damage control crews sprayed water and foam on to the flames. They were the easy bit; the sea water cooled the steel and made reignition less likely, the foam blanketed still-burning areas and cut off the oxygen supply to the fires. Deploying the two together took skill and training. If used too soon, the water jets would break up the foam blanket and allow air back to the fuel for the fires. Timing was everything.

The primary fire was another matter. Rocket fuel held its own oxidizers and nothing could put it out. The seat of the fire would just have to be contained until the fuel had burned itself out. As long as the steel around it could be cooled, that was possible.

"Chief, compartment ready to be accessed." The call went out from one of the anonymous figures in the Fearnought suits.

The Duty NCO shuddered slightly to himself. The compartment was one of those in which men had been trapped. They had died, that much was certain, but how? If the compartment was unbreached, the fired would have consumed the air inside and they would have suffocated relatively quickly. If they were unlucky, there would have been an airflow inside. They would have roasted alive as the fires sent the air temperature soaring. Now, the damage control teams would find out.

"Water and foam teams ready. Open her up." The order was terse. If the fire had exhausted the oxygen, any fires inside the compartment would reignite and send a fireball bursting through the opened hatch. That was why the men in Fearnought suits would be stationed there. If there was breathable air inside, then the fires were really out and there would be no fireball.

A sledgehammer knocked the dogs on the hatch opened and the metal oval swung open. There was no burst of flame or fireball. For the men who had been inside, that meant the worst. There were four of them, crowded around the hatch where they had died struggling to get out. They were brilliant orange-red and the CPO knew that their skin would be as hard and crisp to the touch as crackling on a joint of pork. He looked inside, knowing that it was a sight he would never forget. "Compartment clear. Nothing to do here, move on."

Office of the Chief of Naval Operations, Pentagon, Washington DC

"If these figures are correct, the missile hit rates are abysmal."

"Around ten to twenty percent for air-to-air weapons, Sir. A bit more for surface-to-air. Of course we don't know how many misses were actual misses and how many malfunctions. Infra-reds did a lot better than radar homing missiles of course, and skill has a lot to do with it. I suspect novice pilots fired a lot of missiles off when the homing head hadn't properly locked on. That's probably why the surface-to-air missiles did a little bit better. We'd expected this of course; years of Red Sun exercises have told us that missiles aren't the invincible killers than their supporters suggested. That's why we put nuclear warheads on them and carry as many as we can. We knew AIM-7 had severe problems, at least we now also know that the French Matras have the same difficulties."

Admiral Haywood looked through the summaries of the reports that Igrat had brought back from London. "The British seem to be mostly saying that no matter how good the air defenses, a few planes will always leak through. I don't accept that."

"It reflects their limited defense radius Sir." The Seer had studied the papers as well and found them what they implied about British perceptions as interesting as the hard evidence they presented on the air battles that had taken place. "They were basically relying on a single ring of fighters plus horizon-range missile defenses. They had no airborne command and control which limited them severely. Why that is, we're not quite sure. We know Fairey offer an airborne early warning version of the Rotodyne but the Royal Navy don't appear to have used it. Our guess is that they've loaded down the carriers with every strike plane and fighter they had available and left the support birds at home. Understandable, given how far they are down the supply line, but probably not a good decision overall."

"We've got multiple rings of defenses." Haywood sounded almost smug. "Two rings of fighters and at least four of missiles. And we have command and control aircraft of course. It's going to be a lot harder to get to our carriers."

266

"Of course, sir. The big hit the British have come up with is the vertical launch system. They're getting improved reliability on their missiles by keeping them in controlled conditions until the moment of firing and a higher rate of fire. Something I think we should look into. Our existing rail launchers tend to freeze up in really bad weather and keeping missiles exposed on them results in a high dud rate. I think the Brits must be on to something with their alternative system. But, having said that, the real defense of our carriers is the knowledge of what we'll do to any country that tries to attack them The British don't have that.

"It is also interesting to note how well their Buccaneers did. They came in almost parting the wave tops. We've tended to write off coming in at low altitude since it exposes the attacking aircraft to the full weight of an enemy defense, but the Buccaneers came in so low that they made the low altitude attack plan work. Makes one wonder if we should buy some to equip an aggressor squadron. It looks like the Argentine fighter pilots didn't know how to cope with aircraft that were flying at altitudes measured in single digits. We could fund the purchase as a joint service asset. Or we could invite the British to Red Sun."

Haywood nodded again. "We could. It looks like we can take them into account again. Thank you Seer, I'll take all of this under advisement. Of course, everything depends on how well the counter-invasion goes. I'll say this for the Brits; they've certainly come up with some innovative ways of doing things."

Military Transport Drakensburg *San Carlos Water, Falkland Islands.*

"This remind you of the veroordeel border?" Captain Shumba Geldenhuys was wrapped up in a British Army issue parka and several layers of thermally insulated clothing but was still cold. The shore was a dark shadow that lay around them; the only break was the narrow entrance to the inlet. The position had been carefully chosen. The high hills around it offered some level of protection from low-flying aircraft while the vulnerable areas were covered by the destroyers. Ashore, the black of the hills was interrupted by the occasional flashes of gunfire and the lines of tracers.

"Over there it does." Lieutenant Bastiaan van Huis. "A night when the stams are restless and their militias keep shooting at nothing. But it is never so bloedige cold on the border."

"The bloedige Britse moddervoete are clearing the way for us." Lieutenant Randlehoff was surveying the invasion area with night vision binoculars. "It will be warm enough for them in those hills. We can't move the armor until daylight but they can get us on to the beach. Word from Rigsby when we are to land?"

"Too veroordeel soon. They're ferrying the tanks and armored personnel carriers ashore now. We're next and the artillery behind us." van Huis shuddered, partially with cold and partly with the sure and certain knowledge that this time he would be facing fellow professional soldiers.

"You would not say too soon of you knew what is coming to these ships broers." Randlehoff sounded apprehensive. "Work it out for yourselves. The Argies will not fly until dawn, but they will be taking off as soon as the sky is light. That is three hours time.

267

Count an hour to get here. Four hours and these ships will be the targets in a shooting gallery. Count us fortunate to be well ashore by then, broers."

"Do you think the Britse know that?" Private Meade Dippenaar wasn't certain if it was his place to ask but nobody said he couldn't ask questions. Beneath him, chains started to rattle as the first of the Boomslang tank destroyers was lifted up for transfer to a Mexflote landing raft.

Geldenhuys looked at the sleek Boomslang moving as the chains tightened. "Oh, they know it, broer. They know what the dawn will bring all too bloedige well."

Operations Room., HMS Hotspur, *San Carlos Water, Falkland Islands.*

"Air raid warning red, red, red."

"Here they come, right on time." Sub-Lieutenant Hargreaves was back in the Operations Room after grabbing a few hours sleep while the cruiser squadron and its two escorting destroyers rejoined the amphibious force in San Carlos Water. They'd moved in just after dawn. The cruisers had closed on the beach to provide fire support if needed. *Hero* and *Hotspur* had been assigned to the missile trap position at the entrance to the inlet. The attacking aircraft would have to come through that inlet, the cliffs surrounding the water were steep enough to make that axis of attack near-impossible.

Out to sea, the Sea Mirages from HMS *Furious* were trying to intercept the Argentine Ciclones. By the reports coming in and the chatter on the radio, the Navy fighters had done a good job, but there were only twelve left available and there had been nearly sixty inbound aircraft. They'd downed some but, much more importantly, they'd split the rest of the formation into small groups. The Argentine attack would be coming through in penny packets, not a massive coordinated blow. That alone would give the British destroyers trying to screen the amphibious ships a fighting chance.

The main tactical display showed the four Seadart ships covering the entrance to the inlet. *Gossamer* and *Goldfinch* were in the center of the line with the two H class destroyers on their flanks. Each ship had 48 Seadart missiles available. If the Argentine bombers got past them, they would meet a pair of old C class destroyers with Seaslugs before getting to the amphibious ships beyond. Those amphibs were largely empty now, of men at least. The landing force was ashore and already moving inland to relieve the airmech forces that had been inserted the previous day. *That is a small mercy at least,* Hargreaves thought. *I can't honestly think of anything worse than an amphib being caught with her troops still on board.*

He thumbed the intercom leading up to the bridge wings. There was a new piece of equipment mounted there, known by the arcane initials Outfit DEC. Able Seamen Johnson and Tunney were to operate it. If Hargreaves knew his men right, Johnson would be eating something and Tunney would be prophesying a disaster about to befall the ship. "You two, get your gizmo ready. They're coming through."

Four Macchi Ciclones erupted through the entrance to the inlet, their wings tucked right back for maximum speed at low altitude. One turned into a fireball almost instantly as a Seadart from *Gossamer* struck home. It came apart in mid-air. The variable geometry wings separated from the fuselage and spun away as the fuel tanks erupted. The

268

other three aircraft swerved to avoid colliding with the wreckage. In doing so, they dodged a second Seadart from *Gossamer* that missed the lead aircraft by a tiny fraction more than its proximity fuse would compensate. The tail end aircraft wasn't so lucky, it steered right into a shot from *Goldfinch* that left it streaming black smoke from crippled engines. Out of control and losing altitude, it slammed into the ridge and exploded.

That left just two survivors. They were heading straight for *Goldfinch*. A spray of Seawolf missiles erupted from the destroyer's secondary battery, taking out a third Ciclone with what appeared to be multiple hits. The surviving Ciclone screamed low over *Goldfinch*, leaving a barrage of retarded bombs falling round the destroyer. Then, it was away, running down San Carlos Water. Its nose-mounted cannon flashed as it strafed the ships in its way. It was surrounded by the black puffs of anti-aircraft gunfire from the remaining destroyers and the amphibious ships. In between the black balls from the larger guns were a hail of brilliant red dots; tracer fire from machine guns that had been hastily lashed to the railings of the warships. The first lesson of the carrier battles had been well-noted; some of the attacking aircraft would get through. The crews had done what they could to beef up the anti-aircraft barrage to deal with the inevitable leakers.

Some of the fire had taken effect. The Ciclone was trailing black smoke as it swept away and climbed over the hills at the end of the inlet. Hargreaves watched him go, wondering if the pilot would survive the long, lonely flight back to the Argentine mainland. Then he swept the bridge electro-optical scope back to *Goldfinch*. The destroyer had been hit hard. She was boiling black smoke from her center section to her bows and was already listing badly. A closer look showed she was down by the bows. Whether she would survive of not was a question Hargreaves couldn't answer. Another query was running through his mind as he watched *Goldfinch* fighting for her life. *Would the Argentines run out of aircraft before we run out of destroyers?* He wasn't able to answer that question either.

Macchi Ciclone 4-T-189, Over San Carlos Water, Falklands Islands

It was a classic flak-trap. Geography channeled the attacking aircraft through a narrow entrance point. The missile ships were positioned to cover that point with a crossfire. In many ways, it was similar to a land ambush. The answer to it was also similar. One had to attack the jaws of the trap and force them apart to allow the following aircraft to pass through the trap into the mass of amphibious shipping that lay beyond. That was rough on the aircraft that made the first attacks, though.

What made matters worse was that the Ciclone squadrons were battered before this attack had been mounted and looked a lot worse now. Argentina had started with 80 Ciclone bombers and 32 long-range fighters. They'd lost thirteen bombers and twelve fighters in the air battles over Chile and six more of each when Stanley Airfield had been flattened. That had left them with around sixty bombers and fourteen long-range fighters. Then there had been the swirling air battles on the way in as the British Sea Mirages had intercepted the inbound formation. They'd been badly outnumbered but the fighter version of the Ciclone was exactly what the package had said. It was a bomber that had been hastily modified into a fighter by lengthening the fuselage, adding an air-to-air radar and stowage for four radar homing and four infra-red heat-seeking missiles. Deciphering the panicked messages that had come over the radio, Lieutenant Edmundo Salazar knew that his fighter escort had been shredded by the Sea Mirages who had gone on to carve through the bombers. After the Mirages had broken off, presumably running low on fuel and out of ammunition, only forty two of the sixty bombers had been left. Their formation had been broken as they had tried to evade the British fighters and they were arriving over the target area in a thin, steady stream.

Salazar settled his Ciclone down as the entrance to San Carlos Water appeared in front of him. Through it, he could see the ships that were waiting for him. The first aircraft in had hit one of them, she was the center of a massive cloud of black smoke that was masking the ship beside her. However, over to her left was a much bigger destroyer. She was already shooting out missiles aimed at his formation. Salazar selected her as his target and angled over to make his run. He was carrying ten one thousand pound retarded bombs. With the aiming computer on his aircraft projecting their impact point on to his head-up display, his target would be doomed if he could get through to her.

Bridge Wing, HMS Hotspur, *San Carlos Water, Falkland Islands.*

"Look at them go!" Johnson almost yelled in excitement as the Argentine aircraft erupted through the gap in the hills that surrounded San Carlos Water and were met by a barrage of missiles from *Hero* and *Hotspur*. The new group was five aircraft. Three of them went down instantly as more than a dozen Seadarts picked them off. One survivor was heading down the bay towards the amphibious ships. The other had changed course and was heading straight for *Hotspur*. That meant Johnson and Tunney would get to try out their new toy.

It was an odd-looking piece of equipment; a long rectangular metal box mounted on a powered, stabilized pintle. The sighting system was crude, little more than a pair of binoculars wired to one end of the box. It looked a little like an anti-aircraft machine gun from the Second World War except for one salient fact. It had no barrel. Instead, it had a lens where the barrel should have been.

"This damned thing is no good." Tunney's voice was filled with woe at the expected disaster and a sense of delight that one of his tragic prophesies would soon becoming fulfilled. "Why couldn't they have given us a machine gun instead of this thing?"

Johnson ignored him and centered the attacking aircraft in his sights. He pressed the firing button and felt a slight vibration as the Outfit DEC mounting powered up. He was aiming at the cockpit on the inbound Ciclone but he could see nothing that indicated the strange weapon was having any effect on its target. His stomach started to sink in dismay and he wondered if Tunney's doom-laden pronouncements were going to prove correct for once.

Macchi Ciclone 4-T-189, Over San Carlos Water, Falklands Islands

The grey destroyer grew quickly in his head-up display. The white square that marked the projected impact point of his bombs raced across the water towards her hull. She was still firing missiles but they were directed at a third group of Argentine bombers that were already running the gauntlet of missile fire. *She is sacrificing herself to save the amphibious ships.* Salazar couldn't help respect his target for her dedication but mixed in was relief that he would get his own blow in. He noted something curious though. There was what appeared to be a brilliant light on the forward bridge of the ship.

270

That was when the unimaginable happened. Salazar's cockpit canopy erupted into a swirling rainbow of scintillating, blinding color. The intensity was so brilliant that he felt his eyeballs were on fire. In the midst of the torrent of colored light, his head-up display was a searing square of white light that was focussed into his eyes. Utterly blinded and completely disorientated, Salazar instinctively jerked back on the controls. He felt his Ciclone rear up and roll, then it hit the sea at over 600 miles per hour.

Bridge Wing, HMS Hotspur, *San Carlos Water, Falkland Islands.*

"Way-ho!" Johnson screamed in triumph at the spectacular sight. The Ciclone had appeared unaffected by the laser right up to the second when it had suddenly reared up. Its nose had been flung upwards until it had gone past the 90 degree climb position and actually pointed backwards, leaving the fast-moving bomber apparently flying tail-first. One of its wings had dropped as the aircraft started to stall. Then it had plowed tail-first into the sea, fragmenting as it went.

"Beginners luck," Tunney grunted. "We'll never do that again."

Operations Room., HMS Hotspur, *San Carlos Water, Falkland Islands.*

"*Goldfinch* is a gonner, Sir. Abandon ship order has been given. Reports from the Amphibs say that one of the logistics ships has been hit and is going down."

"Which one?" Hargreaves was trying to watch the air plot. The Argentine aircraft were coming through in a thick stream. That meant more and more were escaping the missile fire. He was also watching *Hotspur's* missile inventory. Her Seadart battery, already depleted by the fight against the coastal defense missiles at Stanley was now running critically low. She was firing Seawolfs at the passing bombers, hoping to get lucky. The small missile was intended as a point defense weapon and its ability to handle crossing targets was limited. She hadn't scored with Seawolf yet, although she'd made the Argentine bombers duck and weave.

"*Sir Lancelot.* She's burning. Thank God she got the troops she was carrying ashore." The Surface Warfare Officer was interrupted by another whooping cheer from the bridge wing. "Sounds like Fatso and Tragic are doing well. That's their second kill up there."

Hargreaves nodded. Nobody had had much faith in the Outfit DEC laser dazzle sight that had been put on *Hotspur* for trials. It sounded the sort of idea a mad scientist would come up with; a laser that would blind incoming pilots and cause them to lose control of their aircraft. But, if it had Tragic Tunney cheering, there had to be something to it.

"Sir, *Intrepid* and *Cleopatra* have been hit."

Hargreaves reacted very sharply to the news. *Cleopatra* was an old air defense destroyer that had been re-rated as a frigate. Armed with Seaslugs, she wasn't much of a contribution to the air defense effort. She was considered mostly an anti-submarine asset these days. *Intrepid* was another matter. Being one of the two amphibious warfare transport docks in the squadron made her mission-critical. "How bad?"

271

"*Cleopatra* is finished. She's turning turtle. *Intrepid* reports minor damage. Two one thousand-pounders hit high in her superstructure. Messy, but watertight integrity is being maintained despite being shaken up by near misses. She'll survive."

"What's the raid count?"

"So far, thirty aircraft. We've got eighteen of them, most of the rest have been damaged. It's a long way home for them. Make that thirty-three, another group coming through."

These aircraft had either tried to surprise the ships anchored in the bay by flying over the hills or had seen the carnage in the flak trap at the mouth of the inlet and decided that discretion was the better part of valor. The result was that they crossed the bay high and fast. They were over the fleet before their bombs could arc down and hit the ships below. The bombs overshot and crashed into the beaches and hills beyond. How much damage they did there, Hargreaves couldn't tell but no secondary explosions erupted in their wake. The three Ciclones got away clean, they'd done little or no damage but they'd taken none in return. *A good deal for the crews* Hargreaves thought *although what their commanders will say to them when they get back is another matter.*

"Two more coming through!" The Air Warfare Officer's voice was shaking slightly as the never-ending stream of Argentine aircraft made their runs.

Hargreaves looked back to the inlet entrance to see two more Ciclones running the gauntlet of missile fire. His electro-optical sight showed them to be slightly different from the earlier aircraft. Their fuselages were longer and their noses were differently-contoured. Hargreaves realized they were fighters; either trying to draw fire from the bombers and give them a chance to get in or pilots who felt they couldn't leave the bombers to make the near-suicidal runs on their own. He took a quick glance at the missile counter. *Hotspur* had only sixteen Seadarts left. "Leave those two, they're fighters."

Gossamer was already engaging them, she brought down one with a Seawolf shot but the two fighters were strafing her with their cannon. *They've got good guns,* Hargreaves thought, *Swiss-designed 25mm Oerlikons. Fast-firing and lots of punch.* The sea around *Gossamer* was boiling with the spray of fire from the fighters. One went down but the other got a long, raking burst into the ship's bridge. As if to make good on Hargreave's high opinion of the guns, *Gossamer* unexpectedly went dead. All her radar systems suddenly ceased to work. Beyond her, the Ciclone fighter was weaving through the fleet, firing bursts at any ships that crossed its path. Suddenly, without warning, it just exploded in mid-air. From its position, Hargreaves guessed a six inch shell from one of the cruisers had scored a direct hit.

"Message from *Gossamer,* Sir. By signal lamp. Strafing took out her main databus and electrical supply circuit. Nothing electrical on the ship works any more. They're trying to fix it but until they do, she'd defenseless. The only weapons she has are her 35mm firing under manual control."

Macchi Ciclone 4-S-311, Over San Carlos Water, Falklands Islands

The sky was criss-crossed by tracer fire streaming from the gray ships that sheltered in San Carlos Water. Long gray streams of smoke went straight up from the destroyers. They climbed for a hundred feet or so, then arched over to lunge at the Argentine aircraft in the center of the interlocking mesh of fire. Amidst it all were the great clouds of black, oily smoke from the ships that had been hit and the burning patches on the sea where the Ciclones had gone in. Lieutenant Manuel Devin had taken the whole scene in within a split second of rounding the point that marked the start of his bomb run. He'd also seen something else. The closest destroyer wasn't firing or, indeed doing anything else. Behind him, his weapons systems operator had come to the same conclusion. "Mickey, the nearest ship, her radars are dead."

Dead radars. That means no missiles from her and her guns firing in manual. It's too good an opportunity to miss. Devin made a slight adjustment in course and watched his continuously-computed impact point racing over the water towards the silent ship. "Give her the six belly bombs. We'll hit another ship with the wing load."

He assumed that his WSO had made the necessary arrangements and touched the controls slightly. The CCIP square moved towards the center of the target ship. Just as it touched the ship's side, Devin released his first salvo of bombs. His WSO hadn't let him down. Six five hundred kilogram bombs detached from the racks under the belly and arched down towards the destroyer. Their tail fins split open to delay their impact until the Ciclone was clear. One landed just short. Four plowed into the vertical launch system that occupied the center of the ship. One fell well beyond its target. That didn't matter; Devin saw a massive explosion devastate the destroyer. A great cloud of white smoke billowed upwards, surrounded by great white streamers that soared upwards before arcing back down to earth.

Devin had already turned his attention to the ships in front of him. Priority targets were the fat-bellied amphibious ships but his turn to take out the destroyer had put him in a bad position to make a run at them. Only one was in a good position for an attack and it was already beached and burning. Beyond it was a big warship; a cruiser with a strangely blackened aft superstructure. Devin selected her and brought his Ciclone around to line up on her. Once again, he watched the white square of his bomb sight racing across the water. Once again, he thumbed his bomb release as he flashed over the cruiser. *Tiger Class* he thought, recognizing the twin turrets fore and aft. Then he was gone and climbing away to clear the hills at the end of the inlet.

"You got her Mickey boy." His WSO sounded triumphant over the intercom. "At least two hits dead amidships. Two ships down with one pass, the brass will be pleased."

And so they should be, Devin thought *for there are few enough aircraft coming back to make their claims.*

Argentine Headquarters, Teal Inlet.

"These orders do not make any kind of sense." Colonel Ruiz Maldonado read the message flimsy again and crumpled it between his fingers. "Menendez wants us to attack the British holding Mount Kent with the cavalry regiment while sending our infantry to block the advance from San Carlos. He obviously knows nothing of the ground out here. Mount Kent is almost eight hundred meters high and it dominates all the ground for tens of kilometers around. The British knew what they were doing when they took that place, as long as it remains in their hands we can do nothing.. Yet it is rocks and outcrops without as

273

much as a dirt track to help us get to it. Our cavalry can do nothing there. To take Mount Kent is the job for our infantry. It is only a few kilometers march for them. To hit the British columns advancing from San Carlos, that is a much longer march and a battle of maneuver at the end of it. That is the place for our cavalry."

"Shouldn't we consult with General Menendez?" Captain Arturo Russo was a good aide and adept at filling in the blanks for his commander. Already, he could see a potential disaster for Maldonado looming if Menendez learned that his orders had been changed. "And are the British advancing from San Carlos? The Air Force is claiming they have sunk more than a dozen ships."

"Divide by three, Arturo, always divide by three. They claim twelve so we can assume they have sunk four. And, yes, the British will be advancing. The bombing of their ships makes it all the more necessary for them to do so. They will have lost supplies so they must finish this thing quickly. So must we. With those airborne troops holding every key point of terrain in the island, they will paralyze anything we attempt to do. We should discuss this with General Menendez, yes, I agree, but we do not have time. We must move now. I am the commander on the spot and I must conduct this battle as I see fit. Now, order the infantry regiment to advance south to Mount Kent while the cavalry regiment moves west. The infantry will assault and retake Mount Kent. The cavalry will locate and repel the advance of the British overland force."

Van Huis's Platoon, Hills West of Mouth Kent, Falkland Islands.

"Now these are orders I like." Captain Shumba Geldenhuys was almost chortling with delight. "I like Colonel Rigsby. 'Pick your own ground and fight your own battle in support of the main column.' A commander like him I can live with."

As if in agreement with him, there was a hiss as the sleek Boomslang lowered itself on its suspension so that it was completely covered by the ridgeline in front. Then, its front elevated slightly so that its Mamba anti-tank missiles would clear the ridge when fired. It and the other three vehicles in the platoon commanded by Lieutenant Bastiaan van Huis were positioned so they could rake the Argentine advance with missile fire. The other two platoons and the headquarters section of two vehicles were also concealed in folds of the ground, waiting to take advantage of the Argentine moves as the battle developed.

Van Huis opened his commander's hatch and looked carefully outside. His Boomslang had been positioned just so; far enough behind the ridge to make sure its concealment was as perfect as possible, far enough forward to allow the two missile gunners to see the battlefield with a minimum of dead ground. Behind him, he heard the whine as the two cylindrical missile launchers rotated, shifting the empty tube into the hull so that it could be loaded from the magazine beneath. The loaded tube rose from the hull into the ready-to-fire position. He swept his binoculars around him, checking out the two alternate positions he had scouted. One lay behind his present position, ready to be occupied if the Argentines advanced on the Boomslang. The other lay in front, ready to receive him if the Argentines fell back. He didn't know, yet, which one he would use but he was aware that if he had the decision to make, he would have seconds only to make it. The answer to tank destroyers lurking in ambush was artillery fire on the positions they occupied.

"The observation positions on Mount Kent say the Argentine cavalry regiment is advancing on the British column's position, broer." Geldenhuys was on the radio again. "Estimated strength is fifty one M92 tanks in a single battalion and two battalions of infantry in armored carriers. Their artillery battery is moving to support the infantry attacking the Britse Mariniers so we will not have to worry overmuch about them. This will be a fight to tell your children about, broer."

Headquarters Section, Mobile Column, West of Mount Kent

Fifty tanks. The number rolled around Colonel Rigsby's mind. *And I have fourteen in my main line plus another 14 in the ambush position. Plus the fourteen South African tank destroyers. Do they even things up a bit? And was I right to give that Griqua maniac his head?*

"I hope the Afrikaaners come through Sir." The comment from his aide echoed the thoughts running through Rigsby's mind perfectly.

"You've talked to Shumba. He actually enjoys fighting; says it's the only thing the Griqua do well. God knows, they have the experience we lack." *Keen but green.* The words rolled through Rigsby's mind in a dank echoing dirge. *We've never done anything like this before. At least, not since That Man took our honor away.*

He had his own tanks arranged in a reverse L-shaped ambush. They would engage the Argentine M92s and then fall back. As they did, they would lure the enemy tanks into a fire trap made up from the flanking squadron that was angled off to his left. The Boomslangs were off to his right, he wasn't quite sure where. That sounded strange, even to him, but Geldenhuys knew what the plan was and what his part in it had to be. How he did it was up to him. Off to his right and left were his two infantry companies, providing far-flank cover. Rigsby was gambling that the Argentine officer would make the standard mistake of all novices at warfare and load all his strength into a single punch. *Argentina hadn't fought on the Russian Front and they wouldn't have had the fundamental flaws in the 'expanding torrent' nonsense hammered home to them. God knows, the frozen hell of the Kola Front had to be worth something, didn't it?*

"First Troop reporting Argentine tanks in company strength with infantry support moving on them."

Here we go. Rigsby turned to his map and marked the position carefully. First Troop was out on the extreme right, its four Cavaliers dug in to cover the ground beyond with their long 20 pounders. To Rigsby's eyes, despite claims that it was descended from pre-Second World War cruiser tanks, the Cavalier still bore marks of German heritage. It looked like a Panther and the 70-caliber 20-pounder reinforced the impression. The question was whether the gun would match up to the fast-firing semi-automatic 76mm guns on the American-made M92s. If it didn't, then it would be up to the Boomslangs and their missiles.

First Troop, 14/20th King's Hussars, West of Kent Mountain.

The five M92s were pushing forward towards his platoon positions with the rest of their company in overwatch. Captain Roland Stanford mentally wished himself the best

275

of luck, recognizing that with four tanks against seventeen he was going to need it. "Open fire!"

The 20-pounders cracked. Their high velocity made the sound a high-pitched slap at the ears rather than the deeper rumble of artillery. The 84mm gun was small by the standards of the 120mm-armed Russian and American main battle tanks, but it was still adequate to deal with the light armor the Argentine Army deployed. His gunners had time to aim carefully and pick their shots. The results showed immediately. Three of the Argentine M92s stopped. Two belched black smoke as the crews bailed out; the third was left still and silent. The other two Argentine tanks had the muzzle flash from the 20-pounders to aim at. Their guns cracked rapidly. The barrage was joined by the tanks on overwatch. Stanford winced; a boiling cloud of black smoke told him that at least some of the rapid flurry of 76mm shots had struck home.

That was when something else also struck home. Stanford had the impression of something streaking across his vision, then a ripple of explosions along the Argentine overwatch positions. For a moment he thought he was getting unexpected air support. Then his mind clicked into gear and he realized what was happening. The Argentine overwatch position had been flanked by expertly-placed tank destroyers that were going about their business with grim efficiency. The first salvo of eight missiles had taken out five of the M92s and caused the rest to start firing smoke in an effort to avoid the destruction that was engulfing them. Perhaps the smoke had saved some. The second salvo of missiles took out only four of the survivors.

Up on the ridgeline used by the Argentine armor, the overwatch position was in utter chaos. Nine of the twelve tanks had been knocked out in a few seconds. Two of them were the company headquarters vehicles. Stanford watched with something close to glee as the two surviving tanks that had been probing his position backed up under cover of their smoke clouds and tried to rejoin their parent unit. They were finding that difficult. The shattered remnants of that unit were also retreating fast.

Van Huis's Platoon, Hills West of Mouth Kent, Falkland Islands.

"Get out of there broer. Go to the forward position." Geldenhuys's voice over the radio was urgent.

"Ahead of you." Van Huis was as good as his word. His Boomslangs were already accelerating backwards, sliding through the rocks as they abandoned their firing positions. The roar of the diesel engines and the whine of the missile launchers reloading was suddenly joined by the howl of inbound artillery fire. The positions they had just evacuated were swallowed up in a mass of white smoke, interlaced with the black clouds of shell bursts. Van Huis heard the rattling as fragments of rock and steel bounced off the Boomslang's armor. "Artillery inbound."

"Mortars, broer. If it was artillery you would have known it. Those are mortars from the infantry. That the crews are laying smoke to protect the tanks instead of supporting their infantrymen tells us much."

The four Boomslangs moved off to the right, heading for their pre-scouted advanced position. From there, they would be able to fire into the rear of the Argentine attack force as it surged forward. Van Huis recognized the pattern that was developing as a classic encounter battle. British and Argentine forces, both moving forward, had collided. The honors would go to the force that could use the ground best. With their long-range anti-tank missiles, the company of tank destroyers were a vital part of the British battle plan. As befitted one of the heirs of South Africa's largest arms producing conglomerate, van Huis felt quietly confident that his initial volley of missiles alone would guarantee a large follow-on order for his company. Of him actually living to see that order, he was far less confident.

Headquarters Section, Mobile Column, West of Mount Kent

"My God, our Griqua friend came through for us." Rigsby was fascinated and a little appalled by the chaos caused by the missile volley. The Argentine tankers had been a bit too confident, a bit too convinced that infantry would not stand against their tanks. *Probably too many years of breaking up demonstrations and deposing governments. Internal security duties could be death on an Army's ability to fight real wars.*

"The Germans taught the world what a well-placed, well-commanded unit of tank destroyers could do to an armored force when the chips were down." Major Albert Fitzgerald threw in the historical comment to cover his own shock at the devastation the South Africans had wrought on the lead company of the Argentine cavalry regiment. *The devastation we have wrought,* he corrected himself; *two thirds of the men in those Boomslangs are British.* Then he stopped and corrected himself again. *And not a few of the British are descendents of the Germans we took in after The Big One. Churchill was right when he called for magnanimity in victory. Now, that gesture is paying off.*

"Stanford is falling back right now. If the Argies follow him in, we'll have them in a pocket; under fire from both sides and the front.

Cross's Platoon, Hills West of Mouth Kent, Falkland Islands.

"Make yourself calm." Sergeant Anders Lehmkuhl spoke quietly to the young British officer. His grandfather had spoken of the bravery of young British officers who had fearlessly exposed themselves to fire in order to lead their men. And how those brave young officers had died from the fire of 7mm Mausers in the hands of expert shots. They had the time to do this thing right. Van Huis's Platoon had drawn fire from the battalion mortars and it would take time for the battery to retarget. Behind them, the two missile gunners were using their electro-optical sights to try and pick out the command vehicles.

"Take them when you are ready, jongmens." Geldenhuys's voice over the radio was calmly reassuring. Cross's Platoon had been almost back-to-back with van Huis's. Together their missile salvoes would drive a wedge through the Argentine formation, splitting one of the Argentine infantry battalions away from the tanks in the center of their line.

"All vehicles, prepare to fire on three. One . . . . two . . . . . three." Despite being safely under cover, Cross ducked as the front of the Boomslang was covered in flame when the two missiles streaked out from their launchers. They dipped, then picked up speed as they crossed the two thousand yards of open ground towards their targets. Their targets were small four-wheeled armored personnel carriers. They were barely more than armored trucks armed only with a 7.65mm machine gun in a one-man turret. They had no real place on a battlefield dominated by tanks and missiles. The Mamba missiles tore them apart,

277

sending them tumbling and burning into the rocks. Through his surveillance sight, Cross saw wheels detaching from the burning hulks and rolling down slopes until they tumbled and fell sideways into the rocks.

The second flash of flame made him duck again, causing him to forget that he was securely inside the Boomslang's command cupola. "Back, let's get out of here before the Argies do something we might regret."

The Boomslangs backed away, spinning on their suspensions and heading forward. In front of them, the British infantry in their Bulldog armored personnel carriers were also moving forward into the gap carved by the Boomslang's missile fire. The whole Argentine left wing was crumbling under the impact of the assault. The troops there were milling around helplessly. The destruction of their command facilities made any attempt to organize a defense against the British assault hopeless. In the encounter battle that was taking place, the British force was quickly moving to dominate the battlefield.

First Troop, 14/20th King's Hussars, West of Kent Mountain.

The fast-firing 76mms were killing him. The Cavaliers would get off single shots and receive half a dozen in reply. That disparity had already cost him three of his four tanks. Stanford guessed that his own wagon would be next. After the probe by the first company of Argentine tanks had been pushed back, the other two companies had funneled into the gap and they'd made short work of his troop. There had been no repeat of the missile salvo that had crucified the first group of enemy tanks. Stanford guessed that the Boomslangs were repositioning. That was what tank destroyers did. They would fire from ambush and then slip away to repeat the dose at another time and place.

His own tank was also repositioning, driven out of its previous hull-down location by the advance of the Argentine M92s. He was running out of options. The ground behind him was open and if he fell back from here, he would be caught exposed and the M92s would make short work of him. And of the rest of A Squadron, what was left of it. They'd started with 14 tanks. Now they had five. Stanford took another quick look through his commander's sight and slumped slightly with relief. B Squadron had entered the battle at last and its flanking fire was pouring into the Argentine tanks. Then he saw the thing he valued most of all, the salvo of more than a dozen missiles tearing across the ground and decimating the Argentine formation. Best of all, the missiles were coming from behind the Argentine formation, closing their tanks in a ring of fire.

Geldenhuys's Company, Hills West of Mouth Kent, Falkland Islands.

"We have them Sir." Geldenhuys's communication was terse and to the point. His company formed a triangle, van Huis's Platoon at the point, Cross's Platoon as its right base and Randlehoff's Platoon reinforced with Geldenhuy's own two-vehicle headquarters section as its left base. That triangle was a wedge that had split the Argentine unit into two and its missile fire dominated the ground for four thousand yards in every direction. One of the Argentine infantry battalions had been severely mauled and was dispersed off to the British right. The other infantry battalion was virtually untouched and it was acting as a pivot covering the retreat of the surviving Argentine tanks. Geldenhuys had the picture of the battle set in his mind. He could see that an Argentine disaster was unfolding before him. The remains of the cavalry unit had only one place to go and that was back to Teal Inlet. Geldenhuys knew that would suit Colonel Rigsby perfectly. There, they would be out of

278

the way and could be finished off later. The way to relieve the air-mech unit holding Mount Kent was open.

Geldenhuys's train of thought was interrupted by a crackle on the radio. "Cross here. The Argentine infantry is retreating to the south. Permission to pursue?"

"Negative broer. That is no work for your tank destroyer. Leave the Britse moddervoete to that. You stay where you are and give them covering fire with your missiles if they need it. Acknowledge."

The deflated and disappointed note in Cross's voice was almost comical. Another young British officer with dreams of glory that, today, would go unfulfilled. "Acknowledged. We will remain in place and give covering fire."

The radio crackled again, this time the column's headquarters command net. "Well done, Geldenhuys. For your information, the enemy is in full retreat to Teal Inlet. Mount Kent is under heavy attack and we are ordered to proceed there with dispatch. The good news is that the Air-Mech unit at Goose Green been relieved by C Squadron and the Iniskillings. One Para is repositioning to Mount Pleasant while we speak while the gunners are moving into place with Two Para along Wireless Ridge and Tumbledown."

"Thank you, Sir." Geldenhuys hesitated before asking the next question. "What do you want us to do now?"

"Follow at a distance and provide cover with your missiles. My God, you people earned your pay this day."

Cabinet Office, 10 Downing Street, London

"The dispatches are in, Prime Minister." Admiral Charles Gillespie spoke somberly in the darkening Cabinet Office. It was late evening and the gloom was almost tangible. "From Admiral Chupe at the beachhead and Brigadier Strachan at the airheads."

Prime Minister Newton poured himself another glass of whisky and steadied himself. "What's the damage?"

"From the beachhead? The destroyers *Goldfinch* and *Gossamer* plus the frigate *Cleopatra* have been sunk along with the landing ships *Sir Galahad* and *Sir Lancelot*. The cruiser *Lion* and the assault ship *Intrepid* have been damaged. Over four hundred men known to have been killed. We also lost six aircraft shot down. Argentine casualties are at least fifty aircraft. Admiral Chupe says that the landing force was ashore by the time the air strikes started but a considerable quantity of fuel and ammunition was lost on the two landing ships. He adds that the remaining air defense destroyers are running low on ammunition. If the Argentine Air Force comes back tomorrow, his ships will have a hard time of it."

"Is he withdrawing?"

"Absolutely not. He says the Navy will be there to support the Army for as long as is necessary. He adds that debts must be repaid, Prime Minister."

Meaning that the British Army died in 1942, covering the Great Escape and now it is the Navy's turn to cover the Army. Newton looked at his glass and found it disturbingly empty. He refilled it and inspected the contents carefully. "What about ashore?"

"There, the news is good. Goose Green has been relieved and the Air-Mech Brigade has repositioned to occupy Mount Pleasant. That area fell without a significant fight. The northern column advancing from San Carlos met an Argentine cavalry unit and defeated them, pushing them back to Teal Inlet. The column is now moving on Mount Kent to relieve the Air-Mech force holding that area. Brigadier Strachan reports that the Argentines are assaulting his positions there but they have made no ground and the position is strong. He is confident of the outcome. The guns have arrived overlooking Port Stanley and are ready to commence the bombardment of the Argentine defenses."

General Pitcairn Howard looked at the map that dominated the Cabinet Room. "That all depends on what happens at San Carlos tomorrow. If we lose more amphibious ships and supplies, we won't be able to exploit our gains today. We'll be stuck with troops scattered all over the island and no way to support them."

"We still have the second amphibious group at sea to the east of the Islands. They can cover the landing force." Gillespie wasn't that convinced; the two assault carriers were fully committed supporting the air-mech forces.

"Perhaps. Whatever happens next, we have to hang on. We can't roll over when the going gets hard, not again."

There was a communal nodding of heads. This time, nobody would be proposing an armistice that stopped short of victory.

"Gentleman, there is one other piece of business we have to consider today. I fear the East Fife Question has reared its ugly head again." Sir Humphrey Appleday had a file nearly three inches thick in his hands. Seeing it Gillespie and Howard both groaned.

"What is the East Fife Question?" Newton was curious. He'd heard of this dilemma but he'd never been present at previous meetings when it had been raised.

Sir Humphrey cleared his throat. "Well, Prime Minister, the temporal environment of the sequence of events that have become collectively known as the East Fife Question appear to date back to the latter days of July 1940. According to the generally-accepted collegium of events, a small convoy of lorries and a Humber staff car on the strength of the Sherwood Foresters Regiment of Infantry but apparently requisitioned by members of the Auxiliary Police without the assignment of the necessary documentation or authority . . . . ."

"Stolen by the Blackshirts." Newton hissed the name of his old enemy.

"That may be so depending on the viewpoint of the interlocutor, Prime Minister, but to continue. The officer purportedly in charge of that alleged Auxiliary Police unit requisitioned complete loads of fuel for all of his vehicles, paying for the fuel with a requisition draft for the due and correct amount, inclusive of purchase and motor fuel tax. The petrol station owner accepted what he assumed was a legitimate draft in good faith and presented it to the local police administrative establishment for the proper remuneration. The officer responsible for the conduct of financial affairs in the local Scottish Police force pointed out this draft was from an Auxiliary Police unit and an English one at that. That being the case, the draft was outside the remit of his responsibility and so he referred it and the bearer to a higher authority. The matter was referred up the chain of responsibility without any resolution.

"The petrol station owner would not let the matter drop and an investigation into his claims was started. This showed that the alleged Auxiliary Police Unit not only had no authority to requisition the petrol, the unit itself had no organizational existence. Indeed, all its paperwork proved to be forgeries of such a primitive nature that it strained credulity acceptance of their veracity was so easily forthcoming. For the last four decades, the file has been circulating around the Ministries with each assiduously denying that it has any responsibility for the purloined fuel. The petrol station owner has long since passed away of course; but his sons and heirs still pursue the sanctity of their inheritance with true Gaelic determination. Put in the simplest of colloquial idioms, they want their money. With interest."

Prime Minister Newton shook his head. This, at least, would take his mind off worrying about the Argentine air attacks due tomorrow. "Very well, Humphrey. Show me the file."

Sir Humphrey smiled to himself. He was one of a select group who knew what had actually happened that evening in East Fife although he would never admit that fact. It had become a game for he and his fellow civil servants to keep the East Fife Question file circulating, to see how thick they could get it before somebody actually came up with a satisfactory solution. "Yes, Prime Minister."

Officers Mess, Argentine Air Base, Puntas Arenas, Argentina

It was one thing to hear how few aircraft had returned from the strike at San Carlos; it was quite another to see the Mess afterwards. The Squadron had a listed strength of eighteen aircraft. Each Ciclone had a crew of two, so the long mess table had 36 seats. Six were unused, representing the three crews lost during the Chile confrontation. That left thirty place settings on the table. Sixteen of those place settings were completed by a wreath of evergreen branches and a single candle. It was a stark reminder that two thirds of the aircraft sent out by the squadron had failed to return. Of the seven aircraft left on the apron, four were shot up so badly it was questionable if they would be ready for flight tomorrow. The ground crews would be working all night but the Ciclones that had returned were in too bad shape for anybody to count on them being ready for another strike.

Lieutenant Manuel Devin stepped into the Mess and walked along the table, pausing by each candle to make the sign of the cross for the crewman it represented. He had returned from the strike still keyed up from the adrenalin rush caused by the low-altitude pass over the British ships. That had deflated as he and the rest of the base personnel had stood by the runways, waiting for the surviving Ciclones to return. As minutes had ticked by into hours, the extent of the losses had become impossible to deny. He stood behind his seat as the unit chaplain said a prayer for the souls of their comrades who had not returned. Nobody had any illusions about the shot-down pilots surviving. They would either have flown into the sea at high speed and died with their aircraft or ejected into the criss-cross hail of gunfire. There were other whispers as well. It was claimed that some of the British ships carried a death-ray. One touch of its beam and it was all over for the crew who flew its victim.

The way the air crew were spread along the mess table meant that speaking would have been difficult, but nobody was in the mood to do so. The mess stewards went down the survivors of the group, serving the soup. Devin looked down the array of faces, noting how few of them seemed to be present in anything other than the physical sense. He turned slightly as a bowl of cazuela gaucho was placed in front of him. He waited until each man had been served, then took his spoon and carefully tried the chicken soup. "This is very good. The staff have done us proud tonight."

His words seemed to break the spell of the half-empty mess. The surviving aircrew started eating, slowly and carefully; as if their bowls would suddenly erupt into anti-aircraft fire and a hail of British missiles. Devin looked around. The squadron commander and all three flight commanders had gone. With a suddenness that shocked him, he realized he was the most senior surviving pilot in the squadron. As he spooned up the last of his cazuela gaucho and watched his bowl being replaced by a plate of parrillada he found himself wondering who would be the senior officer after tomorrow's strike. Or if there would be a squadron left to have a senior officer.

Hangar Deck, HMS Furious, *Off the Falkland Islands*

"Jerry, a word, if you please." Ernest Mullback turned around, to see the CAG standing behind him. The man's voice seemed to echo in the hangar deck. The surviving aircraft, six Sea Mirages and a dozen Buccaneers, were struck down for overnight maintenance. Eighteen aircraft; the survivors of the eighty brought down by the two carriers. The resthad been blown up by missiles, ripped up by rapid fire guns or vanished in the fireball of exploding fuel tanks.

"Max?" Mullback sounded stunned. Commander Frances looked at him carefully. All the pilots, the ones that were left, had the same expression on their faces. Vacant somehow.

"Jerry, your Highball birds. The hangar erks have worked out a way to wire R-550s on to your wing pylons. Frankly, with the Argie fleet neutered, your Highballs aren't much use to us right now while the air defense suppression aircraft and bomb trucks are. So, you and yours will be taking over the fighter role. You'll be doing CAP tomorrow while the remaining Mirages intercept the inbound raid. We've got to stop them Jerry; the amphibs off the beachhead are wide open. Another good Argie strike gets through and they're finished. We don't think they'll come after us out here, but if they do, your Bananas will have to do what you can."

Mullback nodded dully. "Very good, Max. The other birds going on strike?"

"At dawn. The booties are on Mount Kent. They're being attacked by Argie infantry in regimental strength. They're holding them off but they'll need air support. Right now, that position is critical." Frances paused. "Everything is critical. The amphibs at San Carlos, the booties on Mount Kent, the assault carriers backing them up and the Paras overlooking Stanley. I can't think of anything that isn't critical right now. I'm told Albie and the Incredible Bulk have got Rotodynes up flying CAP. You'll just have to do the best you can. We've got nothing left."

282

Mullback snorted gently. "I'll roust the boys out and we better talk to the Mirage pilots. Get some suggestions on how to do this fighter thing."

Mount Kent, Falkland Islands

"Over on the left. They're coming through the gap in the rocks." The light machine gun fired a burst into the rock pile over on the position's left. The Argentine troops trying to infiltrate through the gaps were caught and tumbled backwards. Strachan didn't fool himself that they had been wiped out. At best the burst had caught one or two. As if to confirm his thoughts, a grenade arched out from behind the same rocks and exploded a few feet to the right of the machine gun next. Fortunately, the thick boulders absorbed some of the blast and sent the rest skywards where it would do little harm. The explosion caught the attention of a Chevalier crew though. The two 120mm recoilless rifles threw high explosive rounds at the source of the grenade. In this battle of rifle, pistol, knife and hand grenade, the 120mm rounds were heavy artillery indeed. The orange flashes as the shells exploded lit up the rocks and Strachan saw a figure being hurled backwards. Or, he thought he did. It could have been a trick of the light, a few random shadows somehow linked into an image.

Another image caught his eye. Another figure coming through the rock pile that formed the left of his position. The target image was wrong. It had the long rifle of the Argentine infantry, not the short, stubby British L1 bullpup. He already had his trusted old Webley revolver in his hand and he felt the comforting heavy kicks as he fired two .455 shots. One of them connected and he heard a gasp as the figure fell. Strachan aimed carefully and fired again. The target stopped moving. *It never hurts to shoot a corpse*, the old adage ran through Strachan's mind as he placed a fourth shot into the man's head. There would be no doubt about that one, the slow, heavy .455 was a deadly bullet. That was why Strachan had stuck with the Webley all these years. He broke it quickly, dropped the empty casings and reloaded.

Above him he heard the slow, heavy thudding of the 15mm BESA machine gun mounted on a Boarhound armored carrier. Calling it armored was a joke. It had the same paper-thin steel as the Chevalier but it did have the heavy machine gun mounted in a protected turret. The rounds ricocheted off rocks and howled away into the darkness. He didn't know what the crew had seen but they had night vision sights in the turret and something must have attracted their attention. He hoped it was Argentine. In the confusion of a night infantry battle, it was all too easy to shoot up one's own men.

"Colonel Hartmann's compliments, Sir, and the Colonel says if you are finished playing private, could you honor him with your presence at the CP?" Sergeant Harper had a smirk on his stained and dirtied face.

"Cheeky Hun bastard." Strachan chuckled and shook his head. "This area seems stabilized. Let's go. Lieutenant, make sure you keep that rock pile under surveillance. Don't hesitate to use the armor if the Argies make a serious push. That's what we've got it here for."

The young Lieutenant nodded and made a quick survey of his position. By the time he had finished, Strachan and Harper had slid away. They looked back quickly and saw him moving some of his men to cover the position a bit better. The Argie push had come close to dislodging the Marine platoon, but it had been beaten back. "That young man promises well."

"They all do, now they have a little experience under their belts." Harper agreed. "Colonel Hartmann thinks we're settled in for the rest of the night now. The relief force is a couple of miles down the road and he believes the Argies will disengage rather than get caught between us."

Strachan nodded as he climbed up through the rocks that littered the slopes of Mount Kent. "Sounds right to me. Just as long as we don't get careless."

Argentine Headquarters, Stanley.

"The damned fool did what?" Menendez could hardly believe the disastrous news.

"He attacked the relief column with his armor, Sir." Fernandez shook his head. "The British tank destroyers tore the cavalry unit apart. Colonel Maldonado says the tank destroyers were present in at least battalion strength. They ripped up the tank battalion and drove back the mechanized infantry. He sent his leg infantry to attack Mount Kent. They lacked the firepower to break through and they were too closely mixed in with the British for effective use of artillery. He's ordered them to disengage; they were about to be hit in the flanks and rear by the British armor."

"The fool. I ordered him to block the armor with the infantry. Those missile-shooting tank destroyers would have been almost useless against them. And the cavalry with its armor would have shot the British unit on Kent to pieces. That moron has cost us the battle."

Fernandez looked at the map. The British were advancing fast across the island, taking full advantage of the fact that every key piece of terrain had been seized in advance by the airborne forces. The map showed something else. The British guns were already in place overlooking Stanley.

"Maldonado is regrouping at Teal Inlet but he's been badly mauled. We can probably hold Stanley for a while, Sir."

Menendez looked at the map as well and sighed. "Those guns will tear us apart and there will be nothing we can do about it. And do you want to be under another bombardment like last night's? There is something else to consider." His finger tapped Stanley. "These houses are full of civilians and are made of wood. The British guns will tear them apart as well. If the airbase here was still operational, it might be worth holding on, but it isn't. And won't be, not for a long time."

Menendez thought again, weighing odds and numbers. The answer was one he didn't like but couldn't avoid. "We have an obligation to protect those civilians. If there was any military objective to be gained by exposing them to British artillery fire, then we could justify doing so but there is not. Contact the British headquarters by radio and tell them I wish to discuss terms."

CHAPTER FIVE
CONSOLIDATION

Anti-aircraft Battery, Stanley Airfield, Falkland Islands

"Destroy all the codes and IFF information." Major Grigorio Mazza looked around the control cabin for his Scudo air defense system. The radar fire control screens were blank. The radars themselves had been destroyed by the Buccaneer strikes and the naval bombardment two nights earlier. The missile launchers had gone completely but three of his six twin 47mm anti-aircraft guns had survived. Before he had received his orders from General Menendez, he had ordered his men to reduce the height of the sandbag walls around them so they could fire at ground targets. Privately, Mazza was glad it hadn't come to that. With the British guns on the hills that dominated Stanley, his display of resistance would have been short before the artillery took him out.

"Is it really all over Sir?" One of the privates seemed on the verge of tears. Whether from the humiliation of surrender or relief that the prospect of sudden death had receded, Mazza wasn't quite sure.

"For us, yes. General Menendez has negotiated an honorable surrender. We cannot hold on here without support and with the airfield gone, there is no point in trying. Now, swing the barrels of the guns up to 90 degrees elevation." That was part of the surrender terms. The British Brigadier had known how much damage the fully-automatic 47mm guns could have done and had insisted they be placed in a posture that removed the risk they presented. To Mazza, the elevated gun barrels looked like arms raised in surrender.

It took only a few minutes for the British airborne forces in their armored vehicles to appear. Some diverted to the positions held by the infantry battalion. Others made a straight line for the airport and its defenses. Mazza stayed in his control van. It only needed one fanatic to take control of his guns and there would be two massacres. One would be of the British troops taking the surrender of the Argentine garrison; the other the surviving British wiping out the Argentine troops they would believe had betrayed their word. So he stayed at his guns until there was a pounding on the van door.

"Everybody out, gentlemen, if you please." The words seemed forced and strained, as if the speaker was using phrases carefully dictated by somebody else. Mazza sighed and left his command console, stepping out of the van into the bright sunshine outside. The contrast made him blink and his eyes started to water. That didn't stop him recognizing the light tank and a pair of armored carriers that were covering his unit. A squad of British troops, lead by a sergeant in a maroon beret decorated with black paratrooper wings, went inside. A couple of minutes later the Sergeant came out.

"Hey, you. Argie officer. Is this yours?" The Sergeant held out the picture of Mazza's wife and son.

"It is. Thank you Sergeant. That was kind of you."

"Tuck it away safe. The booties will be here soon and those bastards will nick anything not nailed down." The Sergeant gave a slightly twisted grin and disappeared into the control van. Mazza put the picture in his wallet and shook his head. It sounded as if the relationship between the British Army and Navy was no better than anywhere else.

Casa Rosada Presidential Palace, Buenos Aires, Argentina

"Traitors! Kill them all! Send the Air Force to bomb them." President Galtieri screamed the orders out in a voice that ricocheted around the Presidential Office and echoed outside. At his desk in the anteroom, an aide heard the sound, thought for a second and then picked up a telephone. He had come to a decision and there were calls he had to make.

"The Ciclone Squadrons aren't available, Your Excellency. They took too many losses yesterday and too many aircraft are damaged. It will be tomorrow before they can strike again."

"Then use the other aircraft." Galitieri was still bright red with rage and shaking with anger. "We have other bombers."

"They do not have the fuel to get there and back. And they have no escort. The British carrier fighters will cut them down."

"So the Ciclones must fly regardless. Send the orders."

Officers Mess, Argentine Air Base, Puntas Arenas, Argentina

"Lieutenant Devin, we have orders. The Army on the Malvinas has surrendered to the British. We are to send every available aircraft to bomb them."

Devin shook the sleep out of his eyes. "Bomb the British? Their ships or the troops ashore?"

"Neither. Our orders are to bomb our own men." The disbelief in the adjutant's voice was unmistakeable.

Cold water splashed on his face did not make the orders more acceptable. Devin stared at the image in his mirror and thought with astonishing speed. "How many aircraft are left?"

286

"Seven."

"And four of those were down for their periodic maintenance. That was why they did not fly yesterday, right? When will they actually be available?"

The adjutant got the message loud and clear. "At least tomorrow, possibly the day after. If we get the needed parts."

"I thought so. And the aircraft damaged yesterday?"

A sad shake of the head and a sound of teeth being sucked. "In a bad way. Spares you know, we are short of spares. Perhaps tomorrow?"

"So we have no available aircraft. Ah well. Acknowledge the orders and say we will comply with them to the best of our ability. Add that we know our duty."

La Avenida 9 de Julio, Buenos Aires, Argentina

Word that the Army in the Falklands had surrendered to the British had spread quickly. It had followed right on the heels of the news that the Argentine Navy had been defeated in a great carrier battle and that thousands of seamen had died in the sinking ships. Together, the two reports had been the last straw. The population of Buenos Aires had poured on to the streets and were marching down the avenues. As they marched, more news had come in and word had spread still faster. President Galtieri had ordered the air force to bomb the surrendering troops and the Air Force squadrons had refused to obey. Rage had joined with grief in the ranks of the crowd.

At the heads of the processions were women, wearing black. They were the wives, mothers, sisters, daughters of sailors who had been in the battle. They did not know if their men had survived or not, but each wore black. If it was not for their own families then in solidarity with those who had lost members of theirs. Their grief was contagious, as was their dignity. This was not a riot for the crowds marched in silence and were all the more terrifying for that fact.

In this part of the city, the crowds were converging on the obelisk that marked the center of the Plaza de la República. Blocking access from the Avenida 9 de Julio to the Plaza was a line of riot police, in close order with their shields interlocked. The soundless image of the procession approaching the police was eerie as the two groups closed. Then, the riot police about-faced and joined the procession. Their shields surrounded and protected the black-clad women at its head.

All over the city, the sight was repeated as the security forces joined the processions and converged on the Casa Rosada.

Outside the Swimmer-Commando Barracks, Puerto Belgrano Naval Base, Argentina

"Lay down your arms and surrender." Some orders were a pleasure to give. Major Facundo Caceres found that one to be in that category.

"Who do you think you are?" The reply from the barracks guardpost was laden with arrogance. What came next was also something that Major Caceras found a pleasure

287

and one that was long overdue. The .50 caliber machine guns on his amtracks raked the guardpost with gunfire, sending it crumbling into the dirt. They surged forward, their bows rising slightly as they crushed the wreckage beneath their tracks.

In front of the armored vehicles, the barrack parade ground was dirty, unswept. The swimmer-commandos prided themselves on being the new elite who did not have to worry about such niceties as policing their barracks. Faced with armored vehicles in the hands of men trained to use them and who had fought others of their kind in open combat, the swimmer-commandos panicked. A few fired shots at the vehicles. Such resistance was quelled by return fire from the LVTP-7s and M92 light tanks. Within a few minutes of the opening burst of gunfire, the Marines were herding the swimmer-commando personnel into their parade ground. There, the prisoners sat, hands on their heads.

Leading his men through the captured barracks, Caceras was quietly shocked by what he found. Not by austerity or any signs of the funding shortages that plagued the rest of the armed forces but by the luxury that surrounded him. He guessed that the swimmer-commandos had been looting the homes of those they had 'disappeared.' That was when he got the message that his presence was required in the basement.

The sound of women crying had reached him before he got there and made him guess what he would find. The basement area had been subdivided into small cells. Viewed objectively, they weren't actually bad conditions as prisons went. Caceres guessed that the intent had been to keep the inmates healthy. It also hadn't surprised him to find out that the prisoners were women. What had shocked him was the number that were in varying stages of pregnancy. His men were unlocking the cells and letting the women out but the prisoners were too terrified to take advantage of the situation.

"Please, my men will take you to a hospital for treatment." Caceras was shocked when his words, intending to be comforting, caused a renewed outburst of misery. He looked around, confused, then picked one woman who seemed to less distressed than the rest. "What is the problem? We are here to help you."

"When our time comes and we are taken to hospital, we never come back." The woman spoke in very poor Spanish that made her words difficult to understand.

For a moment, Caceras assumed that he hadn't heard what she had said correctly. Then the implications of the words sank in. He tried to control his anger. To buy time while he did so, he spoke to the woman. "You are not Argentine?"

"Italian."

"We will call the Italian Embassy and they will take care of you. Are there any other foreign women here?" A couple reluctantly raised their hands. "We will call your embassies as well and they will come here and look after you. Sergeant, get through to the Italian and other embassies, as soon as possible. That means now. And call the Swiss Embassy; get them down here to take care of these woman. They don't trust us and I don't blame them. The rest of you, if you have families or friends who can look after you, we will help you call them."

Caceras had his temper under control by then and turned back to the Italian woman. "You are with child? How far along?"

"I think six months."

"And you have been held here for how long?"

"Eight months."

That confirmed what Caceras had known in his heart. "Very well. At some point please write out all that has happened to you as a statement. Your embassy legal department will make sure it is properly notarized as an affidavit. The people responsible for this atrocity will pay for it. That I promise you."

Conference Room, White House, Washington D.C.

"Over the last few hours, the situation has broken wide open. Mister President, the Argentine armed forces on the Falklands surrendered overnight. Stanley went down first, Teal Inlet followed a couple of hours later. When news got back to Argentina, it brought down the government there. Not so much a coup; that would imply organization. There were mass demonstrations all over Buenos Aires and the security forces joined them. Parts of the armed forces that tried to stay loyal were attacked and disarmed by the rest. Ex-President Galtieri tried to make a run for it, but his private jet taxied out on to the runway, then stopped and waited there until somebody came to collect him."

Director of Central Intelligence Richard McColl paused and shuffled his papers. He had a string of reports from the various civilian and military intelligence agencies. It had long been established that the needs of gaining good intelligence were best served by numerous competing agencies whose varying viewpoints and priorities made for a more rounded and comprehensive picture. This time though, the intelligence data was remarkably consistent.

"So, who is in charge there?" President Reagan sounded confused.

"The truth is that we have no real idea at the moment. Nor, I think does anybody else including the Argentines. The Argentine armed forces appear to be the only organized group capable of maintaining order so no change there. Seer, I don't envy you trying to make head or tail of this situation at the next Friday Follies."

The Seer shook his head. "Something will shake down out of this, Rick. I've got three days to think of some profound-sounding things to say. Fortunately, it's not something that greatly affects us. We have few strategic interests down there and our attitude towards governments is that we deal with the ones we approve of and don't have anything to do with those we find abhorrent. Regime change is not our job unless somebody actually threatens us or our friends."

"I think you two are missing the point." President Reagan sounded both thoughtful and reproving. "The people who are removing the Galtieri regime are the very ones we would have slaughtered if we had bombed Argentina. There is a contradiction here."

"It's one that's been at the heart of our national policy ever since The Big One, Sir." The Seer was also thoughtful, although it was an issue he had considered before. "We don't do war any more. We simply destroy those who threaten us. That was a strategy that evolved during the era of total warfare when the civilian population was an essential part of a country's ability to make war. Even then though, we never actually targeted the civilian population. We took out industry, transportation, fuel supplies and so on. The problem always was that by the time we did that, there wasn't much left. When we took out The Caliphate's biological warfare facilities fifteen years ago, by the time we had finished, there wasn't much left in the target areas." The Seer became aware that Reagan was staring at him curiously. "Family history, Sir."

"Of course. Carry on please."

"We've never really wanted to consider the possibility that something short of a full-scale war may exist. To do so would mean we would have to consider a drawn-out conventional war and that is something the American people will not tolerate. The specter of the Russian Front and more than a million American boys dead in the snow still haunts us. So, even our 'limited response' options are basically full-scale assaults on limited objectives. We still don't target the population, of course, but . . . ."

"That makes little difference." Reagan finished the phrase off for him. "We're still holding the bulk of the population hostage against the acts of their government. Forgive me if I find that unsettling."

"But, if the population of a country are not responsible for the acts of their government, then who is?" McColl asked the question, knowing that its implications could keep philosophers arguing for decades. "Somebody has to be held accountable for what governments do."

"Our strategic position comes out of the Second World War." The Seer picked up the thought. "If the German population had done in 1933 what the Argentine people have done today, we probably wouldn't be having this discussion. Or if the British people had done the same to Halifax in 1940, come to that."

"Yet Halifax did get into power." Reagan sighed. "How long has it taken Britain to recover? And what impact does that have on us?"

"Over forty years." The Seer knew it was a rhetorical question but he couldn't help putting the number on it. "What this means for us is that Europe has become important again. We've essentially ignored them for most of that time; primarily because they were too weak and damaged after World War Two to be of any account. That's changed now. They're back. Algeria showed that for the French and now this South Atlantic War does the same for the British. We're going to have to pay attention to what they say now. A little attention, anyway."

"Not a bad thing all considered. Look into these questions, come up with answers that I can live with. We need a fundamental rethink and now is a good time for one."

Naval Attache's Office, Australian Embassy, Santiago, Chile.

"A visitor for us, Garry." Captain Lachlan Shearston was grinning broadly. "An officer from the Argentine Embassy."

"Argentine?" Graeme Gavin was genuinely shocked. There had been an Argentine Embassy in Chile throughout the recent unpleasantness, but for obvious reasons they had kept a very low profile. "What does he want?"

"We're about to find out I think." An Argentine naval officer in civilian clothes was being ushered in. Gavin took a quick look around the office to make sure everything confidential, classified or embarrassing was hidden. It was, the office was in fit state to receive visitors.

"Gentlemen, I am Captain Roberto Brown of the Argentine Naval Attache's Office. Officially, I am here to thank you on behalf of our Navy for the work carried out by your submarine in rescuing our ditched pilots. We are not unaware of the risks your submarine accepted by carrying out this mission of mercy in an active war zone."

"Thank you, Captain. We will pass your words through to the submarine's commander and crew." The fact that nobody had mentioned the submarine's name was not an accident.

"There is another matter, one that is deeply embarrassing to me personally. You may have heard that there are major political disruptions in our country. These, I must tell you, are of such significance that it is questionable who presently constitutes the established government. Various elements of the armed forces are fighting. Some support the existing government but most aid those who would see it removed from power. As part of the conflict, a force of Argentine Marines occupied the Swimmer-Commando base in Puerto Belgrano and freed a large number of political prisoners held there. What they found was infamous."

Brown handed over a thick file, filled with documents and pictures. "The women rescued by the Marines have been placed in the hands of the Swiss Embassy until they can be properly protected. Australia's care for the pilots who would otherwise surely have died sets an example for us all and leads us to ask another such act from you. Please, circulate these files amongst your allies, help identify the women who died without a name and find their families. Allow them to find some peace at least."

"And you want us to do this for purely humanitarian reasons?" Shearston sounded deeply suspicious.

"No. Not just for that. More importantly, the political situation in my country is finely balanced. If this information becomes public knowledge, if it becomes known how the present government used the state of emergency to profit from this barbarous trade, then it will become impossible for them to remain in power. They know this and are doing everything in their power to ensure the details are suppressed. In the name of common decency, I beg you to make sure they do not succeed."

HMS Argus, *Helicopter Support Ship, Off The Falkland Islands*

Once again, HMS *Argus* knew the sound of a Rotodyne powering down as it unloaded another group of Argentine prisoners. With the airfield at Stanley destroyed by naval gunfire, the survivors of the Argentine garrison were being airlifted by Rotodyne to *Argus* where they were processed and then transferred onwards to the internment facilities in Uruguay. Listening to the noise, Lieutenant Harold Dunwoody wondered how the world could possibly have survived without the ubiquitous Fairey Rotodyne. As the noise level dropped, he returned his attention to the officer sitting in front of him.

"So, you are Grigorio Mazza, and your rank is Major. Serial number 4665352. Your next of kin is your wife, Antonella Mazza, and your address is as given here? Is this correct?"

Mazza sipped his tea, savoring the strong shot of rum it contained. "That is all correct, yes."

"We will be advising the Red Cross of your detention so that Madam Mazza may be informed of your safety."

Dunwoody picked up Major Mazza's wallet to return it to him. As he did so, the picture of Mazza's family fell out on to the desk. A female officer picked up the picture to return it to him. "Your wife and son? He looks just like you." It was a woman's instinctive defense of a wife who might just possibly have something to hide.

Mazza laughed for the first time in weeks. "Thank you for saying so, but my son is adopted."

Dunwoody looked sharply at the Argentine Major, noting that the woman from the Directorate of Naval Intelligence was doing the same. He took a picture out from a file. "Do you recognize this man?"

Mazza was on his guard but the strong dose of rum in his tea had lowered his inhibitions. He honestly couldn't see why this particular piece of information should be guarded. "Yes, that is Captain Alberto Astrid. Why do you ask?"

"Did he have any connection with your adoption process? Did he tell you where the baby came from?"

"He organized the adoption for us. The mother had an affair with a sailor but he was already married and she was too young to care for a baby so the Navy arranged for an adoption. We had to pay for the mother's medical care of course and give her a year's salary for her support while she looked for work after the delivery but that was a small price to pay for completing our family." Mazza looked around and felt his stomach congeal into a solid, ice-cold lump. "Why, what has happened?"

Dunwoody looked at the DNI officer who gave a tiny nod. "Major, I am deeply sorry to tell you this. There is currently a state of major political disruption in Argentina. There is widespread fighting between parts of the armed forces who support the existing government and those who wish to see it removed from power. As part of that conflict, the Swimmer-Commando base in Puerto Belgrano was overrun by Argentine Marines. They discovered a number of young women held as political prisoners on the base, many of whom were in various stages of pregnancy.

"It appears that you and Madam Mazza have been cruelly mislead and cheated. We are reasonably sure that the mother of the child you adopted was a female political prisoner who was raped and impregnated. She was then killed immediately after delivering the child. This appears to have been part of a 'business' run by Captain Astrid. That man has many other crimes to answer for, but this is probably the most shameful. Your Marines have freed surviving prisoners held there and released them to the custody of either their embassies or to the Swiss Embassy for protection. The Marines have also arrested the staff at the Puerto Belgrano naval hospital who were complicit in this business. The authorities are trying to piece together what happened now but you and your lady should prepare yourselves accordingly. We'll try and get you home as soon as we can so you can be with her before the storm breaks."

"I do not believe you." Mazza's voice was a wail of angry and desperate protest.

The intelligence officer produced another file, one that had arrived a few minutes before from the Australian Embassy in Santiago. "Major Mazza, read this file. You will note that it comes from Australia, a neutral country whose only stake in this conflict has been the purely humanitarian act of rescuing shot-down pilots from both our nations. They have no reason to take part in a fraud; they have nothing to gain and, indeed, they would only suffer from so doing.

Mazza started to read the file his face whitening with shock as he did so. About half way through the file, he turned one page then broke down, weeping into his hands. "This cannot be true. Anna called him a saint for what he did for us. How could he do this?"

Dunwoody sighed as the Major was led out. He looked at the DNI officer who was dabbing her eyes. "Well, that made me feel like a real swine. Did you notice though? He, his wife and the child all had blond hair and blue eyes. Not that common in Argentina. Remember that circular about any possible link to a Swedish girl who vanished about a year or eighteen months ago? Isn't she on that list?"

The DNI officer folded her handkerchief away and nodded. "When he saw her picture, that's when he broke down. We had better tell Northumberland Avenue."

The Caledonian Club, Belgravia, London, UK

"Well, you said it would be over very quickly once the counter-invasion started. Even my father wasn't expecting 36 hours, though. He's impressed and that doesn't happen very often." Igrat looked across the table at Sir Robert Byrnes and smiled gently. This would be the last time she would be eating at the Caledonian Club and she was going to miss the exquisite meals she had experienced here.

"Aye, the Army came through aw'right. It has cost us though. Nine ships sunk, six badly damaged and over three thousand men dead. More than sixty aircraft shot down. I tell ye this, Iggie, we cannae do this again now, not for years. Just to rebuild our carrier air groups now will take that much time. And Old Glory is one hell of a mess. I dinnae know if she is worth repairing."

"Well, you might get some help." Igrat was suddenly speaking in the flat tones of The Seer and Byrnes knew that this was word he was supposed to be getting, albeit on an unofficial basis. "If your government feels like asking for it."

"Aye, they might well want to do that. But we'll pay our way. We're standing on our own feet now and standing proud at that. I have words for ye too, for your father. The

293

Swedish girl he was interested in? Karyn Sunderstrom? I think we may ha' a lead on her. The news though will nay be pleasant to hear." Byrnes relayed the news that had come in from Santiago and from the prisoner reception station on HMS *Argus*. After he had finished, he hesitated before continuing. "Igrat, I do na wish to be rude but ye have seen more of this world than I, by a long shot. How could even that apology for a man have done a thing such a' this?"

Igrat sighed. Later, alone and privately she would weep for Karyn Sunderstrom but now was not the time and she masked her feelings. "Robbie, the sophisticated people try to deny it, but there is plain evil in this world. Sometimes it is there in little doses we can overlook but just once in a while we meet the real thing in packages so large nothing can avoid it. Astrid is such a man. I have met such people before and I have suffered for it. What will you do with him?"

"He will stand trial for the murder of Postmaster Walsingham. If found guilty, he will go to prison for the rest of his life. If not, he will na' escape justice. He will be handed over to the Italian Government who have questions to ask about their citizens who disappeared. After they ha' finished, he will go to Spain and then to every other country that has an interest. If he is imprisoned here, then representatives from those countries will come to us. There is an accounting to be paid for what he did, Igrat. He will pay it in full, I promise you tha'."

They broke off the conversation as the carving trolley arrived and the waiter sliced off Igrat's favorite cut of the roasted venison. Byrnes noted that she knew the staff by name now, something that even long-standing members of the Club sometimes did not. By the time their meal was served, Igrat had recovered her composure and looked at her venison with regret. "I really will miss this, you know."

"You don't have tae do so. The invitation is always open to ye." Byrnes looked hopeful but in his heart he knew what Igrat did, that this particular part of their lives was over. For a long time anyway.

"I know and I shall treasure the fact. Just as I treasured my Silver Greyhound but I had to give that back as well when it's time had come. Now, I'm giving you back to Heather. Tomorrow morning anyway. The war's over Robbie, and life must go on as it once did. Heather and I have had a little talk and she understands a few things now. Better than she did anyway."

"She still hates you though." Byrnes didn't like to mention that in case Igrat was offended but he was relieved to see her smiling.

"Most women do. It's men who like me. But, she'll come around." *Well, after she forgives me for stealing a traffic light control board from a Royal Rolls.* Igrat thought. *Sorry Robbie, but in the end that angered her more than borrowing you did, especially since she can't prove I did it.* "I'm leaving tomorrow evening, after the memorial service for the Prince of Wales. I'll be on the Sonic Clipper back to Washington. Make your peace with Heather, Robbie. This time at least. Who's next in line for the throne now by the way? Prince Andrew?"

"Aye. Although it will be many years before he gets to sit on it. The Windsors are a hardy bunch." Byrnes sliced into his Ayreshire ham and dipped the portion in its sauce. "I hope he is a patient man. Now, vashi nush."

"Slainte Mhor."

The Seer's Office, NSC Building, Washington D.C.

"Please sit down, Mrs. Sunderstrom. A few months ago I promised I would hang our ears out in the wind and if we heard any word of your daughter, we would inform you of what we knew. Today, I very much regret to inform you that we have received confirmation that Karyn is indeed dead. She died in the custody of the Argentine secret police. Her body was cremated and the ashes scattered. I am sorry, but the records unearthed during the present disturbances in Argentina are quite conclusive on this point."

Maja Sunderstrom started to sob. Behind her, Lillith quietly slipped out into the small executive kitchen and made an Irish Coffee. Nell had brought the recipe back from Shannon and the drink had become an office staple. The NSA made its own rules, after all. Mrs Sunderstrom sipped the black coffee through the thick cream and coughed at the generous dose of whiskey it contained. Eventually she calmed down. "There is nothing left of my daughter?"

"There is one thing. What you choose to make of it is up to you. We know your daughter gave birth to a son while she was in Argentina. That child has been adopted by an Argentine family. They are, according to the British, an honorable family who will do what is right."

HMS Argus, *Helicopter Support Ship, South Atlantic*

The last Argentine prisoners had been transferred to Uruguay for repatriation and their place taken by released British prisoners on their way back home. Standing on the bridge of *Argus* Commander Michael Blaise still mourned his lost *Mermaid* and those of her crew who wouldn't make it home. He still faced the ordeal of the traditional court martial for the loss of his ship although nobody believed he would receive anything other than a commendation for his last fight against overwhelming odds. His thoughts were interrupted by the bridge intercom.

"Ops room here. The plot is clear now. That Macedonian trawler turned up again, the *Nikogaš Nevidel*. She hung around Stanley for a few hours before dawn and then left." The speaker's voice paused. "At least she is supposed to be on the Macedonian registry, Sir, but I can't find her on it and Lloyds of Bombay don't make mistakes like that."

"Funny that. You're right, Lloyds don't make mistakes. Not forgetting whole ships anyway." Captain Anthony Ralph frowned. He didn't like mysteries.

Blaise sounded thoughtful. "Last cruise we made before West Indies Station was Mediterranean Station, based in Cyprus. We had a lot to do with the Macedonians back then. Even picked up a bit of the language. You know what nikogaš ne videl means in that language?"

295

Ralph shook his head.

"Odd story; a legend really. It means 'the never-seen.' The nikogas ne videl is a sort of folk-lore ghost. You can only see it out of the corner of your eye. If you try to look at it, the thing vanishes. And that is a very good thing because the only time you see it clearly is when you are dying."

HMS Glowworm, King Edward's Point, Grytviken, South Georgia.

The harbor at Grytviken looked even more like a decomposing scrapyard than it had done before the war. In addition to the wrecks of the Argentine ships that now obstructed the decaying wharves, damaged British ships were anchored, awaiting the temporary patching that would allow them to take the long voyage home. If some of them would be able to take that journey. Looking at *Glorious* it was hard to see her going anywhere. Her island was a crushed wreck, her flight deck plowed up by bomb hits, her hull riven by near misses. HMS *Afridi* was alongside her, helping with the repairs. *Afridi* was an old destroyer, destined for the scrap heap but had been hurriedly converted into a forward repair ship. Now, there were more modern destroyers and cruisers lined up waiting for her help.

Glowworm was one of them. She was badly damaged enough to need months of repair work, not badly enough to go to the head of the queue. She would have to wait her turn. Lieutenant Baxter was contemplating the prolonged stay when a voice startled him. "Simonstad."

"Sorry Sir?" Baxter turned to face his Captain.

"We're going to Simonstad in South Africa for repairs. There's not enough yard capacity in Britain to repair the ships that need it. So, we're going to Simonstad when we're seaworthy. Then back to West Indies Station. The Jamaicans have challenged us to a re-run of the pack gun race on our return."

Officer's Mess, HMS Furious, South Atlantic

With the daunting prospect of a blank piece of paper in front of him, Ernest Mullback didn't know what he wanted to say or how to say it. He'd sat down, meaning to put down everything that had happened during the great carrier battle and the operations that had taken place before and after that struggle, but he couldn't do it. The experience was too much to grasp, to much for him to absorb himself, let alone try to explain to somebody else. It had come as a profound shock to him to discover that his mind had become turned around during the fighting. Once he had regarded *Furious* and its shrinking air group as being a strange other-world and his home in England normality. Now, it was the gray steel world of the aircraft carrier that was normal and the concept of home and safety the alien other-world.

The facts were easy enough to put down. By the time the fighting had ended, the British carriers had lost 34 of the 40 fighters they had brought and 30 of the 40 bombers. Alasdair Baillie, Paul Carter and Freddie Kingsman had all gone. The truth was that almost everybody he had known in the squadron had gone. *Furious's* hangar deck was a cavernous tomb now, populated by the ghosts of the pilots and aircraft who had once lived there. *How to explain that to somebody who hadn't been there?*

Mullback was suddenly aware that the world was divided into two groups of people, those who had fought and those who hadn't. The gap between the two was a yawning chasm that defied easy bridging. The language simply ddn't exist to do it. All the literary works that had presumed to bridge that gap had been judged shallow and trite because they had attempted to convey something that language hadn't been created to describe. Mullback couldn't write the letter to his wife that he wanted to write and the letter that he could write, one that she would understand, wasn't what he wanted to say.

If he couldn't say what he wanted, he would say what he could. With that decision in his mind, Ernest Mullback started to write home to his wife.

Bastiaan van Huis's Home, Capetown, South Africa.

"Gesondheid, Bassie and welcome home." As lady of the household, it was the duty of Linda van Huis to welcome her husband home. She watched her brothers and sisters raise their glasses to her husband standing at the head of the table.

"Gesondheit, broers, susters en vriende. And I ask you to welcome our new friends Shumba Geldenhuys and Zander Randlehoff, who join us tonight for the first time."

The clan turned slightly so they were facing the two guests and raised their glasses. "Gesondheit, Shumba en Zander. Welcome to our family circle and know it as your own." Linda smiled as the formal welcome was repeated. The close-knit second generation of the van Huis, McMullen and Vermaak families had caused ribald speculation in the sleazier parts of the world press with scandalized speculation of what went on behind the sealed doors of the family compound. If the American supermarket tabloids and their British equivalents were to be believed, the families spend their time in one long orgy that would have done ancient Pompei proud. In fact, the young couples were exactly what they appeared to be, respectable and almost painfully conventional. Nowhere was it more obvious when they gathered for their evening dinner together. Apart from two couples who supervised the children while they played and monitored the watch on the compound walls, all the family were here, formally dressed for dinner and behaving with an elaborate courtesy that seemed almost a century out of date.

The fact that Shumba Geldenhuys, a Griqua, was one of their guests was the one thing that might have scandalized older parts of the South African community. That was simply a sign of the slow but steady change inside South African society. Even so, Linda van Huis knew that his presence was allowable only at a private function. He would not be at the table if this were a public banquet. That made her uneasy but she was privately convinced that another ten or twenty years would see that change also. In her opinion and that of her husband, that time would not come soon enough.

"Absent friends." The third of the formal toasts was made. A silence fell on the room as the men remembered those who had gone off to war and not returned. Then, the men seated their wives and took their own places. A bubble of conversation filling the room as the servants started to serve.

"Speaking of friends, it is a pity Conrad Cross could not join us." Randlehoff had a job remembering the young British Lieutenant's first name. For some reason, it was treacherously easy to forget.

"He had to go with his unit to Britain." Geldenhuys was quietly proud of the young man who had come through so well. "He is something rare in their army, a veteran. He will have much to teach the rest."

"As do we." Van Huis was unpleasantly aware of the long report he had written on the shortcomings of the Boomslang. There were a lot of changes needed, each one minor in itself but together representing a major reworking of the design. There was also the minor but economically important matter of having all the sales brochures stamped 'Comat Proven' to organize. That would do wonders for the sales of the Mamba and Boomslang. "But the British are back now. This is a good thing, I think. In some strange way, the world did not seem quite the same without them."

There was a general crackle of laughter. Anders Vermaak nodded emphatically. "This is true. So, broers, susters en vriende, I propose another toast. To the Lion Resurgent."

EPILOGUE

Major Mazza's Home, Buenos Aires, Argentina

"Would you like me to come inside with you?" The Swedish Embassy official was deeply concerned for the woman in the taxi with him. It wasn't just the delicate nature of this particular mission but the unrest that saturated the city as a whole. Law and order had almost broken down across Argentina with various different factions vying for power. They did so by any means they believed necessary. That meant inconvenient people tended to disappear. Major Mazza could well consider Maja Sunderstrom to be a highly inconvenient person.

The other two occupants in the car nodded agreement. One was another Swedish embassy official who was technically a member of the cultural attache's department. In reality, he was a member of the Särskilda Skydds Gruppen, the Special Protection Group. It was an elite formation of the Swedish Army tasked with protecting Swedish personnel and interests around the world. The other was an Argentine private detective who had taken on investigating the missing children scandal as his life's work. This case was one of the few where there was even a remotely possible chance of a happy outcome.

Maja Sunderstrom shook her head. "I'd like to go in by myself if you do not mind. Everything that had been said about Major and Madam Mazza suggests they are kind and honorable people. I do not think there will be any trouble."

The SSG officer did not seem convinced on that point but all his training was directed towards spotting possible threats. He recognized that gave him a biased perspective. He nodded reluctantly, got out and opened the door for Mrs Sunderstrom. While she was getting out of the car, his eyes never stopped scanning the street. His senses told him that he and the rest of the party were under covert surveillance. That didn't surprise him. This was a guarded and gated community, something that had grown common in Argentina while the unrest grew ever nearer to a civil war.

Sunderstrom walked down the path leading to the front door and reached out to ring the bell. The door opened before she could do so. Obviously the Mazzas had been waiting for her. She guessed that they had been hoping against hope that she would not come. Perhaps they had fixed on a likely time by which her arrival could be discounted and praying for the minutes to pass until that time was reached. She felt sorry for them, realizing that the agony they were feeling now matched that she had felt waiting for news of her daughter.

"Please come inside, Madam Sunderstrom." Mazza's voice was grave and serious yet she could detect the tremble that lay underneath the words. When she stepped into their house, the overwhelming impression she had was one of how normal it was. She wasn't quite sure what she had been expecting. Martial music perhaps with paintings and pictures of battle on the walls. Instead, the house was indistinguishable in character from her own home back in Sweden. Couches and arm chairs gathered around a television set, side tables with colored magazines on them, flowers in vases, painting of landscapes on the walls. The only difference was the collection of children's toys, mostly boxed up on the floor.

"May we offer you tea or coffee? Or something a little stronger?" Major Mazza was trying hard to be a properly hospitable host to a guest who he could hardly have considered welcome.

"A cup of tea would be very nice, if that is not inconvenient." Maja Sunderstrom was trying to be a considerate guest, despite knowing how unwelcome her presence had to be.

"I have packaged all of Jorge's favorite toys for you. Having his things with him will make it so much easier for him to understand." Madam Mazza had brought a tray of tea in and set it down on a small table. She was desperately trying not to start crying again. Her eyes were deeply reddened. Sunderstrom guessed she'd been counting minutes until this moment came, trying desperately to make each one last as long as she could.

"His name is Jorge?"

"Jorge Tercero." Major Mazza busied himself with inconsequential, unnecessary things while his wife poured the tea. "Jorge is named after my father while Tercero is Antonella's maiden name. He is, he was, their first grandchild."

"Jorge is asleep upstairs at the moment. He will have much travelling to do and he should be well-rested before he starts." Antonella Mazza was trying to keep her voice under control, but the anger and frustration was there.

"We have tickets on a supersonic airliner from Rio de Janeiro to Stockholm. It will only be a four hour flight once we take off." It would be the feeder flight from Buenos Aires to Rio de Janeiro that would take time. The trouble in Argentina was such that the big airlines had suspended flights to the country.

"Machliner or Sonic Clipper?" Major Mazza was trying to make conversation, trying to keep the event as normal as he could even though his voice was cracking. "The supersonic airliners have made such a difference to everything. Anna and I wanted to take Jorge to Italy, so he could hear the Pope speak."

"Come upstairs; we should wake him now." Madam Mazza led the way upstairs to the child's room. Again, Maja Sunderstrom was amazed at how normal it was. It could have been any infant's room, even down to the mobile hanging over the cot.

300

Antonella Mazza reached into the bed and lifted the child gently. Half-awake, he gave a very sleepy "Maman" and nuzzled his face into her chest. Her eyes were streaming with tears.

It was something that Maja Sunderstrom could hardly see since she was crying herself. She made her own decision then, one that she couldn't avoid making now she knew everything.

"Madam Mazza, Major Mazza, may I ask a great kindness of you? Would you mind if I came to see you here in Argentina every year so I can visit Jorge while he grows up? Could you even tell him, when he is old enough to understand, that I am some sort of relative?"

"You are not taking him?" Madam Mazza's face was covered with stunned disbelief, mixed with dawning hope that the loss she had dreaded might not take place after all.

"I am an old lady, living by myself. Looking after a child as well. . ." She hesitated, knowing what she wanted to say but not knowing how to say it. It wasn't helping that both she and the Mazzas were speaking in English, the only common language that they had. "It would not be fair on Jorge. He needs a proper mother and a proper father. He needs to grow up in a real family, not with an old woman haunted by ghosts. You have a beautiful home in a nice neighborhood and you are both already his true parents. This is where he belongs now."

Madam Mazza was crying again, this time with joy and relief and she returned her son to his bed. Quietly, the three adults returned down to the living room. "Perhaps sometime we could come and visit you in Sweden. When normal times return and the supersonic flights run from Buenos Aires once again? Jorge should know the Swedish side of his heritage as well as the Argentine."

"That would be wonderful. Now, I must go. The embassy people are waiting for me outside." Maja Sunderstrom made her farewells and left. She didn't start crying again until she reached the embassy limousine.

The Red Lion Inn, Solihull, Birmingham.

Lieutenant Conrad Cross entered the Red Lion with his father and mother, proudly looking around at the dining room full of guests as they stood up and applauded him. The thunder of applause seemed just like artillery fire somehow. Thus it was no surprise to him that the room exploded. The people inside were melting in the heat as his Boomslang pumped missile after missile into the building. He was burning himself, trapped inside his tank destroyer, just as the Argentine soldiers had been trapped when their tanks and armored personnel carriers had been destroyed by his Mambas. He felt the heat frying him, melting his skin . .

"It is all right, son. It is only a nightmare." Matthew Cross shook his son awake. Allie Cross was standing in the bedroom door, her folded hand in her mouth. "Everything is all right."

"The pub; it was blown up. I blew it up and then my Boomslang burned."

301

"Just a nightmare. Everything is all right. Allie, go back to bed. This is a matter for old soldiers to talk over." Matthew Cross gave a warped grin to his son. "I think that she is upset you dreamed about burning her pub down."

Alice Cross nodded vigorously. She had bought the Red Lion when the previous landlord had retired and the business was thriving. Between her husband's house-painting business and the profits from her pub, the family had become prosperous. The idea that her son had dreamed of blowing one element of that prosperity up was profoundly disturbing for her. Memories of the dreary poverty of Britain in the 1950s were still ingrained. She was about to protest but her husband waved her away before she could speak. "Con, we'd better go down to the kitchen and have a drink."

The restaurant attached to the pub was empty of course. Conrad Cross sat down while his father went into the bar to get a bottle and two shot glasses. "Dutch Schnapps; the German original is extinct, I am afraid.

He poured out two shots and watched while his son sank the first. Then he filled their glasses again. "You were dreaming of the war? That is why you screamed."

"In a way. I dreamed we were here then I blew us up and then I was burning in my tank destroyer. Why should I dream that? We never lost a single vehicle. We never gave the Argentine tankers a chance. We hit them from beyond the range of their guns and before they knew where we were."

"Very sensible." Matthew Cross spoke dryly. "Our tank destroyers in Russia did the same. Only a fool wants a fair fight. With lethal weapons, anyway. Drink up, your glass is empty."

"There were eight or ten men each in those armored carriers and we just blew them apart."

"Not your fault, Con. Did I ever tell you what the Russian Sturmoviks did to our vehicles? Or when the Amis napalmed us?"

Conrad had never heard his father telling real war stories before. He had heard his father tell amusing stories about the pranks he and his friends had got up to, but never stories about the real fighting and what it had been like. Now, he heard them. He told his own stories in exchange, of the Boomslangs cutting the Argentine armor apart, of watching the ships in Bomb Alley being attacked. Half way through the exchange, as the night went on, Matthew Cross got up and staggered to the bar for another bottle of Schnapps.

"Dad, how longs did dreams last before they go away?" Conrad Cross was having problems with his tenses.

"What makes you think they ever will?"

Next morning, Allie Cross came down and found her husband and son sprawled over the kitchen table, sleeping off the schnapps. She shook her head fondly, muttered 'old soldier's business' and made a note to charge them for two bottles of best Dutch schnapps. Business was business, after all.

Officially, the room was empty. The people who had gathered in it did not exist. The organization they belonged to did not exist. Nothing any of them had done had ever happened. In a more real sense, the room was empty because nobody in it knew the identities of anybody else there. They had arrived separately; they would leave separately. The room was darkened so that no faces could be seen. It was possible to tell whether a speaker was a man or a woman but that was all. When they spoke, they did so with a generic Oxford Received-English accent that might or might not be genuine. Even their ages were uncertain. The meeting itself ran according to the format adopted by the Society of Friends. They sat in silence unless one person felt he had something to say. Whoever spoke received a quiet and polite hearing and everybody paused for a minute or more before a reply was made. That allowed for a calm and considered response.

"Too many fuelling accidents." The voice came out of the semi-darkness. The tone was not critical but thoughtful.

After a delay, the reply was couched the same way. "We didn't cause that many of them. We should remember that inexperienced armies normally have a high accident rate without our assistance. The elevated Argentine rate plus our own contributions was too high for comfort. I think the Argentines were getting suspicious towards the end."

There was another silence. The others present guessed that the speaker had headed one of the Auxiliary Units that had deployed south. One team had gone to South Georgia, the other to the Falklands although there was no record of that fact nor would there ever be. Even the trawler that had inserted them and picked them up had vanished. Its assumed identity had evaporated as quickly and as finally as dew on a warm summer's day.

"We must think of other accidents that might befall such forces in the future." A woman's voice this time but that meant nothing. It was quite possible that the teams that might have deployed south had had women as members; only their commanders would know that. Even the crew of the trawler that had briefly been the *Nikogaš Nevidel* would be unable to identify the teams they had carried. Nor would those teams be able to recognize the crew of the trawler. In the Auxiliary Units, complete and total anonymity was the norm. When they had been founded in the early days of 1940, in anticipation of a German invasion, the anticipated 'life' of an Auxiliary Unit had been two weeks. Now, the force had lasted almost fifty years yet they were still an unknown, untouchable ghost. That had been achieved by the strictest attention to security. Back in 1942, innocent people had died to maintain that secrecy.

"We must." Another voice from the darkness. "Also, we must move with the times. There are other targets now that can be equally destructive."

"Telephone lines." The truth was that most who attended these meetings rather enjoyed them. The leisured pace of discussions and the complete anonymity of the speakers meant that ideas could be proposed and approved or shot down on their merits.

"And satellite links." The impression of the attendees thoughtfully nodding was strong. "Communications are a modern army weakness as much as fuel and supplies."

"Batteries. Almost everybody depends on battery-powered equipment these days. If we can find a way of ensuring batteries went flat before they were used?"

Another long pause and when the next speaker brought up the idea, the reluctance in her voice was palpable. "Medical supplies. Perhaps we could poison blood banks or pharmaceuticals?"

"That would make wounded troops reluctant to seek medical attention. A major impact on morale. We should look into this."

There was another pause for thought. "Infect, not poison. Poisoning could be detected as deliberate and would reveal our hand. But septicaemia or syphilis in blood supplies could just be an accident. And the rumor would be as damaging as the deed."

"Good ideas. They will be studied." Nobody quite knew how, but they would be. Somebody, somewhere would get a contract to study the degree of infection in blood banks. Somehow, that information would find its way back to be weaponized.

"Are there other matters?"

"The Government remained firm. Commendably firm. There was no sign of weakness and the ghost of That Man remains in his grave."

The satisfied stir that went around the room was unmistakable. One of the key functions of the Auxiliary Units was to ensure that what had been done by Lord Halifax on June 18, 1940 could never be repeated. If a modern-day Lord Halifax tried, he or she would never survive the drive from Downing Street to the Palace and the Monarch would be spared the duty having their hands kissed by a traitor. *Who shall guard the guards?* A question that might be asked of the Auxiliary Units had they existed, which, of course, they did not. And the reply they might have given, had they existed, was *we guard each other*.

There was another long, relaxed silence. Eventually, another woman spoke. "The Americans have been sniffing around. They have picked up word that we might exist."

The possible consequences of that and how word might have leaked out were contemplated. "Is there a breach in our security?"

Another contemplative pause. "I do not think so. I believe they heard the legends and decided that where there was smoke there might be fire. So they investigated. One of the agents from the Office of Strategic Services was looking around. And asking discrete questions."

"Victim of an accident?"

"In this case no. The agent is a person of importance and an accident would have resulted in a full-scale investigation with all the resources the Americans could throw at it. Also, asking questions and the questioner then dying tends to confirm the importance of those questions. Instead, the investigation was monitored and quietly sealed off from access to any possible leads. As a result, it died from lack of interest."

304

"Very well handled." A male voice from the darkness was filled with approval.

Slowly the meeting petered out. Once the discussions were completed, the attendees left. One by one they quietly slipped away in the darkness. Each left with enough delay between them so they would be lost in the passers-by outside long before the next one emerged. The house they met in had several exits and they were used at random. The need for security and absolute secrecy was maintained at all times, even when whatever was happening had concluded.

The woman who had raised the issue of the American investigation into the possible existence of the Auxiliary Units was one of the last to leave. The approval of her actions had pleased her greatly since handling the situation had been one of her first unsupervised missions. It had not been an easy one for her. In common with all Auxiliary Unit personnel she had training in unarmed combat and other deadly skills that was the best that anybody could receive anywhere. Allowing herself to be thrown around a hotel room by Igrat Shafrid had been hard for her to swallow. Still, she had fulfilled her mission and been praised for her success. With that, a contented Heather Watson adjusted her hat, put up her umbrella against the fine spring rain and unobtrusively mixed in with the civilians on the street.

THE END

2002094R00154

Printed in Great Britain
by Amazon.co.uk, Ltd.,
Marston Gate.